A mile later  was the Pyrami signaled him to tense. There w than a tail-gater trying to scare he ... was doing a good job. This was no terrain for fun and games. The track seemed to get narrower as the light faded and even though she tried not to glance over to her right, she knew what was there. Or rather, what wasn't there. It was a long way down.

The van inched up; suddenly, it touched her. Jess gasped and looked into the mirror again. She froze for a split second. She'd seen the Pyramid's face and he wasn't playing games. He was deadly serious, and she was in trouble.

Jess tried unsuccessfully to swallow. Her mouth was bone-dry; her hands were soaking wet. She concentrated on the ribbon of pavement, willing herself to stay on it, to forget the drop, to think about nothing except surviving for another mile and a half.

The van touched her again, less gently this time. Instinct took over, freeing muscles that would otherwise automatically jerk the wheel. Another touch, then a harder bang. The Skylark was no match for a van. Each time, her car jumped ahead, out of control for moment that seemed like an eternity.

SIDE EFFECTS

Barbara Betcherman

Tudor Publishing Company
New York and Los Angeles

Tudor Publishing Company

ISBN: 0-944276-35-0

Printed in the United States of America

First Tudor printing — January, 1989

To Barbara

Chapter 1

There was no point in rereading the death reports, because repetition wasn't going to change the facts. Period. Jessica Canby slowly closed the file folder and wandered out onto the deck off the bedroom. The heat was overwhelming, even outside; the westerly winds coming off the Pacific did no more than tease the oily air. The ocean itself seemed to share her discomfort, oozing desultorily forward to dampen the beach, then retreating into glassy torpor.

She leaned against the railing, still thinking about the file. "Damn. Damn."

"Something I said?"

Jess turned to smile at her husband. Michael Renfrew was lounging against the glass doors, looking, as always, like the quintessential Southern Californian: lean, tall, tanned, fair-haired. And dry. He never sweated. She, on the other hand, red of hair and white of skin, was damp whenever the temperature rose over seventy. The hell of it was, she'd been born and bred in Los Angeles - and Michael came from Chicago.

"Nope, nothing you said." She sighed. "It's a case. Miguel Aguerra."

"The kid who was murdered in Hollywood last week?"

Jess nodded and went back inside. "Molested and murdered. Ten years old."

"I don't know how you can stand it. If I had to spend my days at the morgue, I'd have to spend my nights at the bottle."

"Oh, you get used to it. Sort of." Jess hadn't been able to keep food down during her first week as a coroner's investigator. Eight years later, she was chief of investigations and considerably tougher.

"So what's wrong?"

She paused. "Well, I have this sick feeling that little Miguel was a chicken."

"Come again?"

"A child prostitute. I think the cops are going to find

out that he worked Hollywood regularly."

"Oh." Michael swallowed and sat next to her on the bed. "Ten years old?"

"The chicken hawks like'em young."

"Spare me the details. My stomach isn't strong enough. I like love stories about fully-grown combatants who don't get paid for panting. Speaking of which," he nuzzled her neck, "how about a little panting yourself?"

Jess grinned and disentangled herself. "We've got to get ready for the party. And I've got to take a shower."

Michael followed her into the bathroom, groaning. "I hate parties. Do we have to go?"

"You do. Aspiring screenwriters definitely have to go to film producers' parties." She stripped off her t-shirt. "God, it's hot! I don't remember a summer like this before."

"Really?" He started to grin. "You've had thirty-five of them. Every summer is broiling and every winter is wet — and every year, Los Angelenos are surprised. You guys have the attention span of a kindergarten kid."

"Guys?" Jess glanced ruefully at the mirror. "Maybe they didn't teach biology in Chicago, but take it from me, guys don't look like this."

He patted her stomach affectionately. "You look wonderful."

"I look like a pear that's gone mad." Pregnancy was a humbling experience. She could barely recall being a thin five-foot-seven person, able to take in her waist and her toes with a single glance. Only the features above the neck seemed familiar — the same strong cheekbones, high forehead, and hazel eyes. But hardly anyone ever looked up at her face any more. From time to time, she checked to see if maybe she'd sprouted acne or spinach between her teeth, but that wasn't it. People just couldn't take their eyes off the bulge. She turned on the water and stepped into the stall.

"Never mind," Michael shouted over the sound of the cascade. "In a mere three months, you'll be skinny again and we'll have the world's most brilliant baby."

"Three months, pet, aren't 'mere' to one who tends

2

to topple forward."

"True. But I don't," he pointed out cheerfully, "so the time will just whip by for me."

He was holding a towel when Jess turned off the faucets. She stepped into his arms for a rubdown. He leaned over to kiss her, lightly at first, then more seriously.

"Mmmm." She moved closer. "What time is Martin getting here?"

"Martin who?"

"Martin-your-best-friend who's going to the party with us."

He ran his fingers down her spine. "What was the question again?"

The towel dropped. "I don't remember."

The doorbell echoed through the house. They signed in unison and reluctantly broke apart.

By the time they got downstairs, Martin Dunphy was in the living room, a stocky, prematurely bald figure in white pants and the obligatory Lacoste T-shirt. "Hi, kids. Hope I didn't interrupt anything."

"Your timing's been lousy as long as I've know you," Michael observed. "I remember in college when you— "

"Uh-uh. No college stories," Jess said firmly. "I already know more about your sordid pasts than I care to."

"Mine, alas, was regrettably unsordid." Martin put an arm around Jess and beamed enthusiastically at her stomach. He was a thirty-seven year old confirmed bachelor, despite which - maybe because of it - he was as excited about the pending Canby-Renfrew as its parents were. "How's our baby?"

"Getting big enough to qualify for the Rams." She patted it. "As you can see."

"Say, listen, I was in Saks' toy department the other day, and I saw this incredible building-block set that —"

"Martin!" Michael was shaking his head. "You've already bought enough toys to amuse half the kids in China."

"It's just a building-block set - no big deal." Martin

stepped out onto the deck, wanting to change the subject. He liked to think of himself as a stone-hearted, hard- nosed, unsentimental banker. "Boy, this is the life! I'd move to Malibu tomorrow if it weren't for that damned drive."

"An hour and change," Jess sighed. "I do it every day."

"And for what? So you can hang out with dead people." Martin made a face. "Ugh."

"Look at it this way. Your clients talk back. Mine don't."

He was unpersuaded. "Anyway, you'll only be there until the next election."

Jess grinned. She certainly hoped he was right. Her father, the late Arthur Rader Canby, had been mayor of Los Angeles for almost two decades, and her earliest memories were of accompanying him to rallies and boisterous meetings. She'd caught the political bug before she was fully toilet-trained. With any luck (and little help from her friends) when the state next went to the polls, a Canby's name would be on the ballot again.

Michael snorted. He regarded politics as something akin to a social disease. "And your eight years at the coroner's office will come in mighty handy. Politicians need strong stomachs."

"They say Caesar could have digested an uncooked mule," Martin agreed blithely.

Jess laughed. The nickname referred to the theory, held at one time by many, that Arthur Canby would hold his office until he made it hereditary. "Never mind maligning my sainted father, you two. Dad might have been - uh - forceful, but the people loved him. He was a real, small-d democrat."

"He sure was." Martin was grinning. "May I remind you that he lobbied to make the beaches public? He gave you this house but he gave them," gesturing, "the right to harass you in it."

"Harass" was only slightly too strong. The Saturday mob right below was loud, messy and frenetic: strutting muscled males showing off for beach bunnies wearing fragments of material that almost constituted bikinis, unreasonably extended families with large picnic lunches wrapped in paper Jess and Michael would have to clean up tomorrow, middle-agers, some pathetically trying to such in sagging stomachs and others letting gravity have its way. And above all, dozens — legions — of whopping children.

Jess sighed. "I admired Dad. There weren't very many politicians like him. But I've got to admit, sometimes I wish he'd been a little less public-spirited."

* * *

Cyril Haberman undeniably threw a good party. The crowd was flushed with wine and sunshine and the chicness of their lifestyle - weekend brunch at a file stars and studio magnates and politicians, all as glossy as the ocean, mounds of pink lobster and rivers of champagne. Hollywood's Beautiful People lived in a reality as perfect as illusion. Hardly surprising. They were, after all, the High Priests of Glamor and Glitter.

Or, Jess muttered to herself, the High Priests of Glitz. It all depended on how you looked at it.

"So," Michael asked, "what do you think?"

"I think we're going to be deafened by the clatter of gold neck chains."

He laughed. "Who was the fool who said money couldn't buy everything?"

"No one in this room." She looked around again. "Must've been come innocent who's never had his teeth capped."

"Or who doesn't know Dr. Wiu."

The surgeon to the stars was leaning against the marble fireplace, somberly staring at a fortyish actress. His expression told the whole ugly story; without immediate surgery, the wrinkles could be fatal.

Jess and Michael smiled at each other as Martin reappeared.

"Well, I did a once-around and I've got to hand it to Cyril. He knows how to find female pulchritude."

"Oink, oink."

"With brains," Martin added hastily. "Beauty with brains. And I noticed that some of the brightest were outside. Shall we?"

He led them through knots of partygoers, vivacious groups of senators and studio executives and industrialists leavened with svelte women who definitely tended toward the young side of thirty-five. Jess was feeling more like a gargoyle than ever by the time they reached the terrace.

It was a backyard, really, a landscaped expanse of flowering tress, intricately laid flagstone paths and outdoor furniture nicer than what most people had in their living rooms. Another feature a vast, curved, black- bottomed swimming pool, seemed to suggest that the ocean lying beyond the sea wall was a mere optical illusion.

There was Malibu and there was Malibu. Jess and Michael lived only a couple of miles away, but to lump together the two beach houses was to suggest that a rubber dinghy had much in common with the presidential yacht.

"Humble," Michael observed drily, "but I guess the Habermans call it home."

Martin leaned forward. "Speaking of Haberman, tell me about your negotiations. Is Cyril going to turn your book into a film?"

"Martin, you only introduced us a couple of weeks ago! We've had a few meetings." Michael shrugged, grabbed two glasses of champagne from a passing waiter's tray and handed one to Martin. "Jess, honey, you want some fruit juice?"

"Not much." She regretfully eyed the bubbly. Three more months of being treated as a child abuser if she so much as considered a drink or a cigarette.

"It'll be a expensive film," Michael continued. "These things take time."

"Look, I'm Haberman's banker. I know his set-up. Trail Productions made money off their last four films. They can afford it - and so can Cyril. He got in on the ground floor of the cable T.V. industry. He's worth a bundle, if you're impressed with millions."

"Hell, I'm impressed with hundreds."

"He'll buy it," Martin insisted. "He loved the book, he told me. And Hollywood's crazy for sick family stories right now."

"Hey," Michael protested. It's not a sick family -"

"*Schmuck*! You want to sell it or you just want to sit around, looking at your good reviews?"

"I'd rather look at them than at the royalty statements."

Jess squeezed Michael's hand. His first novel had been a critical success but reviewers got their books for free.

"Darlings! How are you?" Michael's agent was, suddenly, in their midst. Dan Mercowitz tended to burst in and out like a petite tornado; one almost expected her to arrive, whirling, from the sky. When Einstein said that all matter was energy, it was improbable that even he had contemplated so much energy coming from such a minor amount of matter. She was tiny and very thin, her face distinguished mainly be enormous, dark eyes and a vivid slash of lipstick, her hair was whatever color had seemed, to her that week interesting. Today, she was a blonde. "Martin, wonderful to see you. Jess, sweetheart, what a stunning blouse! My, you are huge now, aren't you? When's the baby?"

Jess opened her mouth to answer, but Dana wasn't listening. She never listened to sentences that didn't have the word "points" in them. She thought Alexander Graham Bell had been put on earth to facilitate deal-making. "Michael, lover, why aren't you circulating? This is a Hollywood party! I know you three have fun together, but that's not what these parties are for."

Michael grinned. "Sorry, Dana. I mustn't have been thinking."

"Well, darling - oh, there's Cyril!" Dana caught their host's eye and waved.

He obediently came over, smiling at Dana as everyone did. Because of the size, what would, in anyone else, have been obnoxiousness made her seem like an adorable child playing at being Hollywood.

Jess watched Haberman kiss Dana and greet everyone else. He was a big man, as befitted a man of substance. His face was middle-aged and not conventionally handsome, but there was a sexy quality about it. It might have been the deep-set dark eyes that concentrated intently on whomever they regarded, or maybe it was, the thick salt- and-pepper hair and the creased cheeks. More likely, it was the air of not having to ask the price of anything.

He appeared delighted to meet Jess. "I knew your father slightly - fantastic man. And I've been hearing good things about you from his friends."

"Thank you."

He looked at her empty hands. "What can we get for you? Tea? Milk?"

"Nothing, thanks, Cyril."

"Well, are you comfortable standing? How about us finding you a chair?"

She smiled and shook her head again. There was a fine line between being made to feel cherished and being made to feel like a freak. Mostly, people crossed that line. "I'm perfectly all right. Thanks."

"Come to think of it, anyone who can do your job must be tougher than you look," Haberman commented quickly. A man who came from nowhere to make a fortune to possess many skills. Like being able to pick up on nuances. "I've been reading about your brilliant work in the Beatty case."

"Beatty?" Dana was at a loss. She read both the *Hollywood Reporter* and the *Daily Variety* every morning, so she considered herself well-informed. She was not, however, quite so scrupulous about 'the *Los Angeles Times*.

"Remember the freeway ax-slayer?" Haberman asked.

Dana brightened. "Yes. It'd make a super movie, don't you think?"

He carried gamely on. "Well, a man named Beatty

killed his wife and made it look like one of the other killings. He'd have gotten away with it - except for Jess."

"Oh." Dana looked at Jess with interest. That would make an even *better* movie. "How did you do that?"

"Tedious detail work, mainly."

The agent's face fell. Detail work didn't sound very visual.   Jess took pity on her. "I found out that Beatty was chummy with a cop - he'd bribed him for inside information about the ax-slayer's MO. I just sort of hung in there until I could prove it."

Haberman smiled approvingly. "It's the sort of tenaciousness we could use in Sacramento." He moved away, stopping only to suggest to Michael that they chat before he left.

Dana patted Michael's arm as it were a pet who'd done a particularly intricate trick. "He's interested, definitely interested. Now sweetie," eyes darting around, "shall we go do some wandering?"

Michael managed to avoid displaying a tasteless amount of enthusiasm, but he did let himself be carried off.

Jess and Martin grinned at each other.

"Haberman carries a lot of political clout," Martin pontificated unnecessarily. "He'll make you governor before you know it."

"Uh-huh. But in the meantime, I think I'll mosey around and make nice to a few senators. Just in case."

* * *

Jess and Michael had a late dinner at home. Alone. In virtual silence. They were well-suited to each other in many ways, not the least of which was the need, after hours of socializing, for catatonic-like silence.

Jess pushed her plate away finally, happily glutted. Red meat might cause cancer, clogged arteries and violence, but hell, nothing was perfect. "I love cow. I'd rather die than be a vegetarian."

Michael looked up from the newspaper. "That's exactly what vegetarians say is your choice."

"Who can trust someone who thinks alfalfa sprouts make a meal?" She tried with only moderate success to hide a burp. "Haberman throws a good function."

"If you like that sort of thing."

"Dana does."

Michael grinned. "You think so? Anyway, you should have liked it. Everyone was waxing eloquent over your success with the Beatty matter."

"Publicity doesn't hurt," she agreed happily.

The telephone shrilled. "Hello? Oh, hi, Joe." Jess's heart sank. Joe Miller was one of her assistant chief investigators and a hell of a nice guy but he probably wasn't calling just to say howdy.

"Sorry to bother, you, Jess, but we've got a big one. A fire and a corpse. I figured you'd want to know about it - the victim is Robert Berrington. *The* Robert Berrington."

"Jesus." She whistled. Berrington was in Haberman's league and then some, one of the real powers in the state. Fancy family, huge fortune, financial empire based on microchips and other incomprehensible scientific doodads. And political connections. Big political connections. Her father had known Berrington, and Jess had met the man herself once or twice. But even a "Caesar" Canby was outranked by a Berrington. "Who's handling it?"

"I just got the call. I assumed - uh - of course, if you don't feel up to it -"

Jess sighed. The chief of investigations was an administrator, but when someone like this died, the ordinary chain of command went by the boards. Even so, she could get out of it if she hadn't made a big point of insisting, as a matter of feminist principle, that pregnancy wasn't a disease and didn't hold one back. From the vantage point of late Saturday evening, not to mention being exhausted, it looked like a foolish principle. "Give me the address and have a van meet me there."

Michael raised his eyebrows. He obviously thought she was being foolish too.

10

"Talk to you later." Jess hung up and shrugged helplessly. "How could I let Bella and Gloria down?"

* * *

The road was narrow, uphill and twisting; massive banks of greenery crowded in on either side as if this were an English country lane instead of a Mercedes-and-Rolls Royce track in Bel Air. Jess passed estate after estate, each worth the entire G.N.P. of a small nation, before finally arriving at the top of a priceless hill.

Police and fire department vehicles were parked along the private drive that wound into the property. Jess left her car outside and walked through the cluster of excited neighbors. The rich, it seemed, were no more immune to the titillation of tragedy than any other community, but they did dress better for it. The dressing gowns on display were worth more that Jess's entire wardrobe.

"Coroner's office." She flashed her ID for the young patrolman at the wrought-iron gate.

"Oh." He looked at her stomach and cleared his throat. "You want a lift up there, ma'am?"

She smiled. "No, I think I can make it." As she passed through the barriers, she noticed two closed-circuit T.V. cameras poking out of the trees. Exotic buds. The kind of security system that would be just the thing if the Russians landed.

A short hike later - a distance of no more than that between the gate-keeper and Balmoral Castle - brought the house into view. It was massive English Tudor-cum-California structure - all beamed walls and leaded-glass windows - set into jungles of palms, orange trees and eucalyptus. Nothing was missing that money could buy - but it was going to take a lot more of the green stuff to repair the damage of tonight's fire. Hoses were still being played on the east wing, and the combination of water, soot and smoke made the mansion resemble a frowsy hooker whose mascara had run at the end of a long night.

11

A portly figure stood on the lawn, directing the emergency teams. It was clothed in a beautifully cut, albeit deeply wrinkled, three-piece suit that hadn't come off the rack. Jess grinned. She knew that suit.

"Evening, Francis."

He turned, displaying a face that didn't go with the outfit. His tailor couldn't be blamed for the sagging jowls and blue-circled eyes, but he could have told Detective Francis Arnheim that crewcuts were not longer the right note to strike on Savile Row.

"Jess. You on this? I'd have expected Harper himself."

"Mmm. He's out of town and I'm minding the store." She spoke without inflection. She wasn't the only person in town who dislike the county coroner, but Colman Harper was her direct superior so she didn't have to take out an ad. "What have we got?"

"A body," he grunted. "A twenty-four-carat body that's giving ulcers to the brass downtown. The call came in about ten-thirty." He looked at his watch. "Two hours ago, and already half the big shoots in town are leaning on headquarters and the other half's waiting to get through.

Jess nodded. They'd be closely watched on this one. Their eyes met, then quickly shifted to stare at the scurrying firemen. Big shots were a bitch.

Jess sighed. At least she'd pulled Francis. Two and a half decades of police work did things to a personality. He was dour, sour, suspicious, cynical. He'd been, doubtless, a superlatively lousy husband and father; rumor had it that his family hadn't talked to him since 1976. He thought little of most people and less of young career women, although, after a few cases with Jess, he'd decided for his own unfathomable reasons to accept her. Still, she liked him; he was a smart cop, as straight as anyone else and, in his own way, good company. She liked him enough to know he'd be horrified to find that out.

"How did the fire start?" she asked.

"The arson investigator's got more tests to do, but he

thinks it got going in the east wing, the housekeeper's suite. Probably bad wiring. It ran through the walls all over the house, but the place looks worse that it really is. Mainly smoke damage."

Jess nodded, then stiffened at a sudden twinge in her stomach. She took a deep breath and covered the moment by pulling out her notebook. "What about Berrington himself?"

"Very dead. In bed." He gestured toward the west wing, where the fire had apparently been vanquished. "Looks like smoke inhalation. No marks on the body. No sign he even woke up."

Not a bad way to go, if you had to go. "Anyone else inside?"

"No. The housekeeper was on her day off. She got back early, which was lucky, because otherwise, the whole place would have gone."

"Not lucky for Berrington," Jess observed drily. She glanced around. The property was heavily treed and enormous. It wasn't likely a neighbor could have spotted the fire. "Okay. It's safe to go into the bed-room wing now?"

"Uh." Francis twisted his lips as if there were more words inside but he couldn't remember how to pro-nounce them.

Jess got the point. "If it's safe for you guys, it's safe enough for me." She mustered whatever dignity was available to a pear on stilts and walked toward the house.

* * *

Berrington had been much more impressive in life than he was in death. The thick eyebrows had been ferocious, the jaw — now dropped — had jutted. Hid bank balance had created the aura of power, the illusion of stature, but it hadn't been able to buy him the full threescore years and ten. Now, on imported sheets, he was just a gray haired object, about five-eight in length, weighing maybe one-eighty. The same ninety-eight cents' worth (before inflation) of chemicals as everybody else.

Jess grimaced and snapped a few Polaroid shots of the body. What was with the philosophizing? It wasn't as if she hadn't seen a corpse or two in her time. Obviously, the silver spoon could do one final thing: it could make some deaths seem more significant than those of lesser mortals.

There wasn't time to delve into the psychology of that. For one thing, there was too much paper work waiting. And for another, she had to admit that Francis's solicitude wasn't entirely out of line. The greasy air and the stink of the smoke were making her nauseated. The sooner she got out of there, the better.

She flipped open her notebook. *Rigor mortis* on a scale of one to four. *Livor mortis*, same scale. Flex, poke, cut. Take the temperatures. Make notes. She became increasingly automatic in her movements as she became more and more queasy.

Suddenly, she sagged against the bed, savaged by a sharp pain in her gut. The room was spinning; her breath was ragged until the dizziness and spasms ceased.

"You okay, ma'am?" A uniformed policeman stood in the doorway.

Jess straightened up, took a deep breath. "Yes. Thanks." Everyone had the occasional meaningless pain, It was a cramp, nothing more. She bent over the body again, the realized that the cop hadn't moved.

He was evidently upset at the sight of a pregnant woman fooling with a corpse; he seemed to be thinking about busting her for unnatural practices. "You shouldn't be in here with that thing," motioning toward what had been a power-broker. "Not in your condition."

Jess forced a smile. "I'm almost finished. I'm all right."

He finally left, still dubious. She stifled the urge to dash after him and admit that 'all right' was a gross exaggeration. The cramp was gone, no need to re-inforce the view that pregnant women couldn't do their jobs. And she was almost finished. It looked straightforward. Berrington hadn't been dead for much more than three hours. His skin was cherry pink, consistent with carbon monoxide poisoning, also known as smoke inhalation. Other than an empty drug vial on the bedside table - and that meant zilch in Chemical City, U.S.A. - there was nothing to suggest a less-thanpeaceful accidental end.

Her pencil faltered. Another spasm. Jess closed her eyes, willing the pain to subside, begging it to subside. Eventually it did. She took more deep breaths, moving carefully now so as not to disturb the precarious equilibrium.

Just follow standard procedures, turn off the mind and let habit take control. Remove the jewelry from the body, put it in a plastic bag; seal the bag, initial it, make a note. One watch, gold and diamond band. New page. One neck chain, gold link. New page. Two rings, one diamond, on sapphire. New page. One vial, empty.

Jess put them all into an evidence envelope, which she sealed and signed. She drew a deep breath. She was beginning to feel a little better. The old body had a mile or two left after all. Enough, at least, to take her through a quick survey of the death site.

It was your run-of-the-mill fantasy suite - so bit you'd have to start for bed before you were tired or you'd never make it. Soft velvet couches, marble tables, a large-screen television, a wall of stereo equipment. Not to mention the oversized antique four-poster and a tapestry or two.

His and her dressing rooms, the latter almost devoid of contents. Mrs. Berrington was either improbably ascetic or living elsewhere. The same could not be said for the mister. His closets were crammed with expensive conservative clothing, all neatly lined up and arranged by color. There were even extra shoelaces on the shoe tree.

The *piece de resistance*, however, was the bathroom. A tub you could swim laps in, a shower spacious enough for the host and twenty of this closest friends. Marble. Mirrors. Gilt. Buttons to push for music, recessed lights and, for all she knew, dancing girls.

The rich *were* different. Jess couldn't conceive of actually using the toilet in such surroundings. It would be like peeing in church.

* * *

Detective Arnheim was still outside on the lawn, thumbs in his vest pockets, glumly not acknowledging the presence beside him of another man. Jess's heart sank when she got close enough to identify the city's most sleazy self-proclaimed "investigative" reporter. Just what she needed to lend the final touch to a late night of death, work and stomach pains. Jerry Katz.

"Jess! Babe! Great to see ya!" He advanced to meet her, arms spread wide. Fate had condemned him to look exactly like what he was, a sharp-nosed ferret with a nasty mind. "It's been too long!"

Jess neatly avoided the embrace, nodded unenthusiastically and turned to Francis. "Has my van arrived?"

"Yeah, over by the stables."

"So you're handling this, babe?" Jerry wasn't discouraged; he'd been snubbed by much more important figures.

"Mmm." She scanned the surroundings, then saw one of her people. "Chester!"

A raw-boned young man with an abysmal complexion hurried over. "Hi, Jess. How are you?"

It was important to go along with the civilities. Chester had low self-esteem and assumed that any lack of friendliness was attributable to his own deficiencies. "I'm fine, thanks. Glad to see you. Listen, the body's upstairs in the bedroom. When you get back to the office, would you order a physical work-up and a blood test?" She belatedly remembered to smile.

Chester flushed happily. "Sure thing, Jess. Right away." He scurried off, right hand caressing the badge at his belt.

Arnheim says it looks like an accident." Jerry popped a thick wad of gum in his mouth as he spoke; it took

Jess a moment to decipher the words.

"Uh-huh."

"Typical cover-up."

Jess sighed. "You carry jumping to conclusions to a length Evel Knievel would be proud of."

"Come on, babe, I wasn't born yesterday."

"I'd always assumed you were hatched," Jess said sweetly.

Francis threw her a warning glance.

Jess sighed again; he was right. Don't antagonize the press, even when said press had many of the characteristics of a small amphibian slightly larger than a frog. "Why do you say it's a cover-up, Jerry?"

"Look, a big honcho like Berrington doesn't die in an accident, right? I mean, a God who gave him broads galore, more power than the Mob and half the gold of Fort Knox, doesn't knock him off in an accident. Catch my drift?"

Jess and Francis exchanged weary glances. It was L.A.P.D.'s finest who answered. "Didn't know you were a religious man, Jerry." Francis took Jess's arm and led her away.

You feeling all right? You look like hell."

Jess rubbed her neck. "I'm just tired. Is the house-keeper still around?"

"Yeah." He inclined his head toward a gazebo overlooking the tennis courts.

"Have the next of kin been notified?"

"You kidding? Everyone but the President's been notified. There's a wife, but she's sick or something. Her doctor's gonna break the news. And the house is in the company's name - some big-deal vice-president's on his way to take charge of the premises."

"Thank God for that at least." The coroner's office couldn't leave a house unattended, and Jess was in no shape to spend hours waiting to turn the keys over to someone.

* * *

The gazebo was a white lacy affair, a structure meant for delicate southern belles sipping mint juleps and holding parasols against the coarsening wind and sun. The only person using it now was a casting mistake. The housekeeper's leathery skin would defeat a Sahara sun and her wispy, yellow-gray hair had been given up on long ago. She was huddled into a ball on a white wicker couch, her hands clasped between bony knees.

Jess cleared her throat.

"Oh!" The head came up. Pale eyes behind thick glasses skittishly surveyed the threat.

"My name is Jess Canby. I'm from the coroner's office." She kept her voice low and soothing. "May I ask you a few questions?"

"Coroner's office. Questions." The repetition was empty, she was just mimicking sounds.

Jess stepped inside. The woman flinched, and Jess pulled a chair toward the entrance, careful not to come too close. "I have a few questions. Is that okay?"

The words began to get through. "I guess."

"What is your name?"

"Lil."

Jess waited.

"Lil Scott. I been with them twenty years." Lil's voice was dull, thick. It didn't sound grief-stricken; she was too numb to put that much emotion into it.

"Well, that's really something. Twenty years." Jess pulled out her notebook. "What time did you get home tonight?"

"Ten. Ten-fifteen. I didn't even see no fire - not till I got inside. Then I smelled it."

"Did you go to wake up Mr. Berrington?"

"No - no, I - well, I -"

"That's all right. I,m not accusing you of anything. I'm just getting the facts."

"Facts." Lil nodded. She watched *Cagney and Lacey*.

"What did you do when you smelled the fire?"

"I called the cops. The police."

"Yes, and then?"

"I came outside. I didn't know he was in there. I

mean, I didn't see no fire or nothing. I just smelled it when I got inside."

"Was there anyone else in the house?"

"Huh?"

"Mr. Berrington was living there. You were living there. Was anyone else living there?"

"Naw. Not now. Just him." Lil's voice didn't communicate a great deal of awe for "him."

"What about Mrs. Berrington?"

"Oh, she left a long time ago. He was happy to see her go - left him free to do what he wanted with the other ones, didn't it?"

"What other ones?"

The housekeeper clamped her lips shut, tense again. Jess made a note and left that for another time. "Did the Berringtons have any children?"

Lil did have emotions, somewhere. Her eyes filled up as she swallowed convulsively.

"I gather there are children." Jess could gather nothing at all, but maybe another approach would be more effective.

"Not now." Even Lil could tell that more was required. She stared at Jess, her face impassive again. "They had a daughter - but she's dead now."

"I see." Jess spoke gently. "When did she die?"

"A month ago, Tuesday. She was a good girl, not like she was theirs at all. I raised her from a babe. The mother of hers cared about her card games and her -" Lil broke off and shifted on the couch. "Lorrie. That's her name. She'd have been twenty-three next month. I told her all that bicycling around would come to no good end. Wandering around at all hours, just a girl alone."

"I'm sorry." Not the Ozzie-and-Harriet-Nelson family from the sound of it. But then, how could three people stay close to each other in a house you needed a map to navigate? "Lil, I'll leave you alone now. If I have more questions, I'll get in touch with you again. Where will you be staying?"

"What?" The woman looked ten years older than she

had when Jess started talking to her. "Where? Why - here! It's my home! Been here twenty years."

Let the vice-president handle that one. Jess stood up to leave.

Lil peered closer, showing interest in her interrogator for the first time. "You're pregnant."

"No doubt about it."

"That's nice." A very tentative smile came and went; she sank back and Jess was forgotten again.

* * *

The pains returned before she was out of Bel Air, and this time they didn't go away so fast. Jess sweated them out at the side of the road, her eyes closed, her pulse racing with terror for her baby. God, just let these pass safely and I'll never smoke another cigarette. Not even one. I'll go to church regularly. I'll do volunteer work in the barrios. I'll never get angry at Michael again. Just, please, please, let my baby be okay.

The agony finally ebbed, but the horror didn't go with it. Grimly Jess drove straight to the hospital and sat in the emergency room, waiting for her doctor and for Michael.

Dr. Constance Hartman, obstetrician and gynecologist, arrived first; she'd almost finished examining Jess when Michael burst into the examining room, his face ashen under the tan.

"Is she okay? Are you okay?" Both of his hands were on one of Jess's holding tight enough to cut off her circulation. "What's happening? Baby, are you all right?"

"Jess is just fine, but you're on your way to having a stroke. Calm down and sit down." Connie's style was something between Mae West and a Mob enforcer. She drawled her orders, but woe betide the patient who disregarded them. Jess adored her. "Jess is a little tired. But then" - she shrugged broad, bony shoulders "who isn't?"

Jess winced. Connie herself was gaunt and red-eyed.

She needed a 3:00 a.m. conference like she needed a hole in her head.

"Gimme a cigarette, Michael." Connie leaned against the sink and lit up, oblivious to or entirely uninterested in the hospital regulations posted above her head that warned "No Smoking". Connie was six feet tall, as lanky as cowboy and affecting much the same style of dress. She wore no makeup on her angular face: no curls disturbed the patrician high forehead, no jewelry softened the pale skin. She was either truly homely or a mind-blowing beauty, and Jess had never decided which. "Jess's pains came from tension and fatigue."

Michael sighed. "Yeah. Well, you tell Jess to slow down. And good luck. I've tried and I've got the scars to prove it."

Connie grinned at Jess. "You don't listen to your lord and master? Sweetheart, you'll never hold a man that way."

"No, but I've got a great set of chains." Jess swung her feet down. "I'm sorry I got you in her, Connie. Hell of an hour for snappy repartee."

Connie waved away the apology and came over to sit beside her. "Enough fun. Listen, the county won't fall apart if you take the occasional nap. Hell, honey, even God took the seventh day off."

"Sure," Jess agreed, "and look at the mess the world's in."

"I'm serious. Auntie Connie is speaking and that means you're listening. I want you take if easier. Take a little time off."

Jess looked away. She couldn't do that and Connie knew it. Michael was working like a dog, but there was only one paycheck coming in. Babies cost money.

Connie read her mind. "I didn't say quit. I didn't say take a leave of absence. Just take a little time, now and then. An hour. Ninety minutes. Start small, build up to a lunch break. You got it?"

"She's got it." Michael brought Jess's clothes over to her. "And if she disobeys, I'll squeal to you."

"That should do it." Connie paused at the doorway.

21

"Those particular pains weren't serious, Jess. But agony is nature's way of hinting you should relax. Look at it this way - I'll be very, very disappointed if you don't cool it. And I trained with Ilsa, the She-Wolf of the SS.

Chapter 2

Jess woke up very slowly, more than usually disoriented but unable to figure out why. Then she got it. The room was glowing with sunshine. Not strange for August, but strange for early morning. She reached for the clock, and then leaped out of bed. Eleven thirty!

"What are you doing?" Michael walked in with a breakfast tray. "Back into bed at once."

"Are you kidding? Do you know what time it is? I'm on duty today I've got a ton of work to do."

Michael shook his head pityingly. "Brain damage. So sad in one so young. No memory at all. You don't remember last night, do you? The pain? Connie?"

"Of course, I do. I feel terrific this morning. Morning? Afternoon, almost. I've got to get to the office."

"Silence, woman!" Michael pointed sternly at the bed. "Back before I wreak havoc."

"But — "

"I already called your office and explained that you won't be in. And you lied to me. Not only are you not indispensable, but I had to talk to six people before I found one who recalled hearing your name before."

Jess started to laugh.

"Here's breakfast. A nice, slimming repast of greasy eggs, carcinogenic bacon, toast collapsing under the weight of its marmalade and coffee with cream."

"Uncle. I cry uncle." She got back under the covers and attacked the plate. Michael stretched out beside her, opening the morning paper to show the headlines.

"Berrington." her mouth was full and it sounded like "Brnnnn."

"His is the name on everyone's lips this morning," Michael agreed cheerfully. "He made front page and the business section. And you will be surprised to learn that your Fearless Leader has been on all three networks assuring the city, state and nation that he's got the case under control."

"Harper hasn't has a media fix in days," she said

sardonically. "If this hadn't happened, he'd have gone into withdrawal." One couldn't accuse Dr. Colman Harper, chief medical examiner (also known as the coroner) of L.A. County, of hiding from his public. Television viewers saw more of him than his staff did, which was fine and dandy as far as said staff was concerned.

"Now, now, Harper's not perfect but neither was his predecessor," Michael said teasingly. "You just liked Lawrence Terrell because he was *your* man."

"He was dad's man, actually. But he hired me and kept on promoting me and I love a man like that." Jess slathered another inch of marmalade on the toast. "Besides, he was better. Harper surrounds himself with legions of yesmen and toadies." She chuckled nastily. "And I can barely bring myself to agree with him about the weather. He'd love to get rid of me but he can't. Hell, I could match him a councilman and raise him a senator any old day."

The telephone interrupted. Jess raised an eyebrow. "See, I told you I was indispensable." She picked it up. "Hello?"

"Hi. Leon here, Jess."

"Hi, is something up?"

"Nah, Chester asked me to ring you. Said the work-up on your stiff's done and everthing's cool."

"Uhhuh." She ignored the terminology. Leon was forensic technician who wanted to be the toughest hombre in the West. For some reason, he figured that the jargon of bad forties movies would get him there. "Everything else under control?"

"Yeah. Barely. Bad night, last night. Kirsch and I cut up six bodies already today. By the way, one was your big shot. No wonder he didn't wake up, he was doped to the gills." Leon yawned loudly. "Six autopsies in one morning. Seven's my record, but six is nothing to sneeze at."

"Uhhuh." She rang off and returned to the toast, reading the paper over Michael's shoulder. "Look at all those inches Berrington rated. When I go, I want to go like that."

Michael laughed. "What's the difference? You're gone. You don't get to see the next day's paper."

"You don't know that for sure." She reached for the business section and skimmed the lead story. "Jesus, I knew he was big but I didn't really grasp the size of it! Berrington Industries is the second largest company of its kind in California and our lad ran it like a oneman show. The stock market's going to go nuts."

"Satellites are big business."

"His were. Lots of fingers in lots of pies. Defense contracts, NASA space programs, communications, cable TV " She put down the paper to finish her coffee. The dead man had had a lot to live for. Odds were, it was a simple case, sleeping pills notwithstanding. An accident, an act of God, *hubris* brought down. It was going to be messy, what with everyone who was anyone watching over her shoulder, but it wasn't going to be taxing. "As I recall, his father had a nice little armaments factory, so Berrington was never poor. But the big millions are fairly recent."

"Millions are millions, babe."

"Nope." Jess's hand automatically went toward the bedside table for a cigarette; she withdrew it when she remembered she was trying not to smoke. "Little millions buy toys like yachts and Rolls Royces and mansions. Big millions buy people and power."

"The question remains," Michael said slowly, "who'd want to buy people and power? That's what politics is all about, and that's what I don't understand about wanting to go into politics."

Jess mentally kicked herself. She'd done it again, stuffed her foot right in there with the toast and jam. "It doesn't have to be that way someone's got to run things."

"Someone's got to get cancer too. But why you? It'll destroy you. It's so goddam corrupt."

She felt herself flushing. "Dad wasn't corrupt."

"I didn't say he was. He was my fatherinlaw and I liked him a lot, but I never knew him as mayor. So I don't know what he was."

"He was a good man, a good politician who cared. If he hadn't been mayor, someone who cared less might have been. I think it matters who's in charge, and you used to think so too."

"That was long ago when we didn't sit around in back rooms smoking cigars and dividing up cities."

"I don't smoke cigars." Bad joke, worse timing. "Look, I've worked for the Democrats all my life. I like politics, I'm good at it, I've paid my dues and it the party offers me an Assembly seat next time, I want to take it."

"If? I thought it was all sewn up? Isn't that why the party hot shots have you running around to rallies and giving speeches?"

"Nothing's sewn up till the votes are counted. But, yes, I've got a good shot at it. Dad's friends have been wonderful to me." She got out of bed. What saint did you pray to for a cigarette to appear between your lips? "I won't do anything you're violently opposed to, but you're not being fair. Four years ago, when we got married, you were an architect. Now, you're a writer. Okay, I went along with your choices. Is it too much to ask for the same treatment?"

He thought about that, blue eyes staring into space. Finally, he sighed. "I'm sorry, babe. I guess I've got quite a bee in my bonnet about politics, but maybe I could at least shut up about it."

Jess came back to cuddle against him. "It's not so bad. Martin's involved with politics and you still think he's wonderful." She nuzzled his neck. "And he's nowhere near as talented in bed as I am."

Michael pulled her closer. "I dare you to say that again."

* * *

There was something almost sinfully pleasurable about a day of utter sloth. But sooner or later, reality had to be faced again, and today it was dinner. Jess puttered about the kitchen, searching for something that could pass as a meal. The fridge was loaded with condiment, but mustard and mint sauce cried out for something to be put on top of. Really, she and Michael could use a wife, preferably someone who didn't loll about in bed all day when there was provisioning to do. And laundry, and cleaning.

"Jess!" Michael's shout preceded him down the stairs. "Dana just called. Haberman wants to meet with us tonight!"

Jess threw her arms around him. "Michael! That's fantastic!"

"It's good now, certainly," her admitted, afraid to tempt fate by going further. "But are you okay alone? What'll you do for dinner?"

"I'm fine, believe me. There's, uh, oh, lots of things." She loved mustard. "I'm so excited - this could be your break."

"I've got to change. We're meeting at - " He paused and grinned. "Guess."

"Well, if it's not McDonald's, it's gotta be the Polo Lounge."

"Hole in one."

* * *

Frozen broccoli, it turned out, wasn't much improved by mint sauce. Jess could speak on the subject with authority. She picked at her plate in front of the television where James Garner was proving to Doris Day that life without a man by your side was a rotten business. Probably, she should be offended by it, but Jess had to admit that the argument, coming from James Garner, had a certain charm.

The telephone cut through the saccharine.

"Hello?"

"Mrs. Canby?"

"Yes."

"This is Lil Scott - Mr. Berrington's housekeeper? I met you - "

27

"Yes, Miss Scott, I remember you." What kind of life led someone to believe that they couldn't be remembered for twenty-four hours? "What can I do for you?"

"It's them, they're watchin' me!" The housekeeper spoke in a high-pitched whine that made Jess hold the receiver away from her ear. "The cops, they don't give a damn, and I figure nobody cares about me, but maybe you'd listen, you bein' pregnant 'n all."

Jess's shoulders sagged. She understood very little of what she was hearing but, the last point was clear enough. "Slow down, Miss Scott. What's the problem?"

"Lil. Call me Lil, ma'am, I don't hold with being called Miss Scott, I know my place."

"Lil. Fine. What's the matter?" If she discovered who at the office had given out this number, a head was going to roll.

"They's been people at my place, and they want me to get out - but I'm not goin'. This here's my home, I been here twenty years, and I got a right. And they asked me questions to see what I know, and they's somebody watchin' me scarin' me and -"

"Lil, I can't arrange for you to stay there. I don't have the power to do that."

"No, maybe not, but I figured maybe you'd listen." Dull disillusion came over the line. "Since I was scared 'n all."

Jess fought the pang of sympathy. It was nine-thirty, goddamit! And she was tired. This wasn't her problem, there was nothing she could do for the old woman. Damn. "Lil, if I come over, will you feel less scared?"

"Oh, yes! Oh, thank you, ma'am! Thank you!"

Jess trudged to the closet. It was a good thing Michael wasn't here: Or Connie, for that matter.

* * *

The gates to the Berrington estate swung open to let Jess in. The place was deserted, silent except for the intermittent sound of leaves brushing against each other whenever the still torpid air stirred. Jess parked in front of the house and stayed put for a moment, vaguely oppressed by the floodlights that played up the grim reminders of fire and death. Black streaks and water stains decorated the facade of the mansion, a line of broken windows grimaced at the trampled lawns. No wonder Lil was edgy. A writer of Gothic tales would kill for this setting.

"Mrs. Canby!" The housekeeper hurried out the front door, her faded hair no more kempt than the previous night but the print housedress somewhat cleaner.

Jess pulled her stomach away from the wheel and ungracefully ejected herself. "Hi, Lil. How are you feeling?"

The other woman clasped her elbows, shaking her head fretfully. "Not so good, not so good. Funny things is happening."

"What sort of funny things?"

"They's a man watchin' me, watchin' the house." Her eyes wouldn't stop moving. "They's tryin' to scare me off."

Jess looked around. "What man?"

"He's here, all right. Down there a piece," Lil whispered harshly, pointing a finger and then hastily snatching it back to the circle of safety. "By them trees. He's here, all right."

Jess glanced at the grove, then back at Lil. The woman's face was white. She was sincere, one had to give her that. Paranoid, maybe; hysterical, maybe but sincere. "The police probably left someone to guard the house. Thieves often follow fires."

"No, no, that's no cop!" The whine was tinged with terror. "He's from the company, I bet. He's tryin' to scare me off."

Jess sighed. "I'll take a look."

Lil stayed well back while Jess walked across the lawn. The thicket of orange and avocado trees lay in shadow, otherwise innocuous enough, fragrant greenery melting into a thicker growth of palms and ferns, pines and almost-bare trunks that had overseen the hillside before Bel Air was even a gleam in a developer's eye.

29

She wandered in, seeing nothing in the darkness, no lurking figures, no glinting weapons, not even tell-tale cigarette butts. Jess shook her head wryly. Who did she think she was, straining over her stomach to peer at the ground? Pocahontas with night vision? Maybe and Indian tracker with a flashlight could make something of the terrain, but U.C.L.A. hadn't offered a course in night-tracking and it wasn't knowledge that a Hancock Park girl was born with.

She took another step forward, then froze, Had that been a noise beside her? A smothered cough? Or just the rustle of leaves? Suddenly, her mouth was dry. When Jane Fonda recommended exercise for pregnant women, this wasn't what she had in mind. Jess started to back out, very slowly, one careful step at a time.

"What's wrong?" Lil called tensely.

Jess took a deep breath and pasted a shallow smile on her face. Everyone knew hysteria was contagious. "Nothing. Nothing's wrong." She returned to the front steps. "Let's go inside and talk."

Lil's glance fell to Jess's stomach. "Oh, yes, I was forgetting. You want a coffee or something?"

"I wouldn't mind a cold drink." She followed the housekeeper inside. Fire damage was everywhere: the air stank of stale smoke, and dust still filtered down from holes chopped in ceilings. The parquet floors, warped under pools of water, were dotted with plaster chips and broken glass that crunched underfoot. Jess shivered. Despite the temperature outside, the gloom gave off a dank chill.

The kitchen, at the back of the house, was a little better. The fire had spared it as had the fire-fighters. For that matter, it apparently had been spared everyone's attention for decades. It was a large square room full of nineteen-forties equipment that blended nicely into faded green walls, black-and-white linoleum marked with forty years of scuffs. Cracked counters, the lady of this manor had been confident she'd never want to use the room.

Jess accepted a Coke in the can while Lil fussed

around, swiping ineffectually at crumbs with a none-too-clean cloth.

"I know he's out there," Lil muttered nervously. "I can feel him. I saw him before and now I can feel him." She nodded ferociously at Jess. "He's from the office - they said no, but he is. They want me out and I'm not goin'. This is my home."

"Who's 'they'?"

"The men from Mr. Berrington's company. That man, Desmond somethin', one of them foreign names." She looked at Jess, suddenly sly. "They think I'm dumb, don't know what's goin' on."

"What do you mean?"

The face turned resolutely away. "Then they went through Mr. Berrington's study and everythin' and locked it, like I was goin' to mix in. And they went through Lorrie's room that was hers when she lived here and my room too! They was rude, real rude, askin' all them questions."

"What questions?" Jess had the helpless feeling that she was never going to get a grip on this conversation.

"About Lorrie and Mr. Berrington. Fool things, like how did he feel when she died."

"Oh. Well, that makes sense, Lil. They want to know if he was so upset that he, uh, set the fire himself." Let someone else take on the chore of explaining to Lil the stock-market implications of a tycoon's suicide.

"Upset? That one? Not him," Lil scoffed contemptuously. "He was sorry when Lorrie died but sorry does no good. He should've listened when she was here, instead of yellin' at her and runnin' around with that floozy and chasin' Lorrie out of her very own house!" Vindictiveness was pouring out, overcoming discretion. "And that mother of hers, her and her bottle! Leavin' two years ago and not botherin' to worry about Lorrie! I brought her up, nobody else. She loved me. When she was down in South America in all them foreign countries, she didn't write her parents, did she? No, sir, she just wrote her Lil." The voice thickened, softened, vengeance trapped in the lump in her throat. "She's gone now. I got nothin' except my home and them letters and they're takin'both away from me."

"Shhh!" Jess hissed, a hand rigidly in the air. There had been a noise in the hall, she was almost positive of it. An intake of breath, a shift of a floorboard.

Lil was holding onto the counter with white-knuckled fingers. "He's there, ain't he? He's there, like I said."

Jess stood up reluctantly. Not a bone in her body wanted to investigate, but someone had to. That someone was plainly not going to be Lil. "Wait here."

The hall was dark; Jess stopped outside the kitchen until her eyes adjusted to the shadows. She was alone, but something wasn't right in the corridor. It took a concentrated effort to pinpoint it. A door was open - she hadn't passed an open door when she came into the house, and there was no breeze to blame.

She groped for a light switch. No, it couldn't be blamed on a breeze, unless breezes had learned how to turn keys. The offending door led to Berrington's study, supposedly locked up after today's executive visit.

Nor did breezes leave a room looking like this one. The heavy oak filing cabinets had been emptied; the drawers of the antique desk were gaping, also empty. Files were strewn all over the broadloom; documents littered the sofas and chairs. Someone had painstakingly examined every single piece of paper in the place.

Jess knelt by the desk, quickly skimming the top sheets of the nearest pile. House records: plumbing bills back to 1973, receipts for reupholstery, medical-insurance slips. She picked up a thick envelope. Inside were canceled checks for a personal account at the Brentwood branch of the Bank of America. Probably no more useful than the records of blocked sinks, but something made her hold onto it. She heaved herself up again and crossed to the french doors on the outside wall. They were shut but not locked - and that was enough for her. The grounds were pitch black at the back, as inviting as a cancer ward. The sleuthing part of the day was over.

Lil hadn't moved a muscle; she was still gripping the

counter as if to hold onto reality. "What was it? Who's there?"

Jess commanded her face to make a smile, but she didn't need a mirror to know how insubordinate it was being. "No one, no one I saw, at least." She kept her tone casual, calm, reassuring. As long as Lil didn't take her pulse, she might get away with the pretense. "Did you happen to see what the study looked like when Desmond left?"

The other woman shook her head. "Wouldn't let me get near it. Afraid I'd steal some of his precious books or somethin'"

"Uh-huh. Lil, it's really eerie here at night. I don't blame you for getting nervous - I wouldn't stay here alone. And you can't live here forever, they'll be selling the house sooner or later. Maybe it would be best if you thought about leaving?"

Lil's eyes darkened at the betrayal, and her shoulders sagged. "Them big shots always get their way," she said hopelessly. "They got everyone in their pockets, I guess. Nobody's gonna listen to me."

Jess couldn't bear the implication. "Look, I'm here. I'm listening. But it isn't up to me whether you're allowed to stay. I'm just saying it mightn't be such a good idea." She cast around for another topic. "You mentioned something about Lorrie's letters?"

Lil wouldn't look at her.

"What about the letters?"

The voice was low, almost inaudible. "They was all I had of Lorrie. They're takin' everythin' away from me, the house and the letters. It ain't right."

"Someone took the letters Lorrie wrote to you?"

The other woman nodded slowly, a single tear escaping to run alongside her nose.

"Who took them?"

"That man I told you about."

Jess was nonplussed an showed it. What earthly use could they be to Desmond-of-the-foreign-name?

Lil's lips tightened. "You don't need to believe me. He took them, that's all."

33

"Lil, if I promise to try to get the letters back for you, will you do me a favor? Will you go stay with a friend?" Jess couldn't keep her head from turning to watch the door. "Will you?"

The pause lengthened. Finally, Lil bowed her head and gave up. "I got a friend who keeps house in Brentwood."

* * *

Jess sat for a long time out on the bedroom deck, sipping iced tea, watching the ocean, and wondering why the Berrington estate had so set her teeth on edge. Okay, the ruined house was desolate, especially at night. yes, there had been a prowler on the premises. But the unease was with her still, and she didn't tend to be a fearful sort. She'd certainly experienced far more dismal settings for death — and forgotten them within the hour. Nor was it Lil's terror. That, looked at now from the vantage point of home an sanity, was easily explained as the rambling despair of a aging, not-very-bright woman facing an uncertain future.

Even so, the Bel Air mansion had got under Jess's skin. Maybe it's atmosphere reflected the unhappy desperation of it's menage. Beams and rafters soaked in years of neglect, disillusion, ambition, hate. Had the Berringtons ever been young and starry-eyed? Had their marriage been a love match, or a merger? Maybe that was why Robert Berrington was dead - a Saturday night alone in the cavernous house, totting up the balance sheet and finding that the bottom line was red, that the emotional hollowness outweighed the stuffed bank accounts.

Jess impatiently shook her head. That was ridiculous. Her own parents had been something less than idyllically happy. Her father was lost in his own pursuits: the polls, the constituents, the press, his cronies. Her mother had turned to Bonwit Teller's. And still, her childhood had been happy, the old Hancock Park house cozy and warm. And her father had died of cancer, not

34

suicide.

She was relieved to hear the front door bang. "Up here, Michael!"

He bounded into the room. "How are you feeling, sweetie?"

"Fine. It's so peaceful out here. How was your meeting?"

He spared barely a glance for the flood lit waves. "It looks like we made a deal!"

"Michael!" She jumped into his arms. "Tell me all about it!"

"Not much to tell. Trail Productions wants to do the movie - and they're happy to give me a crack at the first draft of the screenplay."

They grinned at each other. This was it, the break that almost never came to a writer.

"I've got a close deadline, I'll have to work like a dog." He caught himself. "When the contract's signed. Lots could still go wrong. It takes a couple of weeks to iron out the details."

Neither of them paid the slightest heed to the cavil; still holding hands, they smiled broadly at each other.

"What did you do tonight?" he asked.

"Watched a little T.V. and then Lil Scott called. Robert Berrington's housekeeper." She paused, choosing her details carefully. Some were interesting, other not the sort of thing one needed to tell a husband just about to break into the big-time. "She was frightened, up in that big old house by herself."

"I don't wonder."

"So I drove over - just for a few moments. Just to convince her to go stay with a girlfriend. I couldn't ignore her, a scared old lady out of a job -"

"Okay, okay. Mother Theresa would have done no less."

"Theresa would have brought her home to live."

Michael shook his head. "That's why I married you instead."

Chapter 3

The elevator doors creaked open at the basement level, and Jess strode out. Even after only two days away, the smell of formaldehyde hit her like a kick in the stomach. It was like a hospital odor, but less antiseptic; their "patients" didn't have to worry about getting sicker.

It was a busy morning. Gurneys lined the dingy corridor, the bodies only partly covered by pale green sheets. The corpses looked waxy, not quite real, particularly well-crafted mannequins — though there wouldn't be a big retail market for mannequins mottled with purple patches of settling blood, disfigured by violence or poverty or illness. In quantity, the dead lost the pathos of death - except for the children. Jess stopped by one small black figure, a victim of a car accident, from the looks of it.

"Seven years old." An investigator came out of the common office. "Driving with his nineteen year old cousin in a seventy-nine Buick. No seatbelt. The cousin walked away from it, but he didn't."

"No." Jess sighed, covered up the little head, continued on into the watch-command office. On one side, a glass wall overlooked the clerks who took the first calls about fatalities; at the other end, a counter led to the carport where brown vans arrived with the dead. Lying in between were gray metal desks, closed-circuit TV screens, filing cabinets and dirty linoleum. It was enough to make any self-respecting commercial decorator whimper, but the county didn't spend money on offices not seen by the general public.

Bill Kothner was the senior chief investigator on duty, hunching over the green-and-white daily reports, his reading glasses sliding down his nose. "Oh, hi, Jess. How're you feeling?"

"Fat and lazy."

He grinned and handed over the reports; "No time for sloth today. We've already picked up twenty-three.

If it keeps up, we're going to break our record."

"Swell." Jess flipped through the papers. Bill was a good, if stolid, administrator but he was an ex-jock who kept tabs on the statistics of carnage as if he were a sports announcer. "How many investigators in?"

"Ten. I called for another two about an hour ago."

"Good. Though where we'll put them is another matter." She had thirty investigators working around the clock to handle the actual cases, eight senior investigators who deployed the personnel, three assistant chiefs who spelled her, plus thirty-nine technicians, embalmers, photographers, and record-keepers. All were housed in the basement, a square of offices, cold storage rooms, and labs adequate for half that number. If the Los Angeles death rate continued to climb, they'd be working out in the parking lot.

"Bill." A young first-call officer appeared with a piece of paper. "Senior citizen fell down the stairs at Palmview Retirement Home in Van Nuys. No doctor in attendance."

Bill nodded, scanning the page.

"There've lot of fatalities lately in the old folks' homes," Jess observed quietly.

"Yeah. Maybe we'd better pick this one up and take a look. Maybe they're greasing the stairs."

Jess nodded, satisfied. The coroner had to investigate the death of anyone who hadn't seen a doctor within twenty days or whose doctor wouldn't sign the death certificate. On an average day, fifty or so fell into those categories; about a third were patently self-explanatory and only technically their responsibility. Those were sent directly to the mortuaries and token forms were filled out, the data often acquired by phone. The rest came in through the carport for physical work-ups, autopsies, embalming, paperwork.

"Morning, Jess." A female investigator, plump, freckled, and cheerful, wheeled a gurney inside onto the weigh scale. "I'm bringing in that domestic, Bill."

"Hi, Lynn." Jess did a double take. "Now, that's a big man!"

"Sure is. Mr. Marsacoupolos here is six-three, three hundred pounds and change." Lynn tried to adopt a serious expression. "The missus is four-ten and maybe one hundred pounds. She was tired of being beaten up. That's what she told the cops. Maybe it was his right, maybe it wasn't, but she was tired of it. So she took a frying pan and talked back."

"You dames are getting to be incredible," Bill complained. "It's gotten so no husband's safe, and you dames are enjoying it."

"Now, now, Bill, you know we don't approve of murder." Jess grinned. "You must be tired. Isn't your shift almost over?"

"Yeah. Consuela's — "

"Here! Consuela's here!" A small-boned, dark-haired woman breathlessly dashed in. "Sorry I'm late. Go on, Bill, I'll sign you out. Hi Jess. Lynn."

Bill got to his feet.

"Oh, Bill?" Jess called just before he vanished. "Remember not to annoy Marie now. "

He grunted and left, pretending not to hear the chuckles.

"Consuela, I'll be in my office."

"Sure."

Jess took another look at her. "You don't sound like your usual self. Something wrong?"

"No, everything's fine. "

The words were belied by the tone and the unsmiling countenance. Consuela Martinez was an engaging twenty-eight-year-old who was almost always smiling. She was one of the bright spots in Jess's staff, living proof that sometimes good things happen to good people. She'd started out as a filing clerk upstairs. Not only had she passed the civil-service exam to become an investigator five years ago, she'd been so good at it that Jess was able to promote her to senior investigator in record time. "Consuela, I don't want to pry but — "

"It's the usual." The young woman shrugged, pretending to minimize it. "You know."

"Your father again?"

Consuela took a deep breath. "Yes, and now Guillermo, too. Papa got him to tell me he wouldn't marry me until I quit my job."

Jess looked at her in dismay. Consuela was being torn apart by a father and a fiance who were both rigidly locked into Old World traditions. If a man earned enough, his wife didn't work. "What are you going to do?"

"I guess I'll have to tell Guillermo that I won't give in to blackmail. I don't know how he'll take it, but I'll feel better."

Jess nodded. It was obvious how he'd take it, but there were other fish in the sea. She made a mental note to cast a line or two for Consuela.

The phone buzzed. Consuela answered it, then motioned Jess to wait a moment. "Uh-huh. Okay." She hung up. "Dr. Harper wants to see you the second you get in. Are you in? I'm supposed to let them know."

"Damn. Okay, I'll go up."

* * *

Harper didn't react when Jess knocked at the open door. He was making notes, concentrating deeply so as to prove how incredibly insignificant Jess was compared to the weighty responsibilities of a coroner's life. An unbiased observer would probably consider him handsome, a storybook prince complete with craggy, rectangular face, cleft chin, serious brown eyes, and what looked to be character lines on forehead and cheeks. The effect was somewhat spoiled for those who knew he had no character.

"Yes. Well." He finally raised his head, regarding her as if he'd just received incontrovertible proof that she molested babies. "You're not well."

"I had a minor pain, nothing serious."

"Oh." Another of life's disappointments. Harper's fantasy was that Jess was going to quit in favor of motherhood. "You went out to the Berrington fire?"

"Yes."

"Mmm. Well, Stephen Bowdritch called me this morning. He's taken over the running of the business. Berrington Industries. He was Robert's right-hand man. I knew Robert, of course." Harper liked to split sentences and use three when one would have done. I was more pompous and therefore more "him." "We have to dispose of this case. Expeditiously."

Jess nodded noncommittally.

"Stephen is concerned about the effect of uncertainty. On the company. Naturally."

"Naturally."

He desperately wanted to find insolence on her face. He searched for it for a moment, then gave up. "He has offered any assistance we need. For a fast disposition. I'm giving you to him."

"With or without a dowry?"

"What?" Quick scan again. "The death of one of this city's most important men is hardly grounds for humor."

"I'll wrap it up a quickly as possible — though I assume you want the investigation of the death of one of this city's most important men to be thorough?"

He coughed and hunted around for a piece of paper. "Here. This is the address of their head office. I told Stephen you'd go see him. This morning." Cough, cough. Evident reluctance. "It seems he wants you. In particular. He has heard of you."

Jess said cheerfully, "Yes, I met Robert Berrington a couple of times. At Reg Cruickshank's house, I think." She left the office in a good mood. Cruickshank was on the Board of Supervisors, the county governing body that, among other things, appointed coroners. The reminder of her connections should nicely ruin Harper's day.

* * *

The City of Sprawl, of suburbs and gardens and Spanish red-roofed bungalows, now had a real, honest-to-goodness skyline. The downtown was pretending to be a little bit of New York, glass and steel towers shadowing clogged, narrow streets. Its denizens, dressed for board meetings rather than tennis games, actually trod the sidewalks and, what was more, at a clip unknown in Beverly Hills and Burbank.

Berrington Industries had chosen to make its corporate home at the top of one of the highest high-rises, forty floors up, as if the San Andreas Fault wouldn't dare disturb so much money power. Its offices were a desert of gleaming white modular furniture set against dead-white walls and rugs. Jess wished she'd thought to bring sunglasses.

The receptionist took her name with only a minor amount of condescension and allowed as how she'd pass it on.

Almost immediately a section of the wall slid back. "Ms. Canby?" The beckoning woman was tall, nearly six feet, thin and elegant in an Anne Klein skirt and a simple little silk blouse. Jess followed the undulating, perfect hips, feeling a new and deep empathy for Quasimodo.

A man was waiting for her at the door of a corner office.

"Ms. Canby, I'm Stephen Bowdritch, acting president. Won't you come in?"

"Thank you." Jess shook his hand and accompanied him on their hike across the field of Persian carpet. Bowdritch was average-looking: average height, average middle-age, average gray hair, average horn-rimmed glasses. Only his suit and tie, silk and definitely custom-made, were outstanding, and even they were average get-up for a senior executive.

Bowdritch looked at Jess's stomach and cleared his throat.

"Please sit down." He waved at a chair facing the desk. "Can I get you anything?"

"I'm fine, thank you." She hid a sigh. Bowdritch was going to fuss over her and she knew from experience that there wasn't a thing she could do about it.

"Tea? Coffee Uh — milk?"

Jess smiled. "No, thanks." She opened her briefcase

and took out a notebook. "I won't take up any more of your time than I must."

"Ah. Well." He returned to his tilting, swiveling, rolling leather desk-chair. "I believe we have a mutual friend."

"Oh, yes?"

"Reg Cruickshank."

"Oh, yes." Jess grinned. She'd been telling the truth when she waved the red flag at Harper.

"He thinks the world of you."

"That's very kind."

Bowdritch put his hands neatly on the desk, one on top of the other. "I appreciate your coming here. Things are rather hectic today, after our terrible loss." He paused. "Terrible. I work for Robert for twenty-two years. I suppose he was, in the jargon of the day, my mentor. And friend."

Bowdritch did look as if he was suffering. He was probably never ruddy, but no one's natural color was that sallow. "Please accept my sympathies."

"Thank you. " He took a deep breath. "This company was his creation, and it's up to me to see that it continues to run the way he'd have wanted. Now, especially. You see, Robert's last deal is just coming to fruition. It's enormous — to give you an idea of what's at stake, our company and a few other interests have formed a consortium to build and put up three satellites. Two for communications and one for the Defense Department."

Jess raised her eyebrows. Billions, that's what was at stake. No wonder Bowdritch was edgy about Berrington's death. If the great man had killed himself, investors and customers were going to be very uneasy. "I understand. Uncertainty causes chaos."

"Exactly." He began to perk up. "I see we understand each other."

"Of course, Mr. Berrington was very visible. My investigation will have to be thorough or the press" — she grimaced, thinking of Jerry Katz — "will crucify us."

"Yes, of course. Now, it seemed to me that a joint

42

coroner-police force investigation would be more efficient. So I spoke to a few friends — and I also suggested that you, er, oversee it."

"I see." Detective Francis Arnheim was going to just love the news. "Shall we get started, then?"

"Excellent." He pressed the intercom. "Susan, get Desmond in here, please." He turned back to Jess. "My assistant."

She nodded. "When did you last see Mr. Berrington?"

"Friday. We spent the day in meetings with the consortium. We call it A-COMM, by the way. We're just about ready to launch the satellites, so all of Robert's time was taken up with this project. It's the largest we've ever attempted." Excitement actually moved him to wave his hands in the air once. "Our communications network will cover this entire hemisphere — think of it!"

Unless she was much mistaken, he was slipping her the kind of inside tip that the SEC frowned upon. "How did Mr. Berrington seem to you?"

"The same as always. Energetic, businesslike. He was a rather, er, brisk man."

"He wasn't depressed, if that's what you mean."

Jess turned to see who the new voice belonged to. Its owner was a younger clone of Bowdritch, slightly shorter, slightly less gray, his suit just slightly less chic.

"Ah. Desmond Marchenko, Ms. Canby." Bowdritch motioned the newcomer to sit. "Desmond will handle anything you need."

So this was Desmond-of-the-foreign-name. Jess looked at him with interest, then returned to her notes. "Do either of you know what Mr. Berrington did on Saturday?"

Both shook their heads, Desmond's neck muscles going into play a split second after his boss's did.

"Carol, his secretary, might know," Bowdritch offered.

"Fine — or Mrs. Berrington could help?"

Bowdritch and Desmond exchanged glances. The

older man cleared his throat. "Elizabeth has, shall we say, a problem." He looked meaningfully toward the bar in the corner of the room. "She and Robert haven't lived together in quite a while, anyway. She wouldn't be able to tell you anything, and her doctor, Herbert Zollinger, has asked that we not bother her."

"I see. The housekeeper, Miss Scott, mentioned that the daughter was recently killed in a bicycling accident here in LA."

"Yes, a hit-and-run. Still unsolved. Such a waste — a young girl like that." Bowdritch shook his head, then got the point. "Robert was badly shaken up, of course, but not unbalanced enough to, er, do anything to himself."

"He wasn't the type. As Mr. Bowdritch said. "Desmond beamed at his superior.

Jess nodded, thinking that if Desmond got bored here, Harper would hire him in an instant. "One more thing. I understand that someone from your office was at the house yesterday?"

"Yes." Bowdritch waved toward Desmond. "We needed some files Robert kept at home."

"Uh-huh. Well, Miss Scott mentioned that some of her personal papers were taken, too. Letters she'd received from Lorrie Berrington. Is it possible to get them back?"

"Letters?" Bowdritch frowned. "Why would we want the letters?"

"I wondered the same thing."

"We went through the study, " Desmond said, shaking his head. "We took corporate files — nothing else."

"Yes. I saw the study." She searched for tact. "It, er, was searched very thoroughly. There seemed to be papers all over the place."

Desmond flushed. "Mr. Berrington's filing system, if you could call it that, was rather confused." He looked at Bowdritch. "I'm afraid the men did make a mess but we're sending someone around to clean it up."

"You're quite sure that no one took letters from

Miss Scott's room?" She felt like a fool for persisting. "Letters Lorrie wrote from South America?"

"No, of course not. We didn't go near Miss Scott's room." Desmond grimaced. "That woman's mad. She was hysterical the whole time we were there. She even insisted that the man I left to watch the property was there to spy on her!"

"Well, I suppose the shock of everything's been too much for her," Bowdritch said soothingly. "Poor woman."

Jess nodded. Lil wasn't exactly what juries looked at as the most reliable of witnesses. "I've taken up enough of your time. Can I see Carol?"

* * *

The antechamber to the president's suite was furnished with taste, glamor, and warmth, but it wasn't giving any comfort to the red-eyed woman at the bare desk. Desmond introduced the two of them and scurried away self-importantly.

"No, I don't know what Mr. Berrington did Saturday. He probably worked part of the time." Carol's voice was husky, raw. "But not here. There wasn't anything on the tape when I came in this morning."

"Do you have his appointment book?" The secretary wordlessly handed it over.

"A-COMM meetings on Friday. Captain Wrighter, Friday evening. "Yes." Carol brought out another sheet of paper. "The consortium membership is listed here, if it helps. Captain Wrighter is a military liaison for the Defense Department satellites."

"Tell me a little bit about Mr. Berrington. What was he like to work for?" Jess settled herself uncomfortably on the corner of the desk. Carol was a crisp supersecretary type who, under ordinary circumstances, would probably let her fingernails be torn off before she'd talk about her boss, but grief did something to tongues.

"He was great. I've been with him six years — "

45

The voice broke momentarily. "He worked you hard but he paid you well. And he worked himself harder."

"Is that why his family fell apart?"

"I don't know. Maybe. His wife was a difficult woman."

Jess nodded. "I've heard about her . . . her problem."

"Yes."

"What about Lorrie? The daughter?"

"Oh, she was fine. "Carol's gaze had slid away. She lit a cigarette and examined the burning end as if she'd never seen one before.

"She's dead now." Jess was curious about the response.

"Yes." Pause. "Very sad." Another pause.

"They haven't solved the case — I suppose Mr. Berrington was very upset about that?"

Carol's tongue wet her bottom lip. Her eyes were still fixed on the cigarette.

Jess watched her closely. This wasn't grief. It wasn't tact. So what was it?

"And how are you two ladies getting on?" Desmond was back, acting the hearty man-in-charge. "Has Carol been helpful, Ms. Canby?"

"Yes. Thanks." Jess's eyes were still on the other woman, who was now impassive again. "Just one more thing, Carol. Do you know if Mr. Berrington took sleeping pills before Lorrie died?"

"Pills?" Carol stared. "He never took pills."

"Well, actually — "

"Certainly not in the office, at any rate." Desmond was even heartier, looking at his watch. He wanted to give Jess every possible assistance, but he was a busy, busy man.

Jess got off the desk. "I'd like to take a quick peek into the inner office."

"Sure." He took her arm as if she were an ailing old woman.

Jess whistled as they crossed the threshold. The president of an empire like Berrington's could afford to spend any amount on decoration — and Robert had. She estimated at least a hundred Gs of art, sculpture, and marble. Desmond smiled condescendingly and led her back out.

Carol had vacated her desk, which disappointed Jess. She'd have liked one more chance to put her finger on what was bothering the secretary.

* * *

The County Medical Center complex was located on the east side of downtown near several freeways, not inconvenient for those who didn't live in Malibu. Its inconveniences were those of space. There was none. Hospital beds were at a premium, parking spaces were vied for with a bitterness generally reserved for family feuds, supplies and equipment were housed in jerry-built sheds, rooms everywhere were divided and sub-divided.

The medical examiner's building was no exception. The top two floors barely accommodated the fourteen pathologists, the coroner himself, plus records and assorted labs and conference rooms. Even so, it was more luxurious than Jess's department. In the basement, the chief of investigations had anything remotely resembling an office of her own — and that amounted to a cubicle eight feet square, fast vanishing under mountains of paper.

Jess stood in the doorway and resolved to clean it up. Definitely soon. Maybe next month. Meantime, she could only concentrate on the top layer; presumably, everything else had waited so long already, it could wait some more.

She reached for the telephone. "Detective Arnheim, please."

"Arnheim here."

"Francis, it's Jess."

Grunt.

He'd obviously already been given the word. "Listen, this joint task force crap wasn't my idea."

"Yeah. Well, how you want to go about it?"

"I'm not going to teach my grandmother to suck eggs. You do your thing and I'll do mine. I'm still waiting for the lab and autopsy results. Have you heard from the fire department yet?"

"They say it started in the housekeeper's room. She left a fan on and the wiring in the house was shot to hell."

"Okay. It seems pretty uncomplicated, but I guess there's no harm in taking a fast peek at Berrington's mental state and finances. Let's compare notes tomorrow and see if anything merits a closer look."

"You're the boss." He rang off abruptly.

Jess sighed, then flipped through the telephone messages. She sighed again and dialed another number.

"Detective Amory Garland, please. Jess Canby here."

"Yeah, Jess. What's up?"

"That's what I wanted to ask you. I've got six calls from the press here — about the Aguerra case. You remember."

"I remember."

They were both silent for a moment. Neither was tough enough not to remember a ten-year-old's sex killing.

"Well, what do you have?" Jess persisted.

"My boys are out on the street, talking to the players."

"Got anything to suggest that Miguel was one of them?"

He didn't answer immediately. "Not for Sure."

"I need more than that. 'Not for sure' isn't going to get the reporters off my back."

"I'll know tomorrow."

"You think I'm right, don't you?" Jess wasn't going for compliments; it was understood that it was not gratifying to be right under these circumstances.

Garland sighed heavily. "It's going to be one hell of a mess if the kid was a chicken. I've got the Hispanic-American Society already screaming that we're racists framing their boy." He hung up.

Jess wearily rubbed her forehead and looked at the next messageslip. "Oh, Lord. Budget Chief, City Hall."

"I've got worse news than that."

Jess looked up to see Consuela in the doorway, wearing a solicitous look that Jess didn't like at all.

"I don't want to hear."

"Sorry." Consuela waved a piece of paper. "Jerry Katz is on the phone. He says if you don't take his call, he'll come down and camp out in the hall."

"I'll take it, I'll take it." She allowed herself to light a cigarette, mentally excusing herself to the baby. "Jerry, what can I do for you?"

"Sweetheart, I just want the inside scoop on Robbie's case. And if you give it to me, I'll give you anything. Even my fair white body."

Jess shuddered. She must have been a real bitch in another life to deserve Jerry in this one. "There's no scoop. The report isn't done yet, and when it is, it will be made public like all of our reports."

"Listen, babe, I know something's going down because nobody, and I mean nobody, will talk to me."

Jess bit her tongue. She prided herself on not going for the easy shots.

"I even went up to the house to talk to the old broad," he continued with a chuckle. He thought he was cute, which proved everyone could have at least one fan. "The housekeeper, you know? They wouldn't let me in."

"Who wouldn't?"

"The Berrington Industries hoods who're guarding the gate. Jess, babe, I need you. Haven't I always been fair? Haven't I given you inches of space? I'll give you more, I swear it. The electorate will see nothing but your name from now to the election."

"I'm not running for anything, " she snapped. He wouldn't believe it, it wasn't even true, but the denial had to be made. "Look, there's no story."

"I don't buy that and I'm not going to roll over and play dead." Jerry was getting nasty now. "I'm going to find out what's going on and then I'm going to hang you from the tallest tree in LA. You won't be able to run for dog-catcher. So if you change your mind, give me a ring."

Jess hastily moved the receiver away from her ear so she wouldn't be deafened by the crash at the other end. Jerry would never believe that wanting to sweep up fast was not the same thing as wanting to shove something under the rug.

However, she wasn't going to get anything done fast, sitting around and stewing about Jerry. Jess emptied her briefcase onto the desk and skimmed her notes. The first step was obvious.

Captain Wrighter was at the Long Beach Naval Station. He took her call immediately, proving that important people didn't have to stroke themselves by keeping others hanging. He was happy to talk to her, but he had nothing to say.

Yes, he and poor Robert had had dinner together last Friday night. At Scandia. The food had been excellent and Robert's appetite hearty. They'd talked about the DOD's satellite and, alas, the captain had no idea what Robert was planning to do the next day. Work, most likely. All of them were deeply immersed in A-COMM. No, Robert hadn't displayed the slightest sign of depression. After all, what was there about the prospect of making a billion or two that would put someone off life?

What indeed? Jess thanked him and hung up.

Berrington's daily diary was about as forthcoming. The entries were straightforward: business appointments, suit fittings, society functions. Here and there, telephone numbers without names were scrawled across a page in a man's hand. Just the way a busy, messy executive would do it. But Saturday's page was neat. It was pristine, virgin territory.

The appointment book simply confirmed what everyone said, that most of the dead man's time had been taken up with his A-COMM project: meetings with lawyers, money men, technical experts, FCC administrators, and more lawyers. Jess and Michael knew a few legal beagles and most of them didn't tend to be fun types. Could their constant company explain why someone got tired of life?

She reluctantly decided not and put the book aside. There was no reason not to start on the paper work. Nothing was out of the ordinary. Everyone wanted the case to be simple — *she* wanted the case to be simple — so why look for trouble? The infinitesimal, niggling sense of unease in the back of her mind wasn't evidence.

Jess was navel-deep in case-report forms when Lil Scott called.

"It's not better up here. No better." Lil was upset, tension warring with reproach. "They been back all day, running all over the house."

"Lil, I thought you were going to stay with your friend in Brentwood?"

"I did, but I can't stay while she's workin', can I? I got to have some place to go in the daytime. And the house needs a real good cleanin', I can't just leave the mess like them firemen left."

The whine was hard to listen to. Jess found herself paying attention only intermittently until Lil got around to asking about Lorrie's letters.

"You get them letters back yet?"

"Uh. Well. Lil, I spoke to Mr. Marchenko. Desmond Marchenko. He says they didn't take them."

"You don't believe me, do you?" The housekeeper had a brief flash of insight. "You think I'm one of them crazy ladies, don't you?"

"No, no, of course I don't." Jess spoke with all the conviction she didn't feel.

"He took 'em, all right" Lil said with increasing fear. "I been figurin' something's fishy from the start — and it sure is. Something's fishy, all right."

Jess tried reason. "What was in the letters that would interest Mr. Marchenko? What did Lorrie write about?"

"Why should I tell you? You won't believe nothin' I say," Lil said hopelessly. "It's been fishy since Lorrie died. That's why they never found out who killed her. She knew she was gonna die and so did Mr. Berrington.

I'm gonna be the next to go."

Jess gritted her teeth. "Lil, you're not going to die."

"They want to know what I know. It's them letters; them letters was important."

"How?"

"And I'm gonna show you," Lil continued shrilly, ignoring the question. "I'm gonna show you. You'll see. I'm no crazy lady! They been scarin' me and watchin' me and takin' my letters. I'm no crazy lady!"

The line went dead.

Jess shook her head and replaced the receiver. Poor old Lil. It was hard not to feel sorry for her — but it was even harder to have to listen to her. Jess liked a good conspiracy theory as much as anybody, but she preferred those with some logic behind them. She couldn't make head or tail out of anything the unfortunate housekeeper said.

Still, the conversation brought back her slight discomfort with the case. She'd feel a whole lot better if she knew what Berrington had done with his last Saturday. Surely, tycoons didn't spend entire days alone? Didn't they have friends or something?

She suddenly recalled the canceled checks she'd taken from the ravaged study. They were somewhere on the desk; it took considerable pawing around to find them.

Len's Plumbing. Lil's salary. Neiman-Marcus. American Express. The phone company. Jess grimaced. She could always get the phone records, but that was a tedious task. It was an absolute last resort. Visa. Edison. Utility Hardware. Betty Drummond. Brentano's. Blue Cross. Giorgio's.

Jess stopped dead. Giorgio's! A cool three-and-a-half grand bought quite a lot of lingerie, even at exclusive, overpriced Giorgio's.

She went back to the five-hundred-dollar check made out to Betty Drummond. Who was she? Was she, at this very moment, mourning in expensive black satin? Jess turned the check over. Betty Drummond had endorsed it in a round, childish hand, adding her address and phone number as if she had cashed it somewhere she didn't have an account.

On impulse, Jess looked through the appointment book again. Interesting. Betty's phone number was one of those that appeared without a name.

"If the baby gets any bigger, they'll have to move you into a bigger office."

Jess looked up, delighted. "Michael! What are you doing here?"

"Checking on my favorite ghoul." He lounged against the door frame. "Those gurneys, they make me very nervous. How can you work around all these dead people?"

"Obviously not efficiently." She stared sadly at her In tray, virtually hidden by its contents.

"How's it going? Is all of Los Angeles agog over Berrington's death?"

"Something like that. There's going to be a joint investigation — us and the cops — to get it done fast."

"Ah, good. I'd hate to think of the stock market in a tizzy."

"That's the majority view," Jess agreed. "And I've been assigned to oversee the operation."

Michael raised his eyebrows. Isn't that a bit unusual?"

She shrugged. "If it goes smoothly, it's fine by me. And if it doesn't, it's fine by Francis Anheim. Anyway, there's nothing I can do about it. Stephen Bowditch, the guy who's taken over Berrington's company, asked for me."

"Wheels within wheels."

Now, Michael, don't jump to conclusions. I haven't been bought off yet. The offers won't come in until tomorrow."

He grinned. "If anyone offers in the six-figure range, take it."

"Doesn't look like there' s much reason to pay off. But I'll be delighted if someone thinks differently."

"Enough fun. Where do we go for lunch?"

She sighed. "I wish I could, but — "

"No buts. Connie said you were to take it easier, and I'm damn well going to make sure you do.

"Jess hesitated.

"Lunch," he repeated sternly, "or divorce. Take your pick."

She picked up her purse. "I certainly don't have time for a divorce."

Michael studiously kept his eyes averted from the gurneys lining the corridor as they walked to the elevator.

"You know," Jess said thoughtfully, "Connie also said I was putting on too much weight."

"Mmmm." Four years of marriage had been sufficient to teach Michael that, on some subjects, his lips should be sealed.

"So how about skipping lunch and taking a drive instead?"

"Sure. Where to?"

"Long Beach."

He looked at her in surprise. "You take me to the nicest places."

Jess laughed. Long Beach was forty minutes away and it was the sort of place that, when you got there, you didn't feel you'd achieved anything.

* * *

"Two more blocks and then make a left." Jess was navigating from a faded, almost indecipherable map. "Then a right and we're there."

"Where?"

"I'm not sure," she admitted, looking dubiously out the window. "I was expecting condos or something. I thought maybe we were going to find Berrington's love nest."

"Those words don't come easily to mind in this area," he pointed out.

He was right. The streets were painfully respectable, straight rows of small, square, working-class bungalows, each with a neat postage-stamp lawn and a stiff, joyless flower plot. Curtains were beige, house trims favored faded green. The brilliant blue sky and violent sun seemed out of place, tasteless. The notion of "mistress" was unthinkable.

"There." Jess pointed to one house distinguished from its neighbors only by its number. "That's the one."

They parked and rang the bell. It took a few minutes for the door to be opened. A plump young blonde wearing polyester blue pants and a nylon halter top looked out suspiciously.

"Betty Drummond?" Jess stuck her stomach out. What could be less threatening than pregnancy?

"Yes. Who're you?"

"Jessica Canby from the coroner's office. This is my husband, Michael." No point in confusing her with the difference in their surnames. It wasn't likely that Long Beach matrons kept their own monikers. "Can we talk to you for a minute?"

"I'm kind'a busy." On cue, the wail of a newborn baby filled the house.

"It won't take long. It's about Mr. Berrington. Robert Berrington."

The woman looked confused. "Uh, I read he was —"

"Yes, he's dead now."

"Well, I . . . "

Jess pretended to take that as an invitation. She walked inside with Michael on her heels. The living room was on their right, a cramped rectangle of faded teak furniture, leftovers from the uninspired decor of the fifties.

"Lovely house." Jess wasn't above stretching the truth.

"Uh, it's just rented. Ted's with the navy so we just rent." Betty was still in a bewildered fog. "There wasn't room on the base so they got us this place."

"May I sit down?" Jess stuck her stomach out again.

"Oh, yes, I guess." Betty looked around vaguely, now obviously wondering how these two strangers came to be there.

"Your baby's crying. Would you like to get him?"

"No!"

The shout echoed. You didn't have to be a psychiatrist to see there was something wrong. Their hostess had a soft, unformed face, round chin, no cheekbones to speak of. But her eyes were two decades older than the rest of the features.

"Sit down, Mrs. Drummond."

The authority in Jess's voice worked. The blonde sagged into an ocher chair, her frame losing shape as if the bones had turned to rubber.

"How did you know Mr. Berrington?"

"I never did. Ted, my husband, did."

"But Mr. Berrington wrote you a check for five hundred dollars."

The baby's wail was getting louder. Its mother was increasingly distracted, her head turning back and forth between the doorway and her unwanted visitors.

"What was the check for?"

"I — Ted — " She stood up suddenly. "I gotta take care of the baby."

"Of course."

Betty paused indecisively, biting her lip. She'd hoped they would take their cue and leave. The baby was shrieking now, almost choking on the high notes. Betty looked at them again, then hurried out with something that sounded like a sob.

Michael and Jess exchanged puzzled glances.

It was several minutes before Betty returned, carrying a tiny bundle in a yellow blanket. Michael had become a sucker for anything under a year old; he immediately crossed the room.

His fatuous beam froze and his voice was tight as he said, "She's adorable, Mrs. Drummond."

Jess didn't understand until she joined them and saw the cleft palate.

"They say they're gonna fix her up. Operate on her. A little thing like this, they're gonna operate on her." Betty's voice broke.

"The doctors are wonderful with that kind of thing," Jess said reassuringly. "It'll be fine, you'll see." She had to force herself not to hold her own stomach protectively.

Betty collapsed into a chair again, staring fixedly at her child. "Ted says the service'll pay for everything. He says we've got the best doctors and hospitals there are. But that doesn't help much, does it? When your baby's not right?"

"No, no, it doesn't." Jess swallowed.

Betty raised her wet eyes to Jess's stomach. "Is that why you're here? Does he," pointing at Michael, "work with radar too?"

"Radar?"

"Ted's gonna be mad at me. No one's supposed to know."

Jess took a deep breath and grabbed for the reins of the interview. "Ted works with radar?"

"Yeah, at the Long Beach Naval Station. He's petty office, first class. Probably gonna be chief petty officer soon. She spoke flatly, displaying no obvious pride. "That's why it happened to the baby. They say no, but me and Lee-Anne and the others, that's what we think."

Michael was leaning intently forward. "Tell us about Lee- Anne and the others."

Jess looked sharply at him but he didn't meet her eyes.

"Lee-Anne's baby's got one of those funny feet. You know, uh . . . " She cast around for the word.

"A club foot?"

Betty nodded. "Yeah, that's it. A club foot. And some of them have things wrong with their hearts, and some of the others have the same as Julie." She held her baby closer.

"And all of them are navy people?"

"Kenny Washington, that's Lee-Anne's husband, he's a helicopter pilot. She's older than me, and she's lived on a lot of bases. She's the one who told me about the sicknesses."

Jess and Michael were silent for a moment.

Finally, Jess found her voice. "How many babies are sick?"

It's not just babies. Lots of people get dizzy and headachy and they lose their memories. And strange things happen to their eyes — they bleed and everything. And they get pains in their chest." She was talking fast now, letting it pour out. "Somebody said there was some kind of change in the blood — I dunno, I didn't understand it, but it's the babies — " She broke off at the sound of a key in the lock. "Oh, no! That's Ted! He's gonna be mad, I 'm not supposed to talk about it!"

The door opened and a stocky young man in uniform strode in. He stopped at the sight of the three of them. "Who're these people Betty?"

She was on her feet. "From the government. I didn't want to tell them, Ted, they just came and asked and . . . " She started to cry.

"They got no right to just come in here." He glared at Michael. "You got no right to bother my wife!"

Jess stepped forward, trusting that naval men didn't hit pregnant women. "Mr. Drummond, I'm from the coroner's office."

He paled. He knew, if his wife didn't, that the coroner didn't handle people who were merely sick. "Is it Kenny? Did he die?"

"No, not as far as I know." Who was this Kenny, and why should he die? "I'm here on another matter — I'm here because of Robert Berrington."

The name didn't soothe the young man. He flushed angrily. "What's it got to do with me?"

"I'd like to know why Mr. Berrington wrote your wife a check for five hundred dollars."

The room was silent while Ted watched Jess through narrowed eyes.

"Tell them, Ted," Betty pleaded. "You said — "

"Put the baby in bed," he ordered. "You don't need to show her off."

Betty's head bowed, and she obediently left with the little yellow bundle.

There was nothing Jess loved to see as much as a husband browbeating his wife. "Mr. Drummond," she repeated icily, "why did Mr. Berrington write that check?"

He stepped back and opened the door. "I'm gonna tell you and then you're gonna get out. I worked on his car — I do a little extra work to make a little extra money. I'm not supposed to moonlight, so I get the checks made out to Betty. And you can damn well sic the government on me, I don't care!" The door slammed on her promise not to.

* * *

Neither of them spoke until they were back on the freeway, heading north. Michael broke the silence, speaking grimly. "That poor woman. What hell. "

Jess protectively stroked her stomach. "Damn. Someone should get to the bottom of that."

He looked at her, surprised. "Surely you can. You spend hours on a millionaire's accident. You can take a little time to look into something serious."

She avoided the entire issue of how he saw her job and focused on the immediate point. "It's not a question of time, it's a question of jurisdiction. The coroner's office can't start messing with the military."

"Unofficially, then. You can ask around unofficially."

"I'd get chewed out, even if I could get hold of information in the first place, which I couldn't."

"Jess, your pals are highly placed. Your connections can get you in anywhere."

She didn't answer immediately.

"Christ! You're pregnant, you must have some feeling for what that poor woman's going through. You keep saying that politics isn't always corrupt, that lots of political figures are great human beings. That it matters who's in charge. Well, prove it to me."

She sighed. "I'll see what I can do, okay? I'm damn sure it won't be much but I'll see what I can do."

Michael didn't look satisfied but he dropped the subject.

* * *

A gang war, two suicides, a young overdose, a knifing, and a multi-car pile-up. The gurneys were stacked up in the hallways; the investigators moved at a run, and Jess didn't get back to the Berrington case until five-thirty. She'd had a clerk collect a copy of the *Times* clipping file. Berrington had figured prominently in the news over the last twenty-five years. The papers didn't tell her much about how he died, but they did give her a sense of how he'd lived. Very well. He was too rich to count his money, and he could be proud of the fact that he'd made most of it himself. He'd joined his father's business in his twenties and had parlayed a comfortable living into a space-age communications empire. His labs and factories were leaders in developing and manufacturing satellite components — which made him a leader in a field necessary to the military, to NASA, to communications in general. The new technology was growing at a staggering rate; it was becoming to America what the automobile industry had been for the first half of the century.

And A-COMM was the natural next step for Robert. The consortium didn't just manufacture the satellites, it owned them. When they were launched (any day now, it seemed) the partners would be overlords of an international communications network that would make them practically another government.

As his financial status grew, so did his social status. His marriage hadn't hurt. Elizabeth was a Cartwright, and the Cartwrights (oil and agriculture) were what passed locally for aristocracy. The wedding pictures showed the perfect couple: he, with heavy, authoritative looking eyebrows, smiling coolly in a tuxedo that fit like a second skin, his blonde bride, a patrician fantasy in lace and satin, slim as a reed, as poised as the best finishing schools could make her.

Their life together appeared to be a round of society functions, fund-raisers, opera and ballet benefits. Robert thickened only slightly, gaining more in self-assurance and substance. Elizabeth was a sadder story. The slimness stiffened into thinness. The triangular smile seldom showed. The shiny blonde faded over the years, until finally, she wasn't in the pictures at all.

At seven o'clock, Jess closed the file. Well, she knew Robert better now. Which took her where? She sighed and went to the bathroom to repair her hair and makeup. It seemed only appropriate that tonight she was attending a function that would also be recorded, for the dubious interest of posterity, in the society pages.

* * *

The gargantuan Hancock Park mansion was only a few blocks from the house where Jess had grown up. The area was an older one, midway between Beverly Hills and downtown, but, at one time, on a much higher plateau than either. The homes were still elegant, but tough neighborhoods surrounded the area on all sides, and it took considerable courage — or perhaps snobbishness — to remain. Jess would have liked to indulge herself in a brief detour of remembrance, but she was too late to do anything but hustle inside.

The hostess had turned her house over to this month's most chic charity and the guest list read like a kidnapper's wet dream. There was still a prejudice in Los Angeles society against the city's most famous business, but tonight industrialists, bankers, and good blood mingled with entertainment moguls and the requisite number of famous faces. Even so, Jess noticed that most of the stuffed-shirt-and-pearl-necklace set were talking only to those celluloid faces wrinkled enough to have become respectable.

She accepted a glass of wine and wandered through the salons, looking for Richard Simon. She found him on the stone terrace, talking to several members of the Pasadena Garden Society.

"Jess!" He excused himself from his conversation and came over. "Hello, my dear. How are you?"

"Fine. Sorry I'm late."

They smiled affectionately at each other. Richard was a small-boned dapper man with the lean, fit body of a forty-year-old, and the creviced face of a man twice that age. His real chronological age was sixty-six — in fact, he'd looked the same for as long as Jess could recall, which was all of her life. He and her father had been best friends, so she thought of him as an honorary uncle. Since her father's death, he'd become her political angel as well. He was a major fund-raiser for the Democrats, a power in the National Committee, and therefore, ideally placed to be her sponsor and adviser.

"Is Michael here?"

"No. He's busy tonight."

"Ah." Richard smiled. He knew as well as she did that Michael would travel far to avoid these affairs. "How is he?"

"Great. It looks as if he's sold his book to the movies — to Cyril Haberman."

"Oh, really? Cyril and I go way back, you know. Good businessman. He saw the future in cable TV long before most." Richard took Jess's arm and steered her toward the thick of the party.

Most of the guests had settled in the room that was presumably the living room, although its grandeur was somewhat too daunting for any real living. The builder had wisely assumed that the occupants wouldn't want to hide their money under a barrel, so he had installed twenty-foot ceilings, a lustrous marble fireplace big enough for a whole cow, and floor-to-ceiling leaded-glass windows looking out to floodlit lawns with immaculate borders and lush shrubbery.

"Jess, Richard, good to see you." A man with a jutting jaw and a bite that would derange an orthodontist detached himself from a conversation and came toward them. Reg Cruickshank was extremely tall and extraordinarily ugly, so ugly that it was hard to tear one's eyes away from the gaunt, pock-marked face. He was unforgettable, which hadn't hurt him at all with the electorate. They persisted in returning him to the board of supervisors, which made Reg one of the five most powerful people in the county. "How're you doing?" He moved his hand as if to pat Jess's stomach, and then, sensibly, thought better of it.

"Fine."

Richard echoed her and waved for a waitress. "Fresh drink, Reg?"

"Sure. "

They both looked silently at Jess.

"No more for me," she said. Her wine glass was empty, and she'd just have to live with that.

"How's the coroner's office?" Reg asked genially.

She grinned. "You should know." She turned to explain to Richard. "Reg and Stephen Bowdritch got together and suggested to the coroner that I mastermind the Berrington investigation."

"Terrible thing," Richard said, shaking his head.

"Terrible." Reg smiled at Jess. "But we're happy the case is in such reliable hands. What did you think of Stephen?"

Reliable hands. Thank heavens Michael wasn't here. "He seems pleasant enough."

"Not the man Robert was, unfortunately. Perhaps a bit soft."

Richard agreed. "Robert always depended on Stephen, but — well, being the number one man is another story. We'll see."

"I've been trying to get a picture of Berrington in my mind," Jess Commented. "I met him a couple of times, but — "

"You met him at my house, didn't you?" Reg received a nod and continued, "He was a winner. Everything he touched turned to gold."

"It sure did," Richard sighed. "I always bought on his tips. We'll miss Robert. He was a Republican, of course, but reasonable."

They all grinned. In California, the movers and shakers cut their deals without much regard to party affiliations.

"So," Jess asked casually, "there'd be nothing wrong

with his finances?"

Richard was surprised. "Nothing."

"Why do you ask?" Reg eyed Jess speculatively. "Was there something fishy about his accident?"

Fishy. Lil's word. It made Jess hesitate fractionally before shaking her head. "I'm just being thorough."

"As always." Reg smiled, but there wasn't as much approval in his voice as the words suggested.

"To move on," Richard said quickly, "we're going to have a star-studded audience at the sculpture garden opening this weekend."

"It's rather ironic," Jess pointed out with amusement, "dedicating a sculpture garden to Dad. He didn't know Michelangelo from Moore — and he cared less."

"No doubt," Richard agreed cheerfully. "But Arthur isn't here to pound the table and yell about artsy-fartsy pretension, so we'll do it anyway."

Reg laughed. "Caesar was a pragmatist. He'd have kept his mouth shut for something that would give his daughter so much exposure. All the papers in the state and a good many from out of state will be there."

Richard smiled noncommittally. "The press just loved Arthur." They all knew that Jess was likely to run for the state Assembly but these things were better left unsaid.

"You'll give a speech, I imagine?" Reg asked Jess, unabashed.

"Yes. "

"A daughter's eulogy or a political one?"

She smiled. "I'll certainly talk about Dad as I remember him, but I thought I might also say a few things about the water situation. It was one of Dad's main worries, after all." Los Angeles's water problem was chronic and acute; it was the perfect issue for an aspiring politician. It ought to be. The keenest political minds in the party had suggested it for Jess.

None of this had escaped Reg. "The timing's exceptionally fortuitous, isn't it? I'm told that the governor's ready to appoint a commission of inquiry to look into the water mess. The commission members will certainly get a great deal of coverage." He was pointedly watching Jess.

"I suppose it will depend on who's appointed," Richard said vaguely, as if he hadn't spent a good part of the last month lobbying on Jess's behalf. "Jess, I assume your mother and Michael will be at the opening?"

"Yes. Mother's coming in Saturday morning."

"Virginia's coming to town?" Senator Uhuri joined the group. He was perfect for his role: rotund, pink of cheek, white-haired, and congenitally jovial. "How wonderful! I haven't seen her in years. How is she? For that matter, how are you?" He looked her over and suddenly noticed the belly. "Well, now, isn't that something? A grandchild for Caesar." His tone became avuncular.

Jess smiled and wondered if the others had caught the new note of condescension. Why did some men think that brain cells had to go to make way for a baby? "We're all fine, thanks. Mother lives in Texas now, seems to quite enjoy it."

"No accounting for taste." Uhuri was a native Californian who affected disbelief that anyone took any of the other forty-nine states seriously. "I'll have to ask her why at the opening." He turned to the men. "Well, now, why don't we wander down to the library? Some of the boys from Sacramento who are in would like your opinion on a couple of matters."

"We'd love to." Richard took Jess's arm casually, making the point that they'd *all* love to.

The senator took another dubious look at Jess's midriff and led the way.

* * *

Jess walked into her living room and started to grin. Three of her favorite men were sprawled out in the midst of empty tortilla chip bags, the remnants of a quart of chocolate-chocolate-chip ice cream and a veritable brewery of beer bottles. "Is anyone in this room still conscious?"

They all smiled back but none attempted the tricky feat of getting up. Michael was lying on the floor, his long legs propped up against the sofa. Martin Dunphy lay full-length across the sofa, the pin-striped banker's suit crumpled, unbuttoned, and looking like a candidate for the Salvation Army box. The third man, lanky, lean, and long-haired, had wound his legs into an intricate lotus position on the floor near the fireplace.

Jess went over to him first. "Alan!" She clumsily bent to kiss him. "It's been a long time!"

"Sure has. How are you doing, man" He patted her stomach. unselfconsciously. Alan Dickson was one of the few people who could do that without risking an assault charge. Jess and Michael had known him for years. He was a genuine hippie, a refugee from the present who'd been a drop-out, a flower child and a peacenik, and who staunchly refused to notice that that era was long gone. He and a few others like him lived in a time warp on one of the last extant communes in America, just a few miles away in Topanga Canyon.

"I'm doing wonderfully." Jess gave kisses to the other two and then sank gratefully into a soft, deep armchair. She grinned again at the room. "I feel as if I'm back in college."

"Ah, yes," Michael sighed wistfully. "The good old days." He brightened up. "But here we all are again — sitting around, shooting the shit, getting plowed. Nothings changed."

"You won't say that in the morning," Jess pointed out cheerfully. Twenty-year-olds could stand a lot more punishment than almost-forty-year-olds. "What were you guys talking about?"

"Martin and Alan were agreeing that the capitalist conspiracy won," Michael informed her.

"Ah." She raised her eyebrows. "Martin should know."

"Yup. He's part of it." Alan didn't speak with malice; he was prepared to accept the vagaries of old friends. "How did it happen, man?"

Martin grinned. "They bought me. Plain and simple. It turned out to be worth more to deal with Washington than to burn it down."

"Money. Oh, yeah." Alan Still didn't really understand. He owned a couple of pairs of jeans, a few shirts and a van. Was it possible that anyone could want more?

"Never trust anyone over thirty, " Michael remembered with a maudlin air.

"I make a point of mistrusting anyone under thirty-five," Martin answered.

"Me too." Jess laughed. "And every year, the age limit moves up."

Alan looked vaguely surprised. He trusted everyone. "Hey. I gotta get going."

Martin wrinkled his forehead and thought about that. "Yes. I think I should too."

Jess helped them both up and pointed out where the door was. "Uh, you guys think you can drive?"

Alan nodded happily an drifted out before she could say anything else. Martin pondered the question for a long time. "I'm almost certain I can — uh, where am I going?"

Jess and Michael started to laugh; she closed and bolted the door. "You're going upstairs, into the spare room."

Eventually, both drunks were settled, and Jess crawled in beside the one that belonged to her.

Michael was half-asleep. "How was the party?" he murmured sleepily.

"Good. You'd have hated it."

"Mmm." He opened his eyes suddenly. "Oh. I ought to tell you. I hope you're not furious."

"About what, sweetie?" She was drifting off herself.

"I tracked down Betty Drummond's friend this afternoon. Lee-Anne Washington."

"Oh yeah?"

"I found her on the East Coast. At Walter Reed Hospital."

Jess was awake now, watching him quietly.

"We didn't talk long. It didn't seem right to bug her."

"How's her baby?"

"It wasn't the baby this time. It's her husband, Kenny. The helicopter pilot." Michael pulled Jess close. "He's got pancreatic cancer. He's far too young for it — but he isn't the first pilot to get it."

Chapter 4

The Department of Health Services was located in the heart of downtown, housed in drab corridors and dull, scratched walls. The same people who were responsible for the coroner's building had apparently decorated here, too. Jess climbed the stairs, trying not to think about what Harper would say if he knew what she was up to. Still, a boss could only scream and shout; a husband could make life hell.

"Carl, may I come in?"

"Jess! How nice!" He was on his feet, a miniature black elf, pointed ears and all. "Sit down, sit down! What can I get for you? Coffee? Tea? Well, uh, milk?"

"Down, Carl." She cut through the fuss. "Sit."

Eventually, they were both perched on chairs, beaming at each other across the government-issue metal desk.

"What brings you here? Not that I'm complaining, my dear. How's that handsome husband of yours? Excited? About . . .?" He looked briefly at Jess's midriff, having been brought up in an age when public mention of impending maternity wasn't quite the thing.

"Michael's fine, we're both excited, and I need some information." Carl Weber had been with the statistical unit of the county's health department since time immemorial, and it was generally accepted that his memory held more details than the computers.

"Certainly, certainly." He pulled a pad of paper from its assigned spot. He was the neatest man in the world; mess made him wince, and he'd only been able to bring himself to visit Jess at her office once. "What information do you need?"

"What do you know about radar?"

"Radar?" He blinked. "Radar isn't a county matter."

"No, but I've got a complaint I think I should look into."

"Someone died from radar?"

"Well, no, not exactly." She hesitated. "Have you

heard anything about health problems near radar bases?"

"Oh, my!" He was alarmed now, staring openly at her stomach. "Do you live near a radar base? I thought you lived in Malibu?"

"No. No, it's not a personal matter. But I gather from your voice that you have heard something?"

"Oh," he said vaguely, "rumors here and there perhaps. You know how it is."

"I'd like to know. What are the rumors?"

"Um." He fidgeted with the edge of his notepad. "Jess, radar is a military matter. Federal, you know."

"In theory, but if it causes health problems in the county, then it becomes a county matter. Have there been complaints? Files opened?"

"I'm not that familiar with what Radiological Health does downstairs, except that we don't mix into military matters — and I'm not sure you should either."

Jess watched him for a moment. Carl was seldom perfectly comfortable with people; he preferred his files and statistics and, at home, his seven cats. But he was seldom this uneasy with her. "Who should I speak to in Radiological Health?"

"David McPherson, I suppose."

"Can I use your name?"

His eyes were pained. "I'd rather you didn't."

* * *

McPherson was easily accessible. His office door was open, and Jess was able to watch him work for a minute. He looked like a nice guy, a young redhead with broad shoulders and a trim torso that proved he hadn't been sitting behind a desk forever. .

McPherson looked up and saw her. "Hello. Can I help you?"

Jess returned the friendly smile. "Jess Canby from the coroner's office."

"It's super to meet you! I read about the Beatty case — swell job you did. Come on in."

"Thanks." The desk and chairs matched Carl's exactly but the litter on every available surface reminded Jess of her own filing system.

"When is it due?"

"What? Oh, the baby. In three months."

"Great." He grinned. "My wife and I just had our first. A girl. Seven pounds two. She's just beautiful — it's incredible, isn't it?"

"Birth?"

"Yes, I went through it with Judy, and — " His voice faded as he recalled the event with awe. "Hey, I'm sorry. You're probably here on business."

"I had something like that in mind," Jess agreed. "Actually, I'd like to know if your section has had complaints dealing with radar."

"Oh, that's not — "

"A county matter," she finished for him. "Yes, I know that. But radar is a form of radiation, isn't it? And your section is Radiological Health and radiation causes health problems. So the uninformed public might well get in touch with you."

"Well, I can't say they never do," he admitted. "But they're in the wrong place, when they do." His tone became professorial, out of keeping with the pug nose and freckles. "Radar is radiation, but not all radiation is the same, you know."

"I know nothing about it — except Madame Curie was a great scientist and an example to us all."

"Mmm." Cheerful, ingenuous, adorable, he might be. Willing to joke about his field, he was not. "There are two types of radiation: ionizing and nonionizing. The dangerous kind is ionizing — X-rays, for example. The waves bombard us at frequencies so high that they actually change — damage — our cells. 'Course, I'm simplifying this."

"And I appreciate it but — "

"Now, radar is nonionizing, which means that its frequency is much less. It doesn't damage our cells. Uh, it doesn't damage our cells in the same way," he amended, as if Jess had caviled. "I'll grant you that

71

there's conjecture about what it does do."

"Conjecture or differing opinions?" Jess was quick to latch onto a point she understood. "Some experts think it's dangerous?"

"Oh, generally only the fringe element. Nothing's been proven."

"I see. Have you had complaints from people who've jumped to the conclusion that radar is causing them health problems?"

McPherson hesitated a bit too long.

"You have," she said flatly. "What sort of complaints?"

"The files are classified."

"What?"

"Classified. Look, this is a military matter. I mean, radar isn't used much by the general population, now is it? So we can't touch it with a ten-foot pole."

"But people have come to you and — "

He leaned forward and tried another toothy smile. "I'm going to be frank with you. I'm not even supposed to say this much, but the complaints don't amount to a hill of beans. The best scientific minds are quite sure about that."

Not everyone had the same notion of frankness. "Except for the fringe element," she reminded him. "As Albert Einstein was considered to be at one time."

He stiffened. Right before her very eyes, he was turning from a laid-back advocate of natural childbirth into a bureaucrat. "The files are classified. Subject closed."

"David, those are county records and I'm a county official. Surely we can work something out? Off the record."

He shook his head, stubbornly.

She was fast losing her temper. "I know we like to keep the taxpayers who pay our salaries from poking around in our affairs, but I've got a right to see those files."

"You do not!" He flushed, not entirely comfortable with the brusque techniques of rejection. "The feds ordered us to close the records and that's what we've done. Take it up with them." He looked longingly at the door he wished she'd use.

"Okay, I'm going." It seemed a shame to leave him happy, so she added, "but I'll be back."

Jess was on the bottom flight of stairs when someone came down behind her and an arm tentatively brushed her shoulder.

"You're really with the county?" A plump brown-skinned woman in vivid coral pants stood behind her. The woman spoke in a low voice, just a trace of Mexico still in her speech. "I signed an oath not to say things to the public."

"I'm with the coroner's office." Jess fished out her badge.

"I heard you in the office."

"David McPherson's office?"

"Yes." The woman looked around nervously. "I heard what you said about — " the voice became a whisper " — about radar."

"Yes?" Jess moved closer, increasing the intimacy.

"Someone should do something, I think."

"There have been complaints, then?"

"Oh, yes. But I don't know much about them. Except — "

"Yes?" Jess felt the familiar tension in her stomach; she always had it when she was onto something.

"You should talk to people at the North County Clinic in Pasadena. They could help you, I think."

"Why? Are they investigating radar too?"

"That's all I know, what I told you." The woman looked around again and quickly started back up. She didn't pause even when Jess called her thanks.

* * *

She dialed Reg Cruickshank's private number before she even sat down behind her desk. "Reg? Jess Canby here. I need a favor."

"Sure."

"I've run into some red tape over at Health Services and I need help to cut through it."

"County or state?"

"County. That's why I thought of you. Some complaints have been filed about radar — I don't have much to go on. I don't know the names of the complainants or even the exact nature of the health hazards they're specifying, but I'd like to see those files."

"Who did you talk to over there?"

"A nice young bureaucrat named David McPherson. He's in Radiological Health. We had a lot of fun talking about babies because he's just had his first, but when push came to shove, he said the files were classified and there was no way he'd let me near them."

"I see." Reg paused. "Well, I'll give it a shot, but it sounds like a military thing. You know how forthcoming the military are."

"Sure. The wouldn't want it bruited about that the public they're sworn to defend might be in danger from the radar bases that should be defending them. And maybe they're right, maybe there isn't any danger. Still, I'd like to know more about it."

"Okay. You may have to go higher than me, though. What God couldn't accomplish in LA County, you asked a supervisor to try.

"Thanks, Reg."

Jess made her way to the watch-command office for the morning report. Consuela was on duty, handling two phone lines, a trainee investigator, and a small pile of backed-up first-call slips. She grinned at Jess over the receivers cradled on both shoulders, wound up the conversations, and spun around in her chair.

"Morning."

"Hi." Jess was pleased to note that Consuela was much more chipper than she'd been yesterday. "Where's Joe?"

"Here." Joe Miller loped in, a lanky graying stork, complete with long thin beak and round black eyes.

"Good morning." Jess peered at her assistant chief. "Jesus, Joe, what did you do with your day off? You look like hell."

He grinned. "The face isn't perfect, but at least my body's lean."

"True." She felt like a mack truck. "Okay, team, fill me in on the carnage and pillage."

Last night wasn't too bad." Joe glanced down at his clipboard. "One grim pile-up on Mulholland Drive. The kids are drag-racing up there again."

Jess frowned. "I thought the LAPD had that under control." She accepted the report and skimmed it. "Damn. What else?"

He handed over the summary. "Twenty cases."

"Uhhuh." She flicked through the papers. "Consuela, what's outstanding this morning?"

"So far, nine greens and six whites." Green report forms were used for the cases that went directly to the mortuaries. White sheets were those for bodies that came into the office for the full treatment: physical work-up, autopsy, embalming, cold storage. "Seven investigators in, two down with flu, and I didn't have the heart to insist they get out of bed. We're holding our own."

Jess wasn't surprised. When Joe and Consuela were in charge, the office always held its own.

"Now for the personals." Joe was chuckling. "Rumors are going to start about you and a certain police detective who calls you constantly."

Jess didn't get it for a minute. "Oh. Francis Arnheim?"

"Uh-huh." He chuckled again. "He says he dares not take one more step on the Berrington case without his marching orders."

Jess sighed. "How pissed off did he sound?"

"Pretty pissed off."

"Swell. Okay, thanks, Joe. I'll take over now. You can go home."

"Yeah." He paused at the door. "By the way, Our Leader wants to talk to you." Joe was as fond of Harper as Jess was. "He called about twenty minutes ago from his modest cottage."

Jess an Consuela laughed. Harper lived in a fourteen-room, five-thousand-square-foot cottage in Beverly Hills above Sunset. He'd married money and he hardly flaunted it at all.

Jess placed the call from her own office. "Dr. Harper?" She hunched her shoulder to hold the receiver while she sorted through the morning's barrage of memos. "Jess Canby."

"Yes. How is the Berrington case coming?"

"I'm working on it. Shouldn't take much longer."

"You don't have longer, " he said brusquely. "I told Stephen Bowdritch that it would be on my desk today."

"It's possible. There are a few odds and ends to tie up, but — "

"Really, I cannot comprehend what odds and ends there might be. This is a very simple matter! I can understand that in your . . . condition, you have difficulty accomplishing everything, but this case has priority."

She counted to ten so that the flush of red-eyed fury would subside. It didn't. "My condition, as you call it, would slow me down in the Boston Marathon, but it has nothing to do with my job." If only she knew someone who broke legs for a living.

"One certainly hopes not. In which case, I fail to see the problem. It is a simple accident. An accidental fire. An accidental death. What could be simpler?"

Only your mind, Harper. "There still remains the question of Mr. Berrington's mental state. He was drugged, after all, which leaves open the possibility of suicide."

"Suicide!" It was a bellow. He could see his social standing slipping as they talked. "Are you out of your mind? Whatever gave you the ridiculous idea that he was drugged?"

"The autopsy. He was drugged to the gills, to quote Leon de la Pena."

"You are not on top of this case. At all." Prissy disapproval leaked through the telephone wire. "There were no drugs found in the autopsy. I have a copy of the report. Right here. If you were . . . in control, you'd have read it too."

Jess frowned and searched the In tray. The autopsy report was indeed there, under a two-page memo from the County Hall of Administration cautioning county employees not to waste paper. Jess scanned the report: " . . . carbon monoxide saturation in the blood, 50 percent. Death caused by asphyxia due to inhalation of smoke." Nary a mention of drugs.

She slowly put the document back on the tray. "There was a drug vial by the bed."

"I don't know anything about that. But he was not drugged. He died in an accident. And I want that report today. Do you understand me?"

Jess replaced the receiver very gently.

* * *

Leon a la Pena was checking inventory in the cold storage rooms. There were generally between three and four hundred corpses stacked on the open metal shelving, and it was considered extremely poor form to misplace even one of them.

"Morning, Leon." Jess smiled as an afterthought.

"Morning." He wasn't thrilled to see her.

"I want to talk to you."

"Uh, here?" His eyes darted nervously like those of a rabbit faced with a fox.

"Sure. We won't disturb them." She looked at the body bags. "I haven't finished." He flourished the clipboard. "The doctors want the inventory check done first thing."

"I'll take care of the doctors." She stood between him and the door, and, at the moment, she made a very effective roadblock.

"What happened to the blood-analysis results in the Berrington case?"

"They're in Records."

"Do the mention drugs?"

He swallowed: he was looking unusually pale for a dark-skinned person. "Drugs? No, I don't think so."

"Funny. You told me Berrington was doped to the gills."

"Did I?" He flushed. "Well, if I did, I made a mistake. Must've been thinking about some other stiff."

"Leon."

He sighed, a scratch sound. "Really."

"What's going on in here?" A very young man in a white lab coat stopped at the doorway, his lips set disapprovingly against socializing within earshot of the dead.

"Doctor Kirsch!" Leon's welcome was undoubtedly the most effusive the unadorable pathologist had ever received.

It was rewarded with a curt nod. "Jess." Another nod. She technically outranked him but he had a framed diploma on his office wall that told him he was outranked only by God.

"Hi, George." Jess stepped out of the chill. "You did Berrington's autopsy, didn't you?" She was undoubtedly wasting her time, because Kirsch was Harper's prize toady, but there was no harm in beating her head against a stone wall. At the very least, it would feel great when she stopped.

"Yes, I did. And I cannot file the death certificate until I have your reports in hand."

"Uh-huh. In your autopsy, weren't there signs of drugs?"

"No, certainly not."

"Leon said - "

"Leon made a stupid, careless error in his lab work." Kirsch glared at the technician. "Careless. There were no drugs at all — didn't you read my autopsy report?"

"Yeah." And as fiction went, it wasn't bad. Forget it."

* * *

Jess sat beside Chester in the investigators' office and stared disbelievingly at the pile of objects on his desk. One watch, one neck chain, two rings, a pair of white silk pajamas. Nothing remotely resembling a drug vial.

"Let's go over this again, Chester. You brought in the evidence envelope I gave you.".

"Yes." Chester was subdued. He hadn't yet decided if the cross-examination was a hostile act or not. "I brought it in and I took it upstairs to the evidence room. I took the pajamas too, after I undressed the body."

"Did you look inside the envelope?"

"No, how could I?" You signed the flap yourself — I didn't want to break the seal." He pulled the envelope, now slit open, toward him. "See, the seal hasn't been damaged."

The naivete was charming. Drugs and valuables evaporated from the evidence room with a regularity only temporarily by periodic staff dismissals. "Okay. Thanks."

"I did just what you told me."

"Yes, of course." She faked a weak smile and got to her feet.

"Are you sure it was in here?" He followed her into the hall, emboldened slightly by the smile. "Maybe it wasn't in here, you just thought it was or something."

"Maybe." She walked back to her office, deep in thought. Maybe Chester was right. She'd been woozy with stomach pains. Could she have forgotten to take the vial? Or worse, imagined it? She quickened her pace, cursing herself for a damn fool. The notebook would answer the question, of course.

It was still on her desk. Jess flipped the pages, then flipped through again. Nothing between the pages describing the jewelry and the pages of notes taken during her interview with Lil. Nothing. She must be going crazy.

* * *

Francis Arnheim was at his desk when she telephoned. "My report's almost ready, Jess. I'll send it over in an hour or two."

79

"Sure, no problem. Uh, Francis, when you looked at the body, did you notice something on the bedside table?"

"What kind of a something?"

"Well, tell me what you saw. I don't want to put words in your mouth."

He paused. "I'll read you my notes."

"If you like."

"Bedside table, printed. Lamp with shade, printed. Ashtray, four butts, Merit lOOs, printed. By the way, the prints were all Berrington's."

"Uh-huh. Was that it?"

"My notes go on to describe the fire damage in the bedroom."

"I see." She let out her breath. "I saw an empty drug vial on the table. I'm sure I did. I could swear I did."

He didn't say anything.

"Well, I'm almost sure. I thought I picked it up, took possession of it, made a note — but I've got nothing to back me up. I must be hallucinating."

He grunted.

"And you didn't see a drug vial" she persisted.

"I guess not. Otherwise, it would have been in my notes."

Jess frowned. An interesting way to phrase it. She leaned back, staring blindly at the desk. Suddenly, she stiffened and grabbed her notebook again, turning it toward the light. "Hot damn!"

"If that's all, Jess, I'll get back to work."

"Hold on just a second." She peered closer at the pad, then sighed with relief. "Okay, buddy, what's going on?"

"What do you mean?"

"Francis, neither of us has time for this shit. I made that note and I can prove it. The very next page of the notebook shows the imprint of my pencil. There was a drug vial there and I saw it, and if I saw it, so did you."

He didn't speak for a long minute. "Jess, why make yourself crazy over this?"

"You get along by going along, is that it?"

Pause.

"Francis, I don't like being made into a fool."

"It's better, sometimes, than making yourself into a shit-disturber. Look, what's the difference if some tycoon dies in a fire or sets the fire himself? I'm not saying he did, mind you. I'm saying 'if.' "

"What's the difference? Oh, just a few sentimental trifles like truth and principle."

"Truth. Principle." He wasn't being sarcastic; he was trying out the words. "Yeah, well, I got cases where assholes rape kids or drive their Mercedes over people and run away. If I'm gonna push back and shit-disturb, I'm gonna be very picky about where I choose to do it."

She was silent. Francis was talking about reality. Was this the cause for which she should risk her career? "See you around, Detective."

Consuela was buzzing. "Jess, you got two calls waiting — Detective Amory Garland on three and Lil Scott on four. Want to take them?"

"Want to is far too strong. Thanks." She pressed the button for Garland.

"I got news, Jess." His tone said plainly that it was all bad. "You were right. The Aguerra boy worked Hollywood between Wilcox and Cahuenga."

"Oh, damn it to hell! "She threw down her pen and belligerently picked up a cigarette. The baby would survive one cigarette. "Do his parents know yet?"

"No. We'll tell'em today."

"Okay, we'll sit on it till they know." She sighed and pressed the next button.

Lil started to splutter immediately. "Where do they get off, sayin' it was my fault? How could you let them do this to me? I thought you was my friend!"

"Hold on! Do what to you? What are you talking about?"

"They're sayin' I caused the fire!" Lil said shrilly. "They're blamin' it on me, and the newspaper people has been botherin' me all day!"

"The fan in your room caused the fire." Jess hastily

81

rephrased that. "The wiring in the house caused the fire. Nobody's blaming you."

The woman wasn't listening. "It ain't fair! It wasn't my fault — my room wasn't even burned!"

"The fire went through the walls, Lil. Please believe me, nobody blames you."

"No? Well, I don't have no fan, Miss Smart-pants! I don't have no fan, never did. What do you think about that? It's a frame, that's what it is, a frame!"

"Lil, calm down. Listen to me." Jess was frowning, even as she tried to soothe the woman. If it wasn't Lil's fan, then Berrington himself must have put it in her room, and Jess wasn't ready to open that Pandora's box. Not until she thought it all over very, very carefully. "Nobody's blaming you. I promise. Nobody."

The forceful voice got through. Lil subsided slowly.

"Well, it ain't my fault. I didn't have no fan."

A blessed silence finally fell. Jess waited it out, reluctant to say anything that might set the housekeeper off again. When Lil eventually spoke, she'd changed tack. "You know them letters? Lorrie's letters?"

"Uh-huh."

"You won't believe me, I know that, but they was important. It was that trip to South America, that's why Lorrie died."

"What happened in South America?"

"She wrote them letters so somebody'd know. She trusted her Lil to keep'em safe," she quavered "And I tired, you know. I tried."

"Yes, of course you did," Jess said with as much patience as she could muster. "But what happened in South America?"

"I didn't understand it much 'cause I don't have no schooling. I don't understand them scientists and stuff but I know somebody who'll tell you I'm right."

"Who?"

"She'll prove I'm right. You don't believe me, but she'll tell you, if you come with me."

"Come with you where?"

"Will you? They's up to something," the woman

pleaded, outrage now gone from her voice, replaced by fear. "Will you come with me?"

Jess shut her eyes. She could have chosen to work with lepers in Ethiopia. But no. She had to take the hard road.

Chapter 5

Jess waited for Lil in the east end, beside the freeway exit for Santa Fe Avenue. It was stiflingly hot in the Skylark, even with all the windows open, but she couldn't use the air-conditioning. When the car salesman had been rhapsodizing about the fuel economy of four-cylinder engines, he'd neglected to mention that when idling or, for that matter, in stop-and-go traffic, they tended to heat up. A minor point hardly worth noting — if you lived in Nome, Alaska.

The closest thing to a breeze was the disturbance of air caused by traffic easing onto Highway 10. It was air you could see. California emission-control standards were touted as the toughest in the world, but you couldn't tell it by East Los Angeles where cars of recent vintage were as rare as a blonde.

Someone honked. Jess didn't bother to turn. Chicano men in this neighborhood were always honking at a lone female. Or at each other. It just added one dimension to the cacophony of whistles, shouts, and screaming babies. The noise level in the *barrios* was somewhat higher than on the other side of town, the local feeling apparently being that if it wasn't worth yelling, it wasn't worth saying at all.

The honk persisted until she wrenched her soaking back away from the seat and looked behind her. Lil was hunched nervously over the wheel of a small green Chevrolet.

They drove in tandem into Boyle Heights, a shabby community that reflected the Mexican notion of zoning. Car wreckers and radiator shops shared blocks with restaurants and homes; immaculately landscaped, tiny frame houses neighbored unpainted ramshackle slums.

Lil's destination was Brooklyn Avenue, the center of town, a commercial melange of grocery stores, countless shoe stores, travel agencies advertising cheap bus fares to parts of Mexico Jess had never heard of, taco stands, and pool halls. The sidewalks were jammed with listless shoppers. All the faces were brown; the *lingua franca* was Spanish.

Jess's air-conditioning had just begun to hint at cool air when Lil pulled over to a meter. Jess carried on through an intersection and found another parking space a block away. She rolled up the windows, hid her portable tape recorder in the glove compartment, locked all four doors and said goodbye to the car. With any luck at all, it wouldn't be here when she got back, and the insurance money would buy a '75 Lincoln that guzzled gas and kept one cold.

Lil was waiting on the corner in front of a grimy, graffiti-covered bank, clutching her purse to her chest and looking out anxiously for Jess. The traffic light was red. Jess was pressed into a crowd of tired mothers and their fretful babies, her eyes fixed balefully on the housekeeper. This had better be good. Good enough to explain why she wasn't, right this moment, on her way home to Michael and a cold fruit punch.

Then it happened — a horror movie in slow motion while Jess watched in stunned disbelief. A beat-up Volkswagen pulled up to the curb in front of Lil; two black men slid out, leggy as basketball players, big men with purposeful strides. They headed toward Lil as passersby melted away. Jess didn't understand it until she saw the guns in the men's hands, huge pieces of metal, reflecting the sunlight.

She had one arm out; she shouted into the sudden stillness, but it was no use. The shots shocked her into immobility. The corner was a frozen tableau — only the two men had the will to move.

One turned toward Jess, his gun swiveling with him. He looked directly into her eyes; the gun barked again. She grasped the meaning of the noise only very slowly; even then she did nothing except turn around to see where the shot had gone. The car was tearing away, burning rubber as it accelerated faster than any Volkswagen engine could have done.

Life returned gradually; mutters became shouts; tentative motions became running steps. Nobody wanted to be there when the *policia* arrived. Jess and

Lil were alone.

But only Jess was shaking. Lil wasn't moving at all. Jess finally brought herself to cross the street and kneel beside the heap on the sidewalk. She turned it over and then backed away to retch. She knew it was Lil, but no one else would be able to identify her now. The shots had hit her squarely in the face, almost severing the head from the body.

Jess continued to throw up until nothing was coming up. She didn't have the strength to stand; she waited on her knees for the squad car, to arrive.

* * *

"Let's run it through once more, Mrs. Canby."

Jess closed her eyes, then nodded. It was the least she could do for Lil. God knows, that's all she'd done for her — the least. "Miss Scott wanted to take MR to meet someone because — "

"No, never mind that." Detective Carmichael impatiently waved a pudgy hand with filthy fingernails. Jess could sympathize with a work load that interfered with sleep but surely he could have found a moment in the past week to shower? "That's not important. Just the mugging. "

"It *is* important," she insisted for the tenth time. "It wasn't a mugging — it was an execution! I know. I saw it. I was there !" And she was almost part of it. Jess hadn't been able to bring herself to say that one of the shots had been meant for her. Carmichael wouldn't believe it — and she desperately didn't want to herself,

"Look we get this kind of thing all the time. Muggers in this town drive around looking for little old ladies on street corners." His voice was a growl, underlining the resemblance to a bulldog, lumpy low cheeks and flattened nose. "She had a purse, right?"

"Right."

"And it's gone. Right?"

"Right. But that doesn't mean shit." Jess was tired of acting like a lady. Queen Elizabeth might win

Carmichael's approval, but Jess wasn't going to. "Lil told me she was being watched, and I know she was right. She was sure there was something fishy about Berrington's death, and Lorrie's. And you've got to admit, Carmichael, that three death in one household in a single month is above the national average."

"Look, nobody else thinks there' s anything strange about the other deaths. I talked to Dr. Harper, and he told me that — "

"You talked to Harper?" A surge of adrenaline made her sit up straight for the first time in two hours.

"I had to check you out, didn't I? You come in here, all upset — of course," he hastily added, "anyone'd be upset, especially in, uh, your condition. You come in here shouting about executions. What do you expect? I'm gonna run right down to the mob and ask questions? I get lots of muggings in Boyle Heights, but in twenty-three years with the department, I haven't seen a lot of old lady housekeepers executed."

Jess rested her head in her hands. Harper had already poisoned the well. She could hear the conversation: "A little, shall we say, erratic these days. Hormones, you know, during pregnancy. Emotional, quite understandable, but not reliable."

Carmichael lit a cheap cigar, asking after the fact if she minded.

She wearily shook her head. "Did you at least call Detective Arnheim?"

"Yeah. He's coming down. He was off duty." Carmichael spoke accusingly. A cop's lot was a hard one, and she was making it harder. "Can we go over the shooting one more time? Just the shooting."

Jess was describing the Volkswagen again when Francis slouched in, the blue bags under his eyes bigger than on the night of the Berrington fire, the lines on his face deeper. Even the suit was more rumpled. But next to Carmichael, he was a fashion plate and a sight for sore eyes.

Jess leaped in quickly before Carmichael could render the details of her insanity. "Am I glad to see you! But I am sorry to break into your off-duty hours."

"Off-duty minutes, more like." Francis rubbed his eyes and tried to keep them open. "What's the story?"

Carmichael handed over the murder report, along with the notes he'd made from Jess's interview. The other cop glanced over the papers, then nodded curtly.

"I was there and it was an execution," Jess said flatly.

"Execution." Carmichael was muttering just barely under his breath. "Execution. Gawd."

Francis scratched an ear and gazed at the humming office as if looking for inspiration. "Who was the housekeeper taking you to see?"

"I don't know. She wouldn't give me the name — it was going to be a surprise. Frankly," Jess added bitterly, "I think she figured if she gave more details, I wouldn't go. She figured we were all on the other side."

"Other side? Other side of what?" Carmichael pounded his fist on the desk, disturbing several years of dust. "Other side of what"

Jess ignored him. "She said that Bowdritch's men took letters Lorrie wrote her from South America. She believed that all the deaths were tied to something Lorrie did there — "

"Like what, for instance?"

She met Francis's impassive eyes and flushed. "I don't know. But I think the key to finding out is those letters. Bowdritch wouldn't admit to me that they had them, but now I believe Lil. He might be more forth-coming with you."

Francis was still watching the room as if he'd never seen an assortment of handcuffed juveniles, garishly adorned hookers, and tearful families. "Uh, Carmichael, excuse us for a minute." He took Jess's arm and led her through the pandemonium to an interview room, a small beige cubicle containing one table and two chairs.

"Look, Jess - oh, uh, you wanna sit down?"

"Yes." She chose the least unstable of the chairs.

"Look," he continued slowly, "we both know how it is. It's a tricky situation, even if you're right about what you saw. I got nothing to go on. You know your boss isn't behind you?"

"I've heard it rumored. Go on."

"Well, what do we have? We have a fire, and the fire department's satisfied it was a kosher accident. We have a death by smoke inhalation. No, hear me out." He raised a hand as she started to speak. "I know what you're gonna say. But there isn't any *evidence* of drugs. Not now, and not ever because," he shifted his feet, "too many people are on record as saying there wasn't any. Now, we have a crazy old lady mugged by a couple of hoods in a bad part of town." He sighed. "How does it sound to you?"

Jess swallowed. "Not so good. But," she pointed out, "we also have Lorrie's death and those letters."

"Yeah. Lorrie." He spoke heavily. "I looked into that — I may not be the smartest cop in the world, but I'm not as bad as you think. It was a hit-and-run. She was on a bicycle and the guy who hit her was in a car. Unsolved, like a hell of a lot of hit-and-runs." He shrugged. "Big deal. And the damn letters. Give me a break — give me a *hint* of how those could tie in."

Jess stood up. "You're telling me that you don't think I'm a nut, even if I am pregnant. But you're also telling me that, like it or not, Lil's death is a mugging and there isn't a thing I can do about it."

He said nothing.

"Francis, covering up a suicide is one thing. This is another. Lil was afraid she was going to die, and now she's dead."

"We're not going to cover it up. We're going to try to find those hoods, don't misunderstand me." He was at the door, holding it open for her. "And if it turns out that someone hired them, we'll pursue it."

"But Lorrie's death was an accident and Berrington's death was an accident and those cases aren't going to be reopened?"

He stared into her eyes. "Not today, they're not. And for what it's worth — no, I don't think you're a nut. But I'm not convinced you're right either. Everyone —

everyone — disagrees with you. Have you thought about that? Is it possible that you're not the only person in the entire county who's right?"

* * *

"Jess! Are you all right?" Michael dashed into the garage when he heard the whirr of the automatic door. He looked drawn, tired and worried, and he was the prettiest sight she'd seen in hours.

"Hullo, darling." She headed directly into the comfort of his arms. "I need a really thorough cuddle and then I'll be fine."

"Okay, but Jerry Katz is here. He'd probably want to watch."

"Jerry Katz" She sagged. "Christ, has the news spread so fast?"

"No, you had rotten luck. He was here looking for you when you called from the police station and I couldn't get rid of him."

She walked into the kitchen. "Hi, Jerry."

"Babe! You're okay?" He had his arms open wide and there wasn't room to skirt them. "Come to daddy."

She stiffly allowed herself to be hugged.

"Sweetheart, this is too much. I mean, really, too much." Jerry eventually let her go and trailed after her into the living room. "Hell of a thing for a mommy-to-be to go through."

"Mommy-to-be?" She looked down at herself. The bulge just seemed to grow noticeably every day. "No, Jerry, that's just a rumor. We do it with mirrors."

"Laugh if you want to. I like that." Jerry appealed to Michael. "Dynamite, isn't she? I mean, something like this and she's cracking jokes. Dynamite."

Michael looked like he might commit murder any second. Jess leaped in. "Michael, please pour me a drink. And I don't mean fruit juice."

Jerry was at her elbow. "So, babe, tell daddy all about it."

"Jerry, I'm zonked. Today started about a week ago

and I'm bushed. So be a good boy and go away, okay? We'll talk tomorrow." If she didn't see him coming.

"Keep it brief. Hey, I'm human, I understand. Just keep it brief."

Michael came back with the weakest Scotch and water that had ever been poured. "Give him something, Jess, or we'll never get rid of him — and I'll he doing life."

"Okay." She sank into the sofa. "I witnessed a terrible thing, Jerry."

"Uh-huh." His eyes were avid. Sparkling. It was a horrible sight.

"Two big black dudes wasted a little old lady in Boyle Heights. And for what? For her purse! Can you believe it?"

He was staring at her in dismay. "That's it?"

"That's it. "

"A mugging. That's your version?"

"It's no version. It's what happened. It should be good for a paragraph on page nineteen, so I think it's swell of you to hang around waiting for it. Shows real humanity on your part, Jerry, and poor Lil Scott would be really grateful." She sipped the slightly tinted water.

"Okay, doll, we' re gonna take it from the top." It was hardball now, all the way. "Why did you two go to Boyle Heights?"

"Jerry, I've said all I'm going to say. Unless you care to watch me sleep, you might as well go home."

It was as if no one had spoken. "Why did you go to Boyle Heights?"

Jess sighed. The little creep wasn't stupid. He'd make some of the connections if she didn't put him off the scent. And until she was sure about the connections herself, she certainly didn't intend to be the source of sleazy stories. What she needed was a diversion. "Okay. If you want news, I'll give you a piece. A scoop. On condition that you leave immediately."

Jerry paused, assessing his chances. Michael moved to stand over him with narrowed eyes. "Okay. Deal." "The Aguerra case? The kid murdered in Hollywood?"

"Yeah, I remember."

"Yeah." Jerry had done a "let's-make-our-incompetent-and-crooked-cops-clean-up-this-sewer" story. "He was a chicken."

"A prostitute? Hey!" Jerry was chipper again. "Now that I can use! Mind if I use your phone?" He was at it before either of them had a chance to say no. He slammed it down again after a few moments. "Damn thing's out of order."

Jess and Michael exchanged a grin. Malibu phone service was as solid as the ground on which the phone poles stood. But for once, the telephone company had done them a favor.

"Gotta run." Jerry was out the door, boy reporter in search of fame and fortune.

Michael locked the door so there was no chance he could return, then looked sadly at Jess. "You're sure about Miguel Aguerra?"

"I'm afraid so. Garland told me today." She rubbed her aching neck. "Oh, God, what a day!"

Michael came over to cuddle her. "You poor thing. Tell me the real story about Lil. "

"The real story?" She leaned against him and thought about that. "Who the hell knows? Even *I'm* not sure anymore, and I was there. It looked like a deliberate killing to me but I can't prove it. And no one was willing to listen, anyway. The Berrington case is closed — accidental death by smoke inhalation. Period."

"Our public servants can be real snappy when it comes to a billionaire," Michael observed cynically. "Snappy and unsuspicious."

"Yeah. I guess. Except — there isn't much to go on. Lil wasn't what you'd consider a totally reliable source."

"What do you think? Really think?"

She got up and started to pace. "I don't know. I suppose our boy wonder might have killed himself — I mean, there was some indication of drug use, 'was' being the operative word. The record's squeaky clean now."

"Why would he have done it?"

"I don't know. He seemed to have everything except a decent family life, and men like him don't kill themselves over that. They buy another family." She stood at the glass doors and stared out or a few moments. "And I can see Harper covering up so as to ingratiate himself with the big boys, but even the people I trust don't agree with me."

"Maybe you're trusting the wrong people."

She turned around and came back to sit beside him. "You see too many conspiracies. No, if I were right — and if I got the chance to prove it, which is a whole other thing — all of them but Harper would take their medicine like men."

Michael's expression showed just how little he believed that, but he wasn't going to push the point. "Anyway, I don't like this business of guns and muggings. Even if you're right about suicide — the principle isn't worth getting killed over."

Jess tried not to stiffen. She wasn't going to mention the paranoid belief she had that she'd been a target too.

Michael kissed the top of her head, then began to work his way down. "I'd really rather you hung out with quieter people. Preferably unarmed people. If you feel the need to loiter on street corners, could you stick to Beverly Hills?"

"I'll try." She hugged him. "Say, what's that you're doing to my ear? You have exactly one hour to stop it."

Chapter 6

A copy of the police file on Lorrie Berrington's death was waiting for Jess when she arrived in the morning. There was no indication of how it had reached her desk; Francis must have dropped it off himself. She spared a kind thought for him, then revised it after reading the documents. They said essentially what Francis had said.

Nothing.

She pulled the coroner's report from Records and began to reread everything. On or about 5:00 AM, on July 10, an LAPD patrol had found the body of a female Caucasian, estimated age eighteen to twenty-five, on Mandeville Canyon road. A ten-speed French racing bike was wrapped around her; the collision with an unknown vehicle had sent her and the bike several yards into someone's front lawn.

Dr. George Kirsch had performed the autopsy. Findings: massive trauma including the fracture of both femurs, the clavicle, the right tibia, and the cranium. Two ribs fractured, one penetrating the left lung. Cause of death: crushed cranium, consistent with collision with unknown vehicle. Estimated time of death: 2:00 AM, July 10, more or less instantaneous upon same collision.

Homicide's file was detailed. The road was described as poorly lit, the accident as having occurred on a blind curve. The smashed bicycle showed traces of blue paint, which had been analyzed and determined to be from a standard General Motors paint lot. The deceased had been wearing a bright yellow track suit, in the zippered hip pocket of which were found a checkbook and thirty dollars (two tens, a five, and five ones.) She was formally identified on July 10 by her father as Lorrie Angela Berrington, twenty-two years old, graduate of USC, unemployed, residing at 111 Park Avenue, Apartment 3, Venice.

The chief of police himself had accompanied Berrington to view the body and then held a press conference at which he announced that all the garages on the West Side were being notified to watch for a blue GM car needing body work, that the bereaved father had posted a $10,000 reward for information, that the case was being assigned to Detective Francisco Hernandez, Robbery-Homicide Division, Detective Headquarters, and that the department wouldn't rest until it had apprehended the perpetrator.

Jess reached for the phone, hoping that Hernandez had taken that literally and was on duty at seven-fifteen in the morning.

"Hernandez." It was a hoarse voice.

"Jess Canby from the coroner's office. I'm calling to, uh, update the Lorrie Berrington case. Have there been any developments lately?"

"How lately?"

"Since, uh," she looked at the date on the reports, "since July twentieth."

"Nothing. Why? You got something?" His voice perked up a little. It was hell to receive an assignment directly from the chief and have as much chance of succeeding with it as of winning the Irish Sweepstakes. "Why're you people interested?"

"Did you know that her father died in a fire over the weekend?"

"I read about it."

"Well, I'm handling his case from our end." She hesitated, then plunged ahead. Surely the news about her instability hadn't yet reached every last civic employee? "And yesterday afternoon, the Berrington housekeeper was murdered."

"For real?" He didn't know what to make of it, but he was developing hope that someone would. "Hold on while I get the file." His filing system wasn't the greatest. It took him almost five minutes to return. "Lil Scott? That the dame?"

"Yes. She was shot in Boyle Heights yesterday. It was . . . set up to look like a mugging. It might even have been a mugging." She dripped with dubiousness.

"Bad-luck bunch," he mused. "You got any reason to think it was connected to the hit-and-run?"

Erratic imagination. Hormone imbalance. Irrationality. Take your pick. "Not specifically."

"I dunno. It's pretty far-fetched." Hope was leaking away. "Naw, I don't think we got anything here."

"Maybe not. Just one question — was there anything, anything at all, unusual or unexplained about Lorrie's death? Other than who did it?"

"Nah, nothing. Except — "

She jumped. "Except what?"

Big mistake. Hernandez backed away from the intensity. "I don't know if I should be talking about this. How do I know who you are?"

"Call me back at the coroner's office. Chief of investigations. Jess Canby." She forced her voice to sound casual. Detached. Bored, almost. It was a good thing he couldn't see the holes her fingernails were driving into her palms.

He sighed. "I guess it's okay. Well, we got one sighting of a girl in a yellow sweat suit on a fancy bike earlier that evening. She was seen having an argument with a couple of hikers in the Mojave Desert, about a hundred and fifty miles away."

"How could she have bicycled a hundred and fifty miles in a few hours?"

"She couldn't. So obviously it was some other girl. It's no big deal, except you asked if there was anything — "

"I appreciate it." No big deal was something of an understatement. Still . . . "Where exactly was the sighting?"

"In the Lava Mountains, near a pisshole town called Lava Point. Guy said he saw her about midnight."

Well, that tore it. Nobody could have bicycled across a few mountain ranges and made it to a blind curve on Mandeville Canyon in two hours. You'd need a helicopter. "Thanks." She put the receiver down. Like the man said, it was pretty far-fetched. It would take an accuser more credible than Lil to sell it to the masses.

"Uh, Jess." Consuela stood at the doorway. "Oh, good morning. How are you today?"

"I'm okay." She cleared her throat. "Uh, have you seen the papers this morning?"

"No, I'm bored with the news. It's always bad."

"Worse than you think," Consuela said sadly.

"What — "

"Here." She put a copy of Jerry Katz's tabloid in front of Jess. "Page three."

Jess stared at it as if it were a loathsome object she didn't want to touch. Finally, she gritted her teeth and turned the page. "Oh, shit."

The headline was in big print: Coroner Cover-up in Tycoon's Death?" The first sentence was equally delightful. "A coroner's-office sleuth was investigating the so-called accidental death of billionaire Robert Berrington yesterday when her prize witness was murdered right under her nose." The article went on to raise various pithy questions such as why "an accidental" death was still being investigated, what said sleuth was doing in Boyle Heights, why Lil Scott (made out to be the most tragic heroine since Ophelia) had been put into danger, and why the coroner's office was evading questions. There were, however, sly hints that someone in the office was secretly passing information to the Intrepid Reporter, and it took no great intelligence to deduce that the someone was probably Jess.

Jerry had done himself proud. He'd taken innuendo, rumor, supposition, and fantasy and put them together in the form of a news story. It was all the more infuriating that, in a number of respects, he wasn't that far from the truth.

"Oh, shit," Jess repeated helplessly.

Consuela sat down on the only chair not covered with papers. "How did he get onto it?"

"He was at the house last night. I didn't tell him a thing, but he's got a naturally nasty mind."

"So does Harper," Consuela said anxiously. "He'll try to get you for this."

Jess nodded uncomfortably.

"Jess, what's going on?"

She looked at Consuela for a moment without

speaking, then got up and shut the door. She could use an objective opinion.

Consuela listened silently while Jess filled her in on everything that had happened since Joe called with the news that Berrington's house was on fire. When Jess finished, the other woman sighed and lit a cigarette.

"You don't have much to go on, you know," she pointed out carefully.

"I know."

Consuela nodded and fell silent again for a moment. "Well, even if Berrington killed himself, even if his people are willing to kill to cover that up — which is improbable — and even if Lorrie's death is tied in, which is even more improbable, how are you going to prove it? You have no evidence now, and you're not supposed to go out and look for it. All you're going to do is make trouble for yourself."

"A nice concise summary of the situation," Jess agreed.

"And besides," Consuela added tentatively, "do you really believe all that? Really?"

Jess took a deep breath. "I don't know. I don't want to. God knows, I don't need trouble now." Consuela didn't realize how much was at stake. Jess's political goals were almost within reach — this was no time to antagonize the establishment. "I don't want to believe Lil."

"She wasn't believable. She was nuts! It's much more likely that she was mugged than executed. And if so, what are you left with? A suicide. Big deal."

"That's the majority opinion." And Jess didn't have much to put up against it.

Consuela leaned forward. "Jess, do the damn report. Make everybody happy. Stop looking for shadows under the bed."

Jess didn't have time to answer. The door opened abruptly and Harper poked an angry face inside.

"Morning," Jess said calmly.

"Have you seen the — " He noticed the newspaper on her desk and snarled, "I see you have! Would you care to explain that?"

Consuela stood up, obviously wishing she were somewhere else, but without pushing the coroner out of the way, her exit was blocked.

Jess smiled pleasantly. "I can't explain it because I had nothing to do with it. Jerry Katz came to my louse last night, asked questions about the Scott death, got no answers at all — and wrote that article."

Harper was not placated. "I've had a dozen calls already! The chief of police is furious. The Board of Supervisors wants to know what's going on here. Stephen Bowdritch is beside himself — and I don't blame him!"

Jess shook her head. "I repeat, I had nothing to do with it."

"Why were you out with that insane old woman?" His face was turning purple."

"She insisted I talk to someone about Lorrie Berrington's death. It seemed the fastest way to get her off my back."

"I'd like to know the fastest way to get all these people off *my* back!" he shouted. "And I might point out that this is not doing you any good either! You don't have a friend left in town!"

She controlled herself with great effort. "I suggest we hold a press conference — say, tomorrow morning — and release the Berrington report. That should stop the rumors."

It took a few moments for the words to penetrate the thick covering of what was laughably known as Harper's brain. "Oh. Ah. Well." His splutters subsided; his skin returned to tan. "Ah. Yes. That would be satisfactory."

Jess watched him impassively.

"Fine. I'll tell Stephen that you're being . . . reasonable. Good." He nodded and was gone, leaving behind the scent of his after-shave lotion.

Jess and Consuela looked at each other and broke out in grins. Consuela went back to her desk, still shaking her head and smiling.

Jess made good her promise, starting immediately on the reports, sternly stifling twinges of guilt about Lil. Paper work was the bane of her existence, and these papers seemed worse than usual. She felt as though she were slogging through sour cream; it was a relief when the telephone rang.

"Jess Canby here."

"Senora Canby, it is Roberto Aguerra. The father of Miguel."

Jess swallowed. "Yes, senor. What can I do for you?"

"You see in the newspaper, it say Miguel — " His voice broke. The file said he was forty years old, but he sounded like an old man.

"Yes, I know."

"I no understand. "

She closed her eyes. How did you explain to a grieving parent that his child had been selling his body? "Did the police call you yesterday? Didn't they explain it?" Why hadn't goddam Garland informed the Aguerras as he'd said he would?

"No, no one call. Till today. Today, everyone call."

"Yes. I see."

"Miguel, he good boy." It was halfway between a statement and a question.

"I'm sure he was a good son." Her words caught in her throat. God damn Garland. "But sometimes — children make the wrong friends, get the wrong idea, make mistakes . . . "

"His mama, she — " He gulped. "Senora, you tell me, why is such a thing in newspaper? Is family business."

"Yes, but, well, the police reports are public, and the newspapers have the right to print . . . " Her voice trailed off again. They had the right to print, but did they need to print something like this? And she'd sicced Jerry onto the story. If she hadn't, some other enterprising sleaze of a reporter would probably have gotten hold of it, but that was no balm to her guilt. If you tell a vulture that there's carrion around, you've got to take responsibility for his swooping down on it.

"Now," he murmured helplessly, "now everyone call. Many *reporteros*."

"Senor, you don't have to talk to them. You don't have to talk to anyone. Take your wife and go stay with a friend for a few days — the calls will stop. Do you understand?"

"*Si, senora*, but" — he was almost in tears — "is family business. Now everyone know." He hung up.

Everyone knew. If your name was Aguerra, your life was an open book, but if it was Berrington, your dirty linen was encased in safety-deposit boxes.

Suddenly, she couldn't stand the office for one more second. Harper's after-shave was still lingering, and it stank like complicity.

* * *

It was only a few minutes' drive to Boyle Heights, and it was Spanish turf all the way. East of Union Station, Los Angeles returned to its roots — roots commemorated officially at the touristy downtown plaza of Olvera Street. Pious plaques informed visitors that Los Angeles had been born here, in the old inn and mission. The plaques didn't happen to mention that it had belonged to Mexico at the time. Or that the tourists would have to continue east into the *barrios* if they wanted to see where the descendants of the Spanish founding fathers had been banished ever since America stole California.

Jess parked where she'd parked the day before, a block past the street corner on which Lil had died. Brooklyn Avenue was unmarked by the tragedy. That had been an American matter; this was another country, a country of sun-baked dusty stones and desultory brownskinned people. Even the heat was foreign, not the glittering sharp light of the rest of the city, but a lazy haze that washed out colors and softened lines.

She stood at the light, remembering the event, every

detail as vivid as if it had happened five minutes ago. She could even see the faces of the killers, faces she hadn't realized were so clearly imprinted in her memory.

"*Qui tiene, senora?*"

Jess was jolted back to the present. A middle-aged woman dressed in matrimonial black was at her elbow.

"*Esta enferma?*" The woman was looking at Jess's stomach with concern.

"Oh. No. *Gracias. Me siento muy bien, gracias.*" Jess added a weak smile that was meant to be reassuring.

The woman nodded, patted Jess's stomach with a smile and crossed with the light. Jess smiled again, briefly, heartened by the human touch.

She looked around. Maybe something would leap out as Lil's intended destination. The corners were occupied by a marisco stand, a liquor store, a "discoteca," and the bank in front of which the shooting had taken place. If any held a secret, it continued to do so. And it was possible, very possible, that Lil would have led Jess away from the intersection.

Jess sighed. She couldn't search all of Boyle Heights — not even if she had a clue what she was searching for. The odds were lousy; in fact, they'd have to improve to be merely lousy.

She started toward the record store beside her. The "discoteca" was the least likely of all, and not just because the mind boggled at the thought of Lil inside a place that blared Stevie Wonder with painful decibel overkill. It was improbable that Lil would have waited for Jess across the street only to bring her back.

Jess winced at the assault on her eardrums; evidently, Chicano teenagers were no more keen on understatement than their West-Side peers. The record bins displayed mainly English-language music; the browsers wore blue jeans and T-shirts emblazoned with rock-group emblems. Small wonder that the Hispanic societies ranted about the loss of their own culture.

"Senora?" A salesclerk approached, a slight young man with a punk-rock, partially shaved head, jeans he'd been poured into, and a sleeveless tunic that set off a garish selection of tattoos. He was staring at Jess with something akin to amusement and it wasn't because of her color or her shape. She was easily the oldest person in the store, maybe by a decade.

"Do you speak English?"

"Sure. What're ya looking for?" He was definitely native-born from the sound of it, in the Bronx.

"Were you at work yesterday?"

"Yeah."

"A woman was, er, mugged across the street."

"Yeah, I heard." He sounded bored. Either he was a singularly self-absorbed young man or else shootings were as common here as sunrise.

"She was in Boyle Heights looking for someone." If only she had a picture to flash. The only available one, unfortunately, was the morgue shot, and that just showed where Lil's face had been. "I'm trying to find out who she wanted to see. It's got nothing to do with the mugging," she added reassuringly.

He wasn't reassured. He was backing away, suddenly ostentatiously concerned about his customers. "Nothing to do with me, man. I don't know nothing."

Jess tried with the other member of the staff, a very young girl who felt, unaccountably, that short shorts the size of a wide belt were business attire. What had happened to the Mexican tradition of over-protecting the unmarried female?"

This time, Jess tried another approach. She described Lil as if she wanted to find her, neglecting to mention that all she'd have to do was walk into Cold Storage Room Two.

The girl shook her head. She'd never seen Lil, never heard of her, and could hardly keep awake for the entire discussion.

The liquor store personnel were slightly more engaging, but no more helpful. In the rest of Los Angeles, liquor store clerks were customarily strikingly beautiful young men of uncertain sexual preference. There was no such latitude in the *barrios*. Men were men to a fault. The two behind the counter were barely of an age to shave, but they'd learned their lessons well; during Jess's brief conversation with them, they broke off to leer at two young girls, a matronly woman accompanied by five kiddies under six, and a gray-haired grandmother who scolded them vigorously for it but didn't succeed in altering their faces. Only Jess was spared, presumably because of her condition. Despite the chivalry, neither could tell her anything more than she already knew.

* * *

There were two corners left to try. Jess ate at the marisco stand, cashed a check at the bank, and emerged, with food in her stomach, money in her wallet and nothing else to show for the time. She stood outside the bank for a moment, staring at the spot on the sidewalk that still showed traces of the chalk outline of the body and a few dark spots she didn't want to think about.

She forced her eyes away and took a few deep, shaky breaths. All she was accomplishing here was to upset herself. There was one last possibility at the intersection, a medical clinic above the bank. The stairs were steep, dark, and uninviting, but they were, like Mount Everest, there, and so was she. She sighed and climbed them.

It was a birth control center, determinedly cheerful, with hanging ferns, soft bright couches in the waiting room under posters that suggested in Spanish that women had the right to control their own bodies. No doubt a veiled allusion to the availability of abortions for those *Chicanas* who felt that an annual pregnancy was too much of a good thing.

The clinic was humming; seven women waited in the antechamber as staff bustled in and out of the deeper recesses of the office. It seemed that all the employees were either white or black, not surprising in this community. Residents might be able to sneak in for quick care, but they certainly couldn't get away with trafficking openly with the devil.

"Excuse me." Jess put out a hand to slow down a striding gray-haired black woman. "Have you got a minute?"

"Not right now, honey. Go see Karen at the desk." The woman spoke with brusque kindness. "Over there."

Jess obeyed. Karen was a slight figure, twentyish, with a sallow face that spoke of vegetarian diet and indoor life. She listened to Jess's litany, now routine, with only half her attention, the other half occupied by constantly ringing telephones and a parade of staff.

"Do you know anyone of this description?"

Karen finally focused brown eyes on Jess. "Who are you?" She bristled with hostility.

"Jessica Canby, coroner's office."

"If you want to search our records, get a warrant. These women are entitled to privacy."

Jess paused, seized with a sudden fantasy of Lil coming in to ask for a diaphragm. She collected herself. "No. I, uh, don't think this woman was a patient. She was a bit too old." Say two decades in age and two generations in attitude. Jess repeated the description.

Karen shook her head throughout. "No. And we're busy. Sorry."

Jess sighed and accepted the dismissal. She left, passing a young woman on the stairs who took one look at Jess's stomach and burst into tears.

* * *

The car seemed to know better than Jess what to do next. It took her directly onto the west bound Santa Monica freeway, at which point she realized she was going to Beverly Hills.

It made quite a change from Boyle Heights. Nothing in Beverly Hills was shabby, but even in a city of style and sparkle, Rodeo Drive was astounding. Three blocks of stores that glittered with money; a few of them weren't even available for browsing without an appointment. It was consumerism carried to caricature, and it would have made a socialist weep.

Jess didn't even bother vying with the Mercedes and Rolls Royces for a spot on the street. She went directly into a parking lot where the attendant sneered at the Skylark, dismissed with a glance her fashion sense, and couldn't quite believe her hairdo. Everyone else was a gold-plated marvel, as perfect as plastic surgeons, clothing designers, and Elizabeth Arden could make them. Jess told herself that the result was faceless monotony, and strode into Giorgio's.

It was a Beverly Hills institution, the grande dame of the corner of Rodeo Drive and Dayton Way, a drop-in center for generations of needy West-Side wives with nowhere else to go but the masseur and the shrink. They congregated there in outfits they'd shopped for in order to have nice little outfits for shopping, gossiping on the couches around the coffee table, rummaging through racks of simple thousand-dollar dresses, perking themselves up at the counter of hundred-dollar scarves. They all knew each other, knew whose husbands strayed (everyone's), knew who would soon be undergoing facelifts in contemplation of yet another foray into the marriage market.

Jess was looked at, looked over, and looked away from. She was quite obviously an outsider. She shouldn't have brought her briefcase inside.

"May I help you?" A saleslady dressed appropriately for a hot afternoon in a sequined long-sleeved tunic was at her elbow. "Are you looking for something in particular?"

Jess smiled. "No."

"Ah." The woman didn't seem surprised.

"Is the manager here?"

"Not at the moment."

"Maybe you can help me." She pulled out Berrington's check and her own ID. "I want to find out what this check was for."

The woman looked at the signature and then, with avid curiosity, at Jess. "We were so sorry to learn about his death."

"Yes. You knew him, then? Did he shop here

often?"

"His 'friend' did." The woman was developing a fondness for Jess. This could make a good tale, and good tales were much appreciated around the coffee table. "Do come and sit down, dear. You must be exhausted, carrying all that around."

Jess didn't know if the reference was to her stomach or her briefcase, but she accepted the offer. "Who was Mr. Berrington's friend?"

"A good friend."

"Uh-huh." She'd figured that out for herself. You didn't spend three and a half grand on a stranger. "Do you know her name?"

"She comes in frequently. Well, she did. Now, who knows?" A shrug, a meaningful glance. Sugar daddies were hard to come by in these parlous times. "Modesty."

Jess was taken aback for a moment. Was that virtue being recommended specifically for her? Or was it a suggestion for those who aspired to shop at Giorgio's? In either case, it was an improbable thought for a saleswoman who'd passed sixty long ago and still considered cleavage a viable option. "Pardon me?"

"Modesty Nichols. That's her name. She's a lovely girl — very attractive, of course. Size ten."

"Ah. Do you have her address?" If Modesty could afford to buy three thousand dollars worth of togs, she wouldn't lug them home herself.

"I believe so." The woman pulled a leather-bound ledger out from behind the desk. "Yes, here it is. In Pasadena."

Jess copied it out. Good choice, Robert. Convenient to the downtown office, yet tastefully distant from Bel Air and the Los Angeles Country Club.

"Well, thanks." Jess started to leave.

"Oh, one more thing." The woman had Jess's arm in a vise grip. "I forgot one thing." She paused to heighten the tension. "Modesty was in here in May and she told me — " The voice dropped, the eyes were bright. "She told me she was expecting a baby. Mr. Berrington's baby!"

Jess forced herself to display the expected knowing air. It didn't cost anything to give the woman a little gratification.

* * *

The freeway was a parking lot. How could they call it "rush hour" when nothing moved at all, let alone rushed, and it occurred from before three o'clock to after seven? It took Jess fifty minutes to retrace her steps to downtown and, when she got there, another half-hour trapped in the clot of six freeway entrances and exits. Even the Pasadena Freeway, when she finally headed north through the hills, was sluggish. By the time she parked in chic, renovated downtown Pasadena, Jess was soaked with sweat and ready to kick a small animal.

Modesty lived in a chrome high-rise guarded by a doorman who'd trained at a special Doorman's School that provided Californians with a clipped British accent elegant enough for Buckingham Palace staff.

"Miss Nichols?" The doorman shook his white-haired head regretfully. "Miss Nichols is not at home. If Madam cares to try again, Miss Nichols may be at home to visitors later."

Jess opened her mouth to argue, then thought better of it. She was no match for two thousand years of breeding, even if it had been inculcated in a two-week cram course. And she had another call to make in the area.

* * *

The North County Clinic was close by in terms of distance; it was light-years away in every other sense. It sat at the top of Pasadena on Washington Boulevard, its shabby one-story building sandwiched in between a failing dress shop and a parking lot that wasn't busy because there wasn't much to park for.

This wasn't Pasadena as tourists knew it. They saw the wide, treed boulevards of graceful mansions that flaunted the superiority of families who'd developed California and with it their own extant fortunes. North Pasadena was the bastard child of Horatio Alger, a decaying way-station for those who couldn't keep up and those who'd been kept down.

The clinic's waiting room was a microcosm of the community. White families who remembered palmier days and who couldn't figure out what had happened to hard-working people in fifteen years of inflation sat dull-eyed and passive, sullenly pretending not to see the newcomers. The black and brown faces had started appearing as the area crumbled; they were less sullen because fifteen years ago, they'd had less hope to lose.

Nobody paid attention to Jess, including the nurse-receptionist ensconced behind a glass window that could have used a little Windex. She was examining herself in a small pocket mirror and was obviously disappointed with the spotty complexion and lank hair she saw.

"Excuse me." Jess rapped on the window.

The nurse frowned at the intrusion and looked up briefly. "Have you been here before?" She sounded accusing.

"No, I — "

"Well, you'll have to fill these out." She waved a daunting sheaf of medical forms. "MediCal?" More hopefully. "Blue Cross?"

"I'm not here as a patient." Jess showed her ID. "I want to speak to the doctor."

"Well, I don't know; we're awful busy." The nurse spoke dubiously; she was already hoisting herself up. Credentials were credentials, and she'd been trained to obey authority.

She returned from the back with a tall, extra-ordinarily thin man. His skin was a fragile membrane stretched over pointed bones, the forehead high and knobby, the cheeks sharply etched. He looked two-dimensional.

"This," the nurse announced in a new pert manner,

"is Doctor Frechetti."

"Can I talk to you, Doctor? It won't take long."

He rubbed the back of his neck, a gesture of fatigue more than indecision. He glanced over the assembly. "They've waited this long, I guess they can wait a bit longer." It was as if "they" were deaf and dumb. "Come in."

Frechetti's private office wasn't quite what a young medical student aspired to. It was a small bare rectangle with no natural light, splintered wooden furniture and peeling walls enlivened only by a couple of old framed diplomas and some crayon marks. The crayon marks weren't recent. The kids who'd made them were probably waiting outside now with their own children.

"What is it? Have we stepped on someone's toes?" He didn't act like he gave a damn. Jess could understand that. This wasn't the kind of practice you'd kill to keep.

"No, nothing like that. I'm chief of investigations for the coroner's office and I'm checking out a case." If Harper were here, he'd have heart failure. "I understand that your clinic has treated people who may have been harmed by exposure to radar."

"Radar?" He frowned. "You're thinking of Jackson, I suppose. I thought you people decided he was a crank? I was told to leave the complaint alone."

"Yes. Uh-huh." Her mind was racing, but that just meant it was getting nowhere fast. Maybe if it weren't about a hundred degrees in here, she'd be able to think. "We're following up another aspect of it, nothing to get worried about. I figured it might help to talk to Mr. Jackson."

"I'm still not sure why you're here."

Hardly surprising. She couldn't make sense out of what she'd said either. "I'd like a quick look at Jackson's file." Illegal and illogical. She prayed that Frechetti was a fuzzy thinker who didn't know the law.

"The file?" He stared at her. "I don't have it. You took it."

"The coroner's office took it?"

"No, of course not. Jackson's still alive as far as I know. The Department of Health Services took it." He was becoming suspicious, and any moment he would start asking questions, which would be extremely inconvenient since Jess had absolutely no answers.

She stood up quickly. "Oh, fine. I'll get it from them. Typical, isn't it? The right hand doesn't know what the left hand's doing." That should play. Everyone knew how inefficient government was.

He let her find her own way out. It wasn't hard since the entire clinic would fit into a cloakroom at County Medical. Jess stopped by the nurse's desk.

"Thanks. You run a, er, very smooth operation here."

"Oh, yeah?" The woman looked surprised but gratified. "Doctor Frechetti and I were discussing the Jackson case. You wouldn't happen to have his address handy, would you?"

"Sure thing." The woman was determined to prove just how right Jess was. This was a hell of a smooth operation.

* * *

Wilson Avenue shared more than a presidential name with Washington Boulevard. It displayed the same faded resignation a neighborhood worn out by fifty years of constant change, all of it bad. The original doyennes, frame mansions with Victorian gables and deep verandas, had been invaded by unassuming working-class bungalows, at first respectable and now neglected, their lawns brown, their flower beds denuded. Here and there a screen door stood ajar, displaying broken furniture or old refrigerators on unpainted porches.

The Jackson house was one of the upscale models. It was tiny, but the roof was newish, the yellow trim wasn't peeling, and the front yard resembled grass. Jess pressed the buzzer several times, but to no avail. Life had certainly become more complicated for sleuths now that women couldn't be counted on to be home during the day.

"Hello? You look for someone?"

Jess glanced next door. A tiny Chinese girl was holding open her screen door.

Jess crossed over. Up close, the "girl" was evidently no teenager. Her skin was still perfectly smooth, the pores invisible, but a faint network of fine lines around the eyes and mouth suggested that high schooh was an old memory. "Do you know what time Mr. Jackson gets home? Or Mrs. Jackson?" If there was one.

The neighbor looked puzzled, then wary. "Who you are?"

"I work for the county. This isn't a question of taxes or anything like that," she added hastily as the woman took a step backward. "They're not in trouble. I just have a few personal matters to talk to them about."

The woman examined Jess for a while. The big belly apparently persuaded her that there was no danger here. "The Jacksons gone now. No live here."

"They've moved?"

"Yes, moved." She nodded several times to emphasize how happy she was with Jess's choice of words.

"When did they go?"

The neighbor shook her head, but it didn't seem to mean she was unsure of her facts. "Three month."

"Do you have their new address?"

"No." She shook her head again and sighed delicately. "They no say."

"I see." Jess shifted her weight. The "weaker" sex was hardly an apt designation for people who carried around a badly balanced deadweight for nine months. "Were you friendly with the Jacksons?"

"Perhaps." The woman thought about it. "Yes, with Mrs. Jackson, perhaps."

"By the way, my name is Jess Canby."

"My name, Mary Lee."

They shook on it.

"Mrs. Lee, was Mr. Jackson sick?"

"Oh, yes. Mr. Jackson very sick."

"What was the matter with him?"

"Very bad." Mrs. Lee cast around for the right words. "His eyes, his eyes bleeding. Very bad. They call it . . . " She stopped, her face downcast. "I no remember name. Sorry, lady."

"That's fine. You're being wonderful," Jess smiled. "Did they move away because Mr. Jackson was sick?"

"Yes." Mrs. Lee was delighted with Jess's perspicacity.

"The company, they say they fix eyes. People come to ask questions — people like you, man and girl — and Mr. Jackson, he say company is right. They have to move."

Jess watched her carefully. There'd been something in the way Mrs. Lee had said that, something Jess was to pick up on. She took a flyer. "But Mrs. Jackson didn't want to go?"

. "Ah." Mrs. Lee rewarded her with a broad smile. "Yes, I think Mrs. Jackson not want. She happy here. She like house, she like me; she like doctor. I think she not want to go."

"What company did Mr. Jackson work for?"

The smile faded. Another toughie. "I no know name. He work with machines, I think."

They looked unhappily at each other.

"Ah!" Mrs. Lee beamed again. "Mount Wilson! He work at Mount Wilson — like street. Wilson Avenue."

"That's terrific," Jess said sincerely. "One more question. What are the Jacksons' names?"

"Linda Jackson. And," Mrs. Lee thought for a moment, "and Ron. Yes, Linda and Ron." She pronounced it "Lon."

"You've been a great help."

"Okay, lady." She turned to go inside.

Jess shifted her weight again. "Uh, do you think I could use your washroom?"

Mrs. Lee giggled. "I have six babies." She giggled louder, understanding perfectly.

Sam Spade didn't know how lucky he was. Pregnant detectives were somewhat handicapped by their need to be within sight of a toilet at all times.

Chapter 7

Modesty Nichols wasn't nearly as inaccessible as her doorman like to think. She sounded delighted at the idea of having company, and when Jess stepped out of the elevator onto the eighteenth floor, Modesty was waiting for her in the corridor.

"Hi!" She waved as if Jess was likely to miss a six-foot blonde in a violently pink maternity blouse. "I'm Modesty!"

Jess forced her way through the ankle-deep carpet. "Thanks for seeing me."

"You kidding? I never get to see anybody — I'm happy when the delivery boy brings the groceries. Hey, you're knocked up too! Too much!"

She led Jess inside to a massive living room that was furnished with the unmistakable touch of a society decorator's hand. The carpet was pale gray, the sofas and chairs a deeper gray, the walls and ceilings darker still. It was quietly luxurious, unostentatiously classy, and restful. It was, therefore, entirely at odds with the occupant, who wore the entire inventory of a medium-sized jewelry store, bounced when she talked, and within two minutes of their meeting, had breathlessly confided to Jess that her boyfriend had given her the place and she found it oppressively somber.

"Say, you want a drink or something?" Modesty giggled as she patted her stomach. "I mean, we're not supposed to, but what the hell, right?"

"Right." Jess smiled back. The young woman was definitely adorable; refinement wasn't everything.

"So, how far gone are you?" Modesty poured with a practiced hand. "Me, I'm six and a half months."

"I'm in the same ballpark. Thanks." Jess accepted a hefty tumbler of scotch.

"It's a drag, isn't it? I mean, a kid's gonna be fun and all that, but this business of waiting around for nine months — it's for the birds!" Modesty held up her drink. "Well, down the hatch."

Jess sipped.

114

"You married?" Modesty was looking at Jess's left hand.

"Uh-huh. I just don't wear a ring."

"Neat." Modesty herself wore about six rings, but she wasn't a proselytizer. "You like your husband?"

Jess grinned. "He'll do."

"That's nice." Modesty sighed. "My boyfriend was pretty swell, too, but he's dead now."

"Yes, I'm sorry. I — "

Modesty obviously hadn't had a chance to talk in days. "Yeah. You know, I'm real sorry too. I'm not too good about showing that kind of stuff, but I'm gonna miss him. With the baby coming especially. Yeah, I'm gonna miss him." Her eyes were filling up. "Oh, hell! That's life — you figure you got it worked out and you're always wrong. Right?"

She didn't wait for an answer. "I'm gonna have another drink — just a teensy one." She looked back from the bar. "How about you?"

"I'm fine for now, thanks." Jess hadn't made any substantial inroad in hers yet.

Modesty downed her second and became chipper again." I can't wait to get into decent clothes again. I hate these lousy bags, don't you? I'm gonna buy myself a whole new wardrobe afterwards. My boyfriend left me pretty well fixed. He was real nice, giving me this place and everything. 'Course I'm gonna sell it. I want a place that's a lot cuter. Maybe something all yellow — what do you think?"

"It would be more cheerful," Jess agreed cautiously. She put down her drink. "Modesty, I'm here because of Mr. Berrington."

"Oh, shit!" Modesty stood up and put her hands on her hips. "Jeez, here I thought you were okay and everything. You're from that damn office of his, aren't you?"

"No. I'm with the coroner's office. I'm investigating the fire."

"You work with stiffs? No kidding?" She stared. "Isn't it real depressing?"

"Sometimes. Can I ask you a few questions?"

"Sure, long as you aren't from his office." She sat back down.

"How long did you know Mr. Berrington?"

"Uh, let me think. I met him about two years ago — in Vegas. I love Vegas, don't you? It's a real swinging town."

"Mmm." If God tailored hell to his customers, he'd send Jess to Las Vegas.

"We hit it off right away. He was cute. You know, those eyebrows. I just loved those eyebrows." Modesty giggled. "He was a lot older'n me, of course. I'm only twenty-four, but it's different for men, isn't it? He was still real cute."

Jess grinned. Not everyone would recognize Robert Berrington from Modesty's description.

"I was living at the Beverly Wilshire. I'd just moved to LA from Portland. I had a boyfriend there, but when we split, I said to myself, I said, 'Modesty, Los Angeles is the place for you.' I just love the sun. Anyway, Robert got me this place after a couple of months." She winked at Jess. "It wasn't cheap, but it was cheaper than keeping me at the Wilshire. I like to have a good time, right?"

"Why Pasadena? Do you like Pasadena?"

"No, but I could understand it. I mean, his friends, they're all so stuffy and everything. He probably wanted to stay away from them." She didn't seem offended. "Like that stuffed shirt who works for him. Stephen Bowdritch. He's been real nasty — him and his dried-up wife. What's her name? Oh — Delia. Yeah. Delia Bowdritch. Some name, huh? She acts high and mighty but Bowdritch can't stand her. Robert told me that. Bowdritch stays with her 'cause she's got money and he loves money, but he can't stand her. Well, they tried to take this place away from me, but it's mine. I got the papers and everything."

Jess tried to get the interview back on the rails. "Was there anything that might have made Mr. Berrington depressed?"

"Depressed?" Modesty looked bewildered. "Why would he be depressed? He had tons of money and he had that big company and he had me."

Jess smiled fondly at her. The last point was a strong one. Modesty grew on you.

"And we had so much fun," she continued with a sigh. "We traveled, you know. All over. Europe and the Far East and South America. We went to South America three times," she said proudly. "He had business all over the world, and he was doing something even bigger. He said when it was done, we'd be able to go to almost any country in the world and he'd have business there."

"How did he feel about the baby?"

"Oh, he was real excited. It was great. I figured . . . I figured I'd have to take care of it. You know. But he didn't want me to — he was real happy, not like a lot of guys I know." Modesty spoke matter-of-factly. She wasn't Rhodes Scholarship material, but she knew a lot about character. And the lack of it. "He wanted me to have the baby, and if it was a boy, I think he was gonna get a divorce and marry me."

Jess took a moment to digest that.

Modesty misunderstood. "I didn't push him or anything. I mean, I know I don't fit in too good with his crowd. They like prunes like that Delia Bowdritch or that lush wife Robert had. But he said he wouldn't mind having a fun marriage. He had the other kind. They had the kid but — "

"Did you ever meet Lorrie?"

"Yeah, a couple of times. She was okay. She wasn't a snob or anything. I gave her some advice once, about clothes, you know? She dressed real dumpy." Modesty shook her head. "But the next time I saw her, she was dressed the same way."

"Her death must have upset her father?"

"Yeah, sure. But they didn't get along too good. They had a lot of fights, especially this spring. She was kind of strange. She didn't have a boyfriend, didn't even want one." She was awed at the mere thought. "And she got into a lot of crazy things, you know? And Robert said she spent time with radicals. Communists and stuff. Weird for a girl." She suddenly wrinkled her forehead. "Say, why're you asking all these questions? I don't mind, but I don't get it."

"We check out a lot of accidents," Jess said vaguely. "Make sure there's nothing funny about them."

Modesty shot to her feet. "I knew it! I knew it! That bitch killed him, didn't she? I knew there was something funny about that fire!"

"Hold on." Jess stood up too. "What bitch? What are you talking about?"

"His wife. Elizabeth. I knew she wouldn't let him get a divorce. She didn't want him, but she wasn't going to let me have him. Jesus! I wish I'd been here. He'd have been with me, and the fire wouldn't have worked!"

Jess stared at her as if she hadn't understood the words.

"If I'd been here, he'd have been with me," Modesty explained again. "See, I was in the country." She said "country" the way a Catholic would say "hell."

"The country?"

"Yeah, all the way on the other side of Palm Springs. It was nowhere! This ranch he owned — just me and a bunch of cows. No TV even!"

It wasn't easy to picture the blonde in a rural setting. "Why were you there?"

"He made me go, about three weeks ago."

"Why?"

"He got this idea about it being safer."

Jess stiffened. "How so?"

"I didn't understand it," Modesty shrugged. "Something about death rays in the city."

Death rays. Oh, swell.

"It was his fault, making me go."

Jess nodded impassively. Modesty was more gullible than she'd have guessed. Death rays were a pretty weak excuse for removing someone who'd apparently become an embarrassment. "Uh-huh. Well, thanks for your time. I should get going — do you mind if I use your powder room?"

"Sure." Modesty giggled. "I pee all the time too.
It's being pregnant." She led the way to the appropriate
door. "You take a good look at that wife of his. She
killed him, I bet you anything. She'll get away with it,
too, if you don't do something. Her and her fancy family
will cover it all up."

* * *

Jess thought about Modesty's theory as she drove
toward Mount Wilson. Was that it? Had Robert died
because Elizabeth refused to let him go?

It would explain a lot of things, not the least of
which was why Jess had been discouraged from seeing
the widow. It could even explain Lil's death. Elizabeth
might be a lush and a lost soul, but she was also a
Cartwright, and that would make her seem, to her
people, a lot more important than a garrulous old
housekeeper whose ridiculous suspicions about a young
girl's bike accident threatened to bring down the whole
house of cards.

California was the size of many countries and richer
than most, but it was still run like a family business by
a select clique of interwoven clans, and the Cartwrights
were right up there with the best of them. The establishment would have closed ranks around Elizabeth
faster than you could say "whitewash."

Jess winced. She didn't want to run up against
people like that. She didn't even want to think about it.
Far better to concentrate on the road.

The highway climbed north from La Canada
Boulevard into the San Gabriel Mountains, a shiny
narrow ribbon that twisted as if seeking to escape the
baking sun. Even at five thousand feet, even late in the
day, the heat was blistering, choking the pale plants that
tried feebly to cling to the bleached cliffs. Heat com-
bined with smog to obscure the view until the car was
ten miles into the Angeles National Monument; gradually, white sky turned brilliant blue, and vague horizons

emerged as spectacular pine-studded mountains, great hunchbacked beasts sleeping between Los Angeles and the Mojave Desert.

The vistas after she'd turned onto Mount Wilson Road itself were even more awe-inspiring, but Jess paid them little attention. She was too busy trying to get up the mountain without falling off. The road was filled with blind curves and was often too narrow for two cars to pass. The shoulder was crowded on the one side by overhanging bare stone that, as signs warned and rubble under the wheels proved, didn't want to stay put. On the other side there was more room — more than a mile of it, straight down. Jess kept her eyes on the pavement until she was safely at the crest.

The road forked; she had the choice of Audio or Video Drive and took the latter, slowly cruising up past TV towers, larger and more elaborate than their radio cousins below. It was a bizarre landscape in the middle of the wilderness, a metal forest against the sky, spiky frames studded with strange growths: semicircular white drums, shiny concave dishes, spiny antennae.

It was a ghostly community; Jess saw only a few pickup trucks to hint at the presence of her own species. The towering monsters around her silently watched the sky for signals from unseen satellites and silently relayed their messages to earth, their invisible fingers probing televisions and computers and telephones.

There was something oppressive about the new technology. Jess was relieved to come upon the post office, and even more so to find a real human being inside, a portly civil servant scratching his completely bald head over a crossword puzzle.

He looked up. "I just closed. I'm gonna lock the door in a second." His eyes lit up hopefully. "Say, you wouldn't happen to know a six-letter word meaning muscle relaxant?"

" Oh. Uh . . . curare. C-U-R-A-R-E"

"Yeah, that fits. Wonderful!" He sighed happily and put down the pencil." I'm not too good at them, but they pass the time."

Jess smiled. "I suppose there isn't much to do up here. I was a little surprised to find a post office."

"Well, it's quiet, but I like it. You can think. Not too many people hanging around all the time."

A masterfully restrained description. "You work alone?"

"Uh-huh. Mind you," he leaned forward conspiratorially, "it's slow now, but that might change."

"Oh?"

"You know we're gonna keep on delivering mail, even if there's another war?"

She nodded. The postal service had assured the nation that neither rain nor sleet nor snow — nor nuclear holocaust — would stay them from their rounds. A few nit-pickers had complained that there'd be no one left to write, but that hadn't made a big but that hadn't made a big impression on the postmaster. That wasn't his department.

"Well, this is going to be one of the emergency stations."

"Oh. I see." He seemed perfectly serious about it, and she could feel the corners of her mouth twitching. She hurriedly changed the subject before she lost a friend. "I'm trying to find someone. A man named Ron Jackson. He's a technician of some sort, I think."

"Jackson. Jackson." He pursed his lips. "Oh, wait a minute. Big black guy? Six-four, ex-marine?"

Marine. Military. Radar. Her pulse quickened and she nodded.

"Yeah, that's the only Jackson I know works up here. Haven't seen him in a while, now I think about it."

"How would I find him?"

"He was working for Thalen Satellite. Just up the way, a pale blue building. You can't miss it."

There were a few buildings at the other end of the road and only one of them was pale blue. She couldn't miss it. But she couldn't get inside, either. The doors were locked and the small parking lot empty. The broadcast tower might function around the clock, but feeble, tiny humans couldn't be expected to. She'd have to come back, which meant another chance for Mount Wilson Road to get her.

Jess grimaced, allowed herself a cigarette, and stared at the scenery. It wasn't hard to tell directions without a compass. On one side, the view was of blue sky and green clad cliffs, on the other, brown sky and green clad cliffs. Los Angeles really was a sewer. She put out the cancer stick and turned the ignition key.

A van drove up beside her. It was pale blue, marked with a logo that looked something like a Teutonic letter "T." The driver, a young man with a bad complexion and a long, narrow face, leaned across to roll down the passenger window. "You lookin' for something?"

Jess was already struggling out of her car. "Yes, have you got a minute?"

He didn't seem thrilled, but he did climb down to meet her. Thalen Satellite obviously liked to hire big men. Jackson was one and this was another. The driver stood six feet and change. Lots of change. He had the bulk of a minor Pyramid and something of its shape: small head, big shoulders, bigger chest, enormous hips and thighs.

Jess tilted as far back as possible, trying for eye contact. "Does Ron Jackson still work for Thalen?"

"Jackson?" The Pyramid shifted slightly. "Never heard of him."

"How long have you worked for Thalen?"

"Two years."

"Well, then I'm sure you know him. Mr. Jackson's a tall man, not as tall as you, of course." She spoke sweetly and clearly. Lots of large people were bright, but instinct suggested that this one wasn't among their number. "A black man. I think he's a technician."

"Never heard of him."

"The postman said he worked here."

That threw him. He looked away, then went on the attack. "Who're you, anyway?"

She flashed the ID.

"Just a minute." He held out a hand. "I didn't see it."

Jess handed it over and revised her opinion of him. There might be as much to the Pyramid as met the eye.

He carefully studied the identification card, then reluctantly gave it back. "Yeah. Okay, he worked here for a while. He's gone now."

"When did he leave?"

"Months ago." A shrug. A glance at his watch.

"Do you know his address? Or where he's employed now?"

"No."

"Did he have any friends at Thalen who might know?"

Another shrug.

"I understand he was sick. Is that why he left?"

The atmosphere hadn't been warm. Suddenly, it was frigid. "Why're you asking these questions? What's it to you?"

"Like my card says, I'm chief of investigations at the coroner's office. I'm checking out a case." Jess didn't try to match his hostility, but she packed a lot of authority into her voice. "I should obviously be talking to someone in personnel."

"Where'd you hear Jackson was sick?"

"Around."

"It's bullshit. He was just a lazy niger."

"Not according to his doctor," Jess snapped. She drew a deep breath. Why was she standing here, arguing medicine with this redneck?

She looked back only once, just before turning onto Video Drive again. The Pyramid hadn't gotten back into the van; he was still standing beside it, talking into the handset of a mobile telephone.

* * *

The road was as bad going out as coming in, worse, in fact, because the sun was low and the overhanging cliff threw a shadow that seemed to press against the

car. The odometer crept up with maddening delibera-
tion, and it was still five miles to Highway 2, then fifteen
more to civilization. That was an exaggeration, perhaps.
Could one classify suburbia as civilization? Sure, if it
had cold drinks. The day was still hot as hell.

The was no other traffic on the road, but Jess kept
an eye on the rear-view mirror out of habit. Two miles
later, she noticed a metallic flash behind her; it came
and went, hidden by the angles of the mountain but
clearly moving faster than she was.

A mile later, it was right behind her. It was the
Pyramid, riding on her tail. Jess signaled him to move
back, irritated, then tense. There was nothing she hated
more than a tail-gater. If the sonofabitch was trying to
scare her, he was doing a good job. This was no terrain
for fun and games. The track seemed to get narrower
as the light faded and even though she tried not to
glance over to her right, she knew what was there. Or
rather, what wasn't there. It was a long way down.

The van inched up; suddenly, it touched her. Jess
gasped and looked into the mirror again. She froze for
a split second. She'd seen the Pyramid's face and he
wasn't playing games. He was deadly serious, and she
was in trouble.

Jess tried unsuccessfully to swallow. Her mouth was
bone-dry; her hand were soaking wet. She concentrated
on the ribbon of pavement, willing herself to stay on it,
to forget the drop, to think about nothing except surviving for another mile and a half.

The van touched her again, less gently this time.
Instinct took over, freeing muscles that would otherwise
automatically jerk the wheel. Another touch, then a
harder bang. The Skylark was no match for a van.
Each time, her car jumped ahead, out of control for
moment that seemed like an eternity. Jess tried desperately to recall the road. She'd passed a few turn-off
on the way up; she'd only passed a couple coming down.
If she could make it to the next one, if she could veer
onto it without warning, if he was riding too closely to
follow her . . . If . . . a lot of ifs, but they were all she

had.

Another blind curve taken too fast . . . another bang
. . . another curve . . . And then, ahead, she could see
the turn-off, a sandy ledge just big enough for one car.

She pretended that this was just a kids' game of
chicken. It wasn't for real. The stakes weren't high.
Her adrenaline was coursing just because she was
competitive. If she lost the game, she'd get another
crack at it; she wouldn't sail off into nothingness.

The ledge was coming up alarmingly fast; her eyes
were glued to it, and she didn't dare breathe. At the
last moment, she twisted the steering wheel sharply and,
at the same moment, threw all her weight onto the
brake. It was a few heartbeats before she understood
she'd made it. She was safe — only a few inches from
the precipice, but safe.

The van was further down the road, motionless.
Jess hurriedly reversed and got back onto the pavement.
She was behind him now on higher ground. He had no
room to maneuver. He couldn't turn around; he
couldn't reverse their positions, and he couldn't be
deadly coming backwards up the twisting road. He
could keep her there all night, but she was going to see
morning.

The van still hadn't moved. Jess stayed still too,
waiting and watching. Her heart sank when his door
opened and he came toward her, an enormous figure
carrying an enormous hammer.

She locked the doors and tried to stop shaking.

He stopped a few yards away and stared malevo-
lently at her, slowly pounding the head of the hammer
into one cavernous palm.

Finally, he spoke. "You leave Jackson alone. You
leave things that aren't your business alone." Without
warning, he stepped forward, raised his arm, and
crashed the hammer down on the hood of the Skylark.

Jess jumped and screamed.

"You get it?" He leaned close to the window.

She nodded quickly, still nodding after he'd turned
around to go back to his van. She only stopped nodding

when it was out of sight.

Jess didn't put the car into motion for a long time. His cat-and-mouse game hadn't been meant to kill her. It was just a warning. Somehow, that was the most frightening thing about the entire event.

* * *

The shakes came and went several times as she slowly drove down Highway 2. All she wanted was to be safe at home, firmly attached to Michael and watching something inane on TV. Maybe a game show. Something boring. She craved boredom.

But Michael was out with Haberman tonight. The house was at least an hour's drive away, and she couldn't see herself walking into an empty, black living room. She wouldn't mind a crowd.

Martin Dunphy. He wasn't a crowd and he wasn't Michael, but he was definitely a great consolation prize. She took the freeway to its end and Headed north on Glendale Boulevard, savoring the heavy traffic and garish streetlights.

Martin lived in Silverlake, a semiartistic community on steep hills overlooking a reservoir of the same name. The area had a rustic flavor despite being close to the inner city highrises and just north of the Echo Park *barrios*. The houses featured lots of wood siding and jungles of indoor plants. The residents tended toward huge dogs, battered cars, and ostentatious unostentation. There were few who'd completely given up on the sixties.

Martin was one of those few, but his countrified A-frame at the crest of Micheltorena Street was close to the office. He made certain concessions to the main stream. Nevertheless, he had joined the homeowners' association; he opposed pollution and development, and he had put the work of local artists up on his walls. The latter was a not-insignificant action. Laid-back it might be, but Silverlake was not cheap.

Jess almost cried with relief to see Martin's BMW

parked in his driveway. She left her car on the almost-vertical street, pulling on the emergency brake without any confidence that it could fight gravity, but not giving a damn.

It took Martin a few minutes to answer the door. He'd been in the shower and was holding a towel around his still-dripping form.

"Am I glad to see you!"

"Jess! What's the matter?" He ushered her inside and put the free arm around her. "Honey, what is it?"

She didn't know whether to laugh or cry. "I just had a run-in with King Kong's cousin — only bigger." She found herself shaking again.

Martin was frantic. "Sit down! Calm down! I'm going to get you a drink — if you don't tell Michael."

"Scout' s honor. Scotch — and make it a big one, okay?"

He vanished just long enough to grab a robe, two glasses, and the bottle.

Jess was looking around in dismay when he re-emerged. She'd just noticed that the lights were low, a bottle of champagne sat chilling on the mantel, and despite the temperature, the fireplace was ready for lighting. "Martin, you're expecting company!"

He shook his head. "No, I called and canceled." He forestalled her protests with a smile and a hug. "You're a little more important. Now. Tell me what's wrong."

He was ashen and grim by the time she finished telling him. "Jess, this is crazy!"

"I think so too."

"No, I mean — a murder yesterday, a car chase today !"

"You're just touching on the highlights." Her entire life was out of control. Evidence that vanished . . . The prospect of taking on the Cartwright clan . . .

"And that article in the paper," Martin continued wildly. "Jerry Katz is an asshole. You've got to watch what you say to him, or you'll make enemies, important enemies!"

"I know, I know." She sighed and downed her drink.

"Promise me you'll stop putting yourself on the firing line! No more hanging around street corners and exploring mountains. Please. You're supposed to take it easy! You're having a baby — think of the baby!"

She had to smile at his agonized expression. Martin thought the three of them were having this kid. She patted his hand. "I'll try, honest."

The telephone interrupted his relief. He answered it, said hello, and mouthed to Jess that it was Michael.

She grabbed the receiver. "Sweetie!"

"Jess! Say, am I interrupting anything interesting?"

"Nope, I'm doing the interrupting." She felt badly about the champagne.

"Jess, guess what! The deal's on!" Michael's voice was livelier than it had been in a long time. "Dana and I are spending tomorrow with Cyril, and it looks like we'll be signing the contract!"

"Michael! That's wonderful!"

Martin was pulling her sleeve and hissing, "Tell him. Tell him what happened!"

She ignored him. "When will you be home, Michael?"

"In an hour."

"I'll meet you there." She hung up and cut into Martin's expostulations. "I'll tell Michael — some of it. He's getting his first big break, and if you think I'm going to ruin it by scaring hell out of him, you're wrong. And, Martin" — she stared sternly at him — "you're not going to scare him either."

"He'll kill me if he thinks I've kept a secret — "

"He might. But if you don't, I'll do worse. I'll ruin your life. I'll drop in here in the middle of the night on a regular basis. You'll never get laid again."

He sighed unhappily.

She struggled wearily to her feet. "I'm going home now. There's still time to call your date back."

Martin started to cheer right up.

Chapter 8

It was one of the rare summer mornings when Los Angeles was blessed with smog-free, crystalline air. Jess drank her coffee on the downstairs deck, watching the playful waves reflect blinding sunlight. The coast from Santa Monica to Palos Verdes was sharply visible; she could even see Santa Caterina Island, a great hump straight ahead against the horizon.

It would be a perfect beach day. And it would be perfect hell downtown. By the time she got to the office, the acid blue of the sky would be swathed in brown and the temperature would be steaming. She sighed. The weather wasn't the worst of it. She'd promised Harper the Berrington report for this morning. It wasn't ready, so she had to do some really fast typing.

She finished her coffee and started the day. First was the call to Reg Cruickshank. He hadn't left home yet, so she got through to him without having to sweet-talk a couple of aides.

"Oh, Jess." The supervisor wasn't his usual ebullient self.

"Sorry to bother you so early, but I wondered if you'd had any luck unraveling the red tape at Health Services?"

He didn't answer immediately.

"Was there a problem?"

"Uh, yes, there was. I didn't have any luck at all."

" Damn."

"Jess, this is a military matter. A federal matter."

"I know it is. But I think it's becoming a local problem and so — "

"Jess." Reg interrupted her, then paused. "Jess, it's a delicate issue, and it's not ours. It would take more than a casual request to get those files unlocked."

She thought of the Pyramid. "Yes, I bet it would."

"And it doesn't fall into my jurisdiction, I'm not prepared to get heavy."

"I see," she said slowly. "Who could do it, do you suppose?"

"I don't choose to suppose. Period. And my advice, for what it's worth, is that you shouldn't either. Drop it." His voice was flat and uncompromising. "I've got to go now. See you."

Jess's eyes were fixed on the beach but, until a passing neighbor shouted a hello, she wasn't seeing it.

She woke up and waved, then dialed another number.

"Richard? Jess here."

Richard Simn was an early riser too. He greeted her cheerfully and asked after the baby.

"Fine. Growing fast, I think." She patted the tummy. "I need a favor, Richard." She outlined her desire to look at the radar files. "Reg Cruickshank doesn't want to get involved, and I can't get to see them without stroke."

"Mmm."

Her shoulders sagged. She knew what was coming.

It came. "This isn't your problem, my dear. It isn't within your jurisdiction, so why make trouble you don't need?"

"You should have seen Betty Drummond's face when she showed us her baby" she filled him in. "Richard, I'm pregnant. I can understand — "

"You're pregnant, which is all the more reason not to take this on. You should be thinking about your own future. The timing is terrible, Jess. Next week, the governor will be announcing his appointments to the water-inquiry commission. You're on the short list — if you don't stir up the waters."

"I know."

"And I've had run-ins with the military. You don't want to fight the Pentagon. They can be vicious." He sounded genuinely distressed.

"I don't want to fight them, no, but — "

"I certainly can't justify putting the party on the line for it. If it were even part of your job, I might have a different view, but it's not."

"It's something I feel strongly about."

"I can't stop you from acting, but I can refuse to

help." He said it with kindness, affection, and finality. "This is definitely something you shouldn't touch."

"Uh-huh. Okay, thanks anyway."

* * *

She spent the drive to work sorting out her thoughts. Her feelings were mixed. She didn't want to be a saint, if that meant losing her chance at the brass ring, and she certainly didn't want to get to know the Pyramid any better. On the other hand . . .

She still hadn't made any decisions when she approached the Mission Road off-ramp. The radio news chattered on in the background; she was hardly listening until she heard a familiar name.

" . . . Roberto Aguerra was found this morning in his garage where, police say, he killed himself by leaving his car running. Mr. Aguerra was the father of the young boy murdered in Hollywood last week. Recent newspaper reports have alleged that the dead boy was in the habit of selling sexual favors, and Mr. Aguerra's brother told this radio station that Mr. Aguerra was deeply despondent about the publicity."

Somehow, Jess maneuvered onto Mission Road and into the medical complex without being aware of her movements. She found herself in her parking spot, sitting motionless behind the wheel, the engine still running and the announcer giving last night's baseball scores. She slowly reached out and turned off the radio, then the ignition.

It was a few more minutes before she could bring herself to get out. Roberto Aguerra had crossed the Rio Grande to find a better life for his family. He'd worked hard so he could stay in the promised land. All for his family. The irony was unbearable.

Jess stiffly walked into the building, realizing too late that Harper was holding his press conference in the lobby, in front of the reception counter. She tried to turn on her heel, but he saw her before she got far enough away to pretend not to hear.

"There's Mrs. Canby, our chief of investigations. Mrs. Canby was in charge of the Berrington case."

The crowd of reporters turned; the cameras continued to whir. Jess reluctantly moved to Harper's side.

"I've just told the press that you're through looking into the case and that I'll release your report late today."

"Mrs. Canby." An eager young woman who looked to be barely out of school shoved a microphone under Jess's chin. "Would you sum up the results of the investigation?"

Harper intervened, damned if he'd let Jess steal his show. "Well, we shouldn't speak prematurely, but since we're among friends," the smile showed off both dimples and emphasized the cleft in the chin, "what the heck. It was an accident. Mr. Berrington was overcome by smoke before he even woke up."

"How did the fire start?"

Harper shook his head, sad but philosophical. "In the housekeeper's room. With a fan that shouldn't have been left on."

Jess glanced sharply at him. Lil had been afraid she'd be blamed for it — and maybe Lil didn't care anymore, but Jess did, dammit. "The housekeeper wasn't at fault, of course. The wiring in the house was old and inadequate," she interjected smoothly.

Harper eyed her without warmth, then nodded. "Yes. Of course. We don't blame anyone. Naturally — "

He was interrupted. Jerry Katz pushed his way to the front, his face a snide mask. "Mrs. Canby, that housekeeper is now dead, too. She was shot in Boyle Heights two days ago, in your presence. What were the two of you doing there?"

Jess could feel Harper's tension. She gazed coolly at Jerry and said, "I was off duty. I was doing Miss Scott a favor that has nothing to do with you."

His eyes narrowed. He wasn't taking the snub lying down. "You've been associated with several tragedies lately. Miguel Aguerra was another of your cases — his father has killed himself. Do you have any comment?"

She swallowed and hoped her voice wouldn't break. "No."

"Do you think Mr. Aguerra might still be alive if you hadn't released the information that his son was a child prostitute?"

Jess flushed, feeling sick and soiled. Damn Jerry. Damn her own big mouth. And damn the cameras that were immortalizing her red cheeks. "Are there any other questions?"

"Yes." Jerry paused long enough to let a nasty smile spread across his face. "You were completely forthright about the Aguerra case. Can we expect our report on Robert Berrington to be as . . . complete?"

"When it comes out," she snapped, "it will cover every relevant aspect of Mr. Berrington's death!"

"*When* it comes out?" Mock surprise. "But Dr. Harper just said it will be ready this afternoon."

Harper harrumphed. "Yes, of course, it will."

Something inside Jess had cracked wide open. She couldn't stop herself from overriding the coroner. "The investigation isn't complete yet. But as long as I'm chief of investigations, Mr. Katz, this office will make no distinctions between the rich and the poor!"

"She stalked out, ignoring the excited buzz of the press and the shouted questions. Harper stayed behind, trying to regain control of the situation without admitting that his face was covered in dripping egg.

Righteous fury got Jess out of the complex and Mission Road. Reality intruded a block later. She slowed down and stared unhappily at a sprawling yard of rusted auto parts. Jesus, she'd really put her foot in it this time! She could understand the emotions that had made her blurt that out, but Harper wouldn't forgive her unless he got word that, in remorse, she'd thrown herself from the Mission Road overpass onto the Golden State Freeway.

Her life had gone mad. Or she had. Vanishing evidence, muggers who took pot-shots at her for no conceivable reason, oversized men chasing her off mountainsides, icy receptions from old friends . . . Was she mad? Was it the pregnancy? Or was it just a classic case of paranoia?

Except — even paranoids had enemies. The Pyramid was real. And Lil was really dead.

So was Mr. Aguerra.

No, dammit, she wasn't going to take Librium and apologize to Harper! If the Aguerras had to confront the truth, then so did the high-rollers. Whatever in hell that truth was.

* * *

Dr. Herbert Zollinger's office was only a block away from Rodeo Drive in Beverly Hills, which was very convenient for all concerned. His patients would spend most of their time in the area anyway. The plaque on the wall in the reception area didn't indicate what kind of practice Zollinger ran, but Jess would bet next year's salary that the good doctor gave out enough Valium to sedate the US Marine Corps. He was well paid for whatever he did; fees didn't tend to be small in offices where the carpet was genuine Persian, the sofas were Italian, and the art was real.

"Good morning." The receptionist smiled sweetly at Jess. She bore no resemblance to her counterpart at Dr. Frechetti's clinic. This one was no older than twenty-five, and perfect. Her complexion was flawless, the eyes virtual oceans, and she had a mouth only dead men wouldn't want to taste.

"Good morning. I'd like to see Dr. Zollinger." Jess fished out her ID. "I have a few questions about one of my cases."

"Oh, dear." The dismay was adorable. Jess felt like a heel for giving her trouble.

"We're so busy today."

Jess hardened her heart. "Sorry."

A tiny, heartbreaking sigh. "I'll talk to the doctor."

Jess watched her leave the station. Her figure was neither overweight, nor underweight. Nor was it ordinary.

The woman returned quickly with a delighted smile. "The doctor will see you as soon as he's done with a patient!" She was as happy about it as Jess. Maybe more so.

Zollinger turned out to be typecast: stocky and grizzled, his eyes bright and omniscient behind thick glasses necessitated, one felt confident, by his voracious reading of medical journals. He even had a slight mid-European accent. If he hadn't chosen to care for the needy rich, he would have made a great secretary of state.

"Come in, Mrs. Canby." He stood up chivalrously behind his antique walnut desk. His office oozed comfort and class: thick rugs, glass-fronted bookshelves, a dozen framed diplomas. "Please. Sit down."

"Thank you." She returned his smile. It was a con job, no doubt, but she felt safer and healthier just being in his presence. "I'll only keep you a minute."

"Whatever." He sat too, clasping his hands and giving her 150 percent of his attention.

"You look after Elizabeth Berrington, I understand?" He hesitated.

"Stephen Bowdritch gave me your name."

"Ah. Well, in that case. Yes, Mrs. Berrington is one of my patients."

"I'm investigating her husband's death."

"Most unfortunate." He shook his head sadly. "But I didn't realize there was a problem with it."

"It's just a routine check." She kept her voice casual. "I'd like to talk to Mrs. Berrington."

"Why?"

"To get a picture of Mr. Berrington's mental state at the time of his death." Jess didn't put forward Modesty's theory. You didn't hint at homicide with no more to go on than the suspicions of a woman who also talked about death rays.

"Mrs. Berrington couldn't be of any assistance. She and her husband have been separated for some time."

"Even so, she knew him well. And their daughter died recently, as I'm sure you know. They must have spoken about that — even if only over the telephone."

"Hmm." He looked at his cupped hands, his face a model of deep thought. "I see." He raised his eyes again. "I'm afraid I can' t help you. Mrs. Berrington isn't well. In fact, she's, er, in a facility under my care at the moment."

"Where?"

"I'd rather not say. These places are meant, you know, to offer privacy." He spoke in tones rolling with regret that he couldn't be more forthcoming.

"I'd be happy to have you at the interview, to be sure that she doesn't become too upset." How upset could a widow be who'd left home years ago?

"I'm sorry." He brightened and added, "But if it's any help to you, I saw Robert two days before the tragedy. Socially, not professionally, of course. He seemed in good health and excellent spirits."

Jess paused, then plunged. "Dr. Zollinger, if Mr. Berrington was in good spirits, then why would he have been taking sleeping pills?"

The high forehead creased; he removed his glasses, methodically cleaned them, then replaced them on the long nose. "I'm surprised to hear he was. Robert was known for his aversion to drugs of any sort."

"I found an empty vial beside the bed." Might as well be hung for a sheep as for a lamb. She was already in so much hot water, nothing less than committing mass murder could worsen her situation.

He shook his head with authority. "I have treated Robert too, on occasion. I'm sure I'd have known about sleeping pills. Perhaps you were mistaken about the contents of the vial. Do you have it?"

Her eyes fell. "Not exactly."

"I see." A glint of something came and went in his eyes. "Well, Mrs. Canby, I wish I could have been of assistance."

Not as much as she wished it. Jess started for the door. "Oh, one more question. How long has Mrs. Berrington been at the . . . facility?"

"Four weeks." Zollinger was on his feet. He hadn't

moved a facial muscle, but his gaze seemed different. He simply wasn't as fond of Jess as he'd been when she arrived.

* * *

Adversity made her stubborn, and the day, though young, was shaping up to be full of problems. Goddammit, she was going to find Elizabeth and she was going to discover what had really happened to Robert Berrington, and to hell with them all. Harper and Bowdritch and Zollinger and the entire Cartwright family would be gunning for her, but she had resources of her own. Sure, her friends wanted the answer to be convenient — didn't everyone? — but they were decent, they'd live with the truth if they had to.

The point was, there wasn't much time to play with. When Zollinger thought about the interview, he was sure to ring the alarm, and a ton of bricks would descend on Jess's head. She had to act fast, which meant figuring out what to do next.

She found herself staring into a shop window; it turned out to be a boutique for women with ballooning figures like her own. Jess focused on the vivid cotton outfits. They didn't look too bad on the waxen dummies. Her reflection, in her limp beige skirt and yellow blouse, was a pointed reminder that, dowdy as they'd been to start with, her only two outfits for work were getting worse and worse. Even Michael had taken to looking at them dubiously.

She forced herself to go inside, walking as if marching toward the firing squad. It took two minutes to point to seven outfits and twenty to laboriously drag them on. Each one cost a week's salary, all looked far better on the dummies than on her, and all were shoddily made. Modesty was right. No matter how you cut it, the genus of maternity garb amounted to "lousy bags." Still, a girl had to cover the bulge with something. Jess was paying for the least detestable dress when she got an idea. It was feeble, but it was something.

The shop allowed her to make a credit card call. The telephone rang at the other end, which wasn't a good sign. In general, when her mother's line wasn't engaged, it meant her mother wasn't home.

"Hello?"

She must have just gotten in. "Hi, Mother."

"How nice, darling. How are you?"

"Fine. Just calling to check on the time of your flight on Saturday."

"Four. Didn't I tell you last time we talked?"

"Uh, yes. I was just confirming it."

"Oh, I see." Virginia paused. They tended toward pauses in their conversations. Jess was an only child, but somehow she and her mother had never been close. She'd been more like her father in temperament, outlook, and ambition. Not the way to a mother's heart when said mother was fond of none of the above in her husband.

"Four," Jess repeated. "Good. We'll have a nice dinner, and I'll tell you what's planned for the opening on Sunday."

"Yes. Well."

"One more thing, Mother. Did you ever know Elizabeth Berrington? Robert Berrington's wife."

"Yes, of course. She was a Cartwright, and I went to school with a couple of her cousins. Lovely family, the Cartwrights." Virginia had grown up on the fringes of the establishment and had always wanted that social life for her daughter. Arthur wouldn't hear of it. No way was the populist mayor's daughter going to some snotty private school. "Why do you ask?"

"I'm trying to find her. She's in some private hospital, drying out." Jess sighed, regretting the last detail. She'd been unable to resist pointing out just how fine the Cartwrights really were. Virginia had always evoked the same kind of response from Arthur.

"Why do you want her?"

"I just do, Mother. If you don't want to help, just say so."

The pause this time signified disapproval. Ladies didn't talk to their mothers thus. "Well, if you must — Angela Smythe would know, I'm sure. She moved in those circles and she always knew everything. Do you remember the Smythes? He's in mining. They live in San Marino, I believe."

"Thanks. See you Saturday." Now, wasn't that something to look forward to? Jess dialed again, ignoring the sideways glance of the manager. One dress didn't entitle a shopper to monopolize the telephone.

Mrs. Angela Smythe sounded exactly as Jess remembered her: confident, well-preserved, refined to the point of constipation.

"Mrs. Smythe, this is Jessica Canby. Arthur and Virginia's daughter."

"Oh, yes, of course. How are you, Miss Canby?"

"Very well, thanks. I'm sorry to disturb you, but my mother suggested I call. On Sunday, we're opening a sculpture garden dedicated to my father — "

"Yes, I read that. It's rather far for us to go. Otherwise, of course . . . "

"Uh-huh." San Marino looked down its nose on the West Side. "Well, Mother would like to contact Elizabeth Berrington. She's afraid that by mistake, Mrs. Berrington might not have received her invitation."

"Oh, dear." Mrs. Smythe fell silent for a moment. "Well, Miss Canby, I doubt that Elizabeth would be available in any event."

"Yes. We're aware of her . . . indisposition." Tactful pause, understood by both parties. "But Mother's quite concerned that she be invited at least."

"Yes, I see. Well, I don't have the number, but she's staying at a, er, retreat."

"Do you have the address?"

"Not exactly. It's in Montecito, I've been told. Restview Clinic. It's run by a . . . Beverly Hills doctor. Someone her husband no doubt wanted her to see." The inflections were delicate, but Jess spoke the language. Beverly Hills wasn't quite the thing, and only a nouveau like Berrington would have inflicted it on his wife.

Jess grinned, unoffended. San Marino got its comeuppance when the winds blew. The westerlies, with a fine sense of the ironic, sent vulgar Beverly Hills smog over to Angela Smythe ever day. "Thanks."

"Not at all. And do remember me to your mother."

Chapter 9

Highway 101 cut across the top of the city and then sliced through the San Fernando Valley. The heat was savage and the heavy traffic produced greasy black air that even the most efficient air conditioning system — which Jess's definitely wasn't — couldn't have kept out. Only when the freeway reached the coast in Ventura County did she get relief, and even then it was a trade-off. Cooler, cleaner — but slower. The tourists braked to gawk at the view, which, admittedly, was a gawk-worthy sight — glinting silver ocean, creamy beaches, blue horizon — if you didn't get cranky at the sight of the spiny, jerking oil rigs that crawled up the coast parallel to the highway.

The city of Santa Barbara was the empress of Southern California, a quiet, elegant community of the rich, the very rich, and the very, very rich, with a smat-tering of dowdy streets on the south end for the neces-sary support staff. The freeway slowed right down to a dignified crawl, becoming a six-lane road that severed deeply-treed country lanes and the beach on the west from commercial streets and terraced residential hills on the east.

Montecito was the jewel in the empress's crown. Nominally, it was a Santa Barbara suburb, but the city planners who invented the suburb in the fifties, had never dreamed it could be like this. The roads were gravelly and rustic — if rusticity could be used to de-scribe walled estates, elaborately maintained gardens, Mercedes station wagons, and country stores that sold designer originals.

Restview Clinic wasn't hard to find, but it didn't stand out. It was, like its neighbors, a grand mansion in the Spanish tradition, with pillared courtyards, or red-tiled roof, and mosaic tile wherever there wasn't greenery.

Jess pulled into the discreetly screened parking lot. She wouldn't have trouble picking out her car again. It was the only one that didn't cost fifty grand. She could only hope it wouldn't immediately be towed away.

Talking her way inside proved to be a matter of name-dropping. The head nurse who, like her staff, wore refined civilian clothing, was well-versed in the social niceties. The Canby name was a good entree.

Jess was shown up to a front second-floor suite and let inside the vast living room. She stood quietly for a moment, taking it in. It was over-decorated, crammed with chintz and mahogany and knick-knacks, comforting in the style of a maiden aunt's cluttered drawing room.

Only when a figure stood up did Jess realize she wasn't alone. Elizabeth Berrington was easy to miss, a pale wraith overshadowed by the bright colors and hearty good humor of the apartment. She looked at Jess without speaking; Jess looked back, somber in the presence of the wreck of the *Hesperus*. She barely recognized this woman from the newspaper photographs. The woman had classy, bony features: an aquiline nose, a sculpted high forehead, delicate ears, all of which normally improved with the passage of time. If time wasn't passed with a bottle. Every drink was etched on her person. The body was concave; the arms and neck trembled. Blood vessels stained the cheeks, which were otherwise a faded beige. The eyes were flat and dull, no longer red, but the whites were still tinged the memory of pink.

Jess crossed to her and put out her hand. "I'm Jessica Canby. You know my parents."

Elizabeth made no move to take the hand. She wasn't being rude, just passive, as passive as you could be this side of death.

Jess eventually took the other woman's arm and guided her back to the sofa. The illusion of being alone returned; the vivid upholstery swallowed up the stick figure so that Jess, even sitting close, had to make a determined effort to focus on her.

"How are you feeling?"

Elizabeth looked directly at her. "Better, thank you. I'm better ever day." It was a child's voice, repeating by rote a formula that had worked before.

Jess smiled. "Good. Do you feel up to a few questions?"

"If you like."

"I'm sorry about your husband's death."

"Oh." Utter indifference.

"Who told you about it?"

"Dr. Zollinger."

"What did he tell you?"

"Robert died in a fire." They might have been speaking about the loss of a house plant.

"Yes. When did you see him last?"

"See him last?"

How did one interview, a zombie? "When did you see your husband last?"

"I don't know." Elizabeth looked around vaguely as if someone in the room might remind her. "A long time ago."

"When did you talk to him last?"

"Oh, he called sometimes."

Jess expelled a breath and threw away Modesty's theory. This was not a killer. Murder needed a motivation stronger than apathy. "I suppose you talked to your husband about your daughter sometimes?"

Elizabeth's eyes flickered so briefly that Jess might have imagined it. "Sometimes."

"Is this her?" Jess picked up a silver-framed photograph from the sidetable. Two young girls in private-school uniforms were smiling at the photographer, their still characterless faces round with baby fat.

"Yes." Elizabeth didn't look over. "Many, many years ago."

"Who's the girl with her?"

Elizabeth frowned and wrinkled her forehead. "Oh. I know who it is, I just can't remember. Her friend. They were roommates." She was getting distressed, wringing her hands. "I just can't remember."

"You're doing fine. Don't worry about it." Jess hastily put the picture down. "It doesn't matter. Did your husband get along well with Lorrie?"

"I . . . I don' t know." Elizabeth wasn't calming

down. She was breathing quickly, soft little pants of anxiety. "Not very well. Robert was so hard on her. They were so different."

"Tell me about Lorrie," Jess said in soothing tones.

"I don't know." She somehow mustered the energy to stand. She was between Jess and the window, a silhouette against the bright light. "She was difficult. Such silly ideas, making Robert so angry. Only they weren't really silly, you know," she added with a sudden spurt of shocking anger.

Jess hardly dared to speak. "What were her ideas, Elizabeth?"

The anger was gone again. Elizabeth shook her head and watched a fly swoop in and out of the sunlight.

"Did her ideas have anything to do with her death?" Jess didn't know she was going to ask the question until it was out of her mouth.

The other woman began to back away, her entire body shaking. "No, no, how could they? How could she be right? Robert said she wasn't; he was so sure — and then she died." The last words were a gasp. "Who are you? Go away! Go away, you shouldn't be here; I know you shouldn't!"

Jess followed her as she moved around the room. "Was Robert upset enough about Lorrie's death to kill himself?"

Elizabeth's eyes widened. "Robert, kill himself?" She underwent another mercurial change of mood. Suddenly, she was laughing, quietly at first, then shrilly with a force that didn't seem possible for the frail frame.

The door burst open without warning. Elizabeth immediately froze again, invisible and immobile.

"What is the meaning of this? What the hell are you doing here?" Dr. Zollinger marched in, too furious to maintain the treacly bedside manner. "I told you to leave Mrs. Berrington alone!"

Jess didn't answer. She was watching Zollinger's companion. Stephen Bowdritch was in the doorway, eyeing her as if he had to restrain himself from strangling her.

"I forbade you to come here!" Zollinger's face was no more than three inches from Jess's. "How dare you?"

She wrenched her gaze away from Bowdritch. "I have a job to do, Dr. Zollinger, and in my judgement, I had to talk to Mrs. Berrington." She gently patted Elizabeth's arm. "Thank you for seeing me."

On her way out, she took another glance at the photographs of the two girls. The unnamed friend seemed familiar somehow, but the memory was too deeply buried to drag up.

Bowdritch stepped back at the last moment to allow her to pass. His words reached her when she was in the corridor. "You'll be sorry for this."

Jess kept on going, but the threat, with Elizabeth's renewed, chilling laugh in the background, stayed with her all the way back to the car.

She sat there and smoked a forbidden cigarette, trying to push fear out of her mind and replace it with cool, analytic thought. The trouble was that this problem didn't seem to succumb to logic. She had facts. She had theories. But nothing fitted together. It was no good thinking about suicide. Berrington wasn't the suicidal type, at least not on the basis of anything she'd learned so far. And Elizabeth wasn't the homicidal type. So if the fire wasn't an accident . . . Jess was as far from the truth as ever.

On the other hand, if it was an accident, she was up the proverbial creek. She'd made a horse's ass of herself, and horses' asses didn't tend to get ahead. Trouble-makers got excused only when they were right — and sometimes not even then.

She shivered. She didn't want to think along those lines. She wanted to come up with another way of approaching the case. It was time to look into the financial end of it, and she was in the perfect place to do that without making too many new waves.

* * *

Jess parked a block away from the stock-brokerage

145

firm. It was still a gorgeous afternoon, and Santa Barbara glittered with sunlight, an oasis of palm trees and endless blue skies and tanned, handsome people.

She walked into Loemann's, a single large room of recessed lighting, glass-walled offices and high-tech furnishings. "Hi." She smiled at the bronzed beauty at the front desk. "Is Frank Cavenaugh here?"

"Sure." Beauty dimpled back. "Can I give him a name?"

"Jess Canby." It was a name that was going to surprise Frank, a name from the distant past. At the university, Jess and Frank had been an item. After two years of heavy breathing in the back seats of small cars, it was a wonder that neither had been permanently crippled. He'd been tall and lean and pretty as a picture; it had taken Jess a long time to realize that, in the front seat, Frank was humorless, vain, and far more interested in her family connections than in her charms. His game plan had been thrown for a hell of a loop when she returned the diamond he couldn't afford and told him mendaciously that they'd always be friends.

"Jessica!" He was rushing toward her with outstretched arms and, incredibly, a leer. He skidded to a halt when his eyes took in her shape.

"Hi, Frank."

"Uh, hi. " He started moving again, but more cautiously. "Nice to see you."

"Uh-huh." Frank was clearly not one of those to whom pregnant women were beautiful. "Got a minute?"

"Sure." He was cheerful again. He'd always overestimated the extent of the Canby fortune. "Come on in."

"In" meant further back from the storefront window. Jess settled herself in a sleek chair that was every bit as uncomfortable as it looked and proceeded to hint at some future investment needs." I was in town, so I thought I'd stop by and see how you were doing."

"Good. Great. Things are wonderful."

"Swell," she smiled. "Listen, I'm just doing some research at the moment — there're a few stocks I'm interested in."

"What are they? We've got all kinds of data."

"Well, to start with, Berrington Industries." Frank would eventually put two and two together, but math had never been his forte. It would take a while.

"Good time to buy. The market's edgy now because of Berrington's death, but the company's sound. How much were you thinking of investing?"

"I, uh, haven't fixed on the exact number yet." She smiled winningly, implying a number with lots of zeros. "Tell me about the company."

"Let me get Derry Hooper. He's our communications-industry man." Frank waved his arm from the door of the cubicle. "Derry! Can you come here for a sec?"

Hooper bustled up, a tiny, dainty man with constantly waving hands.

"Jessica Canby, Derry Hooper. Jessica's interested in Berrington Industries stock. Can you fill us in?"

"Excellent choice," Hooper said approvingly, perching lightly on the corner of the desk. "Diversified. Manufacturing, of course. R and D. The subsidiaries do just about everything else there is to do — hardware, software, retail. They've branched into cable TV, DBS, Videotext — you name it."

"I'd name it if I understood it," Jess said gently.

"Oh. Yes, of course." He searched for simple words she might be able to grasp. "Okay. A manufacturer develops and builds a satellite. That's Berrington Industries in this case. They sell it to a company that buys it and contracts with NASA to launch it. The satellite company is a subsidiary." He looked questioningly at her and sighed with relief when she nodded to show she was with him this far. "Now, the satellite has a bunch of channels, which are called transponders. So other companies rent the transponders and use them for things like entertainment programs or communication lines. Again, the other companies are subsidiaries. Finally, we come to the consumer, people who want the packages or the communications systems. So other companies rent the packages, lay cable or set up dishes to receive the signals, and sell them to you and me. You see?"

"I'm beginning to."

"Excellent!" He barely restrained himself from clapping. "Of course, when I say you and me, I mean any user. It could be a household; it could be a business; it could be the government."

Jess nodded slowly. "It's enormous."

"Yes, billions. At least. Trillions." His enthusiasm was as pure as a child's. "Where Robert Berrington was so brilliant was that he grasped very early on where it was going. He's always been ahead of the game — so he has companies on every level of the business. And he's even ready for the next step. Soon, dishes will cost less than television, and everyone will have one."

"So there'll be a market for more satellites and more dishes?" Dishes as common as TV antennas. The implications were staggering.

"Of course. Berrington Industries is going to have to up their manufacturing quotas to meet the demand, and Thalen's going to expand like crazy."

Jess didn't realize she'd moved until she found herself towering over Hooper. "Thalen? What do you mean, Thalen?"

"Why, that's one of the subsidiaries I mentioned." He was leaning nervously away, poised for flight if she should suddenly show violent tendencies. "Thalen buys satellites from Berrington Industries and rents out transponder space to software companies — programmers."

"Thalen Satellite is a subsidiary of Berrington Industries?" Jess spoke slowly and clearly. This, she wanted to get straight. "Is that what you're saying?"

"Yes. Exactly." Hooper was casting beseeching looks at Frank. What kind of kooks did he attract, anyway?

"Thanks. Thanks very much." She rushed out and was halfway back to Los Angeles before she realized that she'd ended the interview in a somewhat unorthodox fashion.

* * *

The receptionist at Berrington Industries remembered for the Jess. "I'm sorry, Ms. Canby. Mr. Bowdritch has gone for the day."

"Uh, no, I'm not here to see him."

"And Mr. Marchenko's out for the moment."

"Actually, I'd like to talk to Carol. Mr. Berrington's secretary. Is she still here?"

"Carol Tuchman? I think so." She buzzed and spoke quietly into the receiver.

Carol appeared almost immediately. She was looking a little better than she had on Monday. The eyes weren't violently red any more, and she'd had some sleep. But nobody would describe this gaunt somberly-clad woman as happy. Would that Jess could inspire such devotion in her staff.

"Ms. Canby."

"Hi, Carol. Call me Jess. Listen, I've got a few questions. Do you have a minute?"

"I was about to go home anyway. There's not much to do in my office these days." The voice was sad. "What's it about?"

Jess moved Carol away from the receptionist. "I got the impression the other day that there was something bothering you. I think that's what it's about."

Suddenly the secretary was looking at her watch and giving the impression of someone who didn't have a minute to spare. "I doubt if I can help you. Now, if you'd like to make an appointment to see Mr. Marchenko — "

"No," Jess said sweetly and firmly. "I want to talk to you."

"Really, I don't think — " Carol swallowed and looked nervously at the receptionist.

"We can talk someplace else. Downstairs? Over coffee?"

"Please, please, just leave me alone," Carol whispered. "Please. You'll get me in trouble."

Jess shook her head. "Sorry."

Carol was greenish; finally, she nodded jerkily.

They didn't say another word until they were settled with glasses of wine in the Lord of Kent, a pseudo-pub in the basement mall of the building.

Carol broke the silence. "I only came to convince you that I can't help."

"Can't? Or won't?"

The other woman leaned forward. "Please, can't you leave me out of this?"

"Tell me what 'this' is and I'll try."

Carol looked away, her eyes fearful and haunted.

Jess hardened her heart by thinking about Lil. "What do you know about Thalen Satellite?"

Carol's head jerked in surprise. This wasn't the question she'd been expecting. "We sell them satellites," she shrugged. "They're one of our subsidiaries. They're part of the consortium Mr. Berrington was putting together for the new satellites. A-COMM."

"Have you ever heard of Ron Jackson?"

"No." She was beginning to breathe easier.

"How about Betty Drummond?"

"Drummond?" She thought a moment and then shook her head. "I don't think so."

Jess changed tack. "I'm trying to get a picture of Mr. Berrington. I just went to see Mrs. Berrington —"

Carol raised her eyebrows but stayed silent.

"I can't meet Lorrie, of course. Tell me about her. What sort of person was she? How did she get along with her father?"

Another nerve that wasn't raw. "Lorrie was rather mixed-up. Very young for her age. Over-protected, you know. Private schools all the way through to USC, so when she got to college it was like getting out of prison. Her marks fell, and she became involved with all sorts of . . . strange things."

Jess looked at her inquiringly.

"You know. Drugs. Not heroin or anything like that. Marijuana, LSD. She hung around with . . . Well, she had a guru for a while. Then there was some back-to-the-land commune she wanted to move into. It drove her father wild."

"They fought a lot?"

Carol smiled weakly. "That doesn't mean much. I didn't get along with my father either, until I grew up. And working together didn't help because — "

"Working together?"

Carol was taken aback. "Yes, she came to the company after graduating. It's no secret. She and her father had arguments — personality differences, I mean — so she resigned last spring."

Nobody had mentioned that little item before. Jess filed it away for future scrutiny. "Lil Scott said the company took away letters she had received from Lorrie — "

That was it. The bell that Pavlov had been dreaming of. Carol's color ebbed away as if someone had attached a suction device to her neck.

Jess tried to control her breathing. "Carol, I have to see those letters."

"I . . . I don't know where they are." Carol was whispering again. "I've never seen them."

"But you've heard of them."

"I . . . I've never seen them. I don't know what they're about and I don't want to know!"

"I suspect they're in either Mr. Bowdritch's suite or Mr. Marchenko's. Do you have keys?"

"No." Carol was a lousy liar.

"Carol."

The woman sighed. "Yes, but I'm not going in there."

"There's something in those letters that explains three deaths — including Mr. Berrington's." Jess didn't have much hope that the appeal would work. She was handicapped by two things: She couldn't offer the slightest explanation of why the letters would be of interest to anyone other than Lil. Second, reason didn't generally have much of an effect on blind terror. The secretary was white and trembling. What the hell was going on? "I need to see those letters."

"I can't help you!" Carol leaned forward, desperation written across her face. "Believe me, I can't help you!"

Jess was about to try again when the other woman gave out a long, strangled gasp. She was staring across the pub.

Jess turned around in time to see Desmond Marchenko walking out.

"Oh, God!" Carol's eyes were enormous. "He saw us!" She bolted from the room.

Chapter 10

Consuela grabbed her the second she stepped off the elevator. "Jess! Thank God! Where have you been? All hell's breaking loose around here!".

"Hold on!" Jess spoke firmly enough to stem the tide.

"What's the problem? And why are you still here? You were supposed to go off duty at noon."

Consuela drew a deep breath. "Yes, but I waited for you." She noticed two loitering technicians eyeing them with avid curiosity and drew Jess into an empty embalming room.

Jess shut the door, then nodded. "Okay, let's have it now."

The other woman suddenly found it hard to talk. She bit her lip and fiddled with a cigarette.

"If it's Harper, I was expecting trouble," Jess said quietly. "I figured he'd be in full war regalia after the press fiasco this morning."

"You're right, but you're understating it. He's been storming around all day, screaming for you, and the phones have been ringing off the hook with reporters who want to ask why you said Berrington's fire wasn't an accident."

"I didn't say it wasn't."

"The press thinks you did. And so does Harper — and the Board of Supervisors. Not to mention the police department, which is very unhappy at being made to look incompetent, and — "

Jess interrupted her. "I didn't say it wasn't an accident. I may have implied I wasn't convinced it was, but I didn't say it wasn't."

"You're splitting hairs and your whole head's going to roll!" Consuela said in exasperation. "Jess, you're my boss, but you're also my friend so I'm going to say this. You're in deep trouble. You can't go around contradicting the coroner in front of all the networks and a sprinkling of independents!"

"It wasn't bright, I grant you, but I think I hit on the

truth. Harper will have to lump it." She summed up her day for the other woman's benefit.

Consuela shook her head, bewildered. "Yes, but what does that mean? What does it prove?"

"I'm not exactly sure," Jess admitted. "But I'll find out."

"You won't have time. Harper won't give you time. He's going to get you for this."

"How's he going to do that?" Jess closed her eyes and sagged against the embalming table. God, she was tired.

Jess!" Consuela grabbed her elbow and helped her up to sit on the cracked leather. "What's wrong? Are you having pains again?"

"No, no, relax. I'm fine." "Fine" was stretching it. After all, Dr. Connie Hartman, who should know, had said that the occasional spasm didn't mean anything but fatigue. "Don't worry about me. I'm tough — and like I was saying, Harper'll have a hell of a time nailing me to the post if I turn out to be right."

Consuela paused, then sighed. "Oh, hell. The cops have got the two guys who killed the housekeeper. They want you to go down and identify them as soon as possible. And, Jess, they're muggers with long records just like everyone figured."

Everyone else, she meant. Jess was impassive.

Consuela silently handed over a blue piece of paper. It was a memo from upstairs. Ms. Jessica Canby, Chief of Investigations, was to report to Dr. Colman Harper, Chief Medical Examiner for the County of Los Angeles, *immediately* upon her arrival back in the office. No possible commutation of sentence, no time off for good behavior, even had there been any.

Consuela was staring at her hands. Jess patted her shoulder and smiled grimly. "The sonofabitch still isn't going to win this one. Remember that. Will you do two things for me?"

"Of course. Anything."

"Set up the lineup for . . . " she looked at her watch, "six. An hour from now. And you have a sister who's a keypunch operator at USC, right?"

"Luisa."

"Can she get a student's file up from the memory bank, do you think?"

"Jess." Consuela's head was shaking again.

"Can she?"

"I suppose so, but you're getting in deeper."

"Would you ask her to stay late tonight? I'd like her to read me Lorrie Berrington's file. It's not illegal, really. I could get permission from her boss if I had to."

"I'll see what I can do," Consuela promised, resigned.

Jess took the stairs rather than the elevator to the second floor; she didn't need the exercise, but it was slower. Harper was standing at the window of the suite, hands magisterially clasped behind his back as he surveyed the haphazard collection of sheds, buildings, and garages that made up the medical complex. When Jess entered, he turned slowly, fixing a malevolent stare on her. He didn't speak until he'd moved to his desk, filled a pipe, and taken a few puffs.

Two could play at that game. Jess stared levelly back and sat without waiting for an invitation.

"Your behavior — " Words failed him. He was dragging at the pipe as though it would keep him from apoplexy.

Jess remained silent. It was always better to hold your fire until the other side had fully exposed itself.

"When I lock over this office, I knew immediately that I had some . . . personnel problems. I hoped they would work themselves out." He hoped she'd get herself out. "I had no idea that you'd endanger the good name of this office!"

The office, actually, had a pretty lousy name. They solved their cases, but they also tended to lose evidence and misplace reports. This was not the time to bring it up, so Jess continued her impassive muteness.

"Stephen Bowdritch has been on the telephone to me this afternoon. He was disturbed yesterday about our — your — delay. Today, he was outraged! As he had every right to be!" Harper narrowed his eyes to show he shared the outrage. "You might be interested to know that Mrs. Berrington has suffered a very bad relapse. Very bad. As a result of your inexcusable invasion."

Jess winced. She didn't give one goddam for Bowdritch's outrage, or Harper's, but she did feel badly about Elizabeth.

"You were told to stay away from her! You were told to do your report and stop making a big case out of a simple accident!" His voice was rising, the rage increasing with her refusal to speak. "You had nothing to go on — it's insubordination, pure and simple!"

"That's not true, and you know it." It was time to speak up. It was definitely time to shut him up. "I had plenty to go on. You know as well as I do that there's been a lot of funny business surrounding the Berrington death — evidence vanishing and —"

"You had your orders!" It was a bellow. "And then, this morning, in front of the press — are you crazy?"

They glared at each other. They'd come to the crux of it. Her mortal sin. Thou shalt not steal thy superior's spotlight.

"You are crazy!" he carried on in a fury. "Suggesting to the press that there's more to this than your insane delusions!" He leaned forward and almost spat the words. "I know you're out for all the publicity you can get, but let me tell you this. You miscalculated. This is not going to help you get elected. To anything!"

"Look, I spoke out of turn this morning, and I'm sorry about that. I was upset about Mr. Aguerra's death, and I — "

"Another example of you courting publicity! I haven't seen the official police report on Aguerra — even if you're right, you had no business releasing that information prematurely!"

"I'm right. Detective Garland told me that the child was a professional."

"Your job is not to feed the press with tidbits of information! Just to get your name plastered across the city!"

Jess took a deep breath. He was correct. That was how he perceived *his* job. Not that she was going to argue this particular point. She already felt sick enough about it. "That may be. But in the Berrington case, we don't know enough yet to say — "

"I don't want to hear you say anything more about it!"

Jess got to her feet. It was hard to be dignified when standing up meant heaving yourself up. "Like it or not, we don't have all the facts."

"I have all I need. Your insubordination is intolerable. I don't intend to tolerate it!"

* * *

"Well?" Consuela trailed Jess into her office.

"I got a pretty plain warning. He's out to get me, all right. But don't worry about it. I can handle Harper." If she found the ammunition to prove her suspicions . .

Otherwise — well, better not to think about that.

She spent fifteen minutes on the phone with Luisa Martinez. It was rather alarming to realize how comprehensive civilian files were, now that machines had taken over for fallible human memories.

Lorrie had nominally majored in American studies, but her interests had been eclectic, ranging from anthropology to modern Russian literature. Put less tactfully, the young woman had no real interests at all, and as her marks showed, she never did discover any.

There was one exception, the seventh semester, when Jess could discern a subtle shift, a slight focusing of attention on a clump of courses that must have put her father right off his fresh-fried lobster: "The Dialectics of Political History," "Marx and the Post-Industrial Society," "Radical Terrorism in the Twentieth Century." Here was a young girl in search of a cause. But she wasn't searching too hard. Her marks didn't improve, and her final semester featured a brief foray into fashion designing.

There were a few non-academic footnotes. Lorrie

had joined the fanciest sorority in her first year and had dropped out within twelve months. She'd participated once in a student demonstration, a short-lived, ill-conceived campaign against USC's complicity in nuclear development. She had almost been thrown out of her dorm for staying out all night four times.

Jess pushed her chair away from the desk. She now knew that Lorrie was an indifferent student who disliked the idea of living through a nuclear holocaust and who'd gotten laid a few times. Wonderful. If she kept up like this, she'd have the whole case wrapped up in a century or two.

* * *

When Jess walked into detective headquarters, Carmichael was interviewing a twelve-year-old member of East LA's *Espantos* gang. The Terrors. The kid was tiny, and his voice hadn't yet changed, but the pile on the desk of what had come from his pockets was certainly *espantando*: brass knuckles, a chain, a six-inch-blade, and scissors that had been filed to a scalpel-fine point.

"Be with you in a sec," Carmichael grunted.

Jess nodded and sat on the other plastic and metal chair. The boy was insisting that he wouldn't talk no matter what tortures were applied to his person. It was clear that Carmichael would have loved to indulge the kid's fantasy, but instead he was forced to repeat over and over again that the LAPD had given up putting juveniles on the rack.

"Detective Carmichael?" A heavy-set black woman strode through the chaos of the office. "Heald from Juvenile. I gotta take Torres away or the public defender's gonna have both our asses."

Carmichael nodded heavily. "Yeah. I didn't think I'd get this much time with him." He waved at the assortment of childish toys on his desk. "Take that shit with you."

Torres was on his feet, grinning impishly, looking

like an adorable nine-year-old. "*Adios*, creep. Told ya' I didn't have nothin' to say."

Jess almost felt sorry for the detective. She watched Officer Heald lead the strutting little figure out. "What did he do?"

"The oldest member of that goddam gang hasn't reached puberty yet. Neither have their victims."

Jess sighed. Baby gangs terrorizing the kindergarten set. It was a far cry from the palm trees and tinsel dreams of Hollywood. "You want me to ID somebody?"

"Yeah. I'll call down for the lineup."

He muttered into the phone while Jess watched the parade. It was really ridiculous how television glamorized detective work. The real McCoy was endless, sad, and exciting only if you thought it would be fun to spend 75 percent of your time at a typewriter. And nobody even looked glamorous. The suspects were seedy and often slowwitted; the police tended toward five o'clock shadow and stained armpits.

"Let's go." Carmichael put down the receiver. "They're ready for you."

The lineup room was in the basement. The grimy rectangular room was divided into a stage, garishly lit with harsh white light, and an observer's cubicle behind one-way mirrors. Three officers were waiting for them in the cubicle. Jess nodded at them; two looked vaguely familiar to her.

"Okay." Carmichael spoke into the microphone. "Bring 'em out."

Six black men slouched across the stage. All were tall, young, and hostile. Four of them had to be members of the department, and it was somehow disturbing to know that you couldn't pick them out, to see how easily they adopted the street-anger of the other two. Jess stood at the window while the men faced forward, then left, right, and forward again.

"Well?" Carmichael was at her side, close enough so she could smell the week's sweat on him.

She took a last look. "No."

"Whadda ya mean, no?"

No. None of them are the right ones. I've never seen any of those men before." She spread her hands. "Sorry. Better go back to the drawing board."

All four policemen were watching her with the kind of impassivity that amounts to disbelief.

She spread her hands again. "I know it's disappointing, but those aren't the guys."

"Take a look at six and two again."

"You just blew the ID, even if I could make it, Carmichael."

"I don't see any defense attorneys here." He grinned at the other officers. "Take another look."

She obliged, then firmly shook her head. "No. No way. I remember the men clearly, and those aren't them."

Carmichael shoved a wad of gum into his mouth. "See you later, guys." He led Jess out. "Let's go upstairs and talk."

Robbery-Homicide was even noisier than before. Two women who were screaming at each other were being kept apart by two burly officers. From the look of the women's clothes and hair, they'd had a shot at making the argument physical before the police intervened.

Carmichael shouted sourly, "Get those broads outa here, Lambert. We got work to do." He sat down behind his desk and swung his feet up, narrowly missing a mug of day-old coffee. He chewed his gum and stared at Jess without talking.

"Carmichael, don't even bother saying it. I'm no virgin; I know eyewitness identifications are dicey. But trust me. I remember the killers, and you haven't got them."

He still didn't say anything, just chewed and nodded ruminatively. Suddenly he reached for the phone. "I'm gonna get Arnheim in. You mind?"

She shook her head.

"Have a coffee while you wait."

In other words, buzz off. Jess wasn't offended; she'd met cops before who took it personally when their witnesses wouldn't follow the script.

* * *

Francis joined her in the lunch room, an orange-walled collection of scratched plastic tables and warped plastic chairs.

"Jess." He sat down without bothering to pour himself some of the dubious liquid they passed off as coffee.

"Hi, Francis. Have you talked to Carmichael?"

"Yeah."

They exchanged a glance without any real understanding.

"Francis, what's the big deal? Carmichael thought he had the right suspects. He was wrong. It happens all the time."

"Yeah."

"If those were the men, I'd have said so."

"Yeah."

Francis was no Demosthenes, but even his repertoire was usually more varied. Jess was getting angry. "That's all you're going to say? 'Yeah?' "

He sighed. "Jess, those are the boys. We got all kinds of evidence. They had the old lady's purse. The Volkswagen belongs to them — in a way." He almost grinned. "They stole it a couple of days before the mugging. And they bragged to their pals on the street; that's how we found them. These are the two guys who shot and killed Lil Scott. Do you understand me?" He was speaking as slowly and clearly as he would to any moron.

"I understand your words," she said stubbornly, "but I don't understand anything else. I was there — and those guys weren't."

"Oh, shit." He got up and lumbered over to the coffee machine.

Jess wearily rested her head in her hands. Kafka had taken over her life.

Francis was back, this time sitting across from her

161

so as not to catch whatever virus had scrambled her brains. "Wanna tell me why you're doing this?"

"You don't believe me?"

"Even their mouthpiece isn't screaming 'foul.' He's already booking a deal — which means that those two dudes aren't complaining either."

"You know as well as I do that once you've got a sheet in this town, especially if you're black, there's no point in expecting justice. That's the game. You get away with a lot of things without being caught. You do a little time now and then for things you didn't do."

"Maybe. But not here. There's too much evidence."

Jess met his gaze and held it. "Not if the eyewitness says otherwise. And I'm going to have to talk to their lawyer, Francis. The sonofabitch should've been at the lineup. I'm going to have to tell him I couldn't make the ID."

"Don't do it, Jess."

"I can live with Carmichael's loathing."

Francis looked away. "Don't go out on this limb. It's going to fall right down."

"Look, I didn't ask for the Berrington mess, and I certainly didn't want it to get complicated, but it did anyway." She wasn't getting a response. "Francis, a lot has happened since that bloody fire. I told you what Lil said. Well, I've got more to tell you. Last night I was at Mount Wilson, and I got attacked by a goon who works for the Berrington organization. They're hiding something, and I think it's something they're willing to kill for."

He sighed and scratched his ear.

"Christ!" She got to her feet. "I'd have expected more from you. You're not going to help me, are you?"

He spoke sadly. "Nobody can help you, Jess, if you continue like this."

"Well, to hell with you. I'll do it myself. If it's not too much to ask," she added sarcastically, "who's acting for Carmichael's suspects?"

"Benny Shouldice. Works out of the Bradbury Building."

Francis was still staring at the table when she left.

* * *

Michael and Martin Dumphy were waiting for her, already seated, at Junior's Delicatessen. She sank down on the banquette beside Michael and leaned into the strength of his arm.

"What's wrong, babe?"

Martin spoke at the same time. "Are you okay?"

Jess grimaced. "I've been better."

"Hi, folks. Ready to order?" The waitress was of that breed specifically designed to wait on tables in delis. She was bulky and blonde, not young, but outgoing. "You look like you need a real good meal, honey." That was to Jess with a motherly beam at the stomach.

Jess wasn't hungry, but she also wasn't up to the argument she'd get if she said so. "Pastrami on rye. Lean."

"And a knish? Or a blintz?" The woman wanted to insist.

"No, thanks. You guys order."

Michael had only a sandwich, too. Martin's list was lavish enough to distract the waitress from the others' meager orders.

Michael waited until she'd bustled off, then turned again to Jess. "What is it, hon?"

"Trouble." She tried to smile, but it didn't come off. "I'm in a lot of trouble if I don't prove the Berrington case wasn't an accident. I just can't get a grip on what's happening to my life! I'm close to losing my job; I've become a pariah in a dozen circles and — nobody believes a word I say!" She shook her head in bewilderment. "I've got Nixon's credibility, all of a sudden."

Martin was frowning with concern. "What do you mean, prove the Berrington case wasn't an accident?"

"I've made waves about the official solution, so I have to prove I'm right — or get known as the lunatic trouble-maker. I'm not a lunatic; I know I'm not." She leaned forward. "Get this — today I found out that

Thalen Satellite, home of the guy in the van — remember him? — and former home of Ron Jackson, is a wholly owned subsidiary of Berrington Industries."

"Oh, my." Michael was astounded. "Coincidence?"

She shrugged.

"Look, kids." Martin coughed anxiously. "Is it really any of your business? I mean, I'm all for good works and charity and all that, but do you need to take this on? Jesus, Jess! Think about the baby — and your job — and," he gulped, "your political future!"

Jess felt as sick as Martin looked about that, so she preferred not to dwell on the topic. "If I get canned, Michael will have to support me. Michael and Cyril Haberman. Did you sign the contract, sweetie?"

Michael and Martin exchanged somber glances.

"Anyone want to tell a simple wife what's going on?"

"Yeah. The deal's off." Michael spoke as if he really didn't mind, but his eyes wouldn't play along.

Jess looked from Michael to Martin and back again. "Why?"

"I wish to hell I knew. We had a great time at lunch — talking about who we'd cast and where we'd find locations. Kisses all around. Any chummier and we'd have been arrested. Then Haberman goes to some emergency business meeting and Dana and I spend an hour drinking to success. Haberman comes back around four — and it's no dice. Nice knowing you, don't call us, we'll call you."

Four o'clock. Was it possible? Jess tried to reject the idea that was clinging to her mind like a limpet. "Didn't Dana ask what changed his mind?"

"He left right away. She'll try to see him tomorrow."

"I can't get over it." Martin was greenish. "And I put you in touch with that bastard!"

"It's not your fault, Martin." Jess patted his hand. "You tried; you got Michael the entree."

Martin didn't look any happier. The food arrived and he stabbed the potato salad as if it were Haberman's heart.

"Michael," Jess said sympathetically, "maybe Cyril

had indigestion. Maybe he'll change his mind back tomorrow."

"Maybe."

They all pushed the food around their plates as if they were eating. Jess broke the silence. "This whole thing stinks. Martin, I need your help."

He smoothed down his thinning hair, was already perfectly smooth. "I don't like the sound of that."

"I want to know everything about Thalen and Berrington Industries. In fact, I want to know everything about A-COMM." She fished in her purse and came up with a paper. "A-COMM partners." She read aloud. "CYMA Corporation, whoever the hell that is. Berrington, of course. Two banks — damn shame that neither of them is yours. Frontier Communications and CW Company. I need to know who's behind them, and especially" — she looked at Michael — "if any of them is Cyril Haberman."

Michael whistled.

"You don't listen to a word I say," Martin mourned. "I just explained why this isn't the way to go, why you should be a good little girl for the next little while."

Jess paid no attention. "Meanwhile, Michael and I are going to do a little research into Lorrie's life."

"Jess — "

She cut him off. "Can't you see, Martin? I'd love to be a good girl, but right now — I can't afford it. I'm being screwed!" She waved at the paper in his hand. "Sic 'em, lad." She and Michael slid out, leaving Martin to pay. He was the only one of them with a guaranteed income, after all.

* * *

They say that he who travels alone, travels fastest. Jess's life proved it. Malibu to downtown, Beverly Hills, Santa Barbara, back downtown, East Los Angeles — and now Venice. She was going to check out Lorrie's last apartment while Michael met Alan Dickson. If anyone would know where to find a back-to-the-land commune, it was their friendly neighborhood hippie.

One-eleven Park Avenue proved to be a squat, three-story apartment house only a block from the beach. In either of the bordering communities, Marina del Rey or Santa Monica, the rent would have been astronomical, but if you were prepared to share the street with drunks, rowdies, and the occasional looter, you could live in Venice and save a bundle.

Lorrie, apparently had chosen to do so. One had to give her credit. She could have lived off the more than ample Berrington resources, or for that matter, the Cartwright resources. It was plucky of her to do it on her own. Plucky, brave, and probably a little bit foolish. Jess herself wasn't happy about venturing out of her car. A group of boys was loitering cockily on the littered sidewalk, which wasn't lit because someone had shot out the street lamp.

Eventually, Jess sallied forth and made it into the dingy lobby. No one at apartment three answered her buzz, so she tried the superintendent's bell. A long five minutes later, a stooped gray-haired man appeared in a frayed velvet smoking jacket.

"I'm sorry to disturb you." Jess showed her credentials. "Do you have a minute?"

"Come in." He was aggrieved by the intrusion, but he had an air of always being aggrieved by something. "Come in. You can't stay out there; it isn't safe."

She followed him into his flat, a dark basement warren of rooms filled with shabby but once-good furniture and a few quite spectacular Lalique pieces. The place had the tidiness of a finicky old bachelor, the type who pressed his trousers daily but didn't bother to get them cleaned. Everything was in its place, but dusty; the odors of long-ago meals lingered in the still, hot air.

"You want to sit?"

Jess ignored the ungraciousness of the tone. "Thank you, Mr. — ?"

"Poul. Henry Poul."

She took a brocaded high-backed chair and whipped out her notebook. Henry was the type to appreciate officiousness. "How long have you been superintendent here?"

It was the wrong question. Poul pulled himself up to his full five-feet-five or so and threw out a meager chest. "I am not the superintendent. I am the owner of this building."

Jess apologized with as much profuseness as she could drum up, given the hour and her exhaustion.

He finally accepted that she was genuinely remorseful and sat down again. "What's this in connection with?"

"Lorrie Berrington. She used to live in — "

"Yes, I knew the girl. Quite sad. I used to know her family. The Cartwrights, of course." His thin lips pursed; one wouldn't be proud of knowing *arrivistes* like the Berringtons. "Before things became so . . . difficult."

"Ah, yes." Jess hurried on. No doubt his history was truly absorbing, but she would have to live without hearing it. If possible. "She lived in suite three, I understand?"

"Yes. With Miss Grayley. Who still lives there, as a matter of fact. They came, let me think, oh, about a year ago. A little more than a year, perhaps." Now that he'd gotten over the shock of Jess's invasion, he was pathetically happy to have someone to talk to. "They were excellent tenants. Quite unusually excellent. The stories I could tell you about how people live — "

"I'm sure." Jess coughed. "I rang the bell but no one answered."

"No, Miss Grayley is away. I saw her leaving last night with several bags. A male friend picked her up. They both had male friends. This one was quite respectable. White," he added, to underline the point.

Jess nodded noncommittally. Whatever prejudices Henry Poul had formed over sixty years or more weren't going to be erased in fifteen minutes, no matter how impassioned the argument. "Do you know Miss Berrington's male friend's name"

"I don't believe I do." He sighed. "She was always quite polite, of course. Breeding will tell. But she was like most of her generation when it came to introductions. We were brought up very differently — "

"Yes." This could take all night. "Do you know anything at all about him?"

"Well, he was nice enough looking. A big fellow. Tall. But," his eyes blinked a message, "he wasn't quite what one would hope a Cartwright would find. On the other hand," he added with a slight hint of maliciousness, "her mother married oddly."

Jess smiled blandly and closed her notebook. "Well, thank you."

He accompanied her to the door, straightening the smoking jacket with a flutter of pride. "Shall I leave a note for Miss Grayley to call you when she returns?"

"No, it's not necessary. I'll try again."

"Very well." He suddenly frowned, a jerky little grimace. Would you be interested in their break-in?"

"Break-in?" Jess turned back. "When was that?"

"Oh, about a month ago. Yes, a month. Just after the unfortunate accident. I felt quite badly for Miss Grayley. She was so upset about her friend, and then to have to cope with such thing . . . " He shook his head. "But in this area, what can one expect? I'm actually rather surprised that they chose to live here. I was pleased for myself, of course, because one doesn't often get such good tenants, but — "

They were about to repeat themselves. Jess nodded and opened the lobby door.

"You know, Mrs. Canby — "

She stopped, surprised that he'd noted her name.

"I didn't always live like this." He waved a pale hand vaguely. "But when the money went, well, we'd always had property here. When I was a boy, we used to have a summer home in Venice. It was nice then, you know. Canals and so forth. Well, I didn't have any choice, you see."

"Yes, I see," Jess said gently. Poul was a snob, and everyone else in the world had to work, but she couldn't dislike him. It wasn't his fault that nothing in his genes had prepared him for the twentieth century.

Chapter 11

It was Thursday night, not even the weekend yet, but everyone came out to play. The streets were humming, streams of cars relentlessly moving from one side of the city to the other: old cars, new cars, convertibles, pick-up trucks, torrents of them flooding intersections and gas stations. They never seemed to get where they were going, as if driving wasn't the means to an end but the end itself. LA wasn't a place, it was a process, and the car tied you into it. You were as personally involved with your car as with your body; you washed it, filled it with liquids, talked about it, and named it. Jess had once kept a list of personalized license plates. I LUV ME. EX-WIFE. BIG SHOT. LA BUST. She gave it up after seeing I LUV ME. There was nowhere to go when you reached the pinnacle.

She took Washington Boulevard into Culver City. She was as comfortable at the wheel as anyone else, everybody a good driver, a professional driver. The street was bright. Street lamps were almost unnecessary in the radiance of hundreds of headlights and neon signs and the general glow given off by the city, a brightness that could be seen from the desert a hundred miles away. Los Angeles was never dark.

Michael's car was parked right behind Alan Dickson's van in front of the bar. Jess made it a triple flush and went inside. Culver City was no longer the Culver City of Buster Keaton and the MGM players. It was a tired pocket of small businesses and smaller homes ringed by garish commercial strips. A hollow effort had been made to tart up the main drag: bars calling themselves saloons and putting sawdust under cutesy tables, dress stores self-consciously funky, restaurants weighing down their ceilings with hanging plants. It didn't fool anyone; nobody aspired to a Culver City postal address.

The bar was busy. There were two types of clientele, the very young who hoped to get out one day on a cloud of success and the old who'd finally accepted that they were permanently earthbound. They didn't mix; each group depressed the other.

Michael and Alan were right up against the bar, standing but guarding an empty stool as, if it were treasure.

Jess slipped onto it. "Hi, guys."

Michael kissed her. Alan patted her stomach and said "Hey." He looked even more like a hippie than usual. Along with the faded jeans, T-shirt, and workboots, he was wearing a leather headband around the only long hair in the room. He was also starting to grow back the beard he'd once had, and it was at the scruffy stage. He didn't look anything like anyone associated with show business, so the grins he gave to passing nubile women were not returned. Fun was fun, but there was no point in having it with someone who couldn't take you up the ladder.

"Any luck with Lorrie's roommate?" Michael asked.

"No, she's out of town. The landlord and I had a nice chat —" Jess broke off to stare wistfully at the bartender. "I'd love something."

"Fruit juice," Michael said firmly.

The bartender recognized the voice of authority and brought over a battered can of grape juice along with two more beers.

She sighed and turned back to Alan. "What about the back-to-the-land commune? Have you ever heard of one?"

"Yes, sure." He tried another smile in the direction of a small brunette in jeans that had to be giving her a clitorectomy. She didn't even bother to snub him.

"The commune, Alan," Jess prodded kindly.

"Yeah. Well, there's a couple up north near Frisco." Only people who didn't live there called San Francisco that, and Alan, like most Angelenos, wouldn't be caught dead living there. The feeling was entirely mutual; California was really two unfriendly states. "Only one around here I know about. Kind of a strange place."

Jess caught Michael's eye and raised her eyebrows. If a studiously non-judgmental hippie thought it was strange, it had to be from another planet.

"North," he continued. "Up in Simi Valley."

"Oh, lord." That was far, even to a native who didn't think an hour's drive to dinner was out of line.

"Alan said the head honcho is probably a charlatan," Michael told Jess with a grin.

She grinned back. Alan himself had followed many a cult figure whom others might have considered to be charlatans. It all depended on your point of view.

"Yeah, he's surrounded himself with rich people who've got more money and time than sense." Alan downed his beer in a long swallow and ordered another. "The bought him a fantastic spread, I hear. Air conditioning, hot tubs, tennis courts."

"Tennis courts in a back-to-the-land movement?" Jess asked with genuine curiosity. "How did he sell that one?"

Alan shrugged.

"You're more apt to find peace and enlightenment if the body's fit," Michael guessed. "Jesus, Jess — Simi Valley? Long Beach was bad enough."

"Oh, you don't have to go out to Simi Valley." Alan looked surprised. "Lots of the people live in town."

"Do you know any of them?"

Alan considered. "I know a girl who — sorry, Jess — a woman who used to be into it. I don't know if she still is. I'll see if I can find her." He dug a few coins out of his jeans and headed to the phone, pausing a few times along the way to admire the scenery.

Jess and Michael watched for a moment.

"Doesn't Alan have a live-in girlfriend?" Jess asked.

"Always. But they don't last long. I think it gets harder to replenish the supply as time goes by. There aren't many women anymore who want to live a commune in Topanga Canyon with a dozen kids running around that everyone has to take responsibility for." Michael lit a cigarette. "Would you like to take your turn to cook for thirty?"

Jess shuddered and went back to people-watching.

Alan returned with a victorious air. "She's coming

down here."

Michael clapped him on the back with a grin that could catch flies. "Thank you, my good man. The thought of Simi Valley was putting me right off this very fine brew." He waved for two more.

* * *

Sun Avery had been born Candy Steinberg, and significant surgery notwithstanding, she still looked it. She was closemouthed about background details, but Jess put her at about thirty-eight or -nine, divorced, and originally from someplace like Cincinnati. She was thin, almost painfully thin, with eyes emphasized by a great deal of makeup and a close-cropped cap of blonde hair; the tiny buttocks were pinched into designer jeans, tucked into which was a silk emerald-green blouse.

Alan had given up on the crowd in the bar, so he was prepared to settle for Sun. He made a fuss and found a stool for her, then stood over it at a distance that could be measured in millimeters. Sun cooed and preened at the attention, making a lousy effort at pretending she got a lot of it most of the time.

"It's nice of you to talk to us," Jess offered.

Sun nodded without quite looking at her. She preferred to talk to men.

Michael moved closer and won her heart by saying she looked familiar.

You've probably seen me on TV," Sun murmured happily.

Michael nodded vaguely. He seldom watched TV, and he'd certainly never seen her face on it. "Movies?"

"Commercials. Soap — and I did one for beer. Miller Lite. You probably saw it — a waterfall scene with a bunch of guys and girls. I got three close-ups on that one."

"Ah. Mmm." Michael got down to business because Alan was showing signs of getting down to something else. "Did you ever run into a woman named Lorrie Berrington back-to-the-land group you belong to?"

"Belonged to." Sun, it transpired, had discovered that movements were hollow shams compared to the Prior Life movement. "Yes, I remember her. I was there when she broke through."

"Broke through?" Jess asked naively.

"Found it. Enlightenment. Her own center," Sun explained uninformatively. "I talked to her a couple of times. She was a pretty fucked-up girl. I think she ought to consider Prior Life — it's amazing how much more you understand about yourself when you understand where you've come from." She didn't mean Ohio. She meant Egypt in the Ptolemaic years. "She definitely needs Prior Life."

"Do you remember anything she said about herself?" Michael implied that he knew she could remember if she tried, and that, if she did, he'd be very, very grateful. He moved closer. Sun was now covered in men.

"Well, I'd have to think." It was an unfamiliar activity involving screwing up her eyes and biting her lip. "She hated her family, of course. Her parents were awful. Well," she shrugged, "aren't everyone's?"

Jess winced and looked sternly down at her stomach. The kid in there had better not think he could get away with slandering his parents to total strangers.

"She'd had a really bad stretch with her father, I think. She wasn't even talking to him."

"This was when?"

"When?" Sun opened her eyes as wide as the latest lift permitted. "I don't know, early summer maybe. He was something industrial, I think. Corrupt. A real pig. She wouldn't even take his money any more because it was tainted."

"With capitalism?" Michael suggested.

"No, not that." Sun was vaguely shocked. There was nothing wrong with capitalism if you could get on the gravy train. "It was scientific."

"What was?"

"What he was doing. It was bad, somehow. Christ, I don't remember." She gave up with a wriggle.

"What about her friends" Jess asked quickly. "Did

she have any good friends in the group?"

"We weren't into that. You were supposed to be looking into yourself, not wasting time making friends." Sun didn't appear to realize that that might be construed as a devastating critique of the self-realization movement. "There was the guy in Gardena."

All three of them raised their eyebrows.

"I was in this poker club." Sun grimaced. "My parents were visiting. God, the visit set me back years in my analysis! Years."

"The guy?" Michael's patience was fraying.

Yeah. We were down there because that's the kind of shit my parents are into — I saw Lorrie with this guy. He was cute. I really wouldn't have thought she'd do so well. She's dowdier than hell, you know. He was a big one." She might have been talking about a salmon. "Dark, big shoulders, real cute. I got the feeling he really knew his way around the Acropole. Like he was a regular, you know? Steve? George?" She brightened. "No, Joe. Yeah."

"Did you get his last name?"

She shook her head regretfully. He was cute and he'd slipped by.

Michael and Jess left without telling her that Lorrie wasn't fishing anymore.

* * *

Gardena wasn't as far as Simi Valley, but it wasn't exactly on their way home. It was in the exact opposite direction, south on the San Diego Freeway, which was one of the least scenic routes in the Southland. Jess and Michael and about a million other cars passed the airport and the South Bay and dingy towns like Hawthorne and Lawndale. They saw the roofs of factories and oil refineries, beer joints and liquor stores, and all the way, they breathed something midway between oxygen and an oleo-petroleum by-product.

When they finally got off the highway, they weren't much happier. Gardena was one of the few incorporated cities in LA County that permitted gambling; it was noted for nothing else and, in some circles, not much noted for that. Monte Carlo featured evening gowns and jewels, but Jess had never noticed that glamor played a big role in American gambling joints. A single weekend in Las Vegas had settled the issue definitively; she and Michael had been the only ones in the casinos wearing natural fibers and unassuming hues.

Gardena took the word "polyester" and ran it up the flagpole to new heights. Since polyester was flammable, local government would do well to ban open flames within city limits.

There were two strips of poker clubs only a few blocks apart on South Vermont and South Western avenues, and there didn't appear to be much difference between them. The same neon signs flashed the same exotic, inappropriate names, attracting the same nondescript clientele. Suburbia came for the "action," proving that no one in the suburbs knew much about the word.

The Acropole was smack up against a clump of fast-food parlors and a movie theater playing features too tired for television. The club was a vast smoke-filled dungeon of maybe forty round tables and sweating, intense cardplayers. The decor was meant not to distract anyone from serious business, and it succeeded. Faded wallpaper of indeterminate color exactly matched the worn carpet. Hanging lights threw beams onto the cards and deep shadows between the tables. One wall was cut out to form a hatchway to the kitchen. Here, an unconvincing attempt had been made to prove that this was an all-American place, legal, and therefore wholesome. Fake wood paneling supported framed pictures of the Lincoln Memorial and the state Assemble building; a beer-bellied man in dark glasses, presumably the proprietor, shook hands with minor TV and film stars in dusty photographs running askew down the wall.

Only a few of the players were taking breaks from their cards to grab a bite. They'd made an error in judgment, if the skinny hamburgers and greasy fries tasted the way they looked. From the face of the man closest to Jess, they did. He sneered at the food and then at the only visible waitress, a pasty kid in a short white dress that was meant to be a sexy version of the toga. It was the only touch in the room that recalled the club's name.

"You lookin' or playin'?" A hard-mouthed woman sitting near the kitchen was watching them watch the room. She was wearing wrinkled slacks and a lackluster sweatshirt. She might have been a feminist who refused to demean herself in the toga, but more likely was an ex-waitress past her prime, no longer encouraged toward exposure.

"We're looking for someone," Michael explained. "A regular, uh, client."

"Yeah? Who're you?" The suspicion was heavy, as if this were a floating crap game in the middle of Utah.

"A friend of a friend." Jess put on a winning smile.

The woman didn't think much of pregnant Polly-annas.

"Joe. Tall guy, dark-haired — "

"Joe. I know a thousand Joes."

Than was indeed possible. They waited.

Eventually, the woman shrugged and tilted her head toward a table at the far end of the room. "Talk to Greg."

"Thanks." They moved off, stopping once to watch a hand being played under tension so palpable that it reached halfway across the cavern.

After a few moments, Michael nudged Jess, remembering why they were there. She smiled to get past another spectator, an aging blond surfer who seemed as unimpressed with her smile as the ex-waitress had been.

Greg answered immediately to his name. He was a cherub of a gambler, round-faced, round-eyed, and round-hipped. He was delighted to them, no trouble at all.

"You playin' or what?" An old man, unsoftened by the sight of pleasant social interaction, stared grimly at Greg.

"No, deal me out of this hand. I'll be back." Greg got up and led them to a bench against the wall. "Take a load off." He was mainly talking to Jess; Michael could fend for himself.

She did so with gratitude. A lead-lined basketball could drag you down after a while.

"You smoke?" He offered cigarettes all around.

Jess shook her head, though it made no sense to refuse. The air was thick with smoke particles untouched by fans or ventilation systems. In here, breathing amounted to smoking. "Sorry to get you away from your game, but we're looking for someone." She repeated their meager store of information.

"Joe." He repeated the name and thought about it.

A tall man in a garish Hawaiian shirt approached and caught Greg's attention with a quizzical glance. Greg quickly shook his head, and the man backed off.

"Joe." He sighed. "Not much to go on."

"No."

Michael got the point. He pulled a five-dollar bill out of his pocket and offered it casually. "For your trouble. You know, being pulled away from the table."

"Thanks." It vanished instantly. "Joe. Yeah, I think I know who you mean. I remember the girl, too. Just a kid. I haven't seen her in a while."

Jess and Michael exchanged a glance and kept their mouths shut. Information probably got a lot pricier when the idea of death came into it.

"Joe comes in most nights. Nice-looking guy. Good cardplayer. Not great, but good enough."

"Is he here now?" Jess felt the twinge of success. Sam Spade, eat your heart out.

"Not now," Greg said, looking around the room. Visibility was poor, so it was hard to understand how he could be so certain. "It's early."

Only to cardplayers. Jess stifled a sigh and a yawn.

"Thanks," Michael said with a grin. "Let us know when he gets here?"

"Sure, be glad to." Greg started back to his table, pausing to wave vaguely toward the front of the club.

"You can get a drink next door. There's a bar there. Here, there's just coffee and soft drinks; we're not allowed to have booze."

Jess's eyes strayed to the Hawaiian shirt, now talking intently to a baggy suit and tie. They were also not allowed to have bookies, loan sharks, and drug pushers. "Thanks. We're fine."

It was almost two o'clock when Greg signaled Michael and nodded meaningfully at a man approaching the next table. Jess and Michael moved to intercept the newcomer, stopping long enough to pass another bill to the cherub.

Michael touched the other man's arm. "Excuse me. Is your name Joe?"

He looked at them. He was in his late thirties, with thick dark hair, a ruddy complexion, and sharp brown eyes. Sun was right, he was big and he was cute, but there was something about him that put Jess off. Maybe it was the fact that suspicion came easier to him than smiling.

"Who're you?"

Michael looked at Jess. She flashed her badge. It was plainly marked "coroner's office," not "police," but he'd have to have been a speed reader to catch that. "Your name Joe?"

He nodded grudgingly.

"We'd like to talk to you for a minute."

He shrugged and followed them back to the bench.

"We're investigating Robert Berrington's death. You knew his daughter, Lorrie?"

"That's what you want to talk about?"

They nodded.

Joe relaxed. There might be things he didn't want probed, but this wasn't one of them. "Yeah, I knew her. Nice kid. The accident was a damn shame. You wouldn't think a nice kid like that could come from a bastard like Berrington."

"You knew Robert Berrington?" Michael tried too late to disguise the surprise.

"I didn't move in his circles." Joe eyed him with a

snide grin. "If that's what you mean. I worked at Berrington Industries for a while. That's how I met the kid. She was working there too."

"What did you do there?"

"I'm an engineer, believe it or not." The grin again. "I work sometimes, when the cards go bad. I'd have left after a while, anyway."

"How did you leave?"

"Sonofabitch fired me. I didn't work hard enough for him — he figured you should work twelve-hour days for the privilege of getting a check with his name on it. Lorrie and I got friendly after I left — he had a dirty mind, assumed it was more than that. Made him furious, and he couldn't do one damn thing about it." He twisted his lips uncheerfully. "Paid him back."

Jess sighed. Poor Lorrie hadn't been much in her short life except a pawn in everyone else's life. "She was a bit young for you."

Oh, it wasn't like that; she wasn't my type. She just hung around — I guess she liked coming to a place like this for a change. Kicks. And she didn't have many friends. That crazy group, but no friends." He shrugged. "Maybe she hung around because it made her father sore. She wasn't any wilder about him than I am."

Jess touched her stomach. She and Michael might turn out to be less than perfect parents, but they could hardly do worse than the Berringtons. She looked around the room; it was jammed now, every table full and the air steadily thickening with smoke and sweat. The overage surfer in the Hawaiian shirt wasn't playing. He was standing nearby, watching her. Jess frowned and he turned away. Was he a freak for balloon-shaped ladies?

"Why did Lorrie quit Berrington Industries?" Michael was good at sticking to the point.

"She was having a huge hassle with her father. He went nuts over that obsession of hers the last few months."

Jess leaned forward until she threatened to fall over. "What obsession?"

"She never told me much about it. She was into something, seriously into something. She spent hours at the library and in hospitals, and looking for some dame named Sarah. A scientist or something."

"Hospitals?" Michael was leaning forward too. "Why?"

"Visiting sick people. Meeting interns. Who the hell knows?"

Joe was starting to lose patience with the inquiry; his eyes were straying to the table, and his fingers were fidgeting as if they craved the feel of the cards.

"Come on," Michael urged. "Think about it. Why was she going into hospitals?"

"Oh, shit." Joe paused, then carried on with increasingly bad grace. "I guess it had something to do with the old man's company. She hated him, wanted to get away from him, but she was always asking questions about the business. About the technology, especially regional intercepts. That's what I worked on."

"What are regional intercepts?"

He looked at Jess sourly. "You want a fucking lecture now?"

"Just a brief one." She tried for an irresistible smile.

He wasn't charmed but he answered the question. "Satellite signals travel in a straight line, like light. So to get 'em where you want 'em, you relay them from dish to dish in the community."

"Lorrie was interested in that?" Jess was puzzled. "Why?"

"Hell, I don't know. I never asked, and anyway, after she got back from Paraguay, I didn't see much of her." He saw the next query coming. "And no, I don't know what she was doing. They have business there. Maybe it was that. Maybe she wanted to get a tan."

Jess wearily hoisted herself up. "Okay. Thanks."

"Yeah."

She paused, compelled to ask one last thing, though she didn't quite know why. "What was Lorrie going to grow up like? Her mother?"

"No. No way." He spoke emphatically. "She wasn't

that fucked-up. I think whatever she was doing, it was sort of her last chance to get away from the old man, but she wasn't strong enough. It wouldn't have worked. She'd have gone back — but not to be like her mother."

"What then?"

He shrugged. "Rich."

Jess waited, but he didn't elaborate. When she thought about it, he really didn't have to. At that level, "rich" pretty well said it all.

* * *

Michael got in behind the wheel and started the car, but Jess waited a moment before opening her door, taking deep gulps of air. It was still hot and Gardena wasn't smog-free, but it was better than what they'd breathed inside the club. At least she didn't have to chew it.

Another figure left the club. The blond surfer had had enough too. He strode purposefully across the street. Jess turned to get in beside Michael and noticed that the surfer was meeting someone. A big someone. Very, very big and triangular in shape.

"Michael!" She slid in and locked the door. "Michael, the Pyramid's here!"

He swiveled around to look. The Pyramid and the surfer were watching them, too. Nobody made a move for a moment, then Michael pulled away from the curb faster than the local police would have appreciated.

The drive home was interminable. Both of them were silent, tensely watching the highways. Gardena to Malibu was freeway all the way — San Diego north to 10 west until they came out on the Pacific Coast Highway — and the traffic never let up. It was impossible to distinguish among headlights in the fast-flowing, constant streams of cars, so their vigil didn't tell them if they were being followed, it just tired and blinded them.

The clunk of the garage door behind the car was music to Jess's ears.

Michael, too, heaved a sigh of relief. Then he

swore. "Your car's still in Culver City."

"And long may it stay there." She was too tired even to think about it.

Michael unlocked the kitchen door. Jess led the way in, then froze. There was nothing she could put her finger on, but somehow she knew they weren't alone. Michael sensed it too. He pushed Jess behind him and went ahead into the living room. It was dark; she couldn't see what was happening. She took a step forward, and suddenly a dark form hurtled toward Michael.

Jess screamed as Michael fell, and the front door opened. She didn't spare a glance toward the walkway: her only thought was for Michael. She found herself on her knees beside him, desperately repeating his name over and over, even after he'd sat up and started reassuring her that he was fine.

Michael finally quieted her down by hugging her close. "He just knocked me down. I'm okay. There won't even be a bruise. It's okay."

Jess gradually got her breathing under control and let Michael help her to her feet. He turned on a light, and they both stood there, staring wordlessly at the living room. Papers and books were spread out all over the furniture. Jess's desk had been emptied of everything but the paper clips. It looked like the work of the same maniac who'd searched Robert Berrington's study.

Jess backed out and slowly let herself down onto a dining- room chair. The tears came and they wouldn't stop.

"It's okay, sweetheart," Michael crooned, holding her close to his chest. "Nothing's been taken. It's okay."

"I know. It's just all too much. Too goddam much." She fought for control. "I don't cry. It's hormones or something. It's all too goddam much."

He nodded grimly. "I'm calling the cops."

Jess sniffed and snorted at the same time. "They'll be a real help." They'd insist it was a standard break and enter. Police officers she'd worked with for eight years refused to believe her anymore. Strange cops would really shake their heads. "I'm tired of fighting to be heard. I'm so tired. I just can't do it tonight. I want to go to bed."

He practically carried her up.

Chapter 12

Michael drove Jess to get her car in the morning. He was loath to let her out of his sight and it took considerable doing to convince him that last night was last night, but today she wasn't going to fall apart.

"At least you can drop the Berrington case," he argued. "You've got to think about the baby."

The specter of Betty Drummond's baby lay between them on the front seat. Finally, Michael sighed. "I don't know what to say."

"I don't either. We're trapped. Our lives are in tatters and more than that — would you feel safe? Leaving it alone and wondering who's out for us?"

He shook his head unhappily.

Jess leaned over to kiss him. "I'll be at the office later. Call me when you've talked to Martin. Maybe he's found out something about A-COMM for us."

"Maybe." he kissed her back and took a long time doing it.

Every old-movie buff had seen the Bradbury Building a dozen times. On the outside, it looked no different from its companions in the old part of downtown, just another uninspired brick office building in a crumbling neighborhood of third-rate stores with Spanish names, dubious import-export firms, and small-time immigration attorneys.

Inside was another story. Inside was a fantasy of light and ornament, a long-dead rich man's whim. The building wrapped itself around a vast open court that glowed with sunlight filtered through the glass roof five stories up. Dark curls of burnished, wrought-iron grillwork spiraled up around the hall, framing pale tiled staircases and airy balconies, enclosing two free-standing open elevator shafts. The metal gleamed against wood paneling and marble and mellow creamy brick, the foliate ironwork as graceful as the fronds of the hanging ferns. Half of the detective movies shot in Hollywood had used the Bradbury Building; life followed art, and more than a few private investigators pretended to be the Continental Op in offices off the balconies. Otherwise, it was mainly attorneys who paid the stiff price of working in the aristocrat of Third and Broadway.

Benny Shouldice had a large suite on the fourth floor that he was quick to tell Jess, cost a bundle and couldn't have been afforded by most lawyers at the criminal bar. He could handle it because he was so incredible busy that he seldom had a moment to pee, let alone relax. In fact, he was seeing her without an appointment just because he believed in cooperating with the authorities — even thought he was clearly skeptical about a pregnant dame being any authority at all.

Jess's eyes had glazed over early in the litany, a double bonus since it lessened the impact of Shouldice's self-aggrandizement and blurred the detail of his soft, pasty form. He was probably too busy to exercise; apparently he made enough time for sustenance to bring his gut into conflict with his shirt buttons.

"Mr. Shouldice, it's fascinating to chat with you," Jess finally managed to get in, "but I don't want to keep you away from your work. So let's get down to business."

"Sure." He smiled condescendingly, shading his jowls and displaying an improbable number of capped teeth. "What's the deal?"

"You're acting on the Lil Scott murder case."

"Right. You wouldn't believe how many murders I've got going right now. It's at the point — "

"I'm the eye witness," she cut in ruthlessly. "I saw the killing. Carmichael brought me in for a lineup yesterday."

"O, yeah? Yeah, Lewis — he's one of the killers — he said they were shoved through a lineup."

"One of the killers." And that was the defense counsel talking. Jess drew a deep breath. "Well, I didn't recognize any of the suspects."

Listen, don't feel bad. It's hard to remember faces, especially — "

Jess broke in again before he come out with a racist comment. She was as cynical as the next person, but she wasn't ready for racism from a lawyer who undoubtedly mainly handled people of color. "I saw the killers clearly and I remember them. The men Carmichael arrested are innocent."

Lewis and Theodore mug old ladies every day." Shouldice slid a hand over brilliantine hair. "Slid" was the operative word. "Don't feel bad for them. Believe me, they're bad actors."

"Mr. Shouldice, I'm not squeamish," she snapped. "I've worked at the coroner's office for a long time, and I can assure you I'm not squeamish. I'm here to tell you that your clients did not commit this particular crime, whatever their other failings. We have a funny little principle in our low that likes to match up defendants with the right crimes."

He flushed and sneered. "Looked, lady, don't tell me my business. I talked to Carmichael. I saw what he's got against my boys. He's got them cold. Period. He doesn't need your testimony — "

"But surely you do." She was leaning halfway across the desk. "Surely you've got a defense if you've got an eyewitness who's willing to swear to a jury that your clients are innocent."

"Baby, you got a lot to learn!" Shouldice was snarling as if he were angry, but it was strangely unconvincing. "I'll get my boys good deal. If I go in front of a jury, they're going down for a lot of years."

"Not if they're acquitted!" She was on her feet, hands on what used to be her hips. "Jesus, Shouldice, what kind of a lawyer are you?" She paused, then said slowly, "Or should I be asking who's paying the legal bill in this case?"

His head snapped around. He narrowed his eyes, ran them contemptuously up and down her body, then looked away and picked up a cigar. "I don't have anything more to say to you, sweetheart."

She was steaming when she hit the street and she wasn't even trying to conceal it. Mexican families coming out of the Grand Central Market across the street stared curiously at her; a small child mistook the glare for something personal and started to cry. His mother grabbed him up and hurried away with a nervous backward glance. Jess turned toward her car before she was run in for creating a public disturbance.

She called Carol Tuchman from a pay phone in the mall under Berrington Industries' office tower. It didn't seem wise to venture into Bowdritch territory quite so soon after their meeting in Santa Barbara.

"Carol Tuchman?" The receptionist sounded as if she barely remembered the name.

"Yes. Mr. Berrington's former secretary."

"Oh. Yes. I'm sorry, Carol isn't here."

"When do you expect her back?"

"She doesn't work here anymore." A telephone buzz sounded in the background.

"Where could I — "

"Please hold." A click was followed by Muzak.

Jess grimly held. She'd just about decided that the receptionist's inability to remember things included people on "hold" when the women returned to the line.

"Where can I find Carol?" Jess asked quickly, in case the buzzer rang again.

"I'm sorry, I can't give out that information."

"I'm, uh, Carol's cousin from Phoenix. I'm sure she mentioned me. I'm the one who — " Jess's mind race. "I'm the model. You know, the one on the cover of *Bazaar*?" She grimaced wryly. Of all the things she might be, a fashion model was the last. Especially these days. A Freudian slip, obviously.

"The model? Gosh. Gee, I never knew Carol all that well. I didn't know she had a cousin on the cover of *Bazaar*."

"Really? Well, since I'm in LA for a couple of days, I naturally assumed we'd get together." How much of this could she pile on? "I'm out here — talking to the studios. You know."

"Jeez." Even more awe and respect. "Well, Carol's boss died and she, uh, kind of quit. You have her home number?"

"Not with me. Could you — ?"

"I'm not supposed to give out any information about her."

"I'm at the studio, you see, and the number's back at the hotel."

The magic S-word. "Jeez. Well . . . since you're her cousin. 555-3659. Um — what's your name? So I can look for your picture?"

"Leah. Leah Tuchman."

"Funny. I thought Tuchman was Carol's ex-husband's name."

"Really?" This conversation could only go downhill. "Got to run. Thanks for your help." She hung up and stared at the phone buttons. Carol hadn't mentioned she was quitting. She put in another quarter and punched the number.

"The number you have reached is no longer in service. This is a recorded announcement."

Jess listened to the tinny voice repeat the words several times, then dialed again just to make sure she'd hit the right keys. She heard the record twice more and finally accepted that it wasn't lying to her.

She reached for another quarter only to find that her smallest unit of change was a twenty-dollar bill. That was the kind of day it was turning out to be.

Jess climbed the dingy stairs of the Department of Health Services again, crossing fingers in both hands that she wouldn't run into David McPherson. She stepped cautiously into the open front office of the Radiological Health section, feeling vast and unprotected in a sea of low metal desks brightened by only two scrawny potted palms. she sighed happily; she was in luck. McPherson's door was shut.

"Hi. Can I help you?"

Jess smiled at a perky typist in a nineteen-fifties ponytail and a vivid yellow sundress. "Is this the whole of Rad Health?"

"This?" Chewing gum and looking around. "Yup, all the girls are here. The guys are in the offices." Jess winced. Fat lot of progress they'd made in two decades of unceasing feminist vigilance. "I'm looking for someone. Mind if I nose around?"

The typist shrugged. It wasn't her idea of a fun thing to do, but if Jess thought she'd enjoy it, why not?

There were sixteen women in the room. Jess counted them and took a good look at each and every one. They were young, middle-aged, and old, fair and dark, plump and anorectic, white, brown, and black. But none of them was the woman who'd followed Jess out onto the stairs after her first foray here and suggested that she visit the North County Clinic.

She returned to the ponytail. "Is anyone off sick today?"

The young woman glanced over the room. "Nope. Everybody's here."

"There used to be another woman. A Mexican-American, my age, a bit plump."

"Yeah?" She showed little interest in that fact, then she cracked her gum vigorously and nodded. "Oh, yeah. Letitia. She doesn't work here anymore."

Jess was beginning to feel like a contributing cause of unemployment in America. She had only to meet someone for that person to leave her job. "Where did she go?"

"I dunno. I didn't know her hardly at all."

"Do you know her full name?"

"No."

Jess opened her mouth to ask another question when David McPherson's door started to move. She dashed for the stairway, surprised that she could still sprint, trusting that the typist's chronic apathy would return before she mentioned Jess's visit to anyone.

Carl Weber's office was one floor up he was at his desk, prim as ever as he worked on a perfectly aligned pile of incoming files. Jess watched him close on dossier, put it on the "Out" tray and carefully straighten its corners.

"Hi, Carl."

He looked up, initially beaming and then recollecting that Jess's last visit had been unpleasant. He wasn't good with unpleasantness. "Jess, my dear," he greeted her carefully. "How are you?"

She took that as an invitation and sat thankfully. "It's getting harder and harder to carry both of us around." Especially since "around" had lately covered so much territory.

"Yes, of course." He added hopefully, "Is this a social visit?"

"I wish it were."

His face fell.

"Carl, I wouldn't have come to you if I had anywhere else to turn." She couldn't look at the elfin face without pangs of guilt. "I saw David McPherson as you suggested last time I was here, but he wasn't helpful."

"Oh, now, I didn't suggest it. I simply said he was in charge of Radiological Health." Carl was fidgeting, the long black fingers of one hand smoothing down invisible hairs on the back of the other. "I didn't think he would be helpful. This is a . . . delicate area."

He winced at her bluntness.

"Radar, you mean?"

"Carl, I have to see one of the radar files."

I can't show you a classified file, Jessica!" His mouth had dropped open. "You know that."

"I have to see it. It's important, Carl, a question of life and death." And that might even be the strict truth.

"Oh, please, please, don't ask me to do that!"

She felt like a jack-booted stormtrooper. "Just one. I promise — do this for me and I'll never, ever ask you for another thing."

"I can't, Jess. They keep records on who takes those files. They're restricted, even in the office."

"But you could get hold of one."

He swallowed and tried to lie. It was a valiant effort, but Carl simply wasn't up to changing the pattern of a lifetime.

"Carl, would I do this if it wasn't crucial?"

He didn't answer. She couldn't bear the sorrow on his face, so she concentrated on the framed photographs of his cats. "Carl, the Defense Department is way out of line. They've even got private companies protecting their secrets — while people get ill. Very ill. I'm not imagining things. Let me tell you what's been happening."

"Oh, no! Oh, don't do that!" He was on his feet, the head barely higher than when he was seated. "Oh, no! I don't want to know!"

"Okay, okay," Jess said soothingly. "I won't say another word about it. The file might be under 'Ron Jackson' or 'North County Clinic.' "

His head jerked a few times; it finally settled into a fleeting nod.

Jess waited in the office, her mind a blank and, behind the blank, a seething undifferentiated cauldron of confusion.

"Here it is." He skittered back inside, closing the office door for probably the first time in thirty years. "I haven't looked at it, I don't know what's inside."

She nodded and spread it out in front of her. Carl had done his best, because it had been filed under neither name Jess had suggested. It was file under "Mount Wilson." The papers inside were straightforward medical forms, filled out in the almost indecipherable scrawl of Dr. Frechetti. She was able to make out the salient details: Ron Jackson was thirty-eighth years old, of previously good health, and a responsible husband if not an unimpeachably devoted one. He'd been going to Frechetti for years, mainly for regular VD check-ups.

Jackson came from Fort Worth, Texas. He had a high-school diploma, but until joining the Marines his jobs has been menial ones. He'd been, after all, a black in the South. He'd been working for Thalen ever since his discharge (honorable) from the military. His problems had started eighteen months ago. First, pain in his eyes and headaches. Then shooting spasms accompanied by blurred vision. Lately, sporadic but violent bleeding from the eyes. Jess shuddered. It made a horrible kind of sense. Thalen and Berrington Industries did too much business with the military not to cooperate in covering up this sort of mess. And Jackson himself wouldn't know to associate his illness with radar.

She looked up. Carl was pretending to work she recognized it as pretense because the papers in front of him were not neatly piled. "Carl, how did you know to look under 'Mount Wilson' for the file?"

He refuse to meet her eyes. "I cross-reference it, a simple clerical task."

"I'm not the world's tidiest person, Carl, but that means I don't know how to put things away. i do know how to bring them out of someone else's filing system. You didn't just cross-reference it."

He was almost ready to cry. "I got it for you. Isn't that enough?"

"Yes, I guess it is. But Dr. Frechetti labeled Mr. Jackson illness the 'Mount Wilson Syndrome' and I've never heard of that before. I'm curious about how you knew it."

"I just hear things," he said in a faint, sad whisper. "I hear things. Please, Jess, are you finished now?"

She sighed and skimmed the rest of the papers. What she was looking for was in one of them. Jackson's present whereabouts and the name of his new doctor. "Thank you, Carl." She extended the folder. He didn't move so she finally laid it gently on the desk. Carl stared at it while she gathered up her things and left.

Orange County lay just south of LA, a ghetto for the white middle-class fleeing the big city's heterogeneity and risks. Until comparatively recently, the who spread had belonged to a single family; now, it was subdivided into planned communities, cloned houses and condominiums on prime straight-lined roads, landscaped according to rigid mathematical formulas. It was heaven — if blandness and predictability was you heaven.

Pollard Hospital sat in the middle of the county, just off the Santa Ana Freeway near Tustin. At most private hospitals, patents were assured of comfortable surroundings, deferential staff and edible food. Orange County did things one step better. At Pollard, they had English-country-home decor, a positively obsequious staff and a kitchen that probable rated two stars. In cost around two and a half grand a day, but maybe an up-scale death seemed less final than the kind meted out in public institutions.

Jackson himself lay in bed with bandages on his eyes, so the soft-pink walls and bucolic paintings couldn't do much for his spirits. He was a very big man who'd shrunk; the frame was still extensive but the canvas was dwindling. His wife sat beside him, handsome and ebony, a buxom woman with tightly cropped hair and broad shoulders.

"You the lady from County?" Linda Jackson asked uninterestedly when Jess stepped inside.

"Yes." She handed the woman her card, which said "Medical Examiner" instead of the dread "Coroner." "May I sit down?"

Linda nodded toward an upholstered chair on the other side of the bed. She took a good look at Jess's build and smiled wistfully. According to the dossier, the Jackson had no children.

"How are you feeling, Mr. Jackson?" It was a damn fool question, but it slipped out before she had thought it through.

"He's okay," his wife answered quickly. "But he gets tired real quick, so maybe this won't take too long?"

"Not too long." Jess opened her notebook. "Mr. Jackson, when did you first go to Dr. Frechetti with your problem?"

"When the pains started, the headaches. I dunno. A year ago."

"A year and a half," Linda Muttered. Every day of it was etched on her face.

"It wasn't too bad then. Frechetti gave me pills."

"I see." Jess made a meaningless squiggle. "Do you recall how he diagnosed it?"

Jackson shrugged.

"When did you decide to change doctors?"

"I wouldn't have, but Dr. Merton arranged it."

"What made you consult with Dr. Merton?"

"We didn't consult with him. He just come around

and said he had talked to Dr. Frechetti and now he was my doctor."

Jess glanced up sharply. "Dr. Merton came to you? You never called him in?"

"No, I never heard of him before he came around. Say," Jackson asked with growing belligerence, "what's this about anyhow? I don't like nosy questions.

"Just for the records," Jess answered vaguely. "We, uh, we keep tabs on public clinics."

"How'd you come to me?"

"You left the clinic. We, uh, check that out in case there's a problem at the clinic we should know about."

"Oh." He was apparently not cynical enough to scoff at the notion of a paternalistic government worrying about his satisfaction. "Naw, the clinic's okay. I'd have stayed there if Dr. Merton hadn't come around."

"Fine." Another brisk meaningless squiggle. "What made you choose the clinic in the first place?"

"I dunno. It was there."

Jess nodded. She'd expected him to be a little reticent in front of his wife about his VD check-ups; she'd only asked the questions to lend verisimilitude to her cover story. "When did you leave it?"

"May, I guess. Yeah, Dr. merton sent me to his place in the desert in early May. Said it was better, Frechetti couldn't really take care of me."

"Was Dr. Frechetti upset?"

"Naw," he sighed "it was better too."

"And it is," Linda interjected with the heartiness used for the terminally ill. "This place is so nice and we couldn't have afforded it without Dr. Merton and Captain Wrighter and — "

"You don't need to get into that," Jackson cut her off harshly. "She don't want hear about that."

Jess had stiffened. "Captain Wrighter? I think I know him — but isn't he with the Navy? I thought you were in the Marines."

"Two tours. It was an okay life, the Marines." Jackson seemed to want to get off the topic of Wrighter. "I didn't mind it at all, I only come out 'cause Linda got fed up with all my traveling."

"You were gone all the damn time," Linda defended herself. "And got a good job when you got out."

"That was with Thalen Satellite," Jess asked.

"Yeah, seven years I been with them. Tower repairman."

"I guess you got technical training in the Marines," she said as casually as she could, "working with radar and so on."

"Radar?" He frowned. "No, not me. I worked on artillery."

Jess stared. The closest thing she'd had to a theory had just evaporated without leaving a trace. "No radar?"

"No." He was showing fatigue now, the basso voice getting lower.

Jess collected herself and cast around for something else to ask. "Did Dr. Frechetti recognize your problem as soon as you came to him?"

"I dunno. I guess. The pills worked."

"He's a pretty good doctor," Linda agreed sadly. "He helped Ron a lot there, for a while. He helped Mr. Hulak upstairs, and — "

"There you go again," Jackson exploded. "Bringing in all kinds of shit she don't need! You're as bad as old lady Lee!"

"Mrs. Lee?" Jess leaped in to distract him before he decided she didn't need any more information of any kind. "I met her when I went around to you house."

"Damn busybody!"

"She does deep an eye on the neighborhood," Jess agreed with a chuckle to encourage him and a private apology to Mrs. Lee. "She mentioned watching your visitors. The girl, for instance."

"Yeah, damn busybody. It's my business who I throw out! Stupid girl, poking around in my business — asking about things she's got no right to meddle in."

"Ron didn't even know that lady scientist she was asking for," Linda added indignantly. "Keeping him upset, coming around — "

He was about to shout again, so Jess hastily put in,

"Anyway, with all the coming and going, I can see you'd want to get out of the house and live somewhere quiet."

"It was a dump," he grumbled. "Lousy neighborhood, just a dump."

"I liked it," Linda murmured very quietly. "It was my home and I like it."

"Then why did you leave?" Jess asked.

"Ron . . . Ron felt it was better."

"We had to leave, girl, and you know it! Anyway, it'd be too far for you now. Driving down here every day. Tustin's much closer and we can afford it now." Ron clamped his mouth shut suddenly, as if he'd almost made a mistake. "Linda, I'm tired."

She was on her feet instantly. "You got to let him sleep."

Jess nodded reluctantly. Before she could put the pen and paper away, the door opened to let in a sandy-haired, middle-aged man in a white jacket.

"Hello, Linda. Ron." He wore a shallow little smile and spoke condescendingly. "How are we feeling today?"

"Okay. I'm okay, Dr. Merton."

Linda looked as if she could argue the point if she weren't overwhelmed by the combination of medical and spousal authority.

"And who is this? A friend of yours?" Merton peered at Jess over half-glasses, pretending a courteous interest.

"No, a lady from County."

Jess's heart sank.

"County?" His interest was unfeigned now. "Who are you?"

"Jessica Canby, chief of investigations, coroner's office."

Linda's eyes widened at the realization that medical examiners and coroners were one and the same. She looked quickly at Ron, then away, trying not to show wet eyes.

"What, may I ask, does the coroner's office want here?"

Unspecific chatter about routine records wasn't going to do the trick anymore. Jess bought time by glancing over at the Jackson.

"Ah." He took her point. "Let's talk outside, shall we? Ron, I'll be back in a moment."

He followed her into the corridor, a thickly carpeted passageway that highlighted the hotel-like atmosphere of the institution. There was something eerie about a hospital that didn't clatter and that smelled of cologne instead of cleaning fluid.

Merton come right to the point, the bedside manner slipping away with his smile. "What are you doing here?"

She was getting into a lot of trouble, that's what she was doing, but he didn't need to know that. "I'm doing my job, Dr. Merton. Can you tell me something about Mr. Jackson's illness?"

"I cannot." He made no attempt to smooth it over with protestations of medical privilege. "Why do you care?"

"It's an interesting syndrome, don't you think? The Mount Wilson Syndrome?"

"His eyes fluttered briefly. "There is no such disease, Mrs. Canby. A few alarmists make a great deal of noise and fuss, but that's all they are — alarmists."

"Mr. Jackson's case is not unique."

"Perhaps not. Certainly, we are seeing new illnesses all the time as a result of the industrial climate. Smog, food preservatives, that sort of thing."

"And you're interested enough to walk in and take over this kind of case."

"It is an interesting case. I happened to hear of it and I specialize in Mr. Jackson's sort of complaint, so naturally I suggested to his ordinary doctor that I handle it."

"And you went so far as to put him in here," she continued. "The Jackson can't afford it so it's unusually . . . kind of you."

It's nothing of the sort," he said quickly. "His employer pays the bills. I imagine they have company medical coverage."

"For a private hospital?" Jess pointed out politely. "That's sum insurance policy."

"I have no idea what it covers. Possibly the Veteran's Administration helps."

"And then, of course," she continued pleasantly, "there's the cost of Mrs. Jackson's living arrangements. Orange County is considerably more expensive than North Pasadena, wouldn't you say? The VA is certainly open-handed. Or is Mr. Bowdritch footing that bill too?"

Merton was eyeing her with a mixture of distaste and wariness. "I have never met the man so I couldn't say. Now, if you don't mind — "

"How did you come to hear about Mr. Jackson's problem?"

"I can't recall." He was angry. "More to the point, how did you?"

Jess shrugged. This was her cross-examination. "How many cases like Mr. Jackson's do you have?"

"I have no more time for this," he said brusquely. "I want you out of this hospital and I don't want to find you disturbing my patient again. Do you understand?"

Jess didn't have to answer. They were interrupted by a nurse in pale green pants and a bright blouse.

"Doctor!" She was agitated, but even so, the voice was low. "Dr. Merton! It's Mr. Quinn! Please hurry!"

He started away, turning back to glare once at Jess. She remained impassive until he'd vanished and then she took the stairs up fast. Mr. Hulak was in the second room she tried. His decor was exactly like Jackson's, except here the walls here were creamy yellow.

Jess had assumed that Hulak too would be blinded by bandages; she skidded to halt when he turned perfectly clear eyes toward her and waited for an explanation for the intrusion.

"Hi." Her mind raced. "I'm a friend of Linda Jackson. Downstairs, you know?"

"Oh, sure. Hi" he managed a weak movement of his mouth, a grim version of a smile. Hulak was obviously in a lot of pain, the lines of his face deeply routed his hands moving constantly as if to distract his mind.

Jess come closer so he wouldn't have to speak up. "Linda suggested I see you because my husband's got the some thing as you. I, uh, wanted to check out my doctor against Dr. Merton."

"Oh." He looked at her stomach and then away. "Oh, my, how awful. At least I don't have children."

It seemed lousy to lie to someone who was dying and could still find sympathy for a fatherless child. She had no choice, but she didn't like herself much for doing it. "You used to go to Dr. Frechetti too, didn't you?"

He moved his head a quarter-inch up and down.

"What did he diagnose your illness as?"

Hulak looked surprised. "Cancer, of course. Cancer of the pancreas."

Jess drew a deep breath. "How old are you, Mr Hulak?"

"Thirty-four. Don't look it anymore, do I?"

"Sure you do," she lied. He barely looked fifty-four. "When did you get sick?"

"Couple of years ago. Started out just as changes in the blood, then they found the other thing."

"How did you end up with Dr. Merton?"

He shook his head and shut his eyes. Jess gripped the back of a chair while she watched him endure the pain.

Finally, he looked at her again. "Sorry. What did you say?"

How did you end up going to Dr. Merton?"

"He kind of ended up with me. Dr. Frechetti must've called him or something. I just got to the clinic one day and the nurse told me I had a specialist now."

"Where did you work? Before you got sick?"

"I didn't much." He was remembering the good old days. "I had this real cheap apartment on Washington Boulevard, just down from the doctor. I was studying to be a nurse. You think that's funny? A guy being a nurse?"

"No, of course not. Were you in the Service?"

"No." A private shame made him flinch. "I would've but they — they rejected me on account of I wasn't married. Sort of."

Jess found herself patting his hand to reassure him that his sexual orientation couldn't matter less. "Have you ever worked with radar?"

"What?"

"Radar? Or anything like radar?" Something shimmered at the fringe of her mind, an idea so ephemeral that it dissolved as she tried to approach it. "Before you went into nursing?"

"No, I worked for Bullocks for ten years. Sold shoes and belts." He was saved by another vicious spasm.

"Thanks for talking to me," she said gently. "you're a brave man, taking the pain the way you do. Goodbye, Mr. Hulak."

"Bye." His eyes lit up at the thought that someone felt he was a brave man.

Jess waked downstairs in a fog. She couldn't believe that every hint of a traceable pattern had vanished before she could even formulate it aloud. What was the common thread here?

She stopped at the front desk. "Canby. County Medical Center. Can you tell me how Quinn on the third floor is doing?"

A young, pink-cheeked nurse shook her head. "Just gone. Not five minutes ago."

"What a shame." Jess clicked her tongue. "Terrible killer, that."

"Leukemia? Yes, terrible." The nurse shook her head again.

Chapter 13

Jess parked and entered the coroner's building, for once forgetting to greet the security men. Her mind was wholly absorbed with Pollard Hospital. She had something there, she knew she did. Except she didn't have a clue as to what. Her pace picked up. Maybe she'd get a glimmer if she could find out what Merton's relationship was with Stephen Bowdritch and Berrington Industries.

She rounded the courter at a semi-run and skidded to a halt at the doorway of her office. Joe Miller was behind the desk, her face flushed and not quite able to meet her eyes.

Let it not be said she couldn't take a hint. "I guess this means my suspension is official."

He was practically choking with embarrassment.

A voice come from behind Jess. "Harper made Joe acting chief this morning."

Jess turned. "Hi, Consuela."

"I could strangle the bastard!" Consuela was white-lipped, obviously sincere. "He didn't even have the decency to tell you before he did it."

Jess shrugged, hoping that the sick feeling in her stomach didn't show in her face. "Don't worry about it. Harper's going to know he's in a fight, no matter who wins it."

"What do you mean, 'No matter who wins it?' You're going to win — you have to!"

"Right," Jess agreed. The cheerleading team had arrived and she already felt a bit better. "It just slipped my mind for a moment."

Joe had regained the use of his tongue, but his color was still high. "I'll go to my old office."

"Shouldn't you be taking away my ID and kicking me out of the building?" She made her mouth move into what they all pretended was a grin.

"If I tried, the rest of the staff would have my balls for bookends." Joe's grin wasn't much better. "Uh, Jess — we're all sorry as hell about this."

"I know. Listen, Harper's gone too far this time. He can't fire senior management for insubordination."

Joe and Consuela exchanged uneasy looks.

Jess sighed, cleared a space on the desk and perched. "Okay, folks, what aren't you telling me?"

The acting chief immediately delegated the dirty work by clearing his throat and fumbling through reports in the "In" tray.

"It's the Aguerra case," Consuela finally admitted, sagging into a chair and staring at the floor. "They're — he's saying that the boy wasn't ..."

"Wasn't a chicken?"

Consuela nodded unhappily. "They're saying you jumped to that conclusion so you, uh ..."

"So I'd get publicity."

"So you'd get publicity," she echoed faintly. "The Hispanic American Society's screaming bloody murder — racism and well ..." Her voice faded into nothing.

"I imagine they're blaming me for the father's suicide." Jess assisted her. Her hands felt very cold.

"Yes."

Jess bit her lip. This made no sense, so why were her intestines churning? "Amory Garland gave me the dope on Aguerra. I'm clean. It might get messy — and I'm sorrier that hell about offending the Mexican community — but I'm not getting left with this ball."

"Harper said — "

"Harper's been looking for a way to get rid of me ever since he got here, but this isn't it. He can't rewrite reality."

"You're sure?" Hope was dawning.

"Dead sure. I'm going to call Garland now and sock it to Harper."

Joe vacated the spot behind the desk with alacrity, taking up a position immediately behind Consuela.

"Detective Garland, please. Jess Canby here."

"He's not in the office. You wanna talk to his partner?"

"Sure."

Consuela and Joe were barely breathing. Jess tried

to look relaxed while she waited.

"Oh, hi." She sat up straighter as a Texas drawl took over the line.

"Canby? Detweiler."

"Hi. Where's Amory?"

"On vacation for a couple of weeks."

Jess very quietly let out a breath. "When did he go on vacation?"

"This morning."

"It was kind of sudden, wasn't it?"

The answer took a while in coming. "He had lot of vacation time piled up, and the captain wanted him to take some of it."

"Where did he go? It's important I talk to him, Detweiler."

"Maybe, but that's not gonna help. He's gone camping, can't be reached."

"I see." She paused. "Did you work on the Aguerra case with him?"

"No, I just got back from two-week stakeout in Sherman Oaks."

Jess's eyes met Consuela's; both women were grim-faced. "Can you let me see the file? I'll owe you one."

"I like to collect favors, but I can't help this time. The brass took all of Amory's files this morning. Spot audit or something."

Jess hung up, and nobody moved until Leon de la Pena poked in, saw Jess, flushed, and hurried away.

"I found out something about the drugs," Consuela commented, glaring after Leon. "On Monday morning, some time after talking to Stephen Bowdritch, Harper visited the evidence room!"

Jess smiled gratefully. "Thanks, Consuela, but it won't wash. The vial could have vanished any time Sunday or Monday — and hordes of people visit the evidence room."

The other two nodded glumly and trailed out. Jess stared at the empty doorway for a while and then unenthusiastically reached for the telephone. She might as well get this over with.

Harper had some difficulty disguising his glee. "I'm afraid, Jessica, that this time you've gone too far."

"This excuse will not do," she informed him coldly.

"Excuses? A man is dead because you passed a suspicion off as fact! That is not an excuse."

"It wasn't a suspicion. It was a fact — given me by Detective Garland."

"Garland may have shared your opinion, I can't speak for him. But he had nothing to go on either. As you well know."

"That child was not a prostitute!" Harper was losing his cool; the voice was getting louder and shriller. "If you have any evidence to the contrary, show it to me!"

"I don't have it. Garland does. So we'll have to wait until he's back from his mysteriously arranged vacation."

"It's hardly mysterious. You've dragged him into an unsavory mess. His superiors removed him from the dirt that's flying around! In an attempt to protect their department. Which, I might add, is something that I am also trying to do!"

Jess bit her tongue and counted to ten. "I should tell you that I intend to fight this every step of the way. And I intend to win."

She was about to ring off when Harper spoke again, this time in a really nasty tone. "You won't win — because you've made it really very easy for me. I have a number of examples to bring up to illustrate your appalling abuse of power."

Jess stiffened.

"Radar, for example, might well be a glamorous issue for an aspiring politician to investigate. It is not, however, within your jurisdiction. I suspect that the inquiry officer will regard it as a serious offense that you use your office to bully your way into classified files."

She should have seen that coming. David McPherson over at Rad health had obviously trained at the same stoolie academy as Stephen Bowdritch. "Good day."

There was no doubt about it. Harper had her

caught between a rock and a hard place. She'd have to call on all her friends in order to defend herself, and the publicity wasn't going to do her any good; win, lose, or draw.

Was any of this worth it? It would be so easy to quit, to go home and change diapers. And then maybe, by the time the kid was twenty or so, her personality defects would be forgotten and she could reenter public life.

She was so on edge that when the telephone shrilled she almost jumped out of her skin.

"Jess?"

"Michael! Oh, I'm so glad to hear from you."

"Why? What's going on there?"

"I'm suspended." She told him about Aguerra.

He whistled. "Quite a set-up."

"You think so too?"

"I haven't smelled anything like it since we visited Fisherman's Wharf in the heat."

"Yeah." She signed. "And this morning, I went around and got poor Carl Weber in trouble, too. I know the radar investigation is mixed up with Berrington — not to mention with my crucifixion — but I don't understand how."

"We'll figure it out." He didn't make it sound convincing. "Can you meet me for dinner? I'm going to see Dana now."

Her throat constricted. "Any news?"

"Yeah. All of it bad. The deal's definitely off."

She arranged dinner and got off the telephone. Kafka continued to direct their live. Her jaw was set angrily. She had a few card to play and it was time to start dealing.

She started with the Board of Supervisors. Reg Cruickshank, said his assistant, was in a meeting and couldn't be disturbed. No, not even for Jess Canby. No, not even if it was an emergency. Well, yes, he could take a message in.

Jess waited for a long time, her fingers impatiently drumming on the desk top.

"Ms. Canby?" He was back, the cool, calm voice much cooler now. "Mr. Cruickshank has a terrible schedule for the next few days. I'm afraid I couldn't book you in at all. Perhaps, if you try back next week. Say the middle of the week."

"I'll be seeing him before that. The opening of my father's sculpture garden is the day after tomorrow."

"Oh, yes, that's another thing. Mr. Cruickshank wanted me to convey his regrets. Something's come up and it turns out he won't be able to make it."

She was mad enough to chew a cigarette, but she contented herself with smoking it. When she felt her pulse was merely fast, she dialed Richard Simon.

"Richard, I'm in a lot of trouble. Have you heard?"

"My dear." The funeral tone was answer enough. "What in the world has happened? What did you do?"

"I didn't do anything." She reminded herself not to shout. None of this was Richard's fault. "I've been unhappy with the official findings on the Berrington case, as you know. And the goddamn moron who runs this office has set me up for it."

"Has it anything to do with, er, what we talked about the other morning?"

"Radar? Yes, " she admitted, "I didn't take your advice. I looked into it — and by the way, Richard, there's a lot to look into. Anyway, that's tied in too. Berrington or his companies have been shielding the military on this."

"I see."

"Richard, tell me about Stephen Bowdritch."

"Oh, my, Jessica. Can't you leave this alone? I'm sure we could mend the fences if — "

I doubt it. I just called Reg. He wouldn't even come to the phone."

He stayed silent.

"I know he's got to watch out. He can't risk offending the Mexican community the way I've done in the Aguerra case, but unless I prove I'm right, there's no mending possible. Tell me about Bowdritch."

Richard was reluctant, but he did his best. "He's

been with Robert — oh, almost thirty years. He's an engineer, I believe. He mad a good marriage. Delia Houlihan from Chicago, quite a bit of money. Plumbing supplies. Stephen worked his way up with Robert, always number two, of course, but I believe they were very close. Stephen seemed almost to worship Robert."

"But until Robert died, he could never be in first place."

Richard sighed. "I suppose not, but — " He sighed again.

"And now he has to prove himself." That was important. "Look, I need your help in fighting this set-up, and in proving I'm right."

It was a long time before he answered. "Are you sure you're right, my dear?"

"Yes," she lied.

"Well, you'll have to find something concrete to back you up, something more than suspicion, before anyone can help you."

It was an echo of what Francis Arnheim had said. Jess spent a good part of the next few hours going over everything again and again. It still made no sense. She didn't even know what data she needed to make it make sense. Which reminded her . . .

"Martin? It's Jess"

"God, Jess — I've been hearing about you all day! What the hell is going on?"

"You're the seventeenth person to ask. I'll give you the same answer I gave them. I don't have a goddamn clue. Martin, have you done the research on A-COMM?"

"It's hard to get much. They're a pretty secretive lot."

"Even if you have to sacrifice your fair white body for it, I need that information, Martin. One more thing. Can you think of a reason for Berrington to be in Paraguay? A business reason?"

"Paraguay? You sure?" He thought for a while. "Well, it's a great place for fevers and ex-nazis and poverty. I'm sure there's much of a market for any of those."

"Yeah." She sighed. "Okay, well, Michael and I will come over tonight — " She broke off as Francis Arnheim wandered in. "See you later." She put down the receiver.

Francis hitched up his pantlegs and sat.

"Hi." Jess spoke flatly. "I'm surprised to see you here."

"I could say the same thing."

"True," she admitted. "I'm imposing on my staff's good nature."

He grunted. "Since I'm here, why don't you tell me what you're up to?"

She watched him thoughtfully. "Why do you ask?"

"What the hell do you think you're proving?"

"What do you care?" They could keep this up for days.

"Still think Lil Scott was executed?" he asked suddenly.

"I saw the defense attorney." She wasn't ready to answer that one. "Real charmer."

"Like most of them." He glared at her. "Well?"

Jess sighed. They'd known each other a long time, she and Francis. "Yes, I still think so. Can I prove it? No."

"But you're ready to run all over town asking questions and getting crapped on because you *think* so."

She didn't respond.

Francis nodded as if he'd expected no more. Eventually, he stood up. "You're awful exposed — and awful alone."

That little fact was only too obvious. How come she hadn't noticed sooner that her entire life was built around having an office to go to and a title to flaunt? "You really know how to cheer a girl up."

"You get anything in writing from Garland?" He asked casually.

"I wondered if the Aguerra thing was public knowledge. No, I've got nothing in writing — but I'm right. I'm not hallucinating."

"Do you have a theory about what's really going on?"

She watched him for a moment, then shook her head.

"You trust anyone?"

"Whom do you suggest?"

He shrugged. He was ready to allow as how there might be two teams in the game — which was more then most were admitting — but he wasn't applying to join hers.

"You could do something for me," Jess said finally. "I want some information about a telephone number that's gone out of service."

"Okay. Gimme the number."

"I'd rather do it myself." She gazed levelly at him until he grudgingly scratched a number on the corner of a file folder.

"Dorothy." He rubbed a drooping eyebrow. "Supervisor at Pacific Telephone."

"What's the quid pro quo?"

He grunted and stumped out. Jess raised an eyebrow. There'd been the hint of a flush on the sallow face.

Dorothy proved to be a soft-spoken Southerner who displayed incredible enthusiasm at the mention of Francis Arnheim. It was a whole new way of looking at him. Jess tried to picture the cop as an inamorata, but when she came to the point of thinking of him as undressed and tender, she gave it up. No way was her imagination flexible enough for that one.

"555-3659? That's around Sherman Oaks, honey."

"Okay." Jess was agreeable. "Can you pull the file?"

"Hold on."

More time staring at the opposite wall. There was definitely a new crack in it, a gentle reminder that they were perched on land that wasn't committed to staying place.

"Hi. Y'all still there?"

"Sure thing. Did you get it?"

Sure did. The service was canceled yesterday

afternoon. Belonged to Carol Ann Tuchman, 12335 Lafayette, apartment 3, Sherman Oaks. She said she was moving out of Pacific's territory, so we haven't ordered new service anywhere."

"Is there a forwarding address?"

"Well, sure there is honey. We have to send the final bill somewhere, now don't we? It's going to Berrington Industries —"

I've got that address," Jess interjected grimly. All of her roads certainly bypassed Rome. "How long did she live in Sherman Oaks?"

"Seven years." Dorothy chuckled. "Sort of forever by California standard, isn't it? There's no previous service in her name. Was she ever married, hon?'

"I think so."

"Well, then, that's likely the answer. She probably had a phone somewhere in her husbands name."

"Any chance of locating his file?"

Dorothy laughed merrily. Had Jess never dealt with AT and T before? "Nope, no way."

Does it show who canceled service?'

"Says the subscriber herself. 'Course, any gal could call up and say she was Carol Tuchman."

"Okay. Thanks, Dorothy. Francis owes you one." She didn't specify one what.

It was another blank page to add to a thick dossier of blank pages. She was covering a lot of miles, but other than single-handedly underwriting the gasoline business, what exactly was she achieving? Headaches, nightmares, and the right to stand in line at the Unemployment Insurance office, that's what.

Chapter 14

The North County Clinic closed at one o'clock on Fridays. A curling, brown-edged notice said that the doctor would be available again on Monday morning and that, in the meantime, emergency rooms at the county hospital would have to suffice.

Jess got back into her car and, after three attempts, found a phone booth in which the receiver was still connected to the base and both were working. The operator told her that Frechetti's home was listed, which made him one of a very select number of doctors. Maybe he lived in hope that, one day, a private patient would come calling.

The address was in Highland Park, an area of steep hills and unpretentious houses, just west of Pasadena. Skinny pot-holed roads climbed valiantly up through rough scrub and hardy bushes. The houses overlooked the city, in theory. Smog kept it from being a fact. It was a lower-middle-class community still trying to hold onto respectability, but parts of it were on the verge of giving up. For once in his life, Frechetti was in the vanguard. He'd already given up. His tiny bungalow showed all the signs of incipient slum-hood; it had been years since the wood siding had had an intimate relationship with a paint brush, even longer since gardening equipment had penetrated the small yard. Tiles were missing from the roof, giving the impression of a balding, wizened old man waiting docilely for the grim reaper.

Jess parked on the side of the road, half on the brown erstwhile lawn, so that other traffic could squeeze by should there be any. She picked her way carefully to the front door, avoiding cracked flagstones and a couple of desultory lizards. The doorbell was rusty and had apparently been undisturbed for the length of time it took several generations of spiders to spin thick blankets of webs. Jess pushed it anyway, surprised it into a weak but undeniable whine. She pushed it again after a few, uneventful minutes. The whine was weaker the second time.

"Yes?" A man's fretful voice came through the thin door. "Yes? Who is it?"

"I want to talk to Dr. Frechetti?" The voice didn't belong to Frechetti himself; it sounded as if it come from an elderly man in poor health. "It's Jessica Canby."

"Go away, he's not here."

She was getting awfully tired of rebuffs. "No, I won't go away until you tell me how to find him."

"Oh." Silence. The hidden speaker might have been impressed with the resolve in her voice. Or he might just have gone away.

She pressed the buzzer again; it died in the middle of a shrill gurgle.

"Go away?" He was more tentative now.

"No. Please open the door."

"I'm not supposed to. He tells me not to."

"He won't mind," Jess assured him glibly. "Just this once, he won't mind."

The door finally opened. Jess swallowed her gasp. She was facing disintegration in it's purest form.

The figure was male, of that she could be reasonably certain, since he was wearing only gray wool pants and the chest was concave. She could only make a guess at his age, but he wasn't old in years, just in rot. The skin was yellowish, the muscles lax, so that the epidermis drooped as if it was coming away from the bones. He had dark eyes, the large deep sockets rimmed with red, and lines of despair. It was no wonder that Frechetti wanted to prevent him from meeting the public. Doctors were supposed to discourage drug addiction, but the bruised veins and runny nose said that Frechetti's efforts had been, to put it, charitable, insufficiently persuasive.

"I'm Jess," she said, trying for a casual, pleasant, normal voice. "What's you name?"

"Toom."

"Uh-huh." No way of knowing if that was a nickname, a surname, or the answer to an entirely different question. "I'm looking for Dr. Frechetti. He does live here?"

A vague movement of the skinny arms suggested the affirmative.

"He isn't here now?"

Another movement, suggesting the negative.

Jess took a deep breath. She knew he could talk, at least enough to say "Go away." "When will he be back?"

"Soon." There was a flash of life in the eyes, an almost imperceptible lifting of the shoulders.

"Where is he?"

"He's not here."

"Yes, I know that," Jess persisted with the gentle firm voice of and English *sahib* dealing with a backward native. "He isn't here — but where is he?"

"Getting something for me. He'll be back soon." Another spurt of emotion slid across the eyes.

Jess was silent. She could interpret the emotion now. It was hope, the only emotion left to a burned-out junkie. It was becoming clearer why Frechetti was buried away at the North County Clinic.

Toom wiped his nose with a bare arm and went back inside. Jess followed, preparing herself for what would undoubtedly be a seedy decor.

She'd have needed a full year to prepare for the reality. The outside of the house was decrepit; the inside was decaying. The carpet which curled up at the edges, was bare in places and filthy everywhere. The furniture was rudimentary — bare benches and a single stuffed chair with a visible broken spring. There was nothing on the walls except cobwebs, and even they couldn't be seen clearly in the dim light offered by a single shadeless bulb. It was dingy and depressing, but she could have coped with it without the smell. Something was rotting, and it wasn't just Toom. She figured it out when she noticed a box of rat poison in a corner. The box was empty, and the rats had obviously taken their revenge by dying in unswept corners or in cracked walls.

Her stomach threatened to heave; she had to beat a retreat to the doorstep, taking care to leave the door open. She sat on the stoop, waiting. Toom sat inside, watching for his savior with jerky head movements and increasing tension.

The air was thick and hot; Jess's hair was damp at the roots and her blouse was glued to her skin by the time a tired Volvo tottered up the hill. It hesitated with a stutter when it came upon the Skylark, but eventually, lined itself up behind the intruder. The driver's door opened.

Frechetti was a scarecrow, but compared to his roommate, he seemed the picture of health. He stood beside his Volvo and looked at Jess, then his eyes shifted to her left, and he began to hurry toward the house.

Toom was outside, padding ahead on bare feet, too strung out stop shivering. Frechetti reached him and put a protective arm around his shoulders. "Are you alright?" he asked gently.

"Do you — ?"

"I have it. Don't worry. Come on, we'll take care of you." He soothed Toom and drew him into the house, shutting the door as if Jess were invisible.

She didn't move. After another fifteen minutes, Frechetti emerged again. He sat beside her, looking straight ahead and working his jaw silently.

She almost missed the first word, they were spoken so softly. "he wasn't always like that, you know."

"No, I suppose not." She hesitated. "Couldn't he be helped?"

Frechetti made a noise that sounded like a keen. "It's too late for that. It's almost over."

"How did he get so bad?" She was struggling against pity. Toom was one thing; his supplier was quite another, no matter how he was suffering.

"He took one step, then another, and he never decided to turn around." A tear slid down the concave cheek. "Another month, maybe two." It was as if he were talking to himself. "He was so beautiful, so . . . alive. He made me feel . . . things I stopped feeling years ago."

Jess looked away, the battle against pity lost. She wasn't really tough enough for this mission. "I've got a couple of questions."

"I can't help you."

"You don't know the questions."

"Yes, I do." He winced at admitting even that much. "Someone talked to you about me?"

Frechetti didn't answer, which was an answer in itself.

Jess was tense again, looking around as if she expected to see an army of tails. "Look, I know you've got problems, but believe me, you're not the only one. I have to have answer, and I'm not going to leave without them."

"I . . . No. No, I can't"

"Nobody knows I'm here." Please God. "Nobody needs to find out."

He swallowed hard and shook his head.

"What did they say to you? What hold do they have on you?" She knew the answer even as she spoke. "It's Toom, isn't it?"

Frechetti shrugged lifelessly.

Jess took a deep breath and forced herself to go on. "I'm sorry to have to say this, but I don't have a choice. You'll have to risk it with them — because if I don't get what I want, I'll expose you, too. Doctors aren't supposed to procure drugs, Frechetti. If I go to the police, you'll go to jail, and Toom will be institutionalized."

"He can't go to a hospital! He'll die."

She didn't respond.

"Look, he's going to . . . it's all going to be over soon anyway. Let him stay with me; let him stay in a place he knows. he'd be terrified in a hospital, all alone, treated like dirt — you know what County's like for indigent addicts," he pleaded desperately. "Give me a month!"

Jess couldn't meet his eyes. Stalin, too, had acted as if the ends justified the means.

"Why are you doing this? What are you searching for? Truth? Justice?" He spat the words as if they were obscenities.

"Maybe once upon a time I was," Jess said quietly. "Not anymore."

"You'll be hurt — they're watching you! You're only making trouble for yourself."

"I'm being hurt now, Frechetti. I need to find out what's happening to me so I can figure out how to stop it." She hated to say it out loud because that made it real. "I won't be safe until I do."

He shuddered.

"I'm sorry, but you've got to talk to me," she said simply. "I don't want to hurt you or Toom, but I will if I have to."

He looked at his hands, long elegant fingers that could have belonged to a surgeon if the knuckles weren't swollen and the nails grimy. He finally caved in, asking in a whisper, "What are the questions"

"What's the Mount Wilson Syndrome?"

"I made up that name. It doesn't really mean anything — it's just a name for the strange sickness I've been seeing. It's not really a syndrome, because there isn't a common pattern to the syndrome, just a lot of sick people."

"Like Jackson, and Hulak and Quinn?"

"I don't know about Quinn. The other two were my patients."

"Yes, until Merton took them over. Tell me about Merton."

He shook his head helplessly. "I don't have anything to tell you. He turned up one day at the office and kind of offered a deal. He's studying these sorts of people, and he wanted me to give them to him."

"For which he pays you."

"For the patients." He added bitterly, "And for not talking to anyone about it."

"Is he a real doctor?"

"A real doctor? What do you mean? He may not be any good, I don't know about that, but be's a doctor all right."

"When did he first show up?"

"About a year ago."

"What brought him?"

"I don't know. Maybe he heard rumors; maybe he's a witch, I don't know."

"How many of your patients has he taken?"

"Uh — oh, ten, maybe fifteen."

"In a year?" she asked sickly.

"Yes. In a year."

"Do they all go to Pollard Hospital?"

"Pollard? Where's that?"

"A small private place in Orange County."

Frechetti shrugged. "I don't know where he treats them. I don't even know where his office is — I'm not supposed to be nosy. Maybe he doesn't even have an office. I think he's mainly a researcher. His guy once said something about an institute."

"What guy?" Jess hated to ask.

"Big guy. I don't know his name. He's the one who pays me."

"How big?"

Frechetti almost smiled. "Real big. Could've played ball, except he'd probably crowd the field. Not someone," he added fervently, "that you'd want to annoy."

Jess could testify to that from personal experience. She told herself that she could stop trembling if she wanted to badly enough, but her hands were slow to get the message. "I want all the names, addresses, and medical notes on the people you've sent to Merton."

"No!" He stared at her in horror. "No, no way. Absolutely not!"

"Yes." She stared back. "Think about Toom."

"I don't have them," he protested frantically.

"I don't believe you. You're trapped but you're not a fool. You'd have protected yourself — you've got the notes somewhere, Frechetti. Here? Or at the clinic?"

The air slowly went out of him. "At the clinic," he admitted in a choked voice.

"Okay. Let's go." Jess stood up.

"No." He sated still, speaking with flat resolution. "I'm not leaving Toom now. He's in bad shape."

She paused, considering. "Okay. I'll give you until tonight. I'll meet you at the clinic after ten."

The drive down the hill was a lot more nerve-wrecking than the drive up. Even in San Francisco you couldn't have found more perilous slopes. At least traffic was nonexistent. Jess saw only one other car, a dark brown American model that pulled away from the side of the road just after she passed.

She was filling her gas tank at a self-service station on Avenue 54 when she happened to look across the street. Her stomach turned over. The dark brown car was idling in front of a strip joint.

She didn't see it again, but she cold feel the eyes on her all the way into Hollywood. She parked behind Musso and Frank's, a proletarian Buick in the midst of aristocratic Mercedes and Rolls Royces. The little knot of cheerful parking attendants gave her the courage to stay outside and watch for the tail. It didn't appear. Maybe she'd lost it. And maybe the whole mess would go away if she wished hard enough.

The Musso and Frank Grill was the oldest restaurant in Hollywood, a 1919 dark-paneled home-away-from-home for three generations of entertainment and political hot shots and three generations of ogling tourists. Show business had deserted Hollywood Boulevard years ago, but the grill still packed them in. The food was only fair, the waiters were brusque, and the prices were high, but everyone loved the place, including Jess and Michael.

Michael was waiting in the back room with Dana. He looked glum, and the agent looked even glummer. Jess joined them with a feeling of foreboding.

"Glad to see you, darling." Dana's kiss wasn't convincing. I can't stay, but Michael wanted me to tell you what I heard today."

Jess sat down and waited.

"I talked to Cyril and got no answer at all." Dana's brow was furrowed. "I've never gotten so far into a deal and had it blow up so fast. I mean, deals blow up, but not like this! I just can't understand it."

Jess looked at Michael and felt sick.

"I figured, until the news hit the street that Michael's deal was off he was still a hot property. You know, if someone wants you, everyone wants you."

Jess nodded. The corollary, unfortunately, was also true.

Dana leaned forward. "Suddenly, Michael's name is mud. I mean, the second I mentioned it, people went glassy."

Jess was puzzled. "What does that mean?"

"Oh. Well." Dana started to gather up her purse and briefcase. Agents hated to deliver bad news; that was why they were famous for not returning calls. "Well, he's blacklisted. Someone doesn't like him, someone with clout."

"But — that's ridiculous! How could that be?" Jess was spluttering. "How do we handle that?"

"You find out who it is and make up with them, darling." Dana threw a few fast kisses around and skittered away. If Michael was poison, she didn't want to risk being tainted too.

Once Jess filled him in on what she's done with her day, they had very little to say. They got through the meal mainly by taking in alcohol, and for once, Michael didn't seem to notice that Jess was matching him drink for drink.

The waiter eventually brought the check, unbidden. They were taking up space far longer than they should on a busy night when his tips were bound to be good. Michael put some cash on the plate and looked at Jess. "What now?"

"We're going to nose around and start defending ourselves." She put on a determinedly cheerful face and got to her feet. "Come on."

The sun as going down and the Boulevard was waking up. It was no longer what starry-eyed dreamers in small midwestern towns pictured as Hollywood. Hollywood as a state of mind was glamorous; as a place, it was a lot like Times Square in New York without the glitter. It belonged, after dark, to the underclass:

pickpockets looking for strays from the straight world, hookers and johns, rootless teenagers, gangs of bikers, winos, shopping bag ladies. Even the pink stars set into the sidewalk were listless, their color faded under gray dust, the names of the once great often now unfamiliar to all but masters of entertainment trivia.

Jess led Michael toward Wilcox, pretending not to notice his dubious glances at the parade.

"It gets worse every year."

She shrugged. "It looks worse than it is."

He ignored her comment, as it deserved to be ignored. "Do you feel the energy? In street talk, these are bad vibes, man."

"At least the sidewalk's busy. Most places, everyone's inside a car."

He didn't look as if he thought that as a point in Hollywood's favor. Where are we going?"

"To unravel the set-up. The Aguerra boy worked the block between Wilcox and Cahuenga, and we're in luck because I know a fence there."

"What luck." He was walking slower than Jess.

She turned around just as a black woman in a skirt the size of a G-string cosied up to Michael. He shook his head and lengthened his stride.

"Stay with me," he ordered Jess. "This is no place for weak-minded males."

"You won't find the temptation too much for you if you remember that four out of three people on this pavement probably have herpes — or worse." She was grinning as she turned into one of the few stores not for barred for the night. It was a camera store, displaying a melange of video and audio equipment along with, incongruously, a counter of condoms.

"Mrs. Rubinstein?" Jess broke into the reveries of a heavily pimpled youth behind the cash register.

He looked at a battered wooden door at the back of the room. "You want me to get her?"

"I know the way."

He sank back happily on his stool while they walked through the doorway. A plump, pink-cheeked elderly

woman was sipping a cup of tea and studying a newspaper at a long counter covered by cartons of stock.

"Mrs. Rubinstein?"

The old woman looked up suspiciously, one hand
automatically going to her lap.

"Jess Canby, you remember?"

"Oh, yes, darling! How are you? My God, you're
going to have a baby! Wonderful! Is this your lucky
husband? Do you know how lucky you are, to have such
a wonderful girl?" Mrs. Rubinstein had put her gun on
the counter and was scurrying around to clear a bench
and find two more styrofoam cups. "Darling, it's wonderful! A *mechaieh*? You know what that is? A
blessing!"

Michael raise his eyebrows at Jess when the woman's back was momentarily turned.

Jess grinned. He was going to get even more
astounded. Mrs. Rubinstein as a long-time fence. The
police knew it. But she'd decided when she last got out
of prison, on her sixty-second birthday, that she was too
old to do more time. So She'd become cooperative with
the authorities, semi law-abiding, and a positive
caricature of an ethnic grandmother.

"So, darling," the old woman asked, sitting next to
Jess and patting her hand, "What's new? Except for the
baby? Introduce me to your handsome husband."

"Michael Renfrew, Mrs. Rubinstein."

"Renfrew, Canby," she sighed. "This new thing, not
using your husband's name, it's so confusing. I used Leo
Rubinstein's name all my life, since I was seventeen —
and we were married only seven months."

"Michael was fascinated. "What happened to him?"

"Ah, he didn't know curiosity killed the cat." The
old woman shook her head. "He used to ask questions.
Foolishness."

She was looking at Michael, but the point was being
made for Jess. Jess understood it. She'd herd several
versions of the fate of poor Leo, but this was a new one.
Mrs. Rubinstein used her late (former) husband as
means of illustrating something she didn't want to come

right out and say.

"You never remarried?" Michael was having fun. "A beautiful woman like you?"

"Ach," Mrs. Rubinstein nudged him. "such flattery. I'll tell you something, Michael. Maybe forty, fifty years ago, I'm not too bad. Some people thought I was pretty. But old age — you can have it." She was shaking her head again.

Jess broke in. The caricature was getting on her nerves, and this promised to be a useless visit in any event. "Mrs. Rubinstein, we don't want to keep you."

"Keep me? Keep me form what?"

Jess forbore to mention what. "Do you remember a young boy who used to, uh, work outside?"

"Young boy? Working at what?" The pink skin and bright eyes flushed with innocence.

"Working the street. A Mexican child, Miguel."

"Such things." More shakes of the head.

"Do you remember him?" Jess smiled sweetly.

"Me? No, I wouldn't know such a boy." Mrs. Rubinstein's expression didn't falter, but she stared directly into Jess's eyes.

"I see." Jess motioned to Michael that it was time to leave. "I don't suppose the police came around to ask the same question?"

"The police? The police are on the street all the time. All the time. It's the only way a merchant can service a day in such a sewer."

"Right," Jess said drily. "Thanks."

Michael was frowning as they hit the street again. "Jess, did you really think that old doll was going to know about a ten-year-old hooker?"

She snorted. "That old doll, sweetie, went on the streets herself at about Miguel's age."

"Your kidding."

"No. You want to know why she never remarried? Because she was so handy with a knife that most of the men she knew — and they were a tough lot themselves — were afraid of her. Aside from the fact that she was in the pen half the time."

He found it hard to swallow, but he tried. "How did you meet her?"

"Someone too young to remember Ma Rubinstein tried to hold her up."

"Yes?"

"I was a new investigator at the time, so I got to come deal with the remains." Jess grinned a him and hooked her arm into his. "I kind of liked her, no matter what I knew. So whenever I had a Hollywood case, which used to be pretty damn often, I'd visit."

He was still shading his head as they entered a narrow diner. Jess led them to the stools at the counter and ordered two coffees. A tired man with a long beard and a shining scalp brought over mugs of something hot.

"Thanks." Jess pretended to take a sip. "Uh, you know where I can find Pete?"

"Pete who?" The man didn't look at her.

"Just Pete?"

"Never heard of him."

"Well, if your memory gets better, Jess is looking for him."

He shrugged and crossed to the other side of the diner.

Michael looked inquiringly at Jess. "Who's Pete?"

She lowered her voice. "What we politely term a manager of women."

"Christ, how do you know him?" Michael had heard a lot of Jess's stories. They sounded intriguing from the sanity of Malibu, but it was another thing entirely to see her working in these circles.

"The Garter-Belt Killer got one of his girls." The killer had struck two years ago, strangling seven women in the cause of two months with garter belts in which he subsequently dressed the corpses. He'd never been found, but the murders had stopped, so he was now, presumably, the problem of God, or of another city's authorities.

Jess and Michael waited half hour while a few people came and went, mainly teenagers looking for something to do and quickly deciding that they wouldn't find it here. One old crone sat down briefly beside Michael to ask for a glass of water, and being denied it, offered the counterman a singularly inventive string of suggestions.

Michael watched her leave, then leaned toward Jess. "I wouldn't have suspected her of having any interest in water."

"She did have a certain aroma," Jess agreed. She stiffened slightly as the door opened again and a tiny bland man in a white silk suit strutted in.

"Pete?" Michael asked.

Jess nodded.

The newcomer sat at the other end of the counter and ordered tea.

Jess sighed. "Dammit. Another runaround."

"How can you tell?"

"Watch — "

The diner was silent for the few minutes it took Pete to get his tea and drink it. He threw a dollar bill to the bearded man and got off the stool, straightening his tie. He threw a glance in Jess's direction, then a second at Michael.

"He's my husband," she said pleasantly. "How're you doing?"

"Not bad. How about you?"

"Not good."

He nodded. He'd heard. He casually ambled over and looked at Jess's stomach. "Congratulations."

"Thanks. Are you going to be able to help me at all?"

Pete delicately raised an eyebrow.

"How about at least telling me who put the lid on?"

The other eyebrow joined the first.

"Like that, huh?" She sighed. "Do you think it's worth my to try around?"

"I can't say how you should spend your time. Me, I'd go to a movie if I wasn't busy. The new Clint Eastwood's supposed to be great." He nodded at them and walked away.

"Somebody's warned everyone not to talk to you?"

Michael was incredulous. "A whole community can be shut up? Just like that?"

"Just like that."

"Just like what?"

Jess jumped and turned. Francis was beside her, his hands busy with the wrapper of a cigar.

She stared at him thoughtfully for a moment, then gestured toward Michael. "You remember my husband?"

"Yeah, we met last year, right?"

Michael nodded. "At Judge Starlin's retirement party."

"Yeah, right." Francis took the stool on the other side of Jess. "Hell of a neighborhood for you two to be dining in."

Jess looked sourly at him.

"What'cha doing?" He didn't seem to notice the lack of camaraderie.

"We love the ambiance. Okay, Arnheim, was it you?"

"Was what me?"

"Who cut out everyone's tongues?" She amended her statement. "Except for the tongue of the guy who just called you."

He didn't answer, concentrating on lighting the cigar. It had a particular foul odor, the sort you could only buy for a dime a smoke.

Michael coughed and lit a cigarette in retaliation. Jess tried not to breathe.

"So," Francis drawled finally, "nobody give you the time of day, huh?"

"Nobody, and I bet you're real surprised. This town's protecting your buddy Garland like they were the post office hand he was the mail."

Francis looked off into space. The counterman mistook that for a call to service and shuffled over. Francis glared and the man retreated.

"I'm being setup," Jess said sharply, "and you know it."

"I warned you."

Michael was getting angry. He opened his mouth to say so and grudgingly closed it again when Jess looked over and shook her head.

Francis missed nothing, but he didn't seem uncomfortable about the effect he was having. "I told you to be reasonable, and now everything's gotten way out of hand. Christ, it's a goddamn mess!"

"So I've noticed."

He fixed her with a glare. "One hell of a lot of things are happening and they're on my turf and I don't understand them. That makes me very unhappy."

Jess didn't respond.

"It's time for you to tell me what's going on."

She stayed mute. She couldn't afford to answer questions; she needed to ask them.

"Okay." He tried it another way. "What do you *think* is going on?"

She shrugged.

He looked at her with a hard expression. "You're your own worst enemy. Christ, you don't even know how to recognize your friends."

"Like who? Like you?"

"Maybe." He drew deeply off the cigar. "You can't expect anyone to come right out in the open and join your team. Nobody sane is going to do that. But nobody can help you if you keep everything a deep, dark secret."

On the other hand, it was when she'd been garrulous that she'd gotten hurt. "Nice of you to care, Francis."

"I'm just sentimental, I guess."

Jess looked steadily at him. "I guess." She slid off her stool.

Francis sighed. "You're going home, I hope?"

"See you."

Michael took Jess's arm and they walked outside. He maintained a show of unity until they were halfway down the block. "Francis made some kind of sense, you know."

"Michael, you agreed we have to protect ourselves."

"Yeah," he muttered. "That's the kind of guy I am. A damn fool."

Martin was sitting in his living room, happily immersed in financial statements, when Jess and Michael walked in. He looked up and grinned. "Hi, kids."

They nodded glumly and sat.

"Aha." He pushed away his work. "I'm no genius, but I get the feeling you two aren't in a real good mood."

Jess sighed and tried to find a position that would comfortably support the unwieldy stomach. "In the past week, I've been threatened, followed, scared, and suspended. My house has been searched and wrecked. I no sooner appear in an office than the entire staff quits. Evidence evaporates the moment I express an interest in it. My political career is in tatters. Call me a fool, but I'm depressed about it."

Martin looked as if he could easily call her a fool. "And you persist in playing superwoman. I've told you to act like a normal person — stop messing around and talk to the cops about it."

"I talk to the cops more than I talk to Michael," she said bitterly. "We talk constantly. I say something, and then they say I'm wrong. We have a lot of fun."

He searched for words that were both explicit and tactful. Finally, he accepted the fact that they were mutually exclusive. "You're asking for it. How can you expect anyone to listen? You're sure the whole world's wrong, but you don't have a single theory of what's right."

"I do too." She hoped he wouldn't try to force valium down her throat when he heard her idea. "This mess has something to do with Thalen Satellite and — uh — radar."

"Yes. People are getting sick, horribly sick, Martin. Birth defects and cancer and eye diseases, and somehow, radar's causing it."

"Um."

"There's worse to come." Michael joined the

conversation.

Martin gulped. "I think I can take it."

"Jess thinks Lorrie Berrington was on to the same thing."

"Lorrie Berrington's dead."

"Exactly," Jess agreed grimly. "A whole household wiped out by accidents in a single month. We ought to send it in to the *Guinness Book of World Records*."

Martin got up and poured himself a hefty shot of brandy. He took a look at Michael and poured another for him. "I'm just a simple-minded banker. I like the simple things in life. I especially like life. So if there's anything at all to this, let's not and way we did. That's my suggestion."

"Better than your suggestions," Jess interjected, "let's have your information. What did you dig up on A-COMM?"

"Ah. Well, it wasn't easy, but I turned out to be a detective *par excellence*, a veritable Sherlock Holmes, Hercules Poirot, Inspector French."

"You're going to be the late Inspector French in a moment," Michael warned.

"Okay, okay." Martin pulled a pad of paper out from under a pile of graphs. "I got an idea of what their plans are. Big. Really big. And it all started with Berrington. If it had been my project, I wouldn't have killed myself."

"Maybe Berrington didn't' either. Go on."

Martin winced. He really hated the implications. "The FCC regulations are changing — they're going to allow a lot more satellites up in space, and A-COMM has been licensed to take advantage of that."

"What did it cost A-COMM in bribes?" Michael asked sourly.

Michael sniffed. He'd have expected no less from the low form of life called "politician".

"Go on," Jess urged, taking Michael's hand.

"Well, the consortium is going to own a lot of satellites, out that means they'll own a lot of transponders."

"Channels," Jess explained smugly to Michael.

Martin nodded. "They're also doing the programming — some of it's entertainment, but the big stuff is communications."

"Like telephone lines?" Michael ventured.

"Bigger. Picture and sound. They call that videotext. But the most important development, the real money down the road, is going to come form DBS: direct broadcasting form the satellites to dishes. People are going to want their very own dishes — homes and businesses. It's going to be a huge industry, and whether controls the satellites will control it, too. Think of it!" Martin was beaming, his banker's heart swelling at the thought of all that cash in motion. "Thousands, hundreds of thousands of dishes everywhere! You'll be able to send your picture and any message at all to Botswana in microseconds!"

"Why would I want to send my picture to Botswana? Michael asked fretfully.

"So," Martin disregarded the Philistine, "imagine a consortium that builds all the hardware, puts up the satellites, controls the channels, and sells the services to the public!"

"I think we're imagining a very rich consortium," Jess said, her mind boggling.

"Like Croesus!"

"Like a second government. A monopoly. Swell." Michael was scowling.

"No, no," Martin insisted. "There'll be others in it, too. Westinghouse, RCA, loads of them. A-COMM won't have more than, oh, say, half the business. Max."

Jess and Michael looked at each other in shared distaste.

"Fabulous," Martin enthused, oblivious to their response. "A way to hook up every goddamn person in the world!"

"The world is full of people I have no desire to hook up to," Michael said firmly.

"I'm going to make tea," Martin said with a fatalistic sigh, while you two Neanderthals think about accepting the wheel."

They followed him into the kitchen and sat at the table. Martin filled three mugs with water and put them into the microwave oven.

Jess started to grin as he pushed a series on buttons on a panel complicated enough to mastermind a cruise missile. "You don't think a simple kettle on the stove would suffice, Martin?"

"Uh-huh. I'd have been able to wait the whole four minutes it use to take." She came over to watch the second coming and picked up a metallic box beside the oven. "What's this?"

"That? Oh, it tests leakage." Martin turned to the cupboard. "You want Irish breakfast or mint, Jess?"

She didn't answer. She turned the gadget over and over in her hands, staring at it in dawning horror.

"Jess?" Michael was watching her. "What is it?"

"My God!" It's been in front of us the whole time! I'm a moron, a bonafide moron!"

The two men gaped.

Jess backed away form the oven, looking at it as if she expected an attach any moment.

"What is it?" Michael repeated.

"Don't you see?" She held up the box. "This little darling tests for leakage. From the microwave oven!"

The men nodded, no further enlightened.

"You wouldn't bother testing for leakage if it didn't matter." Her voice was rising. "If microwaves weren't dangerous!"

"Michael came over to put an arm around her. "I still don't — "

"Microwaves." She looked at Martin. "Is it off? The oven — is it off?" She was holding her stomach tightly.

"Yes. Uh-huh." He finally moved, taking the offending gadget out of her hands. "Earth calling Jessica. What planet are you on?"

She didn't hear him. "Is radar a kind of microwave?"

"Oh my God!" Michael suddenly grasped the whole

thing. "Yes, I think so."

"And satellites. Do they transmit my microwave?"

"I think so."

They stared at each other; Michael's arm tightened around her.

"That's what's making people sick," she said with a dry mouth. "Especially near radar bases — and Mount Wilson."

Michael nodded. "Where all those big dishes are."

"Yes, the receivers and transmitters. The beams must cut right through the nearby neighborhoods. Dr. Frechetti's clinic is just below Mount Wilson. That's why he sees so many cases!"

Martin was eyeing them as if they'd lost their minds, but he'd be gentle. "If it were true, it would be the story of the decade. It would be all over the front page."

"If people knew enough to put it together." Jess thought about Lorrie. "And how would they? I mean, right now, it's easy to hide. It only comes up near big installations. Military base. Communication centers. It's still only affecting a small number."

"But," Michael continued her train of thought, "when everyone gets a dish — "

"Or when lots more satellites start beaming down—"

"A lot more people are going to get irradiated." He swallowed and sat down heavily.

Martin shook his head. "I don't buy it. You're jumping to conclusions. Hell, you don't know anything about science — and this is far too big to be hidden."

"We have to talk to experts," Michael agreed.

"And it is big." Jess could barely think in terms of millions of dollars. Billions were simply beyond her grasp. "Big enough to be ruthless over."

"It's becoming the backbone of our society," Martin blurted. "Nobody — and I mean nobody — wants to hear this. Think about it. Nobody wants to know. Not the government or businesses," he added cynically, "ordinary people. We all want a hundred TV channels."

Jess closed her eyes. "Nobody wants to hear it, and I bet some of them would do something about a person who refuse to shut up."

Michael's mouth was set in a tight line. "Martin, let's see the list of A-COMM members."

His friend obligingly went into the living room and brought back his notes. "It's and international consortium. I got hold of what I could get from the public records, but it's not complete. I didn't have time to probe further."

"Two banks and Berrington, we already knew." Michael went down the list. "What's Frontier Communications?"

"A Defense Department organization."

"A front, you mean? A DOD front?"

Martin sighed. "Don't get carried away, Mike. The government does business through corporations, some as everyone."

Michael was unimpressed, but he didn't push it. "CW Company?"

"I'm not positive. I think it might be Cartwright Oil."

"Cozy little nest of vipers," Jess Muttered.

"And CYMA Cooperation?"

Martin shook his head. That's more complicated. It's a consortium itself — basically private investors, I'm told. It's next to impossible to get all their names, especially since a lot of them aren't American." He took a deep breath. "Are you two serious about this? You really think if it were true no one would have proved it already?"

"Maybe someone did." Jess's voice was low.

Chapter 15

Modesty's doorman remembered Jess. He smiled genteelly and called up. "She'd like to speak to Mrs. Canby."

Jess took the receiver. "Hi, Modesty. Got a minute?"

"I'm awful busy, Jess." The voice was subdued. "Sorry. Maybe another time, okay?"

"This won't take long. It's very important."

"Oh, I just can't. Really"

"Well, we can wait if you like."

"Oh, I just can't wait!"

Jess frowned. She didn't understand it, but she'd lucked onto a bargaining lever. "Sure, we can wait."

"Oh . . . well, just a minute." The phone was put down with a thud.

"What's the problem?" Michael asked.

"I don't know. Strange. She was so friendly before."

Modesty was back. "Okay, you can come up for a little while. But give me a minute, okay?"

"Sure."

The lobby was exactly what condominium decorators all over the world felt it should be. Heavy chandeliers, thick bland carpet, phony French-provincial furniture, and walls of dappled mirror. Jess turned away form the reflection. The combination of dappling, lighting, and a ripple in the glass made her look like an elephant with a skin disease. Especially next to long, lean Michael.

She stared out through the glass front doors. There wasn't much to see. Few cars, few pedestrians. The occasional Mexican maid sauntered by, returning from an evening off. It was, after all, Pasadena, and past ten o'clock.

"The elevator's here, Jess."

She didn't move immediately because her attention was caught by a man who came from around the side of the building. He hurried across the street, head down. It was dark, and she just caught a glimpse, but he looked familiar.

"Elevator," Michael prodded.

"What? Oh, sorry." She got in.

Modesty was waiting in the corridor again. This time, she was wearing a more sedate maternity gown, green and white stripes that were, unfortunately, horizontal. Her greeting was somewhat harried, almost edgy, but old habits die hard and she did take a moment to smile at Michael and bat her false eyelashes. It set up a gale-force wind.

"Come in."

Jess and Michael stepped inside and looked around the living room, Michael because it was an unexpected decor for Modesty, and Jess because it showed signs of being disassembled.

"You moving?" Jess asked.

"Uh-huh."

"To a yellow apartment?"

Modesty didn't return Jess's smile. "Oh, we'll see. Uh — what did you come for tonight?"

Jess didn't answer immediately. She was looking down the hall. The door to the bedroom was open and near it were two large suitcases.

"Modesty, when are you leaving?"

The other woman fidgeted. "Soon."

"Like tonight, maybe?"

"Yeah, I guess it's tonight."

"That's rather sudden, isn't it? I saw you the day before yesterday and you hadn't decided then."

"Yeah, well, I just decided. You know." Modesty's eyes were darting around, looking for an escape. "Uh, do you have questions or something?"

Michael was looking puzzled. He hadn't met Modesty before, but even he found her manner odd.

"I'm kind of busy." The panic was rising.

Jess crossed to her. "Modesty, what's wrong? We can help you if something's wrong."

"Nothing's wrong!" She shrank away, "Please, I gotta finish packing, so can we get this over with?"

Jess bit her tongue. Any more friendly concern and the woman would die of fright. "Okay. When did you

234

see Lorrie Berrington lat?"

Uh, jeez, I don't know. A long time ago."

"Did you see her about the time of her accident?"

"Uh-uh. She wasn't talking to her dad." Modesty's hand went to her mouth.

"Why not? I know they were having arguments, but I didn't know they weren't talking at all."

"Oh, like, maybe I'm wrong." She was the world's worst liar. "I often get things wrong."

"What did Robert tell you it was about?"

"I don't know; I can't remember." Modesty ran her hands across her stomach. "Uh, I got to pack now."

"Just another question or two," Jess said soothingly. "Was Robert upset about the fight?"

"Well, uh, when?"

Jess frowned. Modesty hadn't understood the question.

"Let's start with before Lorrie's death." Michael came closer to Modesty and smiled encouragingly. "Was he upset then?"

"Well, yeah, a bit. Sure. He thought she was, you know, a bit crazy."

"And after the death?" He smiled to show her she was doing well.

"A lot more," Modesty answered with a trace of her old flirtatiousness. "Yeah, he went wild afterwards."

"I guess it was guilt and so on? His daughter dying when they hadn't talked to each other for — what was it? Days? Weeks? Months?"

"Weeks. A couple of weeks," she nodded. "He was real guilty."

"What else was bothering him, you figure?"

"Well, maybe her nutty ideas were right, you know. Oh!" She paled and skittered further away. She was saying things she didn't mean to say. "Look, you gotta go. I gotta — "

"Pack," Jess finished for her. "Yes, fine. Just one more question, Modesty. Robert was worried about your health, wasn't he?"

"Uh, sure." She gestured to indicate her pregnancy.

"Of course. Michael worries about me, too." Jess smiled casually. "Men don't really understand pregnancy, do they?"

"I guess not." Modesty suddenly giggled. "They know how to get you there, though."

Jess laughed. "That's for sure. So Robert made you go to the country." She tried to put all the loathing into that word that Modesty had used in their last chat.

"Yeah."

"His concern for you was related to his guilt about Lorrie, wasn't it?"

Pay dirt. Modesty's high color ebbed away, and she flinched as if Jess had hit her. "You gotta go now." This time, she meant it. She crossed to the door, opened it, and stood there, an unusually determined expression on her face.

"Lorrie got him worried about you, didn't she?"

"Go on, now." The pitch was rising. "If you don't go, I'm gonna call the doorman."

Michael took Jess's hand. "Okay, Modesty, we're on our way."

Jess stopped inside the doorway. "Wasn't it because of the 'death rays'? Wasn't that why you had to leave the city?"

The three of them were frozen for a moment. Then Modesty sobbed and shoved Jess out. The door slammed shut, echoing down the posh corridor.

Michael was staring at Jess, his eyebrows at the hairline. "Death rays? Did you say death rays?"

She was furious with herself. "Yes, that's what I said. It's what Modesty called them when I was here last. But bright, rational Jessica — did I listen? Oh, no, not me. I looked at the blonde hair and fake lashes and figured she wasn't dealing with a full deck."

"Look, love, at least three-quarters of the population would have figured the same thing. I mean — death rays?"

"You sound like Martin. He think's I'm not dealing with a full deck."

Michael sighed. "Well, I'm with you, but there are

moments when I wonder about us, too."

They turned toward the elevator.

"Jesus!" She'd stopped abruptly again. "I know who that was!"

"Who was?"

"The man on the street."

Michael shook his head.

"There was a man hurrying away form the building when we were waiting downstairs. I knew he looked familiar."

"Are you going to tell me, or am I supposed to guess?"

It was Desmond Marchenko. Stephen Bowdritch's main ass-kiss."

" 'Toady' would be a more ladylike way of putting it." He pretended to be amused, but his hand tightened around hers.

"Where to now?" Michael turned the ignition key. "I suppose it's mad to suggest home?"

"I wish." She looked at her watch. "Dr. Frechetti's waiting for us at his clinic."

"Why would he talk to us? Nobody else will."

"Uh, he'll talk." She decided against burdening him with the sordid details of why she knew he would.

Washington Boulevard was alive with families unable to bear their stifling slum apartments. The air was as hot and as foul as it had been in the daytime; the darkness did no more than give the illusion of relief.

Michael parked a block past the clinic, and they waked back slowly, Jess edgily glancing around in case someone was in their tail. Nobody stood out more than they did — theirs were the palest faces on the street. At each corner, a knot of teenaged boys, black or brown, but never the two together — lounged arrogantly, flicking cigarette butts to the ground and making lewd suggestions to passing women and nervous old couples. But compared to Hollywood, it was a pastoral neighborly scene.

The clinic lights were on, but no one answered the bell. Michael tried the door and found it open.

"I wouldn't leave a place like this unlocked at night," he observed drily. "There might be a couple of people hereabouts with more than a passing interest in the drug cabinet."

"No more than a couple of thousand." Jess was frowning as they walked inside. "Dr. Frechetti!"

The name hung in the air. It died away into nothingness. They looked at each other. Jess took another step forward, then froze. There'd been a distinct sound in the back of the building, a rustle as if something had brushed against a wall.

Something. Or someone?

Michael heard it too. "Dr. Frechetti?"

Silence. They glanced nervously at each other. Michael tilted his head with a questioning look. Jess shook her head sharply. She wasn't leaning without him. If either of them was going to stay and explore, both were. It took Michael another moment to agree. He crept forward, and Jess followed, almost on his heels.

The long corridor was dark. Michael came to it's end and pushed open the door to Frechetti's consulting office. He drew in a sharp breath. Jess was quieter, staring grimly at the body sprawling across the desk. Alive, Frechetti had been pale. Dead, he was a desiccated mummy, a sack of parchment skin and narrow bones.

"Jesus." Michael's Adam's apple was bobbing. "Is he — ?"

"Yes." She was beside the corpse, forcing herself to poke and probe with professional detachment. She couldn't begin to count the number of bodies she'd handled in eight years, but this was the first one she'd do recently talked to. Everyone said that experience with death mattered little when you know the deceased — and Jess was now realizing that everyone was right.

Michael stayed well back, trying not to watch the indignities but unable to keep his eyes form straying to center stage.

Jess turned around when the examination had told her what she'd wanted to know. Except she'd been hoping for different answers. "Michael," she whispered, "He's been dead only minutes. He's still warm."

"How . . . ?"

"She." She moved closer and kept her voice down. "His neck is broken."

"There aren't any stairs," he muttered grimly.

"No, he didn't fall downstairs." She tried to keep form quavering. "Someone crushed his neck. It's hard to be sure without more time, but I think it was done with bare hands."

"Jesus." Michael winced at the image, then remembered her earlier words. "You said a few minutes?"

She nodded unhappily. A few minutes, or even less.

"The rustle we heard — "

"Yes." It was the palest hint of a whisper. "The killer mightn't be far away."

They were rooted to their spots as if the office was a magic island of safety.

Michael finally broke out of the spell. He grabbed Jess's hand and motioned toward the dark corridor. They quietly, slowly, tiptoed toward it. Nothing moved in the shadows; no sounds except their shallow breathing disturbed the heavy air. The lamp of the waiting room sent a puddle of faint light toward them; it was a beacon of safety. They were almost there.

"The cops," Michael breathed into her ear. "Should we call them?"

"We don't have to." She had stiffened, stopped, then pulled Michael backwards with her. A red light had flickered at the corner of her peripheral vision. She leaned forward more carefully, peering around the door jamb. Three patrol cars were just arriving, roof lights twisting and flashing.

Michael took a step forward.

"No!" she hissed. "Come on, the back door!"

"But — "

She was already moving, clumsy because of her size. Michael caught up with her in two strides and they reached the back door together. It was a flimsy wooden slab with no door knob and a loosely hanging, unlocked padlock. They looked at each other with foreboding. There was no way of knowing what waited on the other side.

The police were coming in the front. Jess shoved the door open and strained into the darkness. She couldn't see a thing. The noises from the newcomers were getting closer. She took the stairs without another thought. Michael was right behind her and behind him the door was closed again.

They were alone in a narrow alley used for parking and, apparently, garbage. She smell was strong.

"That's Frechetti's." Jess pointed to the only car behind the building, the dated Volvo. There would have been room for another car to park beside it, a narrow fit for a big car. A van, for example.

"Let's get moving." They ran down the alley, and emerged at the next cross street, only a block form the Skylark.

Michael's hands were tight on the steering wheel; his jaw was clenched even tighter. "I don't get it."

"Join the club."

"I don't get why we had to run away. Look, it's been a hell of a week. You've been threatened and suspended. I've lost a movie . We drive all over hell's half-acre, only to find that on one we visit wants to talk to us. And then we find ourselves a dead man. Okay, I'm a reasonable person. I can accept all of that." He looked at her. "But why do we then have to play Bonnie and Clyde?"

"We couldn't have stuck around. Think about it."

He did and apparently found little solace in it.

"Michael, someone called the cops. They were there too damn fast. And it wasn't a good citizen, because North Pasadena isn't noted for civic responsibility."

"You think we were set up?"

She didn't answer.

"That's what you think?"

"I think it's a real possibility."

"But how would they know — ?" He answered his

own question, eyes suddenly on the rear-view mirror. "You've been followed."

Jess nodded shortly, her own gaze glued to the traffic, her back stiff, as if unseen eyes were piercing it. She tried to blot out the thought that she'd killed Frechetti as surely as if she'd strangled him herself. "I should have realized before I traipsed up to Frechetti's house. "Oh, God — what's going to happen to Toom now?" she said quietly.

"What's going to happen to us?" He gently touched Jess's stomach. "You're in no shape to become an outlaw — or a private eye. We have to go to the cops."

"You're assuming the policeman is your pal." Her tone was bitter. "I used to assume it too, but right now, I wouldn't trust them with the time of day."

"I'm the one who goes for conspiracy theories," Michael pointed out. "You believe in the established order."

"It stopped believing in me." She stared tensely out the window. They were driving down the Pasadena Freeway and there wasn't anything to see except the headlights of other cars and dark hills pressing in on either side. In the daytime, it was green lush, and serene. At night, the road felt like a narrow, menacing tunnel.

"So you don't want to go to the authorities." He was repeating to get it absolutely straight. "You want us to take on the financial community, the Defense Department, and the police force — all on our own?"

She winced. "I don't want to take on any of them. But who can we go to now? Who'd believe us? Even Martin thinks we've got a screw loose. And . . . well, do you want Bowditch and his partners to know what we're thinking?"

"Not if what we're thinking is right," Michael said with considerable feeling. "I could do without the attention."

She shivered, her eyes going back to the road. It was a nightmare.

"If we're right," he added in low voice, "I wish we

were someplace else. Another continent."

Jess fantasized a deserted Tahiti beach. Nobody watching, nobody behind them. Just her, Michael, the baby, and the sun. She reluctantly pushed the picture away. She couldn't afford even to dream about running away. It would mean giving up everything, everything she'd ever worked for — the job, her ambitions, politics. It would all evaporate with her good name. Her father's name. She had to fight back. "Oh, God, I wish I could turn back the clock! I'd close the Berrington file so fast, the papers would vaporize!"

Michael didn't say anything. She bit her lip and shut. They were passing the downtown thicket now; the offices were black, high shells, and the streets were still. The only life in the landscape was on the highway, endless lines of metal boxes pushing forward in their individual discrete pools of hard white light. And every one of them potentially malevolent.

Chapter 16

It was the kind of morning that made a surfer believe in God. The sky was as pure a blue as the spectrum permitted, and even this early the sand was warm and glinting with sunlight. The waves were another blue, edged with white fingers that playfully stretched up in the air and then delicately stroked the beach. Surfriders Beach was jammed by eight, and the water was dotted with boards and blonds. Jess and Michael watched from their deck, breakfasting in silence. By mutual unspoken agreement, they were avoiding the topics that made their stomachs hurt, and no other topics presented themselves.

When they went out and got into the car, Jess took the driver's seat. Michael had done more than his fair share of driving yesterday, and the more sight of the car keys made him greenish.

They swung out onto the coast highway and headed south. The traffic was already backed up coming into Malibu. It was clear sailing going out. Naturally. On a flawless Saturday, eleven million Los Angelenos wished they were at the beach, and a goodly number of them were willing to fight a couple of hours of hideous traffic to get there. Only a fool would head in the opposite direction.

Jess sighed, and swerved to avoid a tourist who'd stopped abruptly in front of her. He was staring toward a particularly nubile sunbather on the beach; his jaw had dropped onto the brake pedal. Summer driving in Malibu was hazardous to one's health. It was almost as bad as winter driving, when the cliffs slid down and the roads washed out. Malibu wasn't the ideal location for someone who couldn't stay home and clip bond coupons. "If we're going to spend all our time on the road, maybe we should sell the house and buy a camper."

Michael had noticed the sunbather too. His excuse was that he wasn't at the wheel. "Mmmm?" He turned back to Jess. "We might have to. There's not a whole lot of cash flowing in these days."

"We've got money in the bank."

"Sure." He did a little mental computing and grinned. "But it's not going to last till the kid goes to college. It'll run out, oh, say, middle of next month."

"Maybe even before then if we deep on giving large hunks of it to the oil companies." She turned into a gas station.

The smog was settling comfortably into its usual niche by the time they arrived in the city. Jess dropped Michael off at the library and inched through Chinatown's visible soot to the coroner's complex.

Harper's spot was, luckily, empty. Jess descended to her office with a fair degree of confidence that no one would throw her out. Nobody did, but the word had obviously spread. Even the genial security men looked embarrassed to see her.

Several of the staff were chatting in the basement corridor. Silence fell when Jess stepped off the elevator.

"Hi, folks." She grinned as if it were a normal day.

Nods were uncertain. Feet shuffled. Eyes found something fascinating about the floor or ceiling. Only Consuela stepped forward. "How are you doing, Jess?"

She smiled and lied. "Just fine. Everything's going to be fine." Her Pollyanna routine was fairly nauseating, but the truth would be even worse.

Consuela pretended to believe it. No one else did.

I'll be coming back one fair day. Soon," Jess said cheerfully. "I'd hate to find out that you were all way behind. So let's get back to work, okay?"

They fled, relieved. Only Consuela held back a moment. "Joe's in this morning. You want to see him?"

Jess shook her head. "Maybe later. I've got a lot of paperwork to clear up." She rounded the corner, opened the door to her office and stared. It had never been well-organized, but this was a disaster zone. It looked as if a kindergarten of vicious four-year-olds had been let loose; the floor was buried in paper, but the desk top was clean. She absently noted that the desk was oak veneer; she hadn't seen it in so long, she'd forgotten.

Consuela was still behind her. She gasped. "Oh, my! What in heaven's name — "

Jess shrugged helplessly. "Ask around and see if anyone unusual come in during the night."

"I'll ask." Consuela shook her head dubiously. "But you know this place. People get busy — they leave security to the security guys. They don't ask what anyone else is doing."

"Give it a shot anyway."

Consuela took a last glance into the room. "You're not even going to be able to tell what's missing."

Jess sighed and closed the door. She looked around sadly. It would take an army of fanatic Dutch housewives to bring order to the room. That or a fire.

To hell with tidiness. She sat behind the desk, ignoring the fact that her feet were resting on the "In" tray, and called the Santa Barbara information operator. Derry Hooper was listed; in fact, three D. Hoopers had telephones. She got the one she wanted on the third try.

"Who?" The stockbroker sounded groggy. Jess had woken him up.

"Jess Canby. I was in your office last week, seeing Frank Cavenaugh about Berrington Industries. I was thinking of buying some stock — you filled me in on the communications industry."

"Oh. Yes. You." He remembered now. The madwoman who'd flipped her wig over the "Thalen."

"I'm sorry to bother you on a Saturday, but I have another couple of questions." Madwomen didn't keep to business hours. "I could drive in to see you, or we could talk on the telephone — "

As she'd gambled, he was willing to tell her anything — if it would forestall a personal visit.

"There are two companies I'd like to know about. CW Company and CYMA Corporation. Have you heard of them?"

"The names are familiar."

"I believe they're partners in the A-COMM venture with Berrington Industries."

"Oh, right. Yes, of course. CW is Cartwright Oil. A holding company."

She wasn't surprised. It confirmed what Martin had thought, and it proved her pet theory, namely that there were really only fourteen people in Southern California and they got around a lot. "What about CYMA?"

"Let me think." His voice wa losing the edge of wariness; this was fascinating stuff, the minutiae of his specialty. "Oh, yes. CYMA's a mixture of corporate and private money. I don't know much about the private people. It's kept fairly quiet, but I believe some of them are South American."

"Paraguayan, by any chance?"

He was taken aback. "It's possible. If so, it would be hard to find out. They tend to be . . . uh . . . secretive about where their money goes."

Or where it came from. "Uh-huh. What about the corporate interests?"

"The founding partner is Tronics, International. An electronics firm that's grown spectacularly in a decade. It's diversified into all sorts of things — movies, video equipment, satellite hardware."

"Is it Californian?"

"Oh, yes. It's the parent company of Cyril Haberman's empire — "

She interrupted him with a bellow. "Cyril Haberman!"

Derry coughed nervously. The madwoman was doing it again. "I must run now. Really." He hung up, presumably to immediately arrange an unlisted phone.

Hot damn! Jess paced, oblivious to the scrunching paper underfoot. Haberman.

"Hi." The door opened and Joe Miller poked his head in. "Jesus!"

"Yeah."

They looked at the devastation for a moment.

"Jess, Consuela asked around. Nobody noticed a thing." Joe shook his head. "I wasn't comfortable — using your office. I'm sorry. If I'd been here, it mightn't have happened."

"Joe, I know you're a glutton for blame, even you really can't shoulder this responsibility." Jess grinned to cheer him up. "Anyway, it was done in vain. I don't even know what's going on — let alone being able to prove it. There wasn't anything here that could interest anyone but a paper recycler."

"That's something, I guess."

Jess noticed Joe's clipboard. "Is that last night's sheets?"

"Uh-huh." He handed it over.

She slid her eyes over all the pages, but the only one she really read was the case report on Frechetti. He'd been brought in at 2:00 a.m.; the investigator placed his time of death at around eleven to eleven-thirty. Good guess. Jess and Michael had found him at eleven-twenty, and he'd been alive until eleven-fifteen at least. She skimmed the rest of the details. Pasadena's detectives assumed it was the word of a druggie looking for a free needle. Nobody was yet asking themselves what kind of druggie could strangle someone with bare hands. Thus far, there were no clues to identify the killer — though the police said that the body had been searched, probably after the murder. And there were indications that someone had been there just before the cops got to the scene. Jess hoped that her flinch wasn't obvious to Joe; she handed him back the clipboard.

The City Library was a landmark of 1925 Los Angeles, a tiered, white stone building topped by a colorful tiled peak. The architect had had some difficulty choosing between Byzantine, Egyptian, and Roman designs, so he'd just used them all, on the Hollywood principle that more is better.

Michael was on the second floor at the card catalogue, dwarfed by the soaring domed ceiling which was embellished with frescoes and supported a massive chandelier in the form of a globe surrounded by signs of the zodiac. He was deeply immersed in his research and didn't look up until Jess tickled his neck.

"Hi sweetie." He kissed her. "How was the office?"

She grimaced. "The wreckers were back. They

trashed my office this time. But they couldn't have found anything; I don't have anything. Except I just learned that A-COMM's a real family affair. The Cartwrights are in on it — and so is your pal Haberman."

He whistled softly. "It's coming together, isn't it?"

She shrugged. Is it? What have you found out?"

They were speaking quietly, but apparently not quietly enough to suit a librarian. A middle-aged man with a big stomach and thin lips was frowning at them.

Michael picked up his papers, and they left the building. Fifth Street was almost empty of traffic, but there were other pedestrians, all Oriental: industrious students intent on closeting themselves in the library; phalanxes of Japanese tourists, now dressed in sued jackets and lizard-skin boots but still laden with expensive cameras, and Chinatown families out for a stroll in the sunshine.

It was hot, and at ground leave, it was possible to pretend there was no smog. Michael turned his face to the sun and wistfully wished they were back home on the beach.

"What about your research?" Jess wasn't as wistful, because it was no fun to sun a bulbous body.

"We're onto something, all right. And it's grim."

"How grim?"

He sighed and started down the hill toward Pershing Square. "I've only been reading for a couple of hours, but I'm convinced that microwaves aren't good for living things."

Jess had to hurry to keep up with his long strides. "So it's not a secret?"

"Not in some circles. There's been a lot of talk — and there's evidence that's damn disturbing."

"That doesn't make sense. If it's out in the open, why bother trying to cover it up?"

He shook his head. "It's not exactly out in the open. So far, it's just talk. No proof. And believe me, you'd need to have proof to get anything done. There's a lot at stake. They started with radar during the war, and the military just fell in love with it. They've found dozens of uses for it — tracking and scanning devices, electronic eavesdropping, guidance systems, jamming equipment. The mere idea of objecting to radar makes the Pentagon break out in a cold sweat. And shielding the equipment would cost a bundle — not to mention the price tag on the lawsuits they'd be hit with if they ever had to acknowledge the danger."

They stopped at the small park in front of the Biltmore Hotel. Pershing Square was a tiny plot of grass that only looked solid; in fact, it was the roof of an underground garage. The buildings that formed the four sides of the square kept it in shadow for much of the day, but right now it was shining and cheerful, which was a sharp contrast to the people using it: skid row residents with crumpled brown paper bags of cheap booze, pasty youngsters probably looking for a fix, elderly indigent's reading newspapers someone else had left behind.

"Radar's one thing." Jess sat on an empty bench, barely noticing the empty beer bottles piled underneath. "We need radar, I guess, and it doesn't blanket the cities. It's the civilian satellites that make me nervous."

"So they should. They're proliferating like mice."

"It gives guys like Bowdritch something in common with the military. They'd all want to keep the lid on the problem" Bowdritch and the Cartwrights and Haberman all in bed with the service. Plus, a bunch of anonymous Paraguayans. Even if it were a king-sized mattress, it must be getting crowded."

"And it is a problem." Michael pulled out his notes and sat beside her. "There are dozens of examples that scare the hell out of me. There's a school back East, for instance, on a hill in the path of microwave-generating equipment. A bunch of the kids got cancer. Three out of eight men working on a radar project developed cancer. Another group got brain tumors and coronaries. Air-traffic controllers get hideous cataracts on the rear wall of their eyes. People living near radar bases complain a lot about nausea, headaches, behavior changes."

"And worse." Jess wa thinking about Betty Drummond.

"And worse," he agreed. "There're problems with babies — a high fetal death rate, miscarriages, sterility. And get this. More female babies are born than male."

She frowned. "It's usually the other way around."

"Normally, yes. But not if the fathers have been exposed to microwaves. Presumably, it affects their sperm."

"In more ways than one."

"Betty Drummond was right. "There are too many birth defects near radar bases for it to be pure coincidence. Take military helicopter pilots. They navigate by flying along microwave beams, and their kids have a lot of problems — clubfeet, cleft palates, heart and circulatory defects."

She shuddered and looked up as if she could see the satellites. How many beams were passing through Pershing Square at this very moment? "Michael, is all this documented?"

"The sicknesses are." The exposure to microwaves is. But the cause and effect is still being debated." He paused as a young girl in torn jeans and bare feet came up to ask for a cigarette. "Sure." He even lit it for her.

She padded off apparently without considering the idea of saying thanks. She rejoined a nervous boy with sunken eyes and twitching limbs. Neither could have been much older than fourteen.

Jess sighed, then wondered if that meant she was hopelessly middle-aged and middle class. How much evidence do they need before they notice there's a problem here?"

"A lot. The authorities are stonewalling it."

"How can they? In the face of this?" She grabbed his notes and waved them angrily.

"Look, I agree with you. But they say — and they've got experts in their team — that there are other environmental factors that cause illness." He wrinkled his nose. "Like what we're breathing, for example."

She sniffed experimentally. It was pretty foul. "Have there been studies of microwaves' effects?"

"Sure. The big ones so far all agree that there's no cause for concern." He smiled sardonically. "Of course, they were all funded by the military."

"Swell."

"Uh-huh. And there's not much scope for independent work. Scientists depend on government contracts. Universities depend on government grants and contracts. Besides, satellites are new. The population you'd want to study is the one around radar bases, but when independent scientists suggest it, the military shakes it's head and mutters about national security."

"There probably would be." Michael looked glum. "Because the little private research there is, is depressing. The list of what microwaves are associated with is longer than my arm. Memory impairment. Serious behavioral changes. Altered blood chemistry. Chromosomal breaks. Heart and central-nervous-system defects. One guy even said he could stop a heart using microwaves."

"Jesus"!"

"And the really sick part about it," Michael added, "is that the Eastern block countries and the USSR have been studying it for years, and their experts are positive that even low doses of microwaves cause all these symptoms."

Jess raised her eyebrow. "Well, then — "

"Our government says that's commie opinion. Red research. Not reliable."

"Last I heard," she said drily, "Communists had the same physiology as us good Americans."

"Apparently not."

Frustration drove her to pace. "What about the EPA? What about crusading environmentalists? Where are all those people who get so upset about clubbing baby seals?"

Michael shrugged. "Probably watching cable TV. Listen, no one is going to listen to the doom-sayers without proof. Incontrovertible proof. Everyone prefers to listen to the optimists — among whom, by the way, is one of your favorite doctors."

"Merton?"

"Yup. Dr. Edward Sanford Merton. He's here, there, everywhere. Giving interviews. Testifying at hearings. Talking to the White House. Assuring everyone that microwaves are dandy and shaking his head over the lunatics who think that the threat of genetic damage might be too high a price to pay for all-night TV."

"It can't work forever," Jess pointed out with foreboding.

Michael was silent.

"Millions of people will be exposed to large amounts of radar. It'll blow wide open, sooner or later."

"Too much later. The damage will be done, and the industry will be in place. Nobody in America has ever had to dismantle a million-buck business. They'll just slap a few Band-Aids and tell us that progress always has a price."

Jess sat down within the comfort of Michael's arm around her. She was suddenly cold, and there wasn't the hint of a breeze to account for it. "Michael, if nobody believes the evidence or the scientists, why would anyone believe us?"

"I don't know," he admitted, "but someone apparently thinks that we pose a threat."

She drew even closer. "I hate that thought."

"It would be nice," he said grimly, "to justify his faith in us."

They were tired of tension, so they avoided talking in the car and concentrated instead on the scenery. Once they'd left the city behind and were climbing the bluffs of the Palos Verdes peninsula, there was a lot to concentrate on. Above was a cloudless sky, below the glinting ocean and clear horizon. In between were the thick pines and immaculate grounds of the community: woodsy, wealthy, Republican all the way. Just to the north lay the swinging singles' beaches, Manhattan and

Redondo, where a major disaster could wipe out, at one stroke, the entire stewardess staff of most of the world's airlines. Inside Palos Verdes, however, sweater sets, hair sprays, and conservatism prevailed. Aerospace executives were as thick on the ground as station wagons. It was a strange location for the Association of Victims of Electronic Pollution.

The organization was run out of the founder's home, a sprawling bungalow that looked to be the result of crossing a Spanish hacienda with a cattleman's homestead.

"Nice view. Nice garden. Nice house," Jess approved. "But it's hard to imagine we're going to find and anti-establishment voice here."

Michael shrugged. "She sounded fairly cranky in the newspaper interview I read."

Before Jess could ask for further enlightenment, an enormous woman waddled toward them from the side of the house. In any city, she would have been noticeable; in Los Angeles, where well-to-do matrons tended toward anorexia, her three chins and pendulous body were show-stoppers.

"Mr. Renfrew?"

"Yes." Michael got out of the car and extended a hand. "And this is my wife, Jessica Canby".

The woman nodded. She hadn't heard that fat people were supposed to be jolly. This one was all business. "I'm Clarissa Hopper. President of A.V.E.P. Follow me."

It was an order, and Jess and Michael fell into step without missing a beat. Clarissa had missed her calling; she should have been a general by now.

They went into the house and followed her into a glassed-in sunroom that overlooked ocean and green hillside. The furniture was comfortably upholstered white rattan, cheery and handsome; and not a piece of it looked strong enough to support their hostess.

Two other people stood waiting for them, smiling.

Clarissa motioned toward the man. "My husband, Howard."

Jess and Michael shook his hand. It was clear case of Jack Spratt and the missus. Howard was tiny, friendly, and about one hundred and fifteen pounds dripping wet.

"And this is Martha Fontaine. Jessica Canby and Michael Renfrew."

The third woman nodded tentatively. Everything about her was tentative — including her lease on life. She would never have been a big woman, but she looked now as if the bones in her body had simply collapsed. She wasn't well; the gaunt face and clouded eyes spoke volumes about pain and suffering.

"Let's sit."

All four of them immediately obeyed. Clarissa took a deep armchair that creaked ominously but didn't dare collapse. The conversation didn't begin immediately. Clarissa was running the show, and she was taking her time, looking Jess and Michael over with eyes that suggested she'd learned long ago that most people were going to prove disappointing and it didn't pay to expect otherwise. Eventually, she decided that the visuals weren't going to give her any more information. She spoke. "You're studying the effects of microwaves?"

Michael nodded. "I came across an interview you gave to the press — about a year ago."

Clarissa sniffed. "I wasted my breath. It had no results."

"Well, we agree with you. We think that microwaves are dangerous, but we're not experts. We need to talk to people who know what they're talking about."

Clarissa looked at Martha Fontaine, a stick figure perched at the very edge of the sofa. "We know what we're talking about."

Jess and Michael exchanged a glance. There was something in their hostess's voice that elude them.

"Can you prove the danger?" Jess decided that bluntness was the only conversational tactic that Clarissa would recognize.

"No." Flat. Equally blunt. "We know that

microwaves cause genetic damage, heart disease, cancer. For starters."

"But we can't prove it." Howard, unpredictably, felt no compunction about interrupting his strong-minded wife. "If by proof you mean something that will make the government take action. You see, there are two kinds of radiation, and you mustn't confuse them. X-rays, nuclear fallout, things like that are obviously dangerous, and we know it. We can prove it. But that's high-energy radiation, and it actually changes our cells."

Jess was about to interrupt; she'd had this lecture from David McPherson at the Department of Health Sciences, and she hadn't understood then. Michael, however, was leaning forward, rapt.

"What's the other kind?" he asked.

"Low-frequency. What we call 'non-ionizing'."

"Microwaves are low-frequency, right?"

"Right. Microwaves, radar, radio, and TV wave, power lines." Howard gestured vaguely at the world. "We're surrounded by it."

"What does it do to us?"

"That's the question. Enough of it will burn us."

Michael grasped that. "Like a microwave oven."

"Exactly. A heavy dose of microwaves cooks us from the inside out. Literally. Low-frequency radiation penetrates further into our bodies that high-frequency waves like X-rays. So the danger's greatest to our guts."

Jess was following it now. "But how do they explain away the symptoms that people get after they're exposed to low doses?"

"Any way at all." She looked severely at her husband. "They find all sorts of excuses."

He flushed and turned to Jess and Michael to explain. "I used to be in the aerospace industry. Hopper Aircraft. I sold out, but — "

"Well, I suppose you couldn't have known, in those days." Clarissa just wanted to remind him of his sins; she wasn't going to beet him bloody over them. "They blame air pollution, the pill, water, viruses we don't know about, smoking . . . " She shrugged. "They're all killers, too, of course."

"Of course." Michael agreed, hastily slipping his cigarette pack back into his pocket.

"My association has amassed hundreds of files on cases that should alarm the authorities." Clarissa was losing steam now in the recollection of all her failures. "No one listens. I can prove that young men have developed brain tumors and heart disease and cancers that are only normal for old men. There are children with blood disorders, changes in the white cell count and in the bone marrow. Leukemia. I have dozens of cases of eye problems — those are particularly well documented. I have the support of ophthalmologist, a few scientists. a lot of citizens." She paused; suddenly she looked smaller. "Nothing helps."

"You tried, Clarissa." Martha spoke for the first time, timidly, as it offering sympathy was a nerve-wracking action. "We all appreciate that."

"We" Jess caught Michael's eye; they were thinking the same thought.

Martha notice their response and nodded. "I suppose I'm on of the files Clarissa mentioned." She was weak and it hurt to talk, but she obviously wanted to. "I used to work for the State Department. I was a secretary for — oh, fifteen years, and I was posted all over . It was, " she smiled shyly, "awful exciting. I saw so many places — Teheran and London and Nairobi . . . and Moscow."

Clarissa was up, moving with sudden grace. She stood beside the other woman, a hand on her shoulder.

"It was in the sixties," Martha added.

"When we didn't believe that our government would stand for Americans being hurt," Clarissa interjected bitterly.

"So we didn't believe the rumors at first," Martha agreed sadly. "You see, the Soviet government was beaming microwaves at the US embassy in Moscow. The official explanation was that they were trying to jam our communications equipment, but apparently it was the wrong sort of beam — and our government knew that."

"The USSR has been studying microwaves," Michael said slowly.

"Oh, yes, I know that." Martha's nod was a little bit more vivacious than her voice. "They'd been finding that microwaves cause depression, headaches, erratic behavior . . . and worse. But we didn't know it — the staff, I mean."

"Then," Martha continued softly, "it was supposed to be over. But so many of us got sick that the story began to leak out and the government had to set up another study. This one wasn't secret — "

"But the results were never made public." Howard's eyes were glued sadly on Martha.

"Never," she echoed. "The official conclusion was that the microwaves hadn't caused any of the diseases."

"They said the water did."

"What?" Jess stared at Clarissa.

"Moscow water," she repeated with a disgusted air. "And stress. But not the microwaves."

"They had to say that," Howard explained, "because we allowed workers to be exposed to doses five hundred times stronger than the beams in Moscow." He expelled a long breath. "Our occupational standard is a thousand times greater than the USSR standard. A thousand times!"

Jess hated to ask the question, but she couldn't see any way around it. "What happened to the staff in Moscow?"

"Cancer." For the first time, Martha's voice held a tinge of bitterness. "Sixteen cases of breast cancer that I know about. I'm one of them."

Jess could feel Michael's tension. His mother had died of breast cancer, and he was a fanatic about it. He insisted the Jess check for lumps at least twice a month.

"And other kinds of cancer. And appendicitis. Bleeding eyes. Cataracts. Blood diseases. Three children had to go home with blood diseases."

The room was silent for a while, until the echo of the litany had died away.

"They covered it up, finally." Clarissa went back to her chair. "They put metal screens on the windows and gave everyone a twenty percent bonus, but — " she shrugged, — "they never admitted it was the microwaves."

"Metal screens. Danger pay. And they claimed there was no danger," Michael repeated.

"Did none of the scientists dispute the results?" Jess was willing to believe that you could co-opt a lot of people, but surely not everyone.

"It's not smart to dispute them." Clarissa wore a sour smile. "It's not healthy."

"They've killed people?" Both Jess and Michael were leaning forward now.

The other three looked aghast.

"No, of course not." Howard found his voice first. "But you'll lose your job — not to mention your government contracts and your position in the scientific world. If you go along — well, there're lots of rewards. Even the victims get paid off."

Martha flushed. "It's hard to fight them, Howard. With the doctor's bills and all."

"I didn't mean you, my dear." He was appalled at his tactlessness. "Of course I don't blame you. What was you choice? To go bankrupt? Nobody would listen to you anyway."

Clarissa nodded heavily. "We've been to all the environmental groups. Government and private. It's always the same story. No dice without proof. There's too much stacked up against us."

"How could we get proof?" Jess asked.

Everyone waited for the leader to answer, and Clarissa waited because she didn't have and answer. She was just beginning to accept that she'd failed, and that there wasn't a reprieve in sight.

Jess looked away. Whoever had figured that she and Michael might be a threat was wrong. The problem was hideous as she'd suspected, but the odds of doing something about it weren't just bad, they were nonexistent. "Well, thank you for your time." She got to her feet.

Michael stood up too, hesitating. "Is there anyone else who could help us?"

Clarissa shrugged. "You could talk to Dr. Liu Shi, if you really want to be depressed."

"Who's he?"

"A geneticist. He used to be on the staff at UCLA, but when his government and private research funds dried up, I think he quit."

"Where can we find him?"

"Van Nuys. At least, he lived there a year ago. He's kind of dropped out sight, so I don't know if he's still there."

Van Nuys was far enough away in miles; it was even farther in spirit. It was the Valley, and that was another world entirely. Los Angeles was more than a state of mind. It was at least three states of mind, defined mainly by the Santa Monica Mountains, which ran east from the ocean to bisect the city. There was what natives considered the real LA, the diverse towns between the range and the ocean. Then there were the canyon communities, in the hills themselves, hardy folk who apparently thought nothing of perching on skinny stilts over unstable earth. North of it all was the San Fernando Valley, the arid flatland trapped between the Santa Monicas and the desert mountains, one the Valley consisted of vast ranching spreads, now there were endless grids of dusty streets filled with greasy smog and populated by the infamous Valley girls.

The telephone directory said Dr. Liu Shi lived on the improbably named Vista Drive, in front of the stucco, three-story apartment building. Jess and Michael parked and walked inside to the central courtyard, a rectangle of drooping rubber trees surrounding a cracked cement patio. A few sunbathers were draped on deck chairs in bright bathing suits, holding fruit drinks, as if to live up to Los Angeles's public image. They were making a determined effort, but they weren't having fun. It was twenty degrees too hot, and twenty miles too far north.

Jess and Michael climbed one of the staircases at the back of the building. Apartment 32 was on the top story, which gave it a better view of the spread of identical buildings and a better taste of the yellowish air. Liu Shi answered the door himself. He was built on a tiny scale, but in perfect proportion. He didn't come up to Michael's shoulders, but his own were straight and square and body was athletic. It weighed about what Jess had at the age of twelve. He himself was somewhere between twenty-five and forty-five; it was impossible to tell from the smooth skin and impassive eyes.

"Hello?" He spoke with a faint breathiness.

Michael introduced himself and Jess, adding that they were friends of Clarissa Hopper.

"Oh." He thought it over. He was a deliberate man who obviously thought things over before acting. "Come in."

They followed him into a surprisingly bright white-walled living room, too small to hold more than two short couches but crammed with vases of flowers and hanging plants.

"Please sit down." Liu Shi himself stayed standing as if that evened out the inequities of their various sizes.

There was apparently going to be no small talk. Michael took a deep breath and plunged in. "Clarissa suggested we see you because we're researching microwaves."

"Ah. " He nodded, and the eyes became even more impassive. "Why?"

"Frankly," Michael hesitated, "I'm writing a screenplay." Jess hid her reaction by coughing. That was very frank, Michael.

"Well," Liu Shi spoke delicately but there was no mistaking a backbone there "I'm afraid you've come to the wrong place."

"We have just a few questions."

Their host didn't want to be unreasonable. He nodded again and sat opposite them, his shoulders still straight and unrelaxed. "I'll listen to the questions."

Jess decided that the screenplay cover story wasn't

going to wash. It was certainly not going to make the scientist chatty. "Look, Dr. Shi, we just spent an hour with Clarissa. We know what she thinks about microwaves, we happen to agree with her, and she thinks you do too. We'll keep what you say confidential, if you like, but it's important that you talk to us. " She eyed him intently. "Very important."

"I don't want the details." He looked away. "I have nightmares enough already."

"So do we." She pushed the advantage. "You lost your search grants because you wouldn't toe the official line, didn't you? You've got no obligation to keep what you know to yourself."

"It isn't a question of obligation. It's a question of having paid for my . . . foolishness enough. I'm tired of the topic, I wish to forget it."

"You can't. Nobody who's dealt with it can."

He looked at her as if he'd like to deny it, but the words didn't come out.

"We won't stay long. Just tell it to us in your own words." He didn't answer for a long time. Finally, he spoke in a calm voice, as detached as if he were talking about someone else. "I was a geneticist. I say 'was' because a scientist without research facilities is merely an unemployed person. I was studying the effects of non-ionizing radiation on genes — do you understand 'non-ionizing radiation'?"

"Yes," Jess said very quickly. She really couldn't bear another science lecture.

"There's considerable evidence that this sort of radiation affects reproduction birth defects, sterility, high miscarriage rate. That was my field — I was attempting to determine if the if the mutations were genetic or if they stopped when the parent was no longer exposed to radiation."

"Because, if the mutations stop," Jess said slowly, trying to reason it out, "then people who are having children can protect themselves by staying away from microwaves."

Shi nodded. "On the other hand, if the mutations

261

are permanent — genetic — "

No one finished the sentence for him but the image was but the image was plain. Mutants watching TV.

"What happens to helicopter pilots after they leave the army?" Michael asked. "Are their babies normal?"

Shi smiled approvingly. "Very logical question. Scientists have asked for that data, but it's classified."

"But — "

"You see, the authorities don't accept that there is any relationship between these problems and microwaves. Radar. Therefore, there is no issue as to whether or not the problems are genetic."

Jess grimaced. That was logical too. And frightening as hell. "But you pursued it and your funds were cut off?"

The scientist didn't even bother to answer that one. "The sad thing is that there is evidence in other countries — the Czechs and the Poles are light-years ahead of us in this research." He smiled without humor. "Of course, the authorities wouldn't want to accept any research, let alone Communist research, that might force them to restrict the use of their new toys."

"Sure," Michael nodded drily. "They just love their big shiny satellites."

Shi waved that away. "There are more interesting things. The radiation is electromagnetic, you know?"

Jess and Michael nodded weakly.

"Ah. Well, think of it as waves of electricity. You can do that?"

The nods were more convincing.

"Our brains themselves work on electrical impulses so it interferes with our own electrical fields using this radiation. We can create mood swings, nervousness, disorientation. We can make people stupid or smarter. We can even use it as a form of mind control."

"Great." Michael scowled. "A new interrogation tool." Shi raised his eyebrows. "Congratulations. You think like a general."

Michael's smile was feeble. "And despite all this, they prevent anyone from researching what's happening to us?"

"I didn't say that." Shi paused, choosing his words carefully. "I'm quite certain that research is being done — against the day when the effects will be obvious."

Jess and Michael winced.

"I've heard rumors." The voice was vague. "There are research contracts, institutes . . . "

Where? Where are the institutes?" Jess asked sharply. Jackson had mentioned being sent someplace in the desert.

"I don't know. My guess would be near big military installations, but I don't know." He was becoming edgy; his relief when the telephone rang wasn't even partly disguised.

Jess and Michael didn't say much while he was out of the room. Their heads were spinning with information overload.

Shi was back, a much-changed man. Suddenly, he was busy and unwilling to meet their eyes. "I must ask you to go now. I . . . I have work to do. I'm sorry. "He nudged them out into the hall.

Michael looked questioningly at Jess. She shook her head. She had no idea what could have come over the man. "Is something wrong, Dr. Shi?"

"No, no, nothing. But you really must go now."

"We have another couple of questions

"No!!" He froze and they stared. It was the first time he'd raised his voice in the interview, probably in the decade. "I'm so sorry. You must go now. Please."

Jess watched him quietly. "Who called you just now?"

He flinched and opened the door without answering.

"What did they say to you?"

"Please. Don't make more trouble for me." His eyes darted around the courtyard as if he expected to see an armed invasion. "Or for yourselves."

She didn't like the sound of that but she planted herself firmly in the doorway. He'd need another couple of men his size to get rid of her without her cooperation. "I have one more question. Have you ever run across a female scientist in the microwave field?"

"Female?" Only half his mind was on the question. He wasn't pretending to be anything other than what he was. Terrified. "Female? Oh — yes, there was one, I can't remember who."

"Try," Jess urged, not budging an inch.

He made a valiant effort. "Uh, Koestler, I think."

"Sarah Koestler?"

"Yes, yes, that's it!"

Jess hesitated a moment, then kept to her part of the bargain. The door shut behind them, closing delicately without the rudeness of a slam. But just so there'd be no ambiguity, the bolt slid across with a clear click.

"Lepers have nothing on us." Michael took Jess's arm as they started downstairs.

"Leprosy can be cured," she pointed out. And people didn't get called and told to stay away from lepers.

Chapter 17

Jess walked through Dr. Shi's courtyard without seeing anything except the pavement. She watched her feet move and thought about Lorrie Berrington looking for Sarah Koestler.

"Uh, Jess." Michael's voice was casual. "Do you know anyone who's bald, has big shoulders, and favors navy blazers?"

"Is this a riddle?"

"No." He stopped her from stepping past the hedge in front of the apartment building. "There appears to be one in our car."

Jess stiffened and looked. She shook her head. "Okay, why don't you wait here? I'll go check him out."

"Sorry, babe. Haven't you heard? Macho is bad form nowadays."

"Who said anything about macho? I was planning on waving a white flag and bursting into tears."

"Come on."

They stopped a few yards away from the car. The man in the blazer opened the passenger seat and got out. Jess felt better. They could handle immaculate portly gents in gray flannels.

"Mr. Renfrew. Ms. Canby."

They nodded.

"Allow me to introduce myself." He started to put out a plump, well-manicured hand, then thought better of it. "Captain Wrighter."

It took Jess a moment to catch on. "Oh, yes."

"I wish to talk to you."

She nodded unenthusiastically. Wrighter motioned graciously that they should feel free to make themselves comfortable in their own car; he got into the back seat.

"Friend of yours?" Michael hadn't taken to Wrighter.

Jess glanced into the car. The Captain's eyes were the same gray as his pants, but they looked much colder. "I don't think so. He's the guy who shared Berrington's last supper."

They got into the front seat and waited. The ball

265

was in the Navy's court. Wrighter took his time. He adjusted his pant legs, shot his cuff and cleared his throat. It was meant to keep Jess and Michael hanging.

When he spoke, his voice was clipped and harsh. "Last week, Ms. Canby, you obtained classified records at the Department of Health Services."

Jess thought about Carl Weber and felt sick.

"That was a flagrant infringement of the Official Secrets Act. I am here to warn you that if you attempt to make any use whatsoever of the information in those records, you will be charged under the Act."

Michael was getting sore. "Okay. You came here to say it and you said it." He got out and opened the rear door of the car.

Wrighter ignored him. "The official who breached security hasn't been let off so easily."

Jess blanched and tried to twist around. "What happened to him?"

"Mr. Weber has been suspended. I believe he is to be fired."

"Carl?" Michael stared at Jess in horror.

"Oh, no! It was entirely my fault — You should take it out on me because — "

The eyes were stone. "That is something you'll have to live with. And believe me, we will take it out on you if you pursue the matter covered in that file. However, Mr. Weber's transgression was an unforgivable breach of his duty, and there is nothing that can be done for him."

"You can't do that! He's worked for the County for thirty-five years !"

"Thirty-seven, actually." There was no leeway in the voice. "I am not here to discuss Mr. Weber."

"No. You're here to flex your muscle," Michael said contemptuously. "Okay, you've done it. You've proved you can follow us around town and you've threatened my wife. Now, get out of the car and scram."

The arrogant facade faltered. Captains ranked just under vice admirals, and they were seldom told to scram.

"I mean it." Michael was six-two, muscular and furious. He was dying for an excuse to take it out on someone who was five-nine, plump and pompous. "Out."

Wrighter sneered, but he slid toward the door. "Ms. Canby, for your information, the ex-Marine whose file you read was involved in a voluntary medical experiment during his service years. He knew at the time he was taking a risk."

"It must have slipped his mind," she said icily. "I spoke to the man and his wife."

"Oh, Mrs. Jackson never knew. That was part of the agreement. We promised, at the time, to take care of all expenses if anything . . . unfortunate developed."

Jess couldn't stand to look at him. She faced the front again.

"Ms. Canby, you should think carefully before you act. You had quite a brilliant future, I'm told." He got out and marched away.

Michael slammed the rear door and got back behind the wheel. "Jess, What can we do for Carl?"

She'd already done quite enough. She swallowed the nausea. "Not much." The victims were really piling up — and for what? For a good cause, but a hopeless one. "I need a phone."

They found one; she made the call and it turned out as she'd figured. She got back into the car. "They're always a step ahead of us." Her voice was bitter. "Jackson's incommunicado. He's either moved . . . or dead."

Michael lit a cigarette and actually offered her one. She took it gratefully.

"Jess, I hate to bring this up, as if you don't have enough on your mind, but it's time to go to the airport."

Her stomach clenched. "Already?" Her mother was coming. She loved her mother. It was just that she was always so damn tense when Virginia Canby was in the neighborhood.

The flight was on time and Virginia was one of the first off the plane. She walked through the gate looking exactly the way she'd looked for as long as Jess could remember: perfect. Her gray hair was pulled back into an elegant bun that emphasized almond-shaped eyes, flawless skin, and a classic oval face. Her clothes might have just come off the ironing board; her makeup was subtlety itself. Jess instantly felt fat, frumpy and unforgivably soiled. How did her mother manage never to sweat? Everyone else in the terminal was glistening.

"Darling." Virginia caught sight of them. It wasn't clear who the greeting was for.

"Virginia." Michael loped over, took her flight bag in hand, and affectionately kissed his mother-in-law.

Jess stayed put, delaying the embrace as long as possible. "Darling." Virginia came up to her.

"Hi, mother."

They hugged, and Jess tried not to cause wrinkles. "You're looking terrific, Mother."

"Thank you, dear." Virginia made no personal comment. She was on record as saying that if you couldn't say something nice, say nothing.

"How was the flight?" Michael maneuvered himself into the conversation.

"Fine."

"Enjoy your visit, Mrs. Canby." A distinguished-looking older man strode by, inclining his head.

"Thank you." It was a Vivien Leigh smile, triangular and unselfconsciously adorable.

Who's that, Virginia? Another conquest?" Michael teased.

"Of course not." She acted as if she were unaware of her effect on men. Perhaps she was. She hadn't enjoyed her first and only marriage; it was highly unlikely that she'd ever felt tempted to try again. "Just a pleasant fellow who sat next to me. Now. Tell me how you two are doing? How's the baby?"

"Heavy, hot and awkward," Jess sighed.

"I was pregnant with you in the summer," Virginia reminded her. "And we didn't have air-conditioning then. I know how difficult it is. Never mind, it'll be over soon."

"If I don't fall flat on my face in the meantime."

They were on the moving sidewalk, being carried slowly down the interminable hall to the baggage area. The airport was busy, and the noise level was as high as the temperature.

Virginia turned her attention to Michael. "How's the writing coming, dear?"

"Well." He hesitated. "There was interest in turning my book into a movie."

"Marvelous!" She saw his face and stopped smiling. "What happened?"

Michael and Jess sighed in unison.

"We'll fill you in when we get home, Mother." Virginia's clear brow creased for a very brief moment. "Is this concerning the trouble you're in, Jessica?"

Jess was still. "How did you hear about that?"

"Richard Simon called me."

A boisterous family with an improbable number of children pushed ahead of them, almost knocking Jess over. She was too surprised by her mother's words to defend herself.

"Move over, sweetie." Michael took her arm. "You're a road block."

"Why, that snitch! What did he say, mother? Why did he call you?"

"I think we should wait until we can talk about it in peace." She smiled at Michael. "I hope you're not planning to cook tonight. I want to take you two out to dinner."

Jess bit her tongue. In all of her mother's visits, Michael had cooked about three percent of the time. Virginia had a poor memory for the dozens of dinners Jess put on the table. It was a not-so-subtle hint that Jess lacked a little something in the womanliness department.

Michael squeezed Jess's hand, and they walked off the sidewalk toward the baggage claim area.

Getting out of the airport involved getting around

the circular road on which the terminals sat. Construction, begun years ago to improve facilities, had become a permanent state of affairs and the semi-inadequate airport was now a full-fledged disaster zone. Jess plucked her shirt away from her damp skin. It had to be a hundred degrees in the car, and, with traffic thicker than devon cream, there was no escape. "Mother, what did Richard say?"

"He's very worried about you, Jessica." Virginia twisted her wedding ring. "What on earth are you up to?"

"It's a long story."

"He says you're destroying your career."

"I didn't think you cared about my political ambitions, Mother."

"You're too old to be told what to do. I never felt your father should encourage you to follow in his footsteps but you didn't listen to me at ten years old, expect you to start now."

Parry, thrust, bull's-eye. Sixty-one years hadn't blunted good old mom's punch at all. "Um. I think I'll have a cigarette, sweetie."

Michael didn't miss a beat. He might head her away from sin in private, but he was true blue in front of her mother. "Sure. Here."

Jess pretended an interest in a tour group, Germans from the sound of it, waiting noisily for their bus.

"Jessica." Virginia insisted on her daughter's attention. "What is going on?"

"You want the good news or the bad news first?"

"The good news."

"The weather's been wonderful."

Virginia waited, then said patiently, "If that's it for the good news, I might as well have the other."

"The bad news is," she blurted it out fast "I'm on suspension and Michael's lost his first big break."

"But why?"

Michael and Jess looked at each other. They silently tossed for it, and Michael lost.

"We've uncovered a conspiracy," he ventured, "that

affects people's health and involves Los Angeles's elite. So we're rather unpopular at the moment."

"Conspiracy?" Virginia had never liked the word; Watergate had made it no more palatable. "Really?"

"Do you know anything about satellites?" Jess asked.

"They use them for weather predictions, don't they? Oh, and I read something about cable television. I'm afraid I'm not exactly an expert."

Michael grinned. "Don't feel bad. You're about three steps ahead of where I was a week ago."

"In a nutshell, Mother, satellites beam microwaves down to earth, and we think that's causing serious illness. Unfortunately, satellites are big business. Big enough to make a lot of people want to cover up the problem."

"A cause. It sounds like one of your father's causes." Virginia spoke impassively, but everyone in the car understood the subtext.

"Well, Dad cared about people," Jess said defensively. "He took on causes because — "

"Because they were good political weapons."

Jess gritted her teeth. "That's a bit hard, isn't it? Sure, Dad was a good politician, but that doesn't mean he wasn't sincere." She was facing her mother and able to see the veiled expression. It might have been cynicism or amusement or anger. Jess had never figured out that particular look, but she knew she liked none of the possibilities.

Virginia looked away first. "I gather that your theories have won you a few important enemies."

"A few," Jess admitted drily.

"I assume that's why Richard called me. He thought perhaps I'd be able to talk sense to you." Virginia added sadly, "I told him you didn't care what I thought."

About a ton of guilt descended instantly. "Of course, I care what you think. But I don't see what else we can do. Dad himself would have wanted us to fight this one — and damn the torpedoes."

"Your father wouldn't have wanted you to throw

away your future for any reason."

Why couldn't she ever call him anything except "your father" "I'd prefer not to throw it away, too."

"Personally, I hate to think of you in politics but, you're my daughter. If that's what you want. . . " Virginia leaned forward suddenly. "Or are you really your father's daughter? Is this one of his complicated double-whammies? Is this going to give you a political weapon? Is that why you're doing it?"

Jess tried to smiled. "I'd love to be able to say yes."

"Because, if it is," her mother continued, "you better remember that it's hurting Michael, too. Your father didn't stop to think that charity begins at home, but I'd hope'd you would."

It was now about a hundred and ten degrees, and barometer rising. "Mother," Jess said carefully, "Michael and I are doing this together. And as far as Dad went, okay, he wasn't a great husband. I know that. But he did care about his people, and he taught me to care. On this one, he'd have risked his position if he'd had to." She didn't add that she and Michael were risking far more than that.

"Neither of us wanted the problem," Michael added. "But we both agree it's got to be played out.

"Virginia nodded expressionlessly.

They were finally free of the airport traffic and on Sepulveda Boulevard heading toward Lincoln. Fifteen minutes to Santa Monica, and thirty more to the liquor cabinet.

* * *

Martin Dunphy jumped up from the patio where he'd been waiting. "Virginia! The love of my life!" She smiled with real enthusiasm. "Martin, darling. It's wonderful to see you!"

Jess felt the same way. The more the merrier, because it kept the chatter purely social. "Come on in and get loaded."

Martin shuddered and followed Virginia inside.

"No, thanks. That drunk the other night with Michael and Alan taught me a lesson. It taught me that my liver has no loyalty."

Michael grinned and fetched the bottle anyway. "You should have seen Dickson the next day. I ran into him in the market — he didn't look any more than, oh, ninety-five years old."

The sun was low and the westerlies were high, so they sat in the living room and reminisced about the old days. Martin and Michael had met each other at the beginning of college; Jess had met them both in her first year, and their third. They'd spent a lot of time at the Canby residence, partly for Virginia's cooking but mainly for Caesar's company. Whenever Jess thought about it, she wondered if her mother always had felt like an also-ran. Certainly, just moments after Caesar's death, she had left his world; she had even gone so far as to leave his state. Jess gulped with guilt.

Guilt bred guilt. She immediately remembered Carl Weber and got up to call him. He was home; he answered on the first ring.

"It's Jess, Carl."

There was a long pause, during which her stomach clenched into a mass of concrete.

"I'm so sorry about what happened." Sorry was such an inadequate word. "Carl, what can I do?"

"You've done enough." The words were much harsher than his voice but he didn't take them back.

"We can fight it. Let's go to a lawyer on Monday and — "

"Please, leave me alone," Carl asked gently. The receiver made no noise at all when he replaced it.

"Jess?" Michael was at her elbow, watching her with worry.

"Was that Carl? What — ?"

She nodded, then shrugged helplessly.

The telephone rang; she picked it up quickly to distract herself. It was Richard Simon, asking if Virginia had arrived yet.

"Yes, she's here. You want to talk to her?" Again?

"No -- I was thinking I'd drive out there. We could all have dinner together." He spoke casually, as if the idea had just occurred to him.

"Sure." Jess was pleasant, as if she didn't know that this was a set-up, an opportunity created by her mother and Richard for the express purpose of drumming sense into the wayward girl.

Jess, Michael, Virginia, and Martin arrived on the dot of eight to find Richard already seated, no mean feat considering that it was Saturday night and beach-side restaurants were loath to seat anyone until the entire party was present. And even then, generally not for an hour or two. Richard and Virginia smiled at each other and ran through the intricate dance steps of what they considered appropriate greetings while the other three waved frantically for the bar waitress.

The mob was packed in wall-to-wall, dating couples, tourists, family groups, hopeful singles. The place was attractive in a sawdust-on-the-floor, saloonish kind of way; the menu featured good fresh fish and adequate seafood, and the service was perky if not perfect. Still, the hordes came for the intangibles that made it an "in" place to be: the ocean that about one percent of the diners got to see from their tables, a decibel level so high that it convinced everyone that they must be having fun, and a guarantee that no one who was even slightly ambulatory needed to leave alone.

They all ordered drinks and swordfish, along with onion rings, french fries, and salads. The bill wouldn't be any more than what a bank teller made in a week. Jess let the others carry the small talk; she fiddled with lettuce leaves and waited for the other shoe to drop.

It crashed when the fish arrived. "Jess, we've got to talk."

"I suspected as much, Richard."

He nodded, sympathetically. "My dear, this mess has to be cleaned up. It has to stop."

"Richard, I didn't ask for it and I want it to go away as much as anyone, but it's not under my control. Or," she added bitterly, "Michael's. We're both paying."

"Which is totally unfair," Virginia broke in. "Poor Michael's a writer, not a politician, he shouldn't be dragged into this ridiculous mess!"

"It's not ridiculous, Mother!" Jess said heatedly. "And it's not my fault!"

Michael took Jess's hand. "No, it's not."

She smiled gratefully at him.

"Fault isn't what I was getting at," Richard murmured tactfully. "It's no one's fault, Jess. You've irritated a good many people you need to get along with, if you're to get along in Los Angeles."

"I didn't start out to ruffle feathers. Jesus, I'd do anything to do it over again. I swear to God, I'd wear a blindfold and earplugs rather than find out what I've found out."

"What is that?" he asked pleasantly.

"What is that?" She took a deep breath. "Okay, you asked and I'll tell you. I think Lorrie and Robert Berrington, not to mention a few other assorted inconvenient people, have been killed to hide the fact that the satellite industry is causing sickness and death."

The words shimmered in the air, echoing unpleasantly so that all pretense of eating vanished.

"Jessica," Virginia said faintly, "that's a bit strong."

"No, it' s not."

Richard drummed his fingers on the table. "Whether or not it's strongly put, it makes no sense. Why would Robert — who was one of the major figures in the industry — be, uh, harmed by his friends?"

"Because they couldn't trust him anymore," Jess said bluntly, "after they killed his daughter."

"Do you have any proof of murder?"

"Oh." Virginia whimpered at the word.

Jess and Michael looked at each other. She shook her head. "Well, not exactly but — "

"Any real proof that the satellites are dangerous"

"Well, it's hard to prove, because — "

"We've obviously proved something," Michael broke in, "because we're being threatened and followed."

"Um. Well. If this . . . conspiracy" Richard said the

word with difficulty" is so keen to kill, and if your investigations were bothersome, uh, why haven't you been — " He threw a quick apologetic glance at Virginia. "Hurt?"

Jess didn't answer. The same question had occurred to her and she'd never let herself think too much about it. The responses made her blood pressure hit the ceiling.

"Look, my dear," Richard pressed his advantage "businessmen aren't ogres. If there was a danger, don't you think they'd care? They live in the city too, you know. Their families live here."

"Businessmen pollute air they have to breathe," Michael argued stubbornly.

"Everything's a question of balance," Richard continued, speaking directly to Jess. "You know that. Perhaps you have hit on something that the industry isn't fully aware of yet. There's always some cost to innovation, but one can negotiate these things, if," he coughed gently — "if one is in a position to be heard."

Martin nodded emphatically. This was a language he spoke. "You have to negotiate. Jess, Mike — it's not as if you're accomplishing anything right now."

Michael scowled. "*Et tu, Brute?*"

"Hell, Mike, all I'm saying is you can't do much while you're a pariah."

"It's great to have supportive friends."

Martin chuckled and shook his head. "You're an idealist; you always were. Well, in real life, we've got to pay attention to *realpolitik*."

"Politics is the art of the possible," Michael said sarcastically. "Yeah, well, we don't buy that."

Jess kept quiet. As a matter of fact, she did buy that — but there was a line, Somewhere, that even a fan of *realpolitik* couldn't cross. Wasn't there?

"You haven't got a thing you could take into court," Richard pointed out. "Jess, think about it carefully. . . As a favor to me. Could you be wrong?"

All eyes turned toward her. The silence grew heavy. Finally, she sighed. "I'm personally convinced that microwaves fry us."

"Could you be wrong — just possibly — about this bloodthirsty conspiracy? Could the deaths be something less melodramatic than murder on a grand scale?" he pressed.

She ran through the list and bit her lip.

Michael had no such doubts. "Richard, you're a friend of ours, but you're forgetting about morality. No career — not even Jess's — is worth sacrificing that for."

"That's not what your father-in-law would have said," Virginia commented.

"Dad had principles!" Jess insisted hotly.

"Of course he did." Richard nodded. "But he was practical. He made concessions when he had to. The real world is a difficult place to live, sometimes, but it is the only address we have."

"Concessions are one thing, but — "

"Big concessions." Richard paused uncomfortably. "Jess, I promised Arthur I'd look after you — and though I hoped I'd never have to tell you this, I think he'd want me to."

Her heart sank. She knew the signs. Something was coming that she could do without.

He took a deep breath and looked at Virginia, who gave him an almost-imperceptible nod. "Arthur made a lot of concessions. Deals. He achieved a lot — don't get me wrong — but to do so, he had to give everyone something. You can't judge him for it there's no man living who's perfectly honest. There never has been."

"What do you mean?" Her mouth was dry.

"Do you remember the battle for legislation to protect the wetbacks in the garment industry? It was a hell of a time — the radicals shouting, the Mexicans protesting, everything in an uproar." Richard's voice tailed off for a moment as he shook his head over the memories. "Well, he lost that battle. There never was reform legislation passed. The sweat shops still exist — virtual slave labor."

"You lose some battles. He couldn't win everything."

Barbara Betcherman

"Bullshit."

Jess froze. She'd never heard Richard swear, not in thirty years.

"He didn't lose it. He threw it."

"I don't understand."

"He gave the fight away. He spearheaded the reform movement — he spoke for all the reformers. They trusted him. So he was able to engineer their defeat."

She shook her head, refusing to believe it.

"I'm sorry," Richard said gently, "but it's true. He knew it couldn't be won — it was a battle that was over before it started. So he used it to get other things. Smaller things, maybe, but something."

"What other things:" Michael looked as if he'd just eaten a lemon.

"Oh, school appropriations. More public beaches."

"You call that a trade-off? Selling the slaves out so that if they ever had a day off they could get a suntan?" Michael asked incredulously.

Richard sighed.

Jess tried to talk, but it came out as a croak. "Did dad know what he was doing from the very beginning?"

Richard nodded reluctantly. "He was approached by the garment workers when they saw the writing on the wall. It meant garment It meant they owed him one — more than one, actually."

She couldn't put the words she was hearing together with her picture of her father. He'd been a knight in shining armor, a vibrant, handsome powerhouse of good humor and energy and kindness He had loved people and the had loved him back. "He lied to all the people who trusted him? He sold his soul to business?"

"Nobody could have won," Richard reminded her. "He figured he could salvage something."

Jess looked at her mother, silently begging her to deny it. Virginia lowered her eyes.

"Did you know, Mother?"

"Some of it."

"You never told me."

"You worshiped your father. You wouldn't have believed me."

It was true. Jess looked away. "The whole damn thing was a fake front. All of it, just a goddam lie."

Richard patted her hand, distressed. "No, that's not my point. You do what you can in this life, Jessica. It's not perfect, but most people are reasonable — you just do what you can."

"For yourself, it seems." She'd never been so tired.

*   *   *

Michael brooded silently until they were in bed. Jess had hoped he'd brood till morning at the very least but he didn't turn out the light immediately. He propped a pillow behind his head and lit a cigarette. "We've got to get into Frechetti's files. We can't prove a thing till we see them."

"I don't know, Michael. I can't think straight."

"You heard Richard. And Martin. And your mother. There's no way of winning this without those records."

"I heard Richard, all right." The bitterness ached like kick in the stomach. "We can't win at all. You were right about politicians, it looks like. Nobody's ever won, playing it straight."

"Babe, don't take it so hard." He put an arm around her rigid shoulders. "What did you expect? Your father was a great guy, but he wasn't a saint. He was a wonderful father and you love wonderful father and you love him and that's swell — but you're too old for hero worship."

"I'm too old to have illusions about what two ordinary people can do. I'm too old to be on the firing line and lose my job and make enemies." She felt about a thousand years old.

"We aren't going to give up just because there's a little tarnish on Caesar's halo." He kissed the top of her head. "I just had an idea. Tomorrow — at the art garden opening — you're going give a speech, right?

There'll be press there, lots of press. I think you should come out and blow the whistle on the whole bunch of these bastards."

She didn't answer.

"Jess?"

"I don't know, Michael."

"Don't use names, that would be slander. Just lay it out for everyone. That should hit the headlines and get us a little action."

A little more action. A little more vulnerability. She slid down and turned over. "I don't know." She closed her eyes and pretended she could sleep.

Chapter 18

What with one thing and another, including depression, terror and no sleep at all, Jess crawled out of bed feeling as if she'd spent the night in a clothes dryer. It obviously showed. Michael and Virginia were having breakfast when she staggered downstairs; they took one look and insisted that she see Connie Hartman immediately.

Jess went to see what the mirror said. It said she ought to see a doctor.

Connie was good-natured about coming into work on Sunday morning. As she caustically pointed out, Jess was becoming more Considerate. This time, it was 10:00 a.m. not 4:00 a.m.

An hour later, Connie tossed Jess her clothes. "You can get dressed now."

"Well?" Michael had been loitering outside tie examination room, obviously shamelessly keeping one ear to the door.

"She'll live, and so will the baby. But she looks like hell."

"You're an obstetrician, not a beautician," Jess grinned. "Stick to your own field."

Connie grunted and went into her consulting room for a cigarette. Michael waited while Jess finished dressing. She didn't take long; there wasn't any point in fussing over pants that had a semi-circle cut out of them and a blouse that looked like a red laundry bag.

They went in after Connie and found her leaning back in the desk chair, long legs on the desk. It was the kind of office that went with the doctor: utilitarian in furniture, stringently, unpretentious, and revealing sentiment only by the fact that two walls were entirely covered with photographs of mothers and the babies Connie had delivered.

She waved the cigarette at them. "Sit down. Well, Jess, my pet, you've got a little explaining to do."

Jess shrugged.

"Call me a fool, but when I see a healthy woman

281

with navy circles under her eyes, an edge in her voice and a blouse buttoned wrong, I get the crazy idea that there's a problem."

Blouse? Jess looked down. "Shit." The buttons were askew. She began to undo them again.

"Not to mention that you've lost weight," Connie added reasonably. "I see very few six-and-and-a-half month pregnant women who are losing weight. I spend most of my time begging them to stop putting it on."

"Begging?" Jess raised her eyebrows. "Begging, Con? Is that an apt description for a doctor who keeps whips and chains in her desk"

"Joking won't get you out of this." Jess and Michael looked at each other.

"Connie," Michael said abruptly, "have you ever heard of birth defects caused by radar?"

"Why? Who's been playing with radar?"

"Not us. Have you heard anything?"

Connie pursed her lips. "I haven't run across it myself, but I know there have been allegations. No proof."

"Has anyone been studying it?"

"I'm sure."

"Who?"

"Hell, I don't know. I'm not a research scientist; I'm an overworked genie who's a year and a half behind in her medical journal reading."

"What if the allegations are true?"

"Look, people will study anything. They feed cotton batting to mice and study that. They take months to study the relationship between the existence of men and the existence of hookers. You think nobody's thought to study radar?" She paused and took a close look at them. "Why are you asking?"

Jess broke in quickly. "You're better off not knowing, Con. Trust us."

"The last time someone said that, I lent him five thousand dollars I've never seen again." She stubbed out her cigarette. "But I don't have thumbscrews with me, so I can't make you talk."

Michael had been watching Jess. He turned back. "Have you ever heard of a Dr. Edward Merton?"

"Should I?"

"He practices in Southern California."

"Ah, then I can't understand my ignorance. Lord, there can't be more than a million or two doctors in Southern California."

"Is there any way of checking him out?"

"You changing doctors?"

"Not unless Jess's eyes start to bleed or she gets cancer."

Connie stared at him, then swung her legs off the desk.

"What's his hospital affiliation?"

"Jess?"

"What? Oh." She looked up from the what she'd been studying, "Uh, I'm not sure. He uses a small private place in Orange County but I think he's mainly into research."

"Research, huh well, you're in luck. I don't date often, but every now and then, a sucker asks me out and the last one is in medical-research funding. Hold on a minute."

She dialed a number and talked for a long time, as brisk as usual until the very end. Whatever was being said as a fare well was definitely not said as one medical person to another. Connie actually blushed and muttered something inaudible before hanging up.

She tried to bluff her way through, but Michael was grinning. She blushed again. "Yes. Well. Uh, he said that Merton's well known and really reputable. He does a lot of work for the government, mainly classified stuff, so he hasn't published much."

"Classified. Government."

"Military. Radar." Michael finished Jess's train of thought.

Connie stared from one to the other. "Is it too early in the morning for you two to form complete sentences?"

"Sorry," Michael apologized. "We're going to study

283

verbs this afternoon. Go on."

"Not much further to go. My . . . uh . . . friend thinks that Merton's field has something to do with cell mutations, but that's a big field. Whatever, he's well-connected. So connected that he never needs private funding, and that's the mark of a real big-timer. Every university in the country would probably give its right arm and two coeds to get him and his team and his moolah."

"His team. Damn!" Michael shook his head. "We should have told you to ask about another research scientist. A woman. Sarah Koestler."

"Sarah?" Connie sat up straighter. "I know Sarah."

"What?"

"There weren't many female doctors ten, fifteen years ago. There used to be an association, Women in Medicine. I met her there. She's a cancer specialist, as I recall. Oh." Connie leaned forward. "Research, not practice. Is she involved?"

He shrugged. "There, my love, you know as much as we do. Where can we find her?"

The doctor, shook her head. "I haven't seen her in, oh, must be four or five years. She was working with Paul Linze at USC, last I knew." She looked at her watch and jumped up. "God! I've got to go! Sorry an emergency."

"A delivery?" Michael's face lit up with the paternalistic gleam he'd lately taken displaying at the mere thought of parenthood.

"No. A blocked sink."

* * *

"You were pretty quiet in there," Michael observed as they walked back to the car.

Jess shrugged.

"Are you feeling all right, sweetie?"

"Yes, it's not that." She didn't meet his eyes. "It's just that I don't want to bring our friends into this. I've learned that lesson."

"Carl Weber, you mean?" He took a deep breath. "Yeah."

"They got into the car."

"Jess, are you up to a little spin"

"To see Paul?"

"You know Paul Linze?" His face brightened.

"He's at the County USC Medical Center. We've worked on a couple of cases together."

"That makes it easier."

"Michael, I just said I didn't want to bring our friends into it." She wasn't even sure she wanted to be in it anymore.

"Look, we're just going to ask him a couple of questions. It won't take long and it isn't the same as asking him to reveal secret documents." He took her hand. "Jess, I know you're upset about Carl but don't overreact."

She only avoided overreacting to that statement by biting down hard. How could she be considered too fast on the trigger when it took a couple of suspensions and a couple of deaths to make her think she'd rather have a safer hobby. Say, sky-diving.

"How do we find Linze?" He took her silence for assent.

Her answer was slow in coming. "He's on the cancer tracking project at USC."

"It's Sunday."

"Yeah, well, if he's not in church, he's probably at work. The word 'workaholic' was invented for guys like Paul."

Linze must have skipped church. He was in the hospital cubicle he called an office, deeply immersed in a medical journal. He looked up and smiled when Jess knocked at the open door.

"Hey, Jess, long time no see." He started getting to his feet. It took a while. Linze was a blond giant, taller than Michael by a couple of inches and broader by at least four. "Say, you've, uh, grown since the Greenberg autopsy."

"Yup," she smiled back. "Thank God, I'm

285

reasonably certain it's not a tumor. Paul, this is my husband, Michael. The proximate cause."

"Nice to meet you." Linze noticed that four of the buttons on his telephone were flashing, and he shuddered. "I better talk fast and go see what's broken loose. What can I do for you?"

"Does Sarah Koestler still work for you" She figured that maybe they could ask the question, satisfy Michael, and get out quickly.

"Sarah?" Paul shook his head ruefully. "No, worse luck. She left — oh, two, two and a half years ago."

"Where is she now?"

"I don't know. She went to do a government project. I assume she's still there."

"Where's there?" Michael took over when it seemed as if Jess considered the interview ended.

"It was a classified job. Some institute - in California . . . in the desert, I think. I'm sorry, I really don't know more than that. She was a strange woman. Brilliant mind but kind of . . . secretive."

"Secretive? About the classified work, you mean?"

"Well, that, of course. But," — Linze cast around for the right words see — "she was brilliant, like I said. There aren't many women in research and it's hard for them. If she'd been a man, she'd have been head of her own project and I guess that, well, it soured her a bit. She never talked about anything except business. I worked with her for almost eight years, and I don't even know if she had a boyfriend. She wasn't married the payroll records told me that much."

Michael nodded, unhappy with the vagueness but recognizing that Linze was doing his best. "What about a guy named Merton?"

"Ed Merton. Yeah, I know him. He's a fantastic scientist — smart as hell. In fact, he was on the project Sarah went to. He met her through me. We were on a panel, Ed and I, and Sarah attended "Then he stole her."

"He's an expert in microwaves, right?" Michael ignored Jess's glare.

The doctor nodded. "The expert. He's called in

whenever there's a question."

"Of danger from microwaves, you mean?"

"Or ensuring their safety." Linze grinned. "It all depends on your point of view."

"Merton thinks they're just swell."

"He should know, he's the expert."

"Other experts don't agree," Michael argued.

Linze shrugged and looked again at the telephone console. Five lights were blinking now. "Look, I'd be happy to talk but I've got to go see what's up."

Jess started to say thanks and good bye. Michael forestalled her. "We'll walk down with you." He took Jess's arm and pretended not to notice she was stewing.

Linze led the way into the corridor. "What are all these questions about, Michael?"

"It's a long story," Michael said evasively. "So you're not worried about microwaves and cancer?"

"I'm sleeping nights, if that's what you mean. The people who think microwaves cause cancer base it on the clusters of cancers the found near radiation exposure. Fine and dandy, except cancer tends to show up in clusters. There can be a lot of reasons for it. You want the set speech?"

"Please," Michael nodded.

"Okay. Cancer's the name for a whole bunch of diseases, and basically we don't know a hell of a lot about it — especially why and where it's gonna turn up. That's the point of my tracking program. I get data from all over the county — about the cancer and the victims, and I feed it into my computers to try to make sense of the patterns."

"How do you determine the norm?" Michael smiled wryly. "If cancer can ever be normal, that is."

"Cancer's normal. We all have to die," Linze pointed out. "But determining the norm means analyzing thousands of variables like age, ethnicity, place of birth, sex, marital status, occupation. The list goes on and on."

Michael was concentrating hard. He wasn't even paying attention to the passing tides of pretty young nurses. "So if you'd expect to find three cases of cancer in a group and you find ten, and if they've all been exposed to microwaves — you've got something."

"That's the theory. But it's unproved. There isn't enough data — our information base is still so lousy that when we say we expect to find three cases, we could just plain be wrong. And maybe it's not the microwaves in the area. Maybe it's the water or the pill or . . . " He broke off to say hello to a particularly ravishing brunette. She gave him a meaningful smile.

Michael was like a terrier with a bone. "But it could be the microwaves."

"Maybe — Linze sighed. "There are so many things it could be. There's another wrinkle that makes work damn near impossible. Chance."

"Coincidence." Jess was enjoying this conversation more than any she'd had in days. "So you're not at all worried about microwaves causing cancer"

"Hell, I didn't say that. I'd rather not have the radiation — I'd rather not have bad air too. But I'm not ready to go back to an agrarian society, given my druthers, I'd rather worry about what time I can get off today to see that adorable nurse." He stopped at the doorway of a large public ward. "I have to get to work now. Sorry. Was I any help?"

"You gave us your opinion." Michael's voice suggested that that hadn't been a great deal of help.

Jess heaped in. "Yes, you've been wonderful. Thanks, Paul."

He smiled and vanished.

Michael shook his head. "Wonderful? He's perfectly prepared to dismiss a whole slew of frightening events and call them 'coincidence' and you think that's wonderful?"

They were attempting to retrace their steps; they should have left a trail of breadcrumbs. The hospital was a warren of hallways and staircases, all identically seedy, and there was a good possibility that they could spend the rest of their lives inside. Jess stopped an orderly for directions. She didn't answer Michael until they found the opening in the maze.

"Michael, Paul didn't say microwaves didn't cause cancer. He just said that no one knows yet, which means maybe we've been overreacting. Just this morning, you told me not to overreact."

"So what do you suggest? You think we should wait until we know for goddamn sure? Christ, Jess, if there's even a suspicion that microwaves do what people think they do — the onus is on Bowdritch and his cronies to prove that they *are* safe, before they blanket us with them."

"I agree that we should be careful about satellites."

"That sentence had all the earmarks of being followed by the word 'but'."

"Okay. But. But even well-meaning scientists aren't convinced yet. so all we've got is talk. Now, why should someone kill to stop talk? And why would they start now — when they haven't done so before?"

"What are you saying"

"Maybe we jumped the gun."

"What the hell do you mean?" He was getting angry. "Drop this tactful 'I'm talking to a maniac' tone of voice and come right out with what you mean!

Jess turned away. "I don't want to make myself crazy by shouting something from the rooftops that's unpopular, unpalatable and unproven."

"You don't want to make trouble," he said accusingly, "be cause it's getting you into hot water. You're actually willing to play along to get ahead! I don't believe what I'm hearing!"

"It's your trouble too. Jesus, Michael, you've been blacklisted in the movie industry. You're a writer — I can probably get some kind of job, but what the hell are you going to do if the studios blacklist you forever?"

"I don't know and I don't give a damn! I'm thinking about our baby and our health and — "

"Enough." She was shaking. "Enough shouting. Let's talk about it later when we're both calmer."

"You can't back away from some fights, Jess," he said in a quieter voice.

"That's what my father used to tell me." The words

she'd sworn she wouldn't say out loud. "And he was a goddamn liar!"

Michael was shocked into silence.

"It's a hard, cold world out there, sweetheart." She took several deep breaths. "I'm not going to freeze to death in the dark. All by myself. I'm not going to be the only lunatic on the block."

She couldn't bring herself to say anything else, so she got into the car and kept her eyes on the road.

* * *

It was almost four o'clock when Jess walked into the Arthur Canby Sculpture Garden with Michael and her mother.

The party had definitely done her father proud. Late-afternoon sun cast clear golden light on flagstone paths and gardens rioting with blood-red roses and purple bougainvillea dustfree brass and marble sculptures glinting with newness studded soft lawns and proved that LA was not, whatever the East Coast thought, an artistic wasteland.

The park was fully in keeping with its good address and the neighboring Brentwood estates, each of which had its own landscaped grounds. Maybe the maids and chauffeurs would enjoy the benches and the cultural uplift. It took a couple of years of pleading and begging to develop a meager piece of green in Watts. The sculpture garden had been proposed by a pal of Caesar's at a political dinner a few months before; the fun raising and organizing had taken all of a month. The delay was entirely due to the fact that flowers and plants grew at the same rate for rich and poor.

"Are we early?" Virginia was frowning at her wristwatch.

Jess shook her head silently. There were a fair number of Brentwood residents standing around; presumably the news about the fall of the Canby name hadn't yet reached them. Politicians and influence brokers were better informed, and few had shown up this afternoon. Even the press gallery was scanty.

"I see." Virginia's eyes slid away from the bad news. "Hello, Richard."

Richard Simon had hurried up with a false air of cheer. He greeted all of them and pulled Jess aside. "We've had a few cancellations."

She nodded sardonically. "I already knew Supervisor Reg Cruickshank had urgent business elsewhere."

"Yes. Well." He coughed. "Senator Uhuri called me this morning, and — "

"Don't bother with the list," Jess said gently. "We should have seen this coming." So much for the theories of Horatio Alger. You worked hard, you paid your dues — and chance blew a raspberry. Horatio had been a pederast, anyway. She should never have trusted him.

Richard was led away by a local stockbroker and Jess was left to surveyed the assembly. There were a few familiar faces. Consuela was standing with Martin Dunphy and Joe Miller, the trio subdued but loyally pretending that this was fun. Dana Mercowitz was at Michael's elbow. The agent was gesticulating vivaciously, but her eyes were raking the lawn for someone she really wanted to be seen with. The only truly happy expression belonged to Jerry Katz, scandal-mongering reporter's glee positively resonated as he made notes of who hadn't shown up.

"Jess, darling." Virginia came over, smiling her public smile. She'd perfected it over a lifetime of similar events, none of which she'd enjoyed. But one did one's duty. "Don't you think you should mix a little!"

"Mmm."

"The speeches will start soon," Virginia pointed out carefully when Jess obstinately held her ground.

Jess forced herself to nod. She was at least ten years past the point when she should be so bloody-minded about her mother's helpful hints. "Yes, of course."

The choice was obvious. She headed directly for Consuela's threesome. "Hi, Folks. I'm supposed to be mixing, so let's look like it."

"Hi, Jess." Consuela's beam wasn't as sunny as she'd hoped. "Uh, I bet your dad would have been proud of this. The gardens are gorgeous!"

"Uh-huh." Jess avoided Martin's eye. They both knew that Caesar's pride would have been determined by the head count. His interest in living things was strictly limited to those that could vote.

"Darling!" Dana announced herself with a burst of kisses and a cloud of perfume that almost obscured Michael in her wake. "Lovely, lovely place. Shame about the turnout it's the weather darling, everyone's at the beach. Hello, Martin, darling. And hmmmm." She threw fast flashes of teeth at Consuela and Joe. "Jess, I'm desolated, but I can't stay — I have so many stops to make today! Michael, love, keep in touch." She meant, don't.

She was gone.

"Dana's got a good grip on her sentimentality," Michael observed ruefully.

The all smiled weakly, Jess more weakly than the others. Instinct warned her of danger approaching from the north-north-west; she turned around and almost fell over Jerry Katz.

"Hi, babe. Mike. Guys." His eyes were sparkling as if he'd just fallen in love. "Jess, maybe you're ready to talk sense now. Maybe you're ready to talk to Uncle Jerry."

She sighed. "Only if you want to talk about the weather."

"Don't be a damn fool! Why let those bastards make you into the patsy? What was Berrington to you that you're gonna let the cover-up bring you down in flames?" He took her elbow. "You could use good press, sweetheart, and I could use the inside scam so let's get together and make music."

Everyone watched Jess. She watched Michael. His lips didn't move, but his eyes said she should consider the offer.

Jess turned away. "Sorry, Jerry. There is no inside

scam."

"You dumb sucker!" He was holding his notebook as if he wanted to throw it at her. "It's time to cut loose!"

It's time to start the speeches. Excuse me."

She and Michael walked to the little podium. Michael's face was set. He stopped her a few yards away. "Your speech is our chance, Jess. There's not a lot of press here, but there's plenty to let people know what's going on."

"Jess." Richard and Virginia joined them. "Shall we begin?"

The opening comments were brief, and Virginia's set piece even briefer. Jess took the microphone and thanked everyone for. Coming. She ad-libbed the rest; there wasn't any point in delivering the political part of her speech, and she couldn't remember what else she'd planned to say. She barely heard what she did say. Presumably a few adequate comments about her father, Brentwood, and horticulture, because the applause was genteel. But she was silent about microwaves, and Michael refused to look at her.

Two currently chic sculptors thanked the donors for this opportunity to display their works, (not to mention) — they didn't — their much-fattened back accounts. A local merchant thanked the sculptors for bringing enlightenment to the masses, and then it was over.

Virginia was as quiet as they were on the ride back to Malibu. Only when the car was back in the garage did she attempt to regain her usual manner. "Let's go to that fancy Italian restaurant, children. My treat."

"Thanks." Michael got out and handed the car keys to Jess. "I'm going to pass. I'm tired."

Jess was too fed up to protest.

"Well," Virginia paused dubiously, "that'll give us an evening alone, Jessica." She seemed to be waiting for a rebuff.

"Super." The heartiness was a trifle overblown, but her mother smiled happily.

"Yes, we haven't spent much time together." After two glasses of wine, Virginia allowed a trace of wistfulness to slip out. "We never developed the habit."

They were both remembering that Jess and her father had been the companions in the family.

"You should have told me about Dad," Jess said finally. "You got the raw end of the deal and it wasn't fair."

"Well . . . you two got along so well."

"You should have told me what he was really like."

"Virginia started to speak, then abruptly closed her mouth."

"What is it, Mother?"

"You're very disillusioned, aren't you?"

"It's about time. I'm a bit old for that much naivete."

You think cynicism's any better?" Michael asked harshly. "Swinging from one extreme to the other? That's better?"

Virginia suddenly caught on to the fact that Adam and Eve weren't even within sighting distance of the Garden at the moment. She looked from one to the other in dismay. "Children!"

"Everyone noticed how defeatist you were today," Michael continued fiercely. "Richard and Martin even mentioned it. Well, it's too late to give up — you won't get back into the fold You'll just encourage the wolves to go straight for your jugular!"

"Maybe." She sighed wearily. "At this point, Michael, I don't give a damn if you're right or not."

Chapter 19

Jess woke with the sun. She automatically snuggled toward Michael, and he automatically put his arms around her without waking up. It was paradise for ten minutes . . . A fool's paradise. Michael stirred when Jess started to get out of bed. His eyes opened; his mouth smiled and then he remembered enough to turn away.

"You want to talk about it?"

"No."

"Michael — "

"There's nothing to talk about." He closed his eyes and pretended to fall asleep again.

Breakfast was lousy. The coffee was weak, the toast was burned, and Virginia was determined to stay away from controversy without staying away from conversation. She was successful, at the price of being obsessive about the weather.

The telephone rang at seven-thirty, interrupting a comparative survey of four decades of summer smog.

Jess sighed with relief and went inside to pick up the receiver.

"Jess! You were right!"

"Consuela? You want to repeat that?" Those were words she hadn't heard in a while.

"Berrington's fire — it wasn't an accident! Harper's admitting it now."

"What? Tell me!"

"Come on in and find out for yourself."

"Consuela, don't you dare leave me in suspense!"

"It was a suicide, and they can prove it! And everyone's oohing and aahing about yet another triumph of that superb and well-known investigator — Jessica Canby." Consuela hadn't decided whether to laugh or to cry. "You're back! Harper wants to see you this morning!"

"I think I can find the time," she admitted.

* * *

"Come in, Jessica." Harper was at the window of his office with Stephen Bowdritch. Desmond Marchenko hovered by the doorway, eyes twinkling as if this was the best day of his life.

Bowdritch wore a broad smile too, an expression she hadn't expected to see again on his face. "Good morning, Ms. Canby."

"Morning." She remained impassive. "I understand you wanted to see me, Dr. Harper?"

"Colman, Jess. I've told you to call me Colman before."

He must be thinking of a previous life. Jess inclined her head and waited.

"Sit down, sit down."

She did. Bowdritch and Harper sat facing her. The third man continued to hover.

"We were wrong and you were right." Harper spoke with the smug self-righteousness of a man big enough to admit fault.

"We owe you an apology, " Bowdritch added.

Jess turned to look at Desmond. He didn't join the chorus, but he did nod.

"I'm at a bit of a loss," she murmured eventually.

"It seems that poor Robert took his own life," Bowdritch said in a low voice. "The pills were his, and of course, he was an engineer. He knew how to arrange a fire. I still don't understand, but I suppose it had something to do with Lorrie's tragedy."

"I see." She waited.

The men were somewhat taken aback. They could have dealt with tears. Verbose gratitude would have been acceptable. Possibly even a stream of invective. But they hadn't contemplated silence.

Harper cleared his throat. "Well, I'll tell you what happened, shall I?"

"Why not?"

"Yes. Er. Well, Dr. Zollinger — "whom I believe you met?"

Jess watched Bowdritch flush. "Yes."

"Dr. Zollinger came to Desmond here and told him that he'd been less than candid. He had been treating Robert for depression after his daughter's demise, but he'd kept it secret at Robert's request during his lifetime. After the fire, well, he believed at first that it was an accident, and for the sake of Robert's memory, he stayed silent. Robert would have been very upset if people had learned about his . . . weakness."

Nods all around. Good old Robert, businesslike and stalwart to the bitter end.

"I presume that Dr. Zollinger now says he prescribed medication for Mr. Berrington?"

"Yes." Bowdritch swallowed. "Sleeping pills. Poor Robert had trouble sleeping."

Poor Robert. Poor Elizabeth. The god fell from Olympus faster than you could say "capitulation". "What happened to the evidence of the drugs, Dr. Harper?" She'd call him Colman when hell froze over — and they took a picture to prove it.

"That was overzealousness, I'm afraid." Harper and Bowdritch turned to look at Desmond.

It was time for him to join the dance. "We felt, well, that it was a red herring. We even considered the possibility that the pills had been, er, — "

"Planted?" Jess offered kindly. "By some publicity hound of a bureaucrat?"

"Oh, no, of course not." Desmond took a step forward, then a step back. "Perhaps by a competitor. And, well, since enormous deals like A-COMM depend on investors' confidence, well — we didn't want a red herring lying around."

Harper forestalled Jess's next question. "The blood analysis was done by one of our . . . less dependable technicians. He's made — errors — before." His is voice hinted darkly that there was even the possibility that Leon de la Pena had been bribed.

"It goes to show," Bowdritch said solemnly, "that everyone is human. Everyone. I wish Robert had felt he could confide in me — we worked together all those year, I thought we were close enough for — " He took a deep breath. "I virtually worshiped the man. I wouldn't have thought less of him for being depressed. After all, his only child . . . "

"When was the latest prescription filled?" Jess asked with an attempt at professionalism despite the tumult of thoughts tumbling around her head.

"It checks out." Harper pulled a typed letter toward him. "Dr. Zollinger wrote out a new prescription four days before the death. Carol Tuchman, Robert's secretary, got it filled the day before. The Friday."

"Carol did I see."

Bowdritch looked sheepish. "She left us very abruptly, you know. I assumed it was because of her sorrow — but actually, she was the only person in the office who knew Robert was seeing Herbert. And she knew, of course, he must have taken the whole bottle — thirty capsules. I suppose she found burden of the secret too much to bear."

Harper nodded sympathetically and then shook his head at Bowdritch. "Of course, I can understand your interest in avoiding trouble, but still removing evidence — "

"Not to mention bribing a forensic technician," Jess reminded him.

"Yes, yes, that too." Harper's mouth tightened momentarily. One didn't want to go too far with a reprimand to a powerful, rich, albeit errant, magnate.

"Well. The upshot is, Jessica, that you were right. Again." He forced a narrow smile, widening it as he turned toward Bowdritch. "Jessica had another little triumph recently. Beatty."

"Yes, the wife killer. I remember the case." Bowdritch nodded appreciatively. "You know your job, Ms. Canby."

But not, apparently, her place. Still, the room was filled with the warmth of letting bygones be bygones. It was downright torrid. "Am I still on suspension?"

"Of course not!" Harper's voice managed to suggest that he'd had nothing to do with the original decree and had always considered it monstrous. "Naturally not.

You're my chief of investigations, as long as," he added conspiratorially, "the electorate allows me to keep you."

The carrot was swelling. In a few minutes, the entire room would be tinted orange. "What about Miguel Aguerra?"

"Oh. That." Harper wouldn't come right out and say that the fate of a blue-collar Chicano didn't prey on his mind. "I don't think you need to worry about that. Mistakes happen."

"Whose?"

"I beg your pardon?"

"Whose mistake — yours or mine?"

He gritted his teeth. "It doesn't really matter, now does it? Well. It's time to get back to work. Life goes on, or in our case," he chuckled, not having made the joke more than a thousand time before, "death goes on."

Bowdritch stood and shook hands all around. Desmond followed a pace behind. Everyone smiled a lot.

Harper showed the two men out and returned to Jess, wearing a satisfied expression.

"We have a lot of reports to go through." He flipped open his calendar. "Let's see. You'll need some time to get back on top of things, and I'm going away this afternoon. I've been asked to act as a consultant for another research institute." Sigh. So many institutes cried out for his magic. "I won't be back until Wednesday night."

"Thursday will be fine."

"Fine."

* * *

The basement staff was all out in the corridors, buzzing with the news and, when Jess appeared, beaming with congratulations. Consuela pushed her way to the front, her dark eyes alight.

"Hail, Caesar!"

Jess's grin froze for a moment. Consuela didn't understand why, but she knew something hadn't gone down right. She was quick to change tactics. "We're so proud of you!"

"Thanks." Jess smiled at everyone and walked through the mob to her office.

Joe Miller was waiting inside with a long baton on top of which was pasted a star. "I hereby return to you the scepter of power." He sighed with exaggerated relief. "This place is a goddam zoo! One more day of your job and I'd have been taken away in a white coat with strings."

"Right. Thanks." She took the baton and kept on smiling.

Joe and Consuela frowned at each other.

Uh, Jess," he ventured, "I didn't like your job much, but I thought you did. Why are we not being treated to a womanly display of tears and giggles?"

"Sorry, I'll practice up tonight."

They nodded weakly and filed out.

Jess's shoulders sagged as soon as no one was around to see. It was trite wisdom that you weren't supposed to look a gift horse in the mouth — but this one was just not so easy to accept. A person sure could change. A week ago, she'd have thrown it right out, and here she was now wanting to swallow it and thinking here she was now wanting to swallow it and thinking about how to sell the decision to Michael. Her stomach hurt again. This time it wasn't the baby.

* * *

Dr. Herbert Zollinger was much happier to see Jess than he'd been the last time they met. He practically oozed delight at her visit. She only avoided being given coffee, tea, a drink or lunch by being firm and insistent that there was too much work back at the office.

"Well." He finally gave up and settled himself behind the desk, clasping his hands on top of it and beaming paternalistically at her. "I imagine you have questions for me."

"A few."

"Before you start," he said ruefully, "let me apologize for not being entirely straightforward before."

An interesting description of a 180 degree turn. "I gather you were trying to protect Mr. Berrington's memory."

"Yes. I'd promised, you see. He was dead — but I knew his business deal was still in the cards. He'd have wanted me to keep quiet as long as possible."

Jess nodded and moved on. "When did you start prescribing medication for him?"

"Just sleeping pills. Robert wouldn't consider valium. He seemed to think valium was an admission of weakness, and he, uh, didn't like to feel weak. Elizabeth took Valium, you see." Zollinger pressed his lips together. "He'd hate to think we were discussing this. He hated weakness."

"He doesn't hate anything anymore. When did he start taking sleeping pills?"

"Just after Lorrie died. He came to see me approximately less that ten days later — but we'd had a couple of less formal chats parties. He approached me at . . . Zollinger cast his mind back — at a brunch, I believe. At Stephen Bowdritch's house. We went out to the pool and talked for, oh, a good hour. I wrote him out a prescription that day."

"This was how long after the bicycling accident?"

"Four days. Five, at the most. Then we ran into each other at the Music Center, and, again, we took a walk and chatted. That was two days later. Finally he made an appointment and came in."

"It would be recorded in your diary?"

"No." Zollinger paused. "He came in after my staff left. He was determined to keep it secret. Determined."

"His secretary knew, apparently."

"Carol always knew how to reach Robert. He was a stickler for being available for any emergency. I suppose he assumed she was perfectly loyal."

"Tell me about his mental state? Were you surprised to learn of his death? Did you think of suicide right away?"

Zollinger sighed and grudgingly nodded. "I'm afraid I did, yes. I knew I wasn't having much luck reaching him in our sessions — he needed much more intensive therapy than a few hour-long talks but he wouldn't hear of it."

"What was his problem? Surely parents get over grief?"

"You don't know much about psychiatry, I see?"

"No," Jess admitted. "I don't."

"It wasn't a single problem. It was a lifetime of emotional repression and guilt and insecurity and so on, things he'd never handled because he refused to believe they were important. Everything came flooding out with Lorrie's death. The death was part of it, but mainly it was a catalyst."

"Well, then, what were his problems?"

"In clinical terms, he was a depressive. He felt he was losing his grip on things, that he wasn't able to control his environment for the first time in his adult life, that his memory was going, that he was getting old and losing his touch."

"Mid-life crisis."

Zollinger sniffed dismissively. "That's too simple. His marriage was a great source of guilt."

"It sounds like it was pretty lousy."

The doctor nodded. Neither wanted to get into Jess's personal investigation of the marriage. "He was contemplating divorce and that was very difficult for him. His circle doesn't subscribe to the notion that what doesn't work should be tossed aside."

"Do you know Modesty Nichols?"

"I knew of her. Robert mentioned her several times. He'd decided to get a divorce and marry her, for the sake of her baby, before Lorrie died."

"Did he also tell you that he was sending her to have the baby in the country — because it was safer in some way?" That one was for Michael.

"He sent her away when Lorrie died. You see, when that happened, his guilt crystallized. He simply couldn't handle the idea of divorce anymore. He wanted Miss Nichols out of the way while he figured out how to tell her he'd changed his mind."

"If he'd made the decision, why would he commit suicide?"

Zollinger smiled proudly as if Jess were a prize pupil.

"That's the crux of it. You're quite right — if a depressed person can make a decision, he's halfway home. He begins to feel in control again. That's the exact issue."

"Uh-huh. " He was charming and open and sincere, and she didn't like him at all. "Then why suicide?"

"The decision simply replaced guilt about Elizabeth and Lorrie with guilt about Miss Nichols and the baby. He couldn't accept that either, so he vacillated back and forth. Eventually, he could see no way out. No way at all."

"Except one."

"Except one," Zollinger agreed.

Jess paused at the doorway. "What's the prognosis for Mrs. Berrington?"

Zollinger shook his head.

* * *

Her mother answered the telephone and told her that Michael wasn't there. "What happened at work, darling?"

Good question. "Um, well, I've got my job back."

"Oh, darling, that's wonderful! I knew it would straighten out.

At the price of her marriage. Jess took a deep breath. No. No way was she going to think like that. "Where is Michael?"

"I don't know, he didn't say where they were going."

"They?"

"He was with another man. That rather nasty reporter who was at the opening yesterday."

"Jerry Katz?" Christ, why would Michael do that?

"Okay, well, I'm having lunch with Richard, but I'll be back by three. If you hear from Michael, have him call me."

What the hell was Michael up to? She tried to focus on it, but her mind was stuck on what he'd say when he found out that Jess was back in favor.

Consuela walked by the office and threw in a cheery grin that faltered at the sight of Jess's face. She came in. "What's wrong? You look like death warmed over, and you should be on top of the world."

"Yeah, I know." She shook her head. "Yesterday, half the city was disappointed in me. Today, it's the other half — including Michael."

Consuela shut the door. "Tell me about it."

Jess brought her up to date, right up to the lack of consensus in the Canby-Renfrew household.

"Oh, Jess." Consuela was unremittingly sympathetic and loyal. "What else could you do? You weren't getting anywhere, except into trouble!"

"Have you got a drug that'll convince Michael? He won't even listen to me."

The other woman looked unhappy. "But it's not fair."

"He'd say that life isn't fair." She looked at her desk. "When he hears I'm back on the job, he's going to think of a lot of C-words. Co-opted. Corrupt. Craven."

"Use your pregnancy."

"Consuela, what a rotten thing to say! That would be totally below the belt!"

Consuela raised her eyebrows.

"Oh, hell." Jess wearily rubbed her forehead. A minor head ache was turning into a full-fledged monster. "I might have to." That's what her father would have done, used whatever weapon lay at hand, then sprouted pious principles. You must have trained at Caesar's knee.

Consuela was silent for a moment. "Jess, you've got to get over that bitterness. So he wasn't perfect. So what? You put him up on a pedestal as a god — no one can live up to that."

"As a little, tin god," Jess said coldly. "Little and tin being the operative words."

* * *

The Los Angeles Country Club was a fair indication that God was no democrat. Its location, once sprawling countryside, was now a substantial hunk of real estate on the western border of Beverly Hills: a parcel a mile and a half long, half a mile wide, in the heart of a city where land was gold. And as if that mightn't have been a sufficiently generous gift to the mighty, He'd arranged that the simple little twenty-seven-hole golf course should sit upon oil. Let the rich get richer.

Jess smiled at the white-gloved doorman and walked into the clubhouse. Superficially examined, the decor was dowdy, with low ceilings, drab carpets, and unmemorable furniture. A closer look said that this kind of dowdiness cost a bundle. Everything was unostentatiously the best, heavily genteel, perfectly maintained.

The membership, too, was maintained. By comparison, Philadelphia's main line was hip. The West Coast was newer and rawer, and sensitive about it, so its society aped Mrs. Astor's four hundred and refused to change. Standards were as inflexible as the women's hairsprayed hairdos. No riff-raff from the entertainment world, no matter how famous. No dark faces, no matter how wealthy. The women were ladies, their daughters were debutantes and pants were a no-no even on the golf course. Men had ruddy faces, hearty manners, sat on each other's boards, and would as be seen nude in public as in a French silk shirt. It would have been ridiculous, except that power was never ridiculous.

The powerful were now having segregated lunches, the men at their own tables, doing business without ever actually mentioning commerce, the women in clumps, picking daintily at salads and talking about staff problems and charity balls. Richard Simon was in his usual privileged spot by the bay window. He got to his feet as Jess approached.

"My dear." He kissed her, looking happier than he'd looked for a week.

"Hi, Richard." Jess sat down and pointed at the bottle of champagne. "What's that for?"

"For the future." He chuckled. He meant for Jess's future, now that she had one again. "And for my golf game. I broke a hundred today."

"Congratulations." Jess grinned. Richard was superlative at everything — except golf. He played three or four times a week, had done so for decades, and was consistently, thoroughly rotten at it. She raised her glass and drank.

"Jessica. How nice to see you. Hello, Richard." Senator Uhuri and Supervisor Reg Cruickshank were beside the table. Both wore the open, sincere smiles of two men greeting two of their very favorite people.

Jess and Richard smiled back. The affection was mutual. It was a love feast, just as if the past week hadn't seen Jess thrown to the wolves.

"Enjoy your lunch." The politicians moved on.

Richard studied his menu. Jess watched him for a moment.

"The news got around rather quickly," she observed gently.

"News"

"About my rehabilitation."

"Yes." He decided to elaborate. "Stephen Bowdritch called a few people this morning. I gather you've made up your, er, differences with him."

Her pause was only momentary. "So it seems."

"Thank God for that." He raised his head to the waitress and ordered a club sandwich.

"Make it two," Jess angered. " And I may as we have some more champagne, Richard. Who knows when I'll get another bottle"

He poured and smiled. "Soon, perhaps. You're back on the list for the governor's water inquiry."

She downed the champagne and drowned the thought of what Michael was going to say.

"Richard, is my stock high enough again for a couple of favors?"

His voice was wary. "What kind of favors?"

"An old friend who works for the Department of Health Services is on suspension because I made him get me some classified information. I want to see him reinstated."

"What's the other favor?"

"It's about Michael. I'd like a chance to talk to Cyril Haberman."

"That's it?"

"That's it."

He beamed with relief. "We can work those out." This was influence peddling was all about. It beat hell out of being asked to fight the makers of the new technology. "Now, let's toast to the governor's commission."

"Okay," she agreed. She'd agree to anything after two glasses of champagne.

* * *

There were all kinds of independent film-production companies in Los Angeles. Some used that title but nestled into the laps of the major studios, living on the lots, paid by long-term studio contracts. Others were seldom paid at all, but hung onto the fringes of the industry in shabby warehouses on tough industrial streets. A few enjoyed both success and independence, and those, true to the not-ascetic spirit of Hollywood, flaunted it. Trail Productions was no less crass than any other. Haberman owned a three-story building in downtown Beverly Hills, the razor-sharp geometric lines attesting to its designer, the most sought-after, ultra-modern architect in town. The stucco walls were as white as capped teeth, the plaque on the door heavy brass like a yacht's anchor, and the door itself an intricately carved mahogany slab. Inside, thick rugs, museum-caliber art and furniture direct from Milan helped cushion the creative spirit from pain.

A soft-spoken male secretary greeted Jess in the reception area. He was a very thin young man with very short blond hair and designer jeans into which he had been fitted with a shoehorn. Following him up the wide staircase, Jess felt like the beast of burden behind a delicate Indian bearer.

"Cyril's in here," he murmured gently, pointing to double oak doors. "Coffee?"

"No, thanks."

"A drink?"

"No, thanks." In a moment, he was going to offer powdered stimulants. "Nothing, thanks."

She didn't expect to find Haberman's office any less self-indulgent than the rest of the premises and it wasn't. The room took up half of the third floor, an intimate expanse of twelve-foot sofas, glass tables and marble floor.

"Jessica." Haberman came forward with outstretched hands. Most of his companies operated in the suit-and-tie world, but he was dressed for today's role in white jeans and a white-and-navy striped jersey. He probably had a closet of costumes in each of his offices. "So good to see you."

"It's nice of you to make the time, Cyril." They smiled lovingly at each other. Cyril adored her too much to have tried to blacklist her husband; she adored Cyril too much to remind him.

"Sit down." He waved at the oversized silk-covered sofas. "Coffee?"

"No, thanks. Your secretary already offered."

"Oh, good." He took a seat beside her. "I must congratulate you on your latest coup."

"Coup?"

"You were right about poor Robert." He hit the exact note, a mixture of admiration for Jess and regret for the deceased. "I understand you always believed it was suicide."

Jess smiled.

"The county loses real talent when you move on to Sacramento," he added smoothly, as if he were referring to something that was, after all, a point of general knowledge.

She managed to smile again. "The rest of the staff is very good, and I daresay Dr. Harper won't miss me."

A brief flicker to indicate shared amusement at Harper's. little personal dislikes.

"This," she said, looking around and changing the subject, "is quite some place."

"Yes, I suppose it is." He followed her gaze as if he was noticing for the first time. "I enjoy this business. I love to work with artistic people."

"Do you have many productions going right now?"

"Three.   Two in development and one in post-production. I think you'll enjoy that one — you must come to the screening next month. We're very excited about it. It's about a lady senator in her forties who decides to have a child."

"Ah." She made encouraging noises.   Women's stories used to be simple romances about teachers or nurses or, for a touch of *cinema verite*, supermarket cashiers. Today, no one would consider a script unless the heroine was a brain surgeon or a judge.

"It's gone very well. I hope the other two go as smoothly."

Here it was, the point of the interview. "I bet they will. You've got an eye for properties."

"I certainly noticed Michael's book as soon as I saw it."

"Yes. It's a shame you had to put it on the back burner."

"Sometimes, you have to take a step back before you can go forward."

"Of course." Jess waited with a pleasant, casual, unharried smile. Her stomach was hurting almost as badly as her head.

"We're thinking of going ahead with it again." He nodded as if she'd expressed incredulity.   "Yes, *Daybreak's* for us — if Michael sees it the way we do."

"I'm sure he does." This time, her smile was genuine. "Have you talked to Dana? She'll be very pleased."

"Dana? Oh, the agent. No, I talked to Michael."
He watched her blandly. "He dropped in today."

"Michael dropped in today?" she repeated stupidly.

Haberman lit a cigarette without offering her one.
"He wanted to discuss something else he's working on.
I suppose it's a new script idea."

"I see."

"I told him I didn't think it would play. I'm afraid
he didn't like my advice, but I really think he should be
concentrating on one thing at a time. He is, after all, a
first-time screen writer."

"Yes. He is." Or was. Or would be. She stood up,
smiling gamely. "Well, thanks for seeing me."

"It was a pleasure. I'm looking forward to seeing
both of you again. Michael and I have a lot to talk
about.   Perhaps we'll have dinner next week?"
Haberman pressed a buzzer on the coffee table. "Brett
will show you out."

The young man decoratively graced the doorway.

"Ah, there you are, Brett. Will you show Jessica
out?" Haberman kissed her cheek and held her hand
with both of his. "Now, you take care of yourself, my
dear."

Brett and Jess traipsed chummily downstairs. She
was now one of the family.

"Get your business done?"

"Yes, thanks."

"Incredible man, isn't he?" A brief gleam of
wistfulness crossed the smooth face.

"Incredible," she agreed with sincerity.

"You know, he's one of the men who's going to
revolutionize the entertainment industry! Satellites and
so on."

"And so on." She coughed. "It's a shame poor
Robert Berrington won't be around to see what their
partnership accomplishes."

"Yes, well," Brett shrugged, "it wouldn't have lasted
anyway."

"Oh?"

"They weren't talking much the last few weeks before Berrington bought it." He opened the front door and, incredibly, widened what had seemed the ultimately wide smile. "Have a good one."

* * *

Eleven million people lived in the area, and about half of them got onto the freeway at the exact moment Jess did. It took an hour and a half to get to the Pacific Coast Highway, and another half-hour to get home. She had more than enough time to rehearse the arguments she was going to make to Michael. Why she was doing the right thing. Why he should do the right thing. Why helping Carl balanced out not helping Betty Drummond.

Her case was word perfect and a thing of beauty in its stark logic. It lacked one thing: an audience. Michael wasn't home.

"Did he call, Mother?"

Virginia was whipping up a casual three-course dinner; cold soup, rack of lamb, new potatoes, salad, mousse. She paused in the middle of decorating the serving platter with dill and parsley. Jess didn't even decorate living rooms. "Yes. Didn't he telephone the office? I told him about your good luck and said he should call you."

Jess fussed over pouring herself a glass of grapefruit juice, so her mother wouldn't see her face.

Dinner wasn't one of the better times between the two women. Jess didn't want to eat, didn't want to talk and couldn't bear the guilt of doing neither. The meal took about a week to get through. The rest of the evening was slow but television covered the silence.

Michael still hadn't come home when Jess went to bed. She started to worry at about two in the morning and by three-thirty she was standing in the bathroom, staring out the window at the highway as if sheer willpower would bring his car down the road.

When the telephone rang, she caught it before the first ring died. It was Martin Dunphy, telling her something that her mind didn't want to accept.

"Michael's in the hospital?" She finally grasped the salient detail. "Michael's in the hospital!"

"He's going to be fine. Really. He had some kind of fight but he's fine. Don't get upset — calm down, Jess. He wanted me to come out and get you."

"To hell with that. I'll meet you there."

* * *

She was inside the hospital at the county medical center in thirty minutes. Martin was waiting at the emergency reception desk, and they went upstairs together.

"Michael!" She rushed through the doorway, flashing her county ID at a dubious nurses, who was about to insist the these weren't visiting hours. "Michael, are you all right?"

He was lying down, smiling reassuringly. "I'm fine, sweetie. Honest. Bruised and furious, but fine."

He was not being scrupulously accurate. Fine didn't encompass hands that were bruised raw, a bandaged head, cracked ribs wrapped in gauze an blood-caked hair. Jess hyperventilated until she was sure she wouldn't burst into tears.

Martin filled the conversational void. "You look like hell."

"Thanks, pal."

Jess wouldn't let go of his arm, but she tried for a light voice. "Did you take on the whole division by yourself or did someone else get to share the fun?"

Michael's flipness deserted him. He closed his eyes.

"What is it? What happened?"

"I was a damn fool."

"Tell me what happened!"

"You're not going to like this very much," he warned.

"I already hate it."

Martin nodded emphatically in agreement and sat on the only chair. It wasn't comfortable, but there

312

wasn't room on a bed meant for one and holding two.

"Well, Jerry Katz came to see me this morning. He had a few questions I couldn't answer so, uh, we decided to go out together and work on them."

"Jerry Katz."

"I told you wouldn't like it. We went to Long Beach to see Betty Drummond again. She and her husband have moved. No forwarding address. We spent a lot of time trying to track them down, but they've just evaporated. Poof! Cloud of smoke, and they're gone."

"Surprise, surprise. What else?"

"I saw Haberman — "

"Yeah, I know. I did too. Go on."

"We did a few hours at the library, and then, tonight, we went to Pasadena to take a gander at Frechetti's files."

"Who?" Martin hadn't heard that name before. They'd spared him the thrill of joining them as accessories to crime.

"Just a doctor," Jess said hurriedly. "Michael, I'd have thought the office would be all sealed up."

"Uh, well, it was kind of locked," he admitted.

"You broke in?" She sagged. "That was a bright idea. I bet it was Jerry's."

"No, actually, it was mine." He avoided her eyes. "Anyway, we got in the back, all right. There weren't any cops around — there wasn't anybody around as far as we could see. But there also weren't any files. The place was cleaned out." He fell silent.

"So in frustration, you and Jerry took after each other? I hope you killed the sonofabitch."

Michael paled.

"God, I'm sorry." She tightened her grip on his arm. "What happened?"

"We drove a couple of blocks, trying to figure out what to do next. I stopped to make a phone call. To you." His voice softened." I felt pretty rotten about things."

"I know. I did too."

"I started to dial you and then I looked back at the

car. Jerry was standing on the sidewalk with this guy — biggest guy I ever saw in my life. A veritable crowd, all by himself."

"Pyramid?" she ventured.

He nodded. "Could be. He was the shape of that guy you pointed out in Gardena."

"And he did this?" She gestured at the bandages, fighting back the tears.

"First he laid into Jerry. It was incredible. It took him about six seconds to beat Jerry into a pulp. I mean it. I stared for a couple of seconds and then I ran over to help. By the time I arrived" — his voice trembled — "Jerry was on the ground and I'd never seen so much blood. It was everywhere. Unbelievable."

"It's the nose," Jess said soothingly. "Nosebleeds always look much worse than they are."

"Not in this case." Michael swallowed. "I got a taste of the medicine. I went for the big guy, and he taught me a few lessons about presumption. I don't think I messed a hair on his head."

"Were there no witnesses? Did nobody help?"

"In North Pasadena?"

Jess nodded. "Just a fantasy. Did you see what kind of car he left in?"

"I didn't see anything. He had me out on the ground in a flash, and then he must've gone back to Jerry because when I woke up, it was just me and this . . . this . . . thing beside me."

Jess could feel his body trembling. She put both arms around him, ignoring the bandages and her own tears that were making them wet.

"The cops came later, with an ambulance. I don't know how long we were there."

The three of them were silent for a long time.

Martin finally asked the question.

"How's Jerry?"

"I don't know. They took him away when we got here."

"They've taken him away again." The voice came from the doorway.

Jess sat up and shook her head. "Francis Arnheim. You do have a habit of turning up in our lives."

"Yeah. Can't bear to stay away." He slouched over and looked sourly at Michael. "You're one hell of a lucky bastard."

"Sure, that's what anyone would say, seeing him in a hospital bed with bruises and broken ribs," Jess said indignantly. "We don't know what to do with all this luck."

Michael wasn't listening to her. "Jerry?"

Francis shook his head; it made his jowls quiver. "He didn't make it. "

No one moved. Nobody even breathed.

"Whoever got him knew what he was doing. Tidy little job. Snapped his spine." Francis chewed on a cigar for a while. "By comparison, the ape kissed you."

Jess's hands were sweating as she clutched the sheets of Michael's bed.

The detective looked around for a chair. The only one was under Martin and he didn't budge. "So. Michael. Wanna tell me about it?"

Michael showed little inclination to do so.

"Pasadena's not my territory," Francis said sourly. "But Berrington was my case, and Katz was looking into Berrington so I'm not asking. I'll haul you in if I have to."

Michael sighed and repeated the story, leaving out the detail of where he and Jerry had been just before the assault.

Francis nodded slowly and spat out bit of tobacco. "So what's it mean to you?" He was talking to Jess.

She shrugged. "Berrington had something to hide."

"He's dead," Francis grunted. "He's out of the equation."

"He is now. But Bowdritch isn't."

"Pretty messy business, knocking people off on city streets." He sniffed. "Helluva risk."

"Unless you've got friends to protect you," Michael pointed out.

Jess shivered. "To serve and protect." The motto of

the Los Angeles Police Department. It hurt to think it, because Francis was a friend. But then, she'd thought Reg Cruickshank was too.

"Even with protection," Francis ruminated, "a smart businessman would need a lot of motivation to kill. It causes talk. I hear tell, Jess, that you got a theory about the motivation."

She hesitated. "I think — we think — we thought —"

"Skip the verb," he growled.

"We thought that satellites posed a health hazard and that Bowdritch would do anything to keep that out of the news."

"Thought." The cop gritted his teeth, then ground them for emphasis. "You saying you don't think so now?"

She stared at Michael and willed him to catch on. "I don't know, but I do know that it's none of our business. We're ready to surrender. He's won." She wondered sadly how soon Bowdritch would hear about that.

"You're stopping this nonsense!" Martin was on his feet, eyes shining with relief.

Francis looked as if he was about to expire from boredom. "You're gonna mind your own business now. This convinced you."

"You got it."

"You're not curious anymore. You're not angry. You're not filled with reformist zeal."

"You got it."

He nodded drily and turned to Michael. "What about you?"

Jess swallowed and prayed that the right answer would come out.

It did. "You think I want to risk the few bones in my body that aren't broken now? Forget it."

Francis switched topics without warning. "Either of you guys know an doctors in North Pasadena?"

They both held onto bland expressions.

"Uh?" Jess asked. "You sick?"

"The doctor I'm thinking of wouldn't be much good

if I were."

Francis and Jess watched each other. It was a game of chicken and they both were good at it.

The detective sighed. "Doctor's name is Frechetti." They shook their heads in unison.

"Funny things, eyewitnesses." Francis made a big fuss out of cleaning a fingernail. "Frechetti bought it Friday night. After I saw you in Hollywood. One or two people described a couple who went into the clinic just about the time he was strangled."

Martin opened his mouth in shock. He shut it again when Michael glared.

Francis was still studying his nails. "They all said the dame was unforgettable, being as how she was red-haired and pregnant."

"Oh, that guy!" Jess exclaimed sarcastically. "Hell, I strangle so many people, I never bother to get their names."

"Personally, I wouldn't figure you for a killer," he admitted. "But as a witness who's not coming clean —

"I have such wonderful rapport with the police," she said sweetly. "Why would I pass up a chance to spend more time with them?"

"The official view is that Frechetti was killed because of drugs," he continued, unperturbed. "Maybe someone wanted what was in the clinic. Maybe the doctor was behind in his payments for the drugs he bought for his pouf boyfriend." He looked up. "Or maybe it's something else entirely."

Jess shrugged.

Michael shrugged.

Francis looked at them with something in his eyes that vaguely resembled sadness. It was probably a dust particle. He finally stood up. "Killing gets easier each time. I hope you know what the fuck you're doing." He lumbered out.

Martin beamed, almost jumping up and down. "You're going to behave yourselves! You two have made me a happy man!"

"Well, don't be." Michael pointed to the door. "Go

see if he's gone, will you?"

Martin did so with the air of a saint forced to cater to madness. "He's gone. What do you mean, don't be happy?"

"Why should we trust Arnheim? Bowdritch owns everyone else — why should Arnheim be an exception"

"But he's Jess's friend!"

"Maybe. He certainly hangs around a lot. Anyway," Michael said dismissively, "we don't have to confide every last detail of our lives to him."

Martin groaned. "Jess, you were just starting to act like a normal human being. You don't go along with this, do you?"

"Sorry. I take a very dim view of someone trying to make me a widow." She touched Michael's arm. "God, do you realize how lucky we are still to be alive?"

"Bite your tongue, woman. Luck isn't reliable."

"No, it's not." She thought about that for a minute. "Michael, why aren't we dead?"

He started to nod. He got the point.

Martin didn't. "Jesus, what are you talking about? How can you talk about being dead?"

"Everyone else is," Jess pointed out. "We're surrounded by thugs, killers, and cutthroats, and we're fine."

"You call that fine?" He waved at Michael.

"Compared to poor Jerry, yes." She felt stirrings of guilt for all her insults. Jerry'd been awful, but no one was awful enough to deserve what he got. "Martin, someone has to be protecting us."

He considered that, then shook his head. "Even if that's so, how long can it go on? You two would exhaust the patience of St. Peter. Jess, think about the baby."

Her eyes were cold. "I'm thinking about a lot of babies. I've had it. They made a bad miscalculation tonight because I'm not going to take any more of their goddam warnings. Those bastards aren't getting away with this. We're not pawns to be pushed around — we've got resources — and by God we're going to use them!"

Martin swallowed in the face of her fury.

Michael reached for her. "I better get some sleep. They'll me go home tomorrow — uh, today — if I feel okay. Martin take Jess home?"

"Jess can make her own arrangements," she said. "That's the difference between me and a Christmas parcel. I can get places on my own."

* * *

The enormity of it all didn't hit her until she was back home. Suddenly, the wind went out of her, and she started shaking from muscles she didn't know she had. It was all she could do to get inside the house.

Virginia jumped up from the sofa. "Jessica! What is it? Where did you go? Where's Michael? What's wrong?"

Jess sighed under her breath. Of all the times for her mother to turn hysterically maternal. "Why are you up so early, Mother?"

"I heard the telephone, then I heard you leave. What's going on?"

Jess gave her a suitably sanitized version. It didn't seem to make Virginia feel better. Twice she went to the liquor cabinet and poured herself courage.

"Jess, you must make Michael stay away from this! Whatever it is!" The words were slightly slurred, but the intensity was but the intensity was sharp. "You have to make him stop!"

"Well, actually," Jess drew a deep breath, "I don't think I can. He wouldn't listen to me, and anyway, it might be too late to try to just walk away. We're like a couple of sardines in the middle of a school of piranha."

"Oh, my." Virginia returned to the liquor cabinet. "You want one?"

Jess shook her head. It might make her feel better, and then she'd be well on the way toward alcoholism.

"Jess." Virginia's voice was tentative. "You're going to have a baby. You can't — well, risk — "

"I can't let Michael fight it alone." She paused. "I want my marriage to work."

"Unlike mine, you mean." The tone was bitter.

Jess bit her lip.

"You think it was my fault, don't you?"

"Oh, Mother. I don't know whose fault it was. You and Dad were so different. I have trouble figuring out why you married in the first place."

"Why?" Three vodkas brought memories back. "We were so young. I was just out of college and he'd just started teaching grade school. We met at a dance." She was smiling into the past. "He was charming, you know. He wasn't like any other man I'd ever met — all that vitality and force."

She got up unsteadily and made her way to the glass doors of the deck. She stared out. "He wanted me a great deal. I suppose I was pretty. And my family was important and well-to-do. Not like he became, but more than the Canbys. I don't know."

Jess watched silently. This was not the Virginia she knew, this woman expressing real emotions and fears, talking without the seamless, isolating patina of social correctness.

"Then," Virginia's voice changed, and she turned around, "then he got the political bug. He became a school trustee at twenty-seven, and he was never mine again. He ran for City Council at thirty-one, and he never lost an election. Not a single one. His constituents thought he was Jesus Christ, Mahatma Gandhi, and Albert Schweitzer rolled into one."

"Fools that they were." Jess abruptly got to her feet. She'd change her mind. She would have that drink after all.

Virginia gazed at her, then looked into her now-empty glass and held it out. "More for me, too."

Jess poured without comment. She'd only seen her mother take more than two drinks once. It was years ago Jess had been a youngster, and she hadn't quite understood at the time. She did now. It was her parents' wedding anniversary, and Caesar had been at a political meeting. He'd just forgotten.

"Mother, your life was the shits."

Virginia winced and downed the vodka in a single swallow. "Jess, you shouldn't — " She broke off, unable to go on with whatever she'd been about to say.

"Well, I won't let it happen to me. I won't let my marriage go down the tubes like Dad did. Politics won't change me like it changed Dad." It was a promise as much to herself as to Virginia. "Or maybe it didn't change him. Maybe he was always a hypocritical bastard."

"No!" The word exploded; Virginia looked as surprised as Jess.

"Mother" She moved over to her. "You're very strange, tonight. Are you all right?"

Virginia stared at her empty glass for a long time. Finally, she put it down on a side table and sat on the sofa, patting the cushion next to her.

Jess obediently sat too. "What is it?"

"I can't let you go on being bitter like this." A single tear ran down her cheek. "I should have told you this on Saturday. What Richard said about your father — it wasn't fair." She paused for a long moment. "Arthur — Arthur let me down, but he was your father. He loved you. He didn't let you down. I can't let you go on thinking about him like this. Jessica, he never sold anyone out. He lost some battles, of course, but he always fought as hard as he could, and when he made concessions it was because he really believed he was doing the right thing."

"Like leaving the Mexicans to a life of slavery?"

"No, no, you don't understand." Virginia closed her eyes and shook her head. "He thought he could slip one past the businessmen who'd set up the deal. He had a flaw — he was terribly, terribly arrogant — but he honestly thought he could beat them. When it turned out he couldn't, he was sick about what he'd given away. He called himself a Judas. I don't think he ever forgave himself. But it was the sin of pride, not — not what Richard let you think."

Jess was hardly breathing. It was too much to absorb all at once. She let the words slide gradually into her consciousness. "But then why did Richard say — "

"He save you the harsh version because he felt it was the best thing for you. To bring you back to your senses. He loves you, he loved Arthur — he wanted to protect you."

To protect her. Jess licked suddenly dry lips and thought about what she and Michael had said about that. Richard had lied to get her to stop making trouble. To protect her.

"And I — " Virginia couldn't meet her eyes. "I didn't stop him because — "

"Because why? Because you thought it was best for me too?"

Her mother shook her head. "That's what I told myself but really, it was because . . . because it was best for me."

Jess was puzzled.

Virginia's voice was barely audible. "I resented him so much, taking everything away from me. Himself, first. And then you." She looked up, ashamed. "Can you understand that?"

Jess nodded and patted her mother's hand, but she wasn't thinking about Virginia. She was suddenly flooded with a white burst of relief; she felt twenty pounds lighter and a decade younger. It wasn't true about Dad. The earth had stopped shifting under her feet.

Chapter 20

Courtroom Seven, was jammed at nine o'clock. The noise level was earsplitting, a pandemonium of angry shouting defendants, urbane lawyers, frantic families and barking police officers.

Jess had had no sleep, and the commotion almost bowled her over. She took a deep breath and pushed her way toward the front.

Benny Shouldice was talking to the Assistant DA, looking every bit as oily as he had in his glamorous office; but here he fitted right in. The prosecutor was a young woman, certainly fresh out of law school if not just out of grade ten. Did they not require attorneys to complete high school anymore? How did they come to be so baby-faced?

"Howdy."

Jess turned sharply as a body pushed between her and a black-clad Mexican woman who was wailing shrilly at a dead-eyed young man.

"Francis. Well, well, well. You're certainly more ubiquitous than sin."

"Did you ever consider that I might be the arresting officer on any of these cases?"

"Are you?"

"No," he admitted lugubriously. He scanned the dock. "That's them."

Jess looked at a clump of soon-to-be-arraigned prisoners. Theodore an Lewis were standing to one side, apparently bored by the prospect and undisturbed. "That's the two they've charged with Lil's murder," she agreed. "That's not the two who did it."

"I didn't figure you'd change your mind."

"You were right."

"I thought you were going to see no evil, hear no evil, and speak no evil anymore."

She looked at him and hoped her flush wasn't obvious. "I'm prepared not to make trouble, but I'm not prepared to see two innocent men go to jail. Excuse me."

"Where are you going?"

She didn't answer, but forced her way through the madness to reach to two black men. "Theodore. Lewis."

They looked at her without changing expressions.

"My name is Jess Canby. I want to talk to you for a minute."

"What about, girl?"

Jess had no idea which was which, and they were going to call the room to order any minute, she didn't have time to sort it out. She arbitrarily decided that the speaker was Lewis. "I'm the witness to the murder you're charged with."

"Oh, yeah?"

She'd raised more interest in other settings with a comment on the weather. "I know you two didn't do it. And I told your attorney that."

The second man raised an eyebrow. "He musta been happy to see you."

Jess frowned. The tone hadn't been serious. "No, no, he wasn't, as it happens. I thought you might like to see me."

No response.

"Look, why would you want to go down for something you didn't do?"

"Who says we want to go down?"

"You're going to — if you don't talk to me. The prosecution's got a lot of evidence, and that's rather strange, isn't it? Since if you didn't kill Miss Scott, there shouldn't be evidence saying you did."

"What are you doing here?" Shouldice was at her elbow, pressing her against the wooden wall of the dock. "You have no right to talk to my clients!"

"I'm not an ambulance-chaser, Shouldice." She let the words hang in the air to suggest who she thought was. "If your clients want to, they can talk to God himself."

Lewis liked that. He flashed a broad grin that would have been engaging but for two missing teeth.

"My clients don't want to talk to you! Do you, boys?"

324

Jess winced, waiting for the Black Panthers to appear and strike the lawyer dead. Nothing happened. Lewis and Theodore were not, it seemed, politically evolved.

"Do you?" Shouldice demanded again.

The two men shrugged. It could have meant anything.

Jess chose to interpret it as a denial of their mouthpiece's statement. "I'm willing to testify for you two. I'll do it voluntarily, but I hope you'll do me a favor in return."

"They do you no favors!" Shouldice shouted. "You leave them alone!"

"You leave me alone!" she snapped. "And stop shoving me. In case you didn't notice, I'm pregnant and babies don't come out when you crowd their womb, they get hurt — which gives their mother a swell cause of action!"

Shouldice looked unimpressed, but he did move back a centimeter.

She returned her attention to the accused. "Who set you up on this? Who's paying your lawyer?"

"What's it to you, girl?"

If they could bend their principles to accept being called "boys" she could show a little flexibility too. "It's a long story. But, basically, I don't want the real killers to get away with this, and to find them I've got to find out who's protecting them."

Theodore yawned.

"It's not right that you get convicted!" she argued passionately.

Lewis joined Theodore's ennui.

Jess took a deep breath, then noticed that Shouldice had relaxed. He was grinning nastily. It slowly dawned on her that the defendants were passing the time by playing with her. "You guys got paid too, didn't you?" she asked carefully. "And you got a deal. You clean your slates of things you did do — in exchange for taking this rap and doing some easy time."

Theodore's eyes flickered before they moved away.

Lewis was already staring in another direction.

"I see." She looked at Shouldice. "How many years are your clients going to do? Three? Four? Out in less than two?"

He shrugged. "Wait and see."

"I intend to." Jess made her way back toward the benches. Francis had secured two very small places for them on the one closest to the front. He was sitting now, watching her approach as if he'd never taken his eyes away during the whole of the fruitless conversation.

"You going to sit or go?" he asked.

"Sit. I always enjoy farces." She sat heavily. "Great little legal system we got here."

He gave no sign that he understood.

"They've done a deal." As if that would come as a huge surprise. "I guess it's not too hard to bargain out a murder in this sewer."

"A mugging that happens to turn into a murder," Francis corrected patiently.

"Oh, right. A mugging that happens to turn into a murder. A gunshot happens to remove an old lady's head. Pure accident. Who'd expect it to be so serious from a distance of a whole twelve inches."

They didn't talk again during the proceedings. A deceptively benign-looking judge took the bench, the chaos subsided marginally while he heard dozens of arraignment. He cholerically set trial dates for the few who pleaded not guilty, and sentencing dates for the rest. The judge's snarls added yet another dimension to the already-rich medley of voices: court clerks reciting archaic legal formulas in bored staccato bursts, police officers thundering data at the female prosecutor as if she mightn't comprehend a gently put sentence, attorneys reeling off set pieces, mothers and wives alternately weeping and protesting.

At ten-thirty, the judge banged his gavel with a nicotine-stained hand an declared a recess. The defendants' dock emptied, Lewis and Theodore loping away as if they admitted falsely to murder every day of the week. Cigarette-craving lawyers fought tiny old women and families with babes in arm for a hasty exit. Benny Shouldice sauntered along in the crush, pausing to catch Jess's eye and wink maliciously.

Jess and Francis held back until there was no more than a fifty-fifty chance of being trampled. They emerged onto the street at the same time as Detective Carmichael. He'd given his all to the case, from the look of him. His face was sagging with weariness, and he didn't appear to have changed or washed since Jess last saw him at the lineup.

"Arnheim. Mrs. Canby." He looked her up and down. "You here for any particular reason?"

"No," she answered coldly. "Except to see if you were actually going to go through with this disgrace."

He nodded as if he'd expected that answer and didn't mind it. "Yeah. See you."

Not if she saw him first. Jess nodded curtly, and Carmichael ambled away.

Francis coughed and pulled out a cigar. "Jess — "

She wasn't any keener on him than on Carmichael. "See you." And given the way things had been going, that, at least, was probably true.

* * *

Michael was dressed and waiting in the hospital lobby. He looked even worse than during the night; the bruises were starting to settle into rich shades of purple and scarlet.

"Sorry I'm late." She kissed him gently on lips that were still split. "Are you sure you're up to getting out today?"

"Damn sure. If I stayed, there's a good chance the hospital would finish what the Pyramid started. They brought me the wrong pills this morning." He put an arm around her despite obvious pain from the ribs.

Jess winced in sympathy and helped him into the car.

"Where are we going?" he asked.

"I thought maybe I'd take you home. Weird idea, I

327

know, but — "

"No, there's no time for me to lie a bed." He pasted on a phony grin. "I feel wonderful."

She raised an eyebrow.

"Fair. I feel fair," he amended. "What did you plan to do when you dropped me off? Because we'll do it together."

"A great pair, we make." She was grotesque and front-heavy. He had to beg every muscle before it would obey his desire.

"We're all we've got."

So true. So sad. Still, nothing seemed to unseat her good mood this morning. She was Arthur Canby's daughter, and she could do anything. "It all started with Lorrie. We've got to remember that."

The car crossed the compound to the coroner's building and defiantly took Harper's spot. It was a very tiny act of defiance; he would still be out of town, so she didn't have to worry about parking stickers, or his reaction to the demise of their short lived entente.

Michael sat at the telephone in her office while Jess joined Consuela at the watch-commander's station. Consuela looked horrified when she realized that Jess and Michael were back at it. She did her own work while Jess telephoned, scowling at nervous first-call officers, emitting waves of disapproval that kept bewildered investigative staff away.

Michael limped in an hour and a half later. "Any luck?"

Jess shook her head.

Consuela sniffed.

"Me neither," he sighed. "Lots of Koestlers in the county, but none of them Sarah."

"She vanished in a cloud of smoke." Jess stretched wearily. She was too old and much too pregnant to miss a night's sleep.

"Between the people who disappear the moment you talk to them and the bodies that turn up all over the place, we're single-handedly emptying LA."

Consuela couldn't bear it. "Jess, Michael. Why are

328

you doing this? Please — come back to the real world. God — Jess, you just got your job back. And look at Michael!"

Jess grinned unsympathetically. "Consuela, think about Sarah Koestler. How would you go about finding a missing scientist? No phone. No address. No medical association ties anymore."

"I don't know." Consuela didn't want to think about it.

The other two eyed her sternly, and she sighed. "You're not your usual inventive selves, are you? Friends, of course. People who used to know her — at the associations, neighbors."

"Of course." Michael grinned at Jess. "We're getting senile. My excuse is my battered head. What's yours?"

She shook her head in disgust. "Hormones, I suppose." Or maybe good humor dulled wit. Her experience was too scanty to say.

Connie Hartman's nurse wasn't enthusiastic about breaking in on the doctor's interview with a patient, but eventually, she capitulated. Probably just to get Jess off the line.

"You okay, Jess?" The voice was more bass than usual. Connie must have had a hard night too."

"I'm fine. We need help, Connie. Sarah Koestler has vanished off the face of the earth, and we have to talk to her."

"Jesus, I haven't seen Sarah in years, and doctors don't just vanish. There's the AMA and — "

"All tested and found wanting. Maybe it needs the personal touch. You knew people who knew her."

Connie sighed. "I'm backed up till Christmas."

"That's not soon enough. We were thinking more in terms of a few hours."

"Important?"

Jess put all the fervor she felt into her words. "It's a question of life and death!"

"Oh, hell. Okay, I'll try, but it'll take the day. I'll call you at home tonight."

Jess was smiling as she replaced the receiver. "I like that woman. I really like that woman."

"Are you ready for another scenic drive?" Michael had a little trouble doing it, but he got himself to his feet.

"Am *I* ready? Who are you trying to kid?" She put an arm around him.

"It's time for Santa Barbara again."

Consuela groaned. "Michael! You can't sit in a car for two hours!"

"Then Jess will drive faster."

* * *

She did her best, but as always, Highway 101 was clogged, and they pulled into Restview Clinic's parking lot two hours and fifteen minutes later. Michael's face was gray from the inevitable bouncing. Jess's wasn't much better from lack of sheep and the tension of trying unsuccessfully to see if any of the zillion other cars on the road had been following them.

They made their clumsy way to the front doors.

"How will we talk our way in?" Michael asked, just as Jess reached for the knob.

She looked at him, then down at herself. "It's a rest home, babe. I have a feeling we'll fit right in — they just won't be able to figure out which one of us is the patient."

She kept her face down and her eyes on the carpet. It was an ostrich's *modus operandi*, but it seemed to work. No one stopped them as they climbed the stairs and let themselves into Elizabeth Berrington's suite.

Elizabeth was in her usual fetal crouch on the sofa, as gaunt and pale as Jess remembered her.

"Is it time for my pills?" The shadowed eyes flickered.

Jess shook her head. "No, we've just come to talk to you."

"Oh."

Michael raised an eyebrow and muttered to Jess,

"Super little witness you've got there."

Jess ignored him and crossed to the widow. "I want to talk about your daughter, Mrs. Berrington."

"I — oh, that makes me tired," Elizabeth said fretfully. "No, not about her. Can't talk about her."

"Sure you can," Jess crooned as she sat down. "You told me about her before. Do you remember?"

"No, I don't. Do I know you?"

"You told me that Lorrie had some funny ideas just before her death. Do you remember that?"

Elizabeth stirred, still barely aware of her visitors. She was deeply immersed in her inner fantasy world.

Jess persisted. "She had funny ideas, and Robert said they were wrong; but they weren't wrong, were they?"

"Oh, I can't remember."

Michael joined them and painfully crouched, his face only two feet from Elizabeth's. "What were the ideas, Elizabeth?"

A male voice kindled reaction. Elizabeth had been brought up to defer to men, and the habits of a lifetime took more than a few carloads of Scotch to erase. "Do I have to remember?"

"Yes, you do," Michael answered firmly, getting into the spirit of the conversation. "You must remember. What were the ideas?"

Elizabeth's long fingers splayed and contracted nervously. "You know. Those complaints. You know."

"Robert was angry, wasn't he?" He tried another approach. "He didn't like her complaining about his business, did he?"

"No, he didn't," she agreed dutifully.

"What were the ideas?" Jess was too tired to restrain herself. It was a mistake. Elizabeth looked straight at her, the eyes widening. "You were here before."

Jess nodded.

"You're not supposed to be here."

"We have to talk to you. We need help from you."

Elizabeth pushed her way past them and stood at a round table covered with china figurines. "I'm not supposed to talk to you."

Michael motioned to Jess to stay put. He followed the other woman and towered over her. "Lorrie needs your help, Elizabeth."

"Lorrie."

He nodded.

"Lorrie's dead." The genteel voice was flat.

"Yes, she's dead. She was killed, and we want to punish the people who killed her."

Elizabeth frowned. "I'm not supposed to talk about Lorrie."

"You have to talk to us. You don't have a choice."

Jess winced at the hint of menace. Then she thought about the Pyramid, the car chases, and Michael's ribs and bit back her protest.

"You have to talk to us. What were Lorrie's ideas?"

Elizabeth looked around distractedly as if she expected the cavalry to swoop in and save her.

"Her ideas," he persisted coldly.

"The machines. That the machines hurt people."

It was hard to hear the whispered words. Jess was straining her ears.

"Her friends — those foreign people — they encouraged her."

"And she was right. So she was killed."

"No!" It was a horrified hiss. "It was an accident. My daughter wasn't killed on purpose!"

"Your husband thought she was."

"Yes, but he was wrong! He was wrong, I'm telling you," she insisted frantically. "Lorrie was crazy — " She laughed with a harsh burst of frenzy. "She was crazy like her mother."

"What did Lorrie say about the machines? How did they hurt people?"

"Burned them or something. I don't know; I wouldn't listen. She came here and I wouldn't listen and then she was dead, and Robert said she was right, and they had to give me something for my headaches. I have a headache now," she subsided.

Michael helped her back to the sofa. "The machines that Robert built, how did Lorrie know they weren't safe? How did she find out?"

"She — I don't know." Elizabeth was silent for a moment.

"That trip she took. She knew for sure afterwards."

"Did she have proof? Could she prove it:"

"I don't know."

"What convinced Robert? Proof that Lorrie showed him? Or was it her death that convinced him?"

Elizabeth shook her head frantically. "I don't know."

Michael leaned forward so her eyes had nowhere to hide. "Which was it, Elizabeth? What she showed him or how she died?"

"Her death and that girl."

Michael paused, puzzled.

"Her roommate?" Jess asked quietly.

"Yes, yes, that girl."

Jess picked up the picture from the end table and studied it again. The roommate's face was still familiar, and she still couldn't figure out why. "What did Robert do after Lorrie died?"

Elizabeth watched Jess, apparently grateful for the soft voice. "He talked to people, I suppose."

"He was worried, wasn't he? He was worried enough to send . . . his friend out of town?"

"His floozie." Elizabeth frowned. "His floozie was pregnant and he was worried about his little bastard."

Someone knocked on the door. Jess and Michael froze.

"Mrs. Berrington."

"Tell her to go away," Jess whispered. "Tell her you're busy."

"She'll come in anyway." Elizabeth seemed surprised that Jess wouldn't know such a basic fact of life.

"Mrs. Berrington, it's time for our nice walk." The nurse spoke with the condescending command that nurses always used for patients, no matter how rich. "Get your clothes on, and I'll come for you in a minute."

Jess and Michael clasped hands with relief. They

333

moved silently toward the door.

"You won't be back." Elizabeth might have been making a prediction or a plea.

They let themselves out after carefully peering into the hall. It was time for a nice walk for everyone; the corridors were busy with anxious-faced inmates herded along by the forced cheer of staff. Michael and Jess must have looked as bad as any of them, because no one seemed to pay them any attention.

* * *

They took the coast road back. It was longer and generally slower except in rush hour, which was anything after three. Besides, it went right past the house, and it seemed like a good idea to stop in and say hello to their houseguest. Michelen wouldn't give their hotel any stars for service.

"That's Richard Simon's car, isn't it?" Michael pointed, trying to sit up like a normal person who didn't hurt all over. "What's he doing here? I thought he had to work long days, bagging money for the party?"

Jess pulled in behind the Cadillac and hurried into the house. Maybe NOW didn't believe in woman's intuition — in fact, she didn't believe in it — but something was telling her that all was not as it should be.

Virginia and Richard were beside each other on the couch. Richard looked anxious, and Virginia looked worse.

"What happened?" Jess stood in the front doorway, realizing that her relief at seeing them meant that she'd actually feared more violence. This was no way to live.

It was Richard who answered. "Virginia had a frightening telephone call this afternoon. She couldn't find you, so she called me."

Michael came in time to hear the last words. He and Jess moved slowly toward the older couple.

"What did the caller say, Mother?"

"He said . . . he said . . . "

Richard took over again. "He told Virginia that if you two didn't start minding your own business again, she'd be at tending your funerals."

Jess and Michael's hands joined.

"Jess," Virginia said in a trembling voice, "he meant it. I could tell; he really meant it. He said you could easily have a car accident; you could even have one today in Oxnard. Lots of bad drivers in Oxnard, he said."

"I see." Oxnard was on the way to Santa Barbara. She'd been given the chance to regain favor, but she'd not been trusted to accept it.

"Virginia," Michael said slowly, "I don't want to kick you out, but I think it would be better if you went home today."

"I can't leave you like this — "

"You'll relieve our minds." He went over to kiss his mother-in-law. "It would be worse for us, worrying about you here. I'd like you to fly out tonight."

"I'll take her to the airport," Richard offered. "You two look dreadful. Completely done in. Virginia told me about last night, Michael. I — " He broke off. "I don't understand; I thought everything was normal again. What's going on?"

Jess couldn't meet his eyes. There was a good chance that he already knew the answer." Richard, would you call and get Mother a reservation? I'll help her pack."

The telephone stopped them all in mid-stride.

Michael picked it up and held it so Jess could listen.

"You're home now. Stay there." The line went dead.

"Who was it?" Virginia stood up, wringing her hands as if she were studying to play Lady MacBeth.

"Nothing, just a wrong number." Michael did his best to smile reassuringly while he and Jess held each other's cold hands.

* * *

"You think Richard's in it, don't you?" Michael

waved a final goodbye at the vanishing Cadillac and looked at Jess.

"I don't know. Oh, God, I hate to think so!" Richard had been part of her life as far back as she could remember. "God, I hope I'm just paranoid!"

"Even paranoids have enemies." They silently went into the house to call Dr. Liu Shi. He was unhappy to hear from them. He finally agreed to listen to Michael's question only to get them off the telephone.

"Have you ever heard of anything in Paraguay — an American installation? A research institute? Military test sites?" Michael cast around for all the possible options. "Anything to do with microwaves?"

"I know nothing. About Paraguay or anyplace else. I'm hanging up now."

"Wait!" Michael shouted to get Shi's attention and hold it for another moment. "Look, this is important. We don't have much time left, and all we know is — "

"You don't seem to know the most important thing. What you're doing, it is very dangerous."

"We don't want to put you in danger. That's why we called instead of coming over."

"I'm leaving anyway. I'm just about to start my new job. I'm only talking to you for one reason — one reason." His voice was intent. "Listen to me. You're the ones in danger. You're about to have a family. Content yourself with that and live a long life."

"What new job?"

Jess pressed even closer to Michael and the receiver.

"I have been fortunate enough to secure another research position."

"Where? No, let me guess. With Merton."

Shi had no intention of discussing his career path. "Leave well enough alone, Mr. Renfrew. Be grateful that you are still . . . healthy." He hesitated. "Pray that it is not already too late."

"Well, it may be," Michael said angrily. "We're asking you one lousy question. We have to find proof before — "

Shi interrupted him. "I will not talk about this any longer. I am not sure if there is any proof, as you call it. I do know that if there is, I'm very lucky I never found it. Finding proof that would be the most stupid thing you could do." He hung up. When they redialed, the telephone rang thirty fruitless times.

Jess massaged icy fingers. Michael put his arm around her, but his body temperature wasn't an improvement.

He finally broke the silence. "How good do you think we could be — at getting away from a tail?"

"Obviously not too good. We don't even see the goddamn things."

He nodded. "Then we'll just have to pretend we're going to Venice to watch the zoo.

* * *

The Venice beach was a carnival of action. Roller-skaters in red, yellow, and blue zipped along the paved boardwalk, performing patently impossible feats. Two basketball games were being played to a female audience more taken with the leggy players than the doings of the ball. Vendors hawked candy and ice cream, T-shirts, and, less aggressively, dope. A young man on a collapsible chair gave legal advice for free. Another counseled religion. A woman passed out pamphlets for a Woman's Free Clinic. It might have been the sixties again, except that in the Sixties there hadn't been a sense that guns, knives, and chains could appear at any moment.

Jess and Michael sauntered along, for once uninterested in the passing trade. They used any excuse at all to turn around suddenly: they moved through the thickest crowd; they changed directions a dozen times. Finally, they slid away from the beach toward Karen Graley's street. No one followed them out. Nobody came down the sidewalk from the ocean. It was a hot, dry evening, and the traffic was all in the other direction.

"What do you think?" Michael asked eventually.

She shrugged. They were babes in the woods, sitting ducks, target practice. But she hadn't been able to detect a tail.

Karen wasn't home but her mail box wasn't full. Jess checked with the landlord. Poul was listening to chamber music and he didn't want to interrupt himself for long, but he did say that his tenant had returned from her trip. He'd seen her last night.

Jess and Michael waited inside the front door, watching the street without showing themselves. It was a long vigil, disturbed only by the comings and goings of other tenants, a scruffy bunch, who bore no resemblance to the silver-spoon set among whom poor Henry Poul had grown up. The thought of his asking these people for rent money was a disturbing one.

Jess was almost asleep on her feet when a trio stopped on the sidewalk outside. The two men were the peacocks, vivid in purple and orange, their lithe bodies tanned and oiled and glinting. Their companion was the little brown hen, her pale skin and neutral hair set off by a sleeveless beige shift.

The men smiled, waved goodbye and trotted off, hand-in-hand. The young woman turned and came up the stairs.

Jess's jaw dropped. She stepped forward as the door opened. "Karen Grayley."

The pale skin became parchment.

"You remember ne, Karen." This was an older version of the girl in Elizabeth Berrington's snapshot, all right. Older and sadder. Karen was only twenty-two or -three, but she wore the air of defeat of someone twice that age. "I talked to you at the Boyle Heights birth-control clinic. I was looking for someone who knew Lil Scott, and you said you didn't."

"I'm — in a hurry." Karen tried to push past, but it took more than a hundred pounds to budge a firmly-rooted pear.

Michael joined the action. "We won't take long if you're cooperative."

The faded eyes risked a quick flash at him, then

turned downwards again. "No, no, I can't. Let me pass."

"You talk to us out here — in public — or inside. It's up to you." Jess had little taste for browbeating, but she was in no mood to be put off. "If I were you, I'd prefer privacy."

The words struck a chord. Karen glanced nervously at the street and nodded jerkily.

They followed her closely. No one spoke until they were on the other side of a green door at the back of the first-floor hall. The living room was standard student habitat, complete with three white walls and one dark brown, oversized pillows on the floor, brick-and-board shelving, and candles stuck in empty wine bottles.

Karen stood in the center, passive, as if she were the guest and they the hosts.

Jess and Michael looked at the cushions and sighed. They'd have to stay standing too, unless someone was willing to bring in a crane.

"Lil Scott was bringing ne to see you when she got murdered for her trouble," Jess said flatly. "It's taken me a while to find you, and my patience has just about worn out." Torquemada making his position very, very clear. "So we want answers."

The other woman watched her, dull-eyed.

"What did Lil Scott think you could tell me?"

No response.

"What do you know about Lorrie's last few months?"

No response.

"What was Lorrie doing in Paraguay?"

No response.

Jess made herself think about the way Lil had looked as she lay on the sidewalk. Then she pictured Lorrie and Robert and Frechetti and Jerry Katz. And Michael. She spoke again, her voice hard. "You're going to answer my questions, Karen. You can't afford not to."

Karen moved then, a little shrug. Apparently even hundred-pound weaklings weren't exactly terrorized by pregnant ladies and bandaged men, no matter how tough they talked.

"You're terrified to tell us anything and I can understand that," Jess conceded. "I'd be scared in your position, too." Hell, she was scared in *her* position. "But you'll give us what we want."

"I can't."

"You have to. We won't beat you or shoot you or slip knives under your fingernails. We don't have to do any of those things."

Karen had paled at the mere rundown of the sort of events that could overtake her.

"We won't do the dirty work ourselves. We just have to let it be known that you're about to give us the information we want. This city's full of people who'd get very nasty if they heard that."

"You wouldn't do that," Karen pleaded.

Jess and Michael stared at her icily.

"Take the risk and see," Michael suggested.

The room was quiet except for the distant shouts of the street people and Karen's ragged breathing.

"Lorrie was looking for proof that microwaves cause illness," Jess said helpfully. "She's not the first person whoever thought so, but she's the first we know of who died for it. So we have to figure she came up with more than suspicions. What did she come up with?"

"I don't know."

Michael eased himself down onto the cushions. "Karen, so many people are dead already." The implication was that it would be a shame if the toll rose by one.

"I don't know — I swear!" Karen inched forward. "She was looking for proof, I know that. But I didn't want to know more that — not after she got threatened!"

Lorrie was threatened?"

"Yes, of course she was. That's how she knew she was living on borrowed time. She even told Lil she was going to die. She knew it and I knew it, and I didn't want any part of it!"

Jess swallowed. So far, Lil was batting one thousand. She'd always spoken the truth and, like

Cassandra, wasn't much thanked for it. "Tell us from the beginning. How did Lorrie get onto it in the first place?"

Karen flinched.

"It was through you, wasn't it?" Jess guessed suddenly. "Through the clinic?"

The young woman spread her arms. "I didn't know what I was saying! I didn't know Lorrie would get so involved." She shuddered at the recollection of just how involved Lorrie had gotten. "She was working for the cable company and hating it. She didn't like business anyway, and — well, that reminded her of her father all the time. She hated him."

"Had she always hated him?"

"Well, it was mixed up. Love, hate — all mixed up. She was like that when I first met her."

"What did you say that started her off on this?"

"I . . . I mentioned — like, you know, it was just a comment. I didn't mean it seriously because I didn't take Herminia seriously."

"Hold it." Michael pointed to the floor. "Sit down, Karen, and take it slowly. Who is Herminia?"

She lowered herself with a grace Jess could only wish for. "This South American woman who came to the clinic a few times. We get lots of South Americans, you know, not just Mexicans. She and her husband were leftists — they came up on the underground railroad. That's what they call it — "

"Uh-huh. Go on."

"Well, she said the villages in her county were being poisoned. People were getting real sick, all kinds of things, cancer and bleeding eyes, and birth defects." Karen frowned. "She even said there were too many girls being born — it's a macho society; they want boys."

Jess cut into the impending lecture on feminism. "This is Paraguay, you're talking about?"

She nodded. "Yes. And Herminia said it was being made to happen — that there was radiation deliberately pointed at the villages. I didn't believe her. Manuel, that's the husband, he hangs out with the crazy people

341

at the South American Club. They see conspiracies everywhere."

"Did Lorrie ever meet Herminia or Manuel? What's their last name?"

"Perreira. Yes, she met them. Or Manuel, at least. But that was later, after she saw this." Karen got up and crossed to a bookcase. She held out a ragged magazine. "It's a medical journal we get at the clinic. It's got an article about microwaves."

Jess knew it. She and Michael had skimmed through it at the library.

"It gave her the idea, and then she found out that her father had some business in Paraguay. She kept on saying that there wasn't any other possible reason — it's such a poor country." Karen stared off into space, remembering. "She got all upset. But I think she was looking for something to make her father notice her. Even if it was just to yell at her. Notice. You know?"

Jess knew. The road that had brought the Berrington family to tragedy was a very long one; there'd been a lot of possible turn-offs along the way, but they hadn't been taken.

"She read this article, oh, I don't know, maybe twenty-five times. She took a day off work just to sit home and read it."

"Did she talk to anyone about it?" Michael asked. "Except you?"

"There wasn't anyone except me. She didn't have friends, really. She was kind of shy and, well, prickly. We got along because we knew each other so long, and because I'm not real outgoing either. Not real popular, you know." She touched her face as if to comfort it for not being quite up to the mark.

Jess refused to deal with the pathos. "What did Lorrie do about the article?"

"She decided to prove it was true, the suspicions. And then she'd go to the papers. Really smear egg on her father's face. So she talked to Manuel and lots of other people. She found lots of other people. Possible victims of microwaves — but she couldn't prove it."

Jess and Michael sighed. They knew the feeling.

"She became obsessed. She quit her job and did it full-time. She even went to her mother for money, and she'd never done that before; but she wouldn't take a dime from her father. She was real upset when she came back from the hospital, " Karen added glumly. "She hadn't seen Mrs. Berrington in a long time."

It must have been quite a shock. Jess imagined seeing Virginia in a shape similar to Elizabeth and shuddered. "She went to Paraguay to prove Manuel's allegations?"

Karen looked away.

"Did she prove them?"

"I don't know."

"When did the threats start?" Michael put in.

"Before she went. Telephone calls, people following her, things like that. I got scared. I made her go to her father. I forced her. I told her he loved her, no matter what things were like with the two of them." Her face was screwed up with intense pain. "I made her go — and he didn't believe a word of it. He said he'd give her money for a shrink, as if she was like her mom! But he wouldn't give her anything if she was going to go on with her ridiculous obsession. That's what he called it. Lorrie stopped talking to me about then. She stopped trusting me — it was my fault!"

"It wasn't your fault," Jess said gently. "It wasn't your fault that Lorrie came from the family she did."

Karen's thin chest was heaving, but she made no noise. It was a long time before she brought herself under control. Jess watched dust filtering across a low-slung beam of sunlight and thought about a twenty-two-year-old poor little rich girl, desperate to strike out against the world and unlucky enough to find a real weapon.

Karen finally started talking again, slowly and quietly. "Lorrie got Manuel to tell her who to talk to in *Asuncion* and other places in Paraguay. When she got home, she got more threats, and then — then she died. I was too scared to do anything."

"You were threatened too," Michael guessed shrewdly.

She nodded, edgy at the reminder. "After she died, and her father came around. He wanted to know . . . about this. He was starting to believe what she'd told him."

"Did you answer his questions?"

The silence answered that one.

"You knew Lorrie had been murdered"

"No, no — not for sure, not till Mr. Berrington died too." She looked up beseechingly. "I don't want to die!"

Jess and Michael stared at each other, but neither said a word. They had no reassurances to offer.

"Manuel came back once. That was after Mr. Berrington died. I told him to go away. I went away, too." She folded her hands in her lap as if a chapter had been closed.

"What about Lil?" Jess asked sadly. "What about the letters Lorrie wrote her?"

I never saw them." Fear was creeping back into the voice.

"What did they say?"

"They broke in here, you know." Her fingers twisted and turned, playing with an invisible skein of wool. "It was a mess, everything upside down and torn and — "

"What did the letters say?" Jess stood over the girl, throwing a shadow over her face.

"I never saw them," she repeated frantically.

"You can guess."

The mongoose saw no escape from the snake. Finally, Karen sagged into a heap. "I didn't want to hear about it; I didn't want to know. But when Lorrie left, she told me she was going to find proof in Paraguay that microwaves were bad — and that people like her father knew it. She said she'd write to Lil, and if she didn't come back, Lil would bring me the letters. Lil wouldn't be able to do anything with them, but I would."

"Did Lil ever come back to you.?"

The tears were beginning. "No, because Lorrie did come back. I guess Lil didn't think she was supposed to do anything after the hit-and-run accident."

It had eventually occurred to her. Jess sighed.

"Karen, who is Sarah Koestler?" Michael asked suddenly. "Did Lorrie ever find her?"

Karen didn't hear him. She was frozen, eyes glued to the door. "Was that a noise in the hall?"

Michael was up, sore muscles, bruises, and broken bones forgotten. He looked through the peephole, then cautiously opened up and peered outside. He turned to Jess and shrugged.

Karen wasn't relieved. "You have to go! You have to! Go away!"

"We will, when you tell us about Sarah." Michael shut the door and spoke coldly, as if he and Jess didn't want to make tracks too. "Who was she? Where is she?"

"I, uh, I — " Karen was frantic. "Some scientist. I don't know — Lorrie didn't tell me what Sarah said — "

"Where can we find her?"

"She was in *Asuncion*, I think. I — " Karen suddenly dashed to the bookcase again and held out a thick volume. "Here! That's all that's left. I don't know any more — please! Leave me alone!"

Michael took the tome and leafed through it. A single page of a three-holed notebook drifted lazily to the floor. Karen bent and shoved it at him. He glanced over it and crossed to show it to Jess. It was a scribbled list of names and addresses. They knew most of them. Ron Jackson. Betty Drummond. Edward Merton. and Sarah Koestler, now of Palm Springs.

"Please." Karen looked as if she might faint with terror. "Go!"

There didn't seem to be any lurking figures in the hallway or in the street, but Jess and Michael held sweaty hands all the way back to the car. It seemed like the longest walk they'd ever undertaken.

* * *

It was obviously too late for a drive to the desert.

Too late for most people, and definitely too late for the two of them. They were hoarse with exhaustion, and Jess was particularly unhappy about Michael's pallor. She turned the key. "Home."

It cost him plenty, but he shook his head. "I'll live, but he shook his head. "I'll live, I promise you. Jess, we don't have time for our beauty sleep. They're closing in on us. They're on our heels now, if we don't keep moving they'll be one step ahead of us.

She looked at the pain in his eyes. She couldn't bear it, but he was right.

The South American Club wasn't hard to find. It was an old Victorian frame house in East Los Angeles that had been built between the wars by simple middle-class folk who'd probably never heard of class warfare and guerilla fighting. The years had pushed the original owners west or north; the house had stayed behind, probably vacant for many years, now a shabby, creaking warren of dingy rooms filled with revolutionary posters and angry-eyed, dark young people.

Several of them were having a meeting in the front room, once an elegant salon meant for teas and sedate conversation. All eyes turned to Jess and Michael when they walked in; the discussion stopped as if the sound track had been cut. Two young men — hardly more than boys — who affected the international khaki Uniform intended to display their political zeal, stepped forward.

"Sorry to bother you." Michael's words were ridiculously genteel, an Oscar Wilde character walking into a John Osborne play. "I'm looking for Manuel Perreira."

The faces were hostile. Two women were nursing babies and watching Jess without a single sisterly thought for the pregnant white oppressor.

"Is Manuel around?" Michael persisted politely.

Jess moved closer to him. They were fools for coming and fools for staying, but she wasn't really sure how to get out gracefully.

One of the would-be revolutionaries came closer.

His arm shot out suddenly, locking Michael in a stranglehold. He barked an order, and another man grabbed Jess's purse.

Jess and Michael managed not to shout or shriek. It was a not-inconsiderable achievement.

The purse-snatcher examined the contents by dumping them contemptuously on the floor and motioning an even younger boy to paw through them. The license was taken out and shown around. Then the library card. Jess's heart sank when her coroner's badge was picked out of the wadded Kleenex and empty gum wrappers.

"I'm not police. Neither of us are." No one had asked, but it seemed wisest to scotch the thought before it got going. "I'm from the coroner's office. Not the police."

She might have been talking to herself. The badge was tossed back on the heap, and the boy went through Michael's pockets. Even less was found. Michael rarely carried even a driver's license.

The man holding Michael released him, then carefully looked them both up and down. His mouth twisted into a sneer. "Take your shit and go."

It was all the hint they needed. They knelt and gathered up their papers. Jess threw caution to the winds and tried one last time. "Do you know Manuel?"

"No."

She looked up. "Don't you want to know why we're asking?"

"No."

She gritted her teeth and extended a hand. He was surprised enough to pull her up. She helped Michael. "He helped a woman named Lorrie Berrington, and we hoped he'd help us, too."

Lorrie's name was the magic word. Black magic. A slight hiss passed through the room, an almost-imperceptible intake of breath that was felt rather than heard.

The man in charge made no movement, but suddenly he was framed by a line of cohorts, a hostile frieze of dark, bony, staring faces.

Michael took Jess's arm. "You know who we are. If Manuel wants to talk to us, he can find us." He spoke with bravado, as if he sensed that a mere whiff of their fear would unleash the anger.

No one followed them into the foyer; no one came to see that they shut the door behind them.

Jess looked back only once. The faces in the front window were crowned by someone's clenched fist. It was the same configuration of impassivity and threat she'd seen on one of the wall posters, a paean to the Sandinistas in Nicaragua.

Michael waited until they were out of the *barrio* before suggesting they stop at a phone booth. "We have to see Manuel. Consuela's family is a cast of thousands — some one must be someone must be able to help."

"Consuela won't be happy, but I'll try." Jess got out.

"You just came from where?" Consuela almost choked on the information. "Gringos can't go in there!"

"Stupid ones can. Consuela, we must find Manuel Perreira. It's very important."

"Who is he?"

"A revolutionary — from somewhere in South America. Maybe Paraguay."

"It doesn't matter. They're all connected, the South Americans. But, Jess, you mustn't go near them again. They're very tough, really tough! Some of the wilder Chicanos hang out there, but mostly it's hard-line South Americans with a lot to hide."

"Really? Funny, they seemed so chatty."

"Jess!"

"Look, we were dumb. We admit that freely. But we were lucky and we got out. Probably because I was an official."

"You fool! That's the worst thing you could be — they blame all their troubles on the American government, and," Consuela added honestly, "there's something to it. The juntas get their weapons from us."

"So do some of the guerillas. And a plague on both their houses. Consuela, can you help us?"

Sighs. Silence.

"Look, I'd rather not have to go back myself, but —"

It was a phony threat because she'd rather have her fingernails ripped off one by one than go back, but it worked. "Don't do that! I have a cousin — "

Jess grinned. You could count on only a few things in this life: Death. Taxes. And Consuela's cousins.

She wasn't so amused when she got back into the car and saw Michael's expression. "What's the matter?"

He gestured down the street. "We're not alone. A blue van just passed us and turned around. I saw it on our way over to the South American Club, but I didn't see the driver that time."

"Oh, Michael." She got the car in motion. "Where do we go? We can't drive around all night."

A pair of high headlights came slowly up the street toward them.

"The freeway, Jess."

She obeyed mechanically, but her heart wasn't in it. Motion and progress weren't the same thing. "The freeway and then what?"

"Then we pretend we've got muscle to flex." He kept his eyes on the headlights behind them. "Let's go see a senator."

"Uhuri mightn't even be in town," she reminded him grimly. "And we've got no reason to think he'd help."

"They can't be sure of that. It might buy us a few hours, Jess."

Life had come down to that; buying an hour of it at a time.

* * *

Senator Uhuri's Los Angeles pad was a basic, four-hundred-thousand-dollar condominium on Wilshire between Westwood and Beverly Hills. A strip of stark, sterile high-rises had sprouted up at Wilshire's widest, grayest point. It was a dandy location for anyone determined to shun the myriad of beautiful settings in Los Angeles and keen to be thirty stories up when the

Big One struck.

Uhuri was home; he answered the doorman's call himself. Jess and Michael could hear his voice on the intercom, reluctantly agreeing to see the visitors.

"Didn't like his manner much," Michael muttered as they shot upwards in a brothel-owner's dream of an elevator.

"Maybe we're getting too sensitive," Jess suggested hopefully.

They weren't. Uhuri answered the door with a face that suggested he'd rather have found the IRS outside.

They followed him into the living room, Jess and Michael sticking close to each other to mitigate the chill. Uhuri stopped in the middle of the room without waving toward the miles of velvet couches or clumps of brocaded chairs.

"I don't have much time, Jessica."

He had more than they did. Jess was tired, frightened, and fed up. "I'm not going to bore us both with a little song and dance, Senator. You have some idea, at least, of what's going on. We're here because we need help."

Uhuri remained impassive, waiting for her to show her hand, probably confident she didn't have one.

"I know that politics is the art of the possible and that money talks and all the rest of the truisms. But Michael and I have run into something that can't be permitted to continue, and we need information — and protection."

Uhuri shook his head ambiguously.

"You were a friend of my father's. Please help us."

That at least brought him to the point of speech. "I've heard your theories."

Michael spoke up. "Have you heard that our lives are in danger? We've been harassed, threatened, followed and scared out of our wits."

Uhuri's eyes were on Jess; they were cold, tinged with disappointment. "You know the facts of life. You can't run around making wild accusations about important people, Jessica."

"And if I shut, will I ever be able to get up again in the morning without wondering if I'll live to go to see night fall?"

"This is preposterous." He was talking for the record now. "Naturally, you've disappointed your . . . backers. Naturally, you're being, well, shall we say, frozen out. But are you really suggesting that respectable people are killers?"

Jess didn't answer.

"If Jess won't say it, I will." Michael took a step forward. "Maybe they don't do the killing themselves, but they hire people who do."

Uhuri looked away.

Jess took a deep breath. "Dad thought a lot of you, Senator. Enough to help you along at the beginning. Please, listen to us. We need help too, now. Right this minute, we're being watched! Time's running out!"

"You're being melodramatic, Jessica. The entire scenario you've been shouting from the housetops is melodramatic."

She ignored that. "We need data. We need to know the relationship between a couple of scientists and the military. We need to see a list of research programs and research institutes funded by the Navy. We need —"

Uhuri was shaking his head. He'd started shaking it midway through her speech. "That's all classified."

"Maybe, but you can get it."

"Maybe, but I won't." He paused. "Jessica, I owe this much to Caesar's daughter. I'm going to give you some very sound advice. You're the best young candidate we've come up with in some time, and we're all very sorry it's worked out this way. Still, if you are very careful, very careful indeed, perhaps some of your bridges could be rebuilt. Perhaps you could make people understand that this isn't a" — he coughed delicately — "a typical time in your life."

Jess patted her stomach defiantly. "I'm pregnant, Senator, not crazy."

He didn't look convinced.

Michael put an arm around Jess. "Senator, what do

you suggest we do about the fact that people are being hurt by microwaves? The fact that, if nothing's done now, in a very short time our cities will be bombarded by microwaves? Pretend we never heard of cancers and blood diseases and birth defects? Is that what you suggest we do?"

Uhuri's jaw was clenched. He finally relaxed it enough to speak stiffly. "That's gross speculation. It's unproved — in fact, there's considerable opinion that it's wrong. You two are acting obsessively, irrationally — "

"There *is* proof" Michael insisted.

"In the East." He stared coldly at them, then strode to open the door. "It's no coincidence that the alarmists who want to hold back progress depend on so-called proof from Communist countries."

They looked at each other and left.

* * *

The van wasn't in sight when they pulled away from the condominium. It hadn't gone away; it was just being more tactful. They saw it again a few blocks behind them as they drove down San Vicente toward the coast highway. The visit had bought them, at best, a very short-term future. Neither of them chose to comment on it.

Michael slowed down to turn left into the garage. Another van was parked at their house, one with a vivid yellow sun painted on the side. Its driver, a lanky familiar figure, climbed down and waved.

"Alan Dickson," Michael observed.

"We'll have to tell him to go home. It's a dangerous business these days, hanging out at our place."

Alan walked into the garage behind the car. "Hi. I was driving by and figured I'd stop a while. Are you guys tired or can you give a weary electrician a beer?"

Michael hesitated. "Alan, I think you'd be better off at the saloon." He took a deep breath and gestured toward the street. "We're being watched. It's a long story, but you don't want to hang out with us right at the moment."

All three were hypnotized by the pale blue van with the Thalen Satellite logo, openly and insolently parked at the opposite curb. At the wheel, the Pyramid, not even bothering to notice the attention.

Michael and Jess reached for the garage opener at the same moment. The door swung down and left them in darkness.

"Hey, far out." Alan didn't sound surprised at the drama. This was the sort of thing he could accept instantly, totally, and unquestioningly. "You onto something like Watergate?"

"Not exactly." Jess didn't have the energy to elaborate; suddenly, she didn't have the energy even to stand. She sagged against Alan.

"Mike, let's get this lady inside. She's zonked out."

The house was dark. It seemed hostile, a different place from the home they'd loved for four years. Jess hugged her arms to her chest as Michael turned on lights and moved through all the rooms, pretending to be casual, as if he weren't looking for intruders.

Alan watched too, his eyes somber and his head nodding slightly.

"Alan," Jess said slowly, "we really meant it. I think you ought to go home. We don't have time to give you the details — "

Alan shook his head violently and held up a hand. He rummaged around in his pockets and came up with a matchbook cover and a pencil stub. He made a few marks and gave it to Jess. "Careful bugs."

She sighed. "Alan, that's a bit — "

Again he shook his head. He made another note. "I'll see." Michael was reading over Jess's shoulder. "Can't hurt."

She shrugged. Alan was certainly up for the job. He was an electronics whiz who was the resource person for paranoid ex-radicals who couldn't accept that time and the FBI had passed them by. She sat down, surrounded by all the middle-class paraphernalia of stable, adult life, watching with disbelief as a tall, skinny, long-haired hippie poked and pried. Alan was muttering happily to himself. This was the good life.

The telephone rang. Jess picked it up.

"Hi, Jess. It's Consuela."

"Oh, hi."

"Listen, my cousin thinks he can find Manuel. He went down to the South American Club tonight, and —"

Jess cut her off. "Consuela," she faltered, not wanting to admit they might be bugged, in case they were, "I'd rather you weren't elicit over the phone."

Alan was beaming approvingly.

A long pause indicated just what Consuela thought of that particular piece of hysteria. "Yes. Well. I was right about those people — they're bad actors. You shouldn't be dealing with any of them."

"I have no intention of inviting them up to dinner. Er, do you have the information?"

"No."

Her heart sank. "Damn."

"But he left a message. Ma — this other person is supposed to contact you through me. You understand?"

"Yes. When?"

Consuela sighed. "I can't promise he will at all. He's a little erratic, apparently. Jess, why are you and Michael doing this?"

"Talk to you later." She hung up and went back to watching the charade, or what she prayed was the charade.

God wasn't at his listening post. Alan found the device in the molding behind the record cabinet. He smiled with the satisfaction of one who has validated his world view and motioned them over to share the pleasure. Then he led them outside.

"You want it left in, or taken out?"

Michael and Jess looked at each other.

"Sometimes, the devil you know is better," Alan suggested.

"I suppose." Michael was undecided.

"It's already done the damage," Alan added. "Maybe you can turn it to our own use."

The damage. "Consuela!" Jess gasped.

They walked with her down to the pay on the sidewalk Surfriders Beach. They were hurrying, but their shoulders were at stiff with the self-consciousness of those who know they're being watched.

"Consuela! Thank God you're home."

"I'm not going anywhere. I'm just reading, being grateful for the peace and quiet for a change."

"Where's your family?"

"At a church meeting."

"Jesus! You're alone!" Jess took a deep breath. "Our house is bugged. I'm calling from a pay phone."

"What?"

"I might be overreacting, but I think you'd be a whole lot safer if you just took off for a couple of days."

"You're kidding." Silence. "You're not kidding." "We're getting closer," Jess said soberly. "They played rough when we didn't know a thing. We've got to be making them hysterical now."

"Then you're the ones in danger! You've got to hide!"

She'd get no argument from Jess. "Indulge me — go away and don't tell anyone where you're going. Call us from a pay phone. No — better yet, call Martin. We'll figure out a way to look after you so you can come back."

Consuela stuttered as the reality hit her.

"Think about the victims," Jess said brutally. "Lil, Lorrie, Berrington, Frechetti — "

"Frechetti?" Consuela asked in horror. "Who's — "

"Promise me you'll get away from there!"

"Okay, but my folks won't like it."

"Your folks don't like a lot about your life. Maybe they'll accept the little things if you lay a really big one on them every now and then." A weak smile.

A weak chuckle. "I'll be in touch. Jess — please — be careful!"

Michael handed her another dime. "Try Connie Hartman. I'd rather she didn't call either. And we know how to get hold of Sarah Koestler. We should tell her not to bother trying anymore."

There was no answer at either home or office.

Jess returned the dime, and they walked back to the house, tensely pretending not to stare at the pale blue van.

Jess hesitated at the front door. She didn't want to walk inside; she wanted, even less, to sleep inside. Michael felt the same way.

"Alan," he said, "it's an imposition, but can you help us get away from here?"

"Sure. You can stay with us at the commune."

"Have you got room for him, too?" Jess tilted her head in the direction of the Pyramid.

"No, but I've got an idea."

Alan drove his van into the garage while Jess and Michael threw a few things into a flight bag. They got into the back, and Alan drove out again. Pyramid was bound to suspect what was going on — but he couldn't know if it was a bluff or a double-bluff. They prayed he'd decide to take his orders literally and stay put.

Alan drove along the highway without saying a word. He turned left to climb Topanga Canyon Road and hooted. "We did it! You're safe!"

For the moment. It wouldn't be hard to find Alan's commune once someone tried. Jess put that thought out of her mind. In the meantime, they'd get some sleep, and maybe things would look brighter when they weren't punchy with fatigue.

Chapter 21

The sound of children's voices woke Jess in the morning. She lay still, comforted by Michael's warmth and the giggles of happy people who had no reason to doubt that they could plan on being happy for a long time. The sun filtered through the rough burlap curtains; it picked up dust motes lazily drifting through the air and settling on homemade wooden furniture. Beams lit up bright cotton pillows on the floor and played in Michael's hair. Alan had given them his bedroom. It took Jess back to days when everyone slept on mattresses on the floor, under unframed posters of Che Guevara and cheap reproductions of Picasso's cubist women. Those had been wonderful days — when everyone saw conspiracies everywhere without actually falling smack into the middle of one.

Michael stirred; they cuddled together, then kissed with growing passion. They forgot where they were, and where they had to go, and lost themselves in each other's bodies, making love with a breathless, sweet intensity that drenched them in sweat and shudders of hot pleasure.

Afterwards, the children's noises and the twitters of birds played softly around them; they were entwined in limbs and sheets, their skin drying in gentle early-morning breezes. Jess tried to be conscious of it all, fixing it in her mind so that no matter what happened, she'd always have this moment.

"Jess. We've got to get up."

She sighed. "Yes."

He put a hand on her back as they stood, and he smiled into her eyes. "I love you."

They kissed again, then dressed and emerged, still smiling, into the large main room of the house. Several communards were at the huge wood-slab table, sipping coffee and gently easing into the day. Alan was among them; he'd obviously explained a bit, because no one looked surprised at the newcomers and everyone was solicitous.

"Coffee?" A buxom blonde with a baby on her hip set two mugs at two empty places.

Jess and Michael smiled and sat.

"We've been talking about it," Alan said after they'd had a chance to empty one cup each and get refills. "We took a vote and we agreed — anything we can do to help you is cool. You can stay here as long as you like, and — "

"Thanks, Alan. "Michael looked touched. "But we're not safe." "Not," he added with determined optimism, "until we clean this problem up. And you've got kids here. It's not your war; there's no reason to put the children in jeopardy.

No one argued when they stood up.

"Is there anything you need?" Alan was looking older suddenly, as reality crept into his world.

"A car. Something they wouldn't recognize."

"They could take the Jeep," the blonde woman suggested helpfully. "I filled it up yesterday and it's in good shape."

"Alan nodded and went to get the keys. On their way out, Jess tried Connie Hartman. She wasn't at home, and the nurse-receptionist sounded puzzled when she said the doctor wasn't at work either.

Jess drew a quavering breath and told herself that Connie was probably treating an accident victim by the side of a road somewhere. She'd turn up.

She and Michael reassured each other several times between the overgrown woods of Topanga and the flat scrub desert outside Palm Springs. Nevertheless, they stopped four times in two and a half hours to try again. The nurse always said the same thing, but she said it with increasing bewilderment.

"We'll find Connie as soon as we get back to LA." Michael promised Jess grimly. "If we have to pay off the whole LAPD."

She pretended to believe they could. "The motel is just off Route 111."

They were driving on what was only technically a highway, a narrow, dusty trail that crossed flatlands of parched, baked rock and weed. Small trailer communities appeared out of nowhere, sparse potted flowers at the entrances pretending that this was maintaining the fiction, dust-covered panels and wilting curtains admitted that they were here because they'd given up, would never get into the Promised Land.

The city came upon them suddenly, the highway becoming a paved street running past red-roofed bungalows and brand-new shiny malls. The air was clear and still, affording a crystalline view of vast blue-tinged mountains that looked deceptively close. The cars and the buildings and the shop windows affected a glossy, wealthy, youthful air; signboards sparkled with promises of resorts and spas. None of it, however, obscured the fact that this was the city of the old, of gray and white hair, sagging wrinkled skin, shapeless bodies. Most of them were women's. Here was incontrovertible proof that men died first. The pedestrian tide was a sluggish current, thick with widows.

Jess looked at the map again, quick to brush away the reminder of mortality. "Two more blocks, then a right."

Lorrie's notation gave Sarah Koestler's address as the Desert Spa, which turned out to be a two-story brick motor hotel in the nineteen-fifties mode. Reception was at the front, a small square cubbyhole of unrelenting Formica. The floor, the countertop, and the chairs were identical drab, beige plastic. An old man, probably a social lion in this town, was reading a tabloid through bifocals. He looked up with mild surprise when Jess and Michael came inside.

"Morning'." It was an old man's voice, with the hint of a deep Texas drawl. "Hot enough for you?"

"Sure is. " Michael grinned. It was unbearably hot, at least a hundred and ten; this was the desert, and the peak of the desert summer.

"You folks lookin' for a room?"

"No, we're looking for someone."

He nodded with resignation. There wasn't much tourist business in August.

"Do you have a guest named Sarah Koestler?"

He pondered the question. "Nope."

Jess's shoulders sagged. They could be in Los Angeles, looking for Connie. "She'd be about forty, I guess, traveling alone. A scientist."

He pursed his lips. "Don't get many scientists in here."

"Any women alone?"

He looked a little taken aback. This was Palm Springs. "Sure. No scientists, though. There's Shirley, but she's a waitress. 'Bout forty."

"How long has she been here?"

He pondered again. "Two, three weeks."

Jess and Michael spoke in unison. "Where is she?"

"Over in the coffee shop. Pays her rent by working here. We had a waitress, but she left last month when this man — "

"Thanks." They were baking in that office. Not even for the salacious details of the errant waitress would they stay a moment longer than necessary.

The coffee shop was actually just a counter fronted by ten stools. There was an old air conditioner over the door; it made deal of noise and dripped industriously onto the floor, but the temperature was still in the Hades range. A plump old woman was carefully eating toast and sipping tea, masticating delicately as if each mouthful was a major meal in itself.

The staff was one person, a tall, bony, fortyish woman in a white sleeveless blouse that displayed muscular brown arms. She leaning against the back of the shop, staring into the distance, lost in her own thoughts. Jess and Michael sat on stools and waited for service.

"Sorry." The waitress came to with a start. She put cups of coffee in front of them without asking, then waited for their orders. Her face was expressionless; in thirty seconds, she'd have forgotten what they looked like, even that they existed.

"You want to eat?" Michael asked.

Jess was starving, and it was lunchtime, but the grill

looked, but the grill looked greasy and the bread stale. "Just a cold drink."

"Two Cokes," he ordered.

They studied the woman in silence for a moment. Her features were regular, not unattractive but not feminine. Their expression made them less so. This was someone who had a lot of definite opinions about a lot of things, and the long lines around the mouth suggested that she didn't tend toward the optimistic viewpoint.

"Sarah." Jess shot the name out abruptly.

The waitress jumped, then tried to recoup too late. "Who? My name is Shirley."

Jess shook her head. "We know you're Sarah Koestler. We've come from LA to talk to you."

The eyes went immediately toward the parking lot, and the body stiffened and rose slightly, as if she was poised for flight.

"We just want to talk to you," Michael added quietly. "We're not here to hurt you. We're on the other side."

"I don't know what you're talking about." Sarah might have been a wonderful scientist, but she was a lousy actress. Her eyes were still warily covering the approach to the coffee shop, and her muscles were still taut. The self-assured, commanding voice was also out of character for a small-town waitress.

"Satellites, Dr. Edward Merton, A-COMM, and microwaves," Michael summed up neatly. "Look, there's no point in pretending you're Shirley, neighborhood hash-slinger. We've had a hell of a time finding you — but Lorrie Berrington left a note."

The eyes fixed on him briefly, hard, assessing, uncompromising.

"Connie Hartman told us about you as well." Jess tried not to flinch at the thought of Connie. "We're friends of hers."

Sarah crossed her arms and leaned against the wall again. "Who are you and what do you want?"

They introduced themselves quickly.

"Miss!" The only genuine customer looked peeved at

being ignored. She held up a handful of change. "I want to pay."

Sarah took care of her, using the moment to think about what she was going to do. She didn't seem to have reached a decision when the old woman left.

"You knew Lorrie." Jess made it sound as if they were sure of their facts had more than a few of them. "She asked the same questions we want to ask — and you answered them for her."

The pause seemed interminable. Finally, the woman lit a cigarette and nodded curtly. "I answered them for her. And for her father."

Jess raised an eyebrow.

"And," Sarah continued evenly, "they're both dead now. That tells me something. If you've got any brains, it tells you something too."

They winced. It was a lesson that was hard to miss and harder to accept.

"We'll just have to take the chance," Michael said finally. "Tell us about microwaves. Are they dangerous?"

More silence. Sarah smoked the entire cigarette without speaking; there was something about the set of her jaw and the self-containment that kept them quiet too.

She stubbed the butt out in the sink. "Yes. Microwaves are dangerous."

"You proved it while you were working for Merton?"

"*With* Merton." The face was stone. "I don't have my own projects because I bleed every month, but I can assure you, I'm more than qualified. I work with people, not for them." It suddenly dawned on her that the pride was a trifle out of place at the moment. She flashed a glance around her, apparently seeing no humor in the irony.

"Sorry." Michael amended the question and repeated it.

Sarah folded her arms across her chest. "The effects of microwaves are well-known. We don't have to spend millions proving that. Even small doses over enough time have significant biological effects."

Jess realized grimly that there was no gratification at all in being right. "Then what is Merton studying?"

"Ways of protecting the population. The causation will be obvious at some point — they'll have to do something. Preferably something that doesn't interfere with the technology and, of course, isn't prohibitively expensive." She appeared to make no moral judgment about it. This was a piece of empirical data, and a fact was neither good nor bad.

Jess wasn't as rational. She had still, deep down, not been able to believe that a so-called respectable person could *know* — and still go ahead. She was breathless with the feeling of betrayal. "God damn them all to hell!"

Sarah looked at her with something like amusement, then turned to make a fresh pot of coffee.

"What about Paraguay?" Michael asked. "Why were you there?"

The broad shoulders tensed. Michael had to repeat himself twice before she faced them again.

"Paraguay?" She spoke the word as if she'd heard it before, but couldn't quite remember what it meant.

"Is there a microwave facility there? A study? An institute?"

"I have no idea."

"You do, because you were there," Jess said flatly. "It's where Lorrie first found you. Merton and the rest of them are beaming microwaves into the villages — probably with the blessing of the government. It's a neat little way to get rid of unwanted Indians, isn't it?"

Sarah didn't answer. A very small muscle in her neck was jumping.

"They're irradiating people deliberately," Jess repeated. "They're getting data there that they won't have here for a decade."

The neck muscle moved faster. Jess studied it, not liking what it was saying.

"You worked there. Watching the villages sicken, didn't you?"

Sarah remained silent.

Michael took over. "We can prove you were there. Lorrie wrote home about you." He didn't mention that the letters were now bedside reading for only Bowdritch and Marchenko. "How did she find you?"

Sarah finally spoke, the tendons in her jaw standing out in high relief. "The leftists, I suppose. They tried to find out exactly what we were doing. They watched us."

"When did you leave Paraguay?"

"Two days after the Berrington girl did."

"Because you were in trouble for helping her?"

Sarah flushed. "I didn't help her. Look, I'm not a social worker, I'm a scientist. I get the facts — it's not up to me to philosophize about the ideal world."

Jess took a deep breath. "The German scientists who worked for us after the war said the same thing. Their job was to get the rockets up — it wasn't their business where they came down."

Michael pressed Jess's arm warningly. "Sarah, you're hiding because someone believes you gave Lorrie proof?"

Sarah's face said that was the question of a fool.

"What proof did she get?"

"I don't know. I — " She broke off. A thought had struck her, and she wanted to work it through. Her voice, when she spoke again, was a little friendlier. "I imagine it had to be pictures. Maybe even copies of internal reports, scientific documents. I've got a couple with me, in fact — if you wait a minute, I'll get them."

She was gone before they could answer.

A minute later, Jess spun around to stare out the front. "Michael, I don't trust the sudden cooperation."

"Yeah." He was out of the coffee shop like a shot.

Jess followed at her best pace, which was slower every day. She found Michael at the side of the road, watching a dark American sedan vanish in the distance.

"Damn it! "He pounded a fist into his palm. "She's gone!"

"Another gig." All she could see now was dust. "Maybe next time, Sarah will be a stenographer."

"That," Michael said slowly, "was one frightened lady."

"One frightened tough lady."

The words reminded both of them of Connie. They wordlessly turned toward the Jeep.

* * *

Midway between Banning and Redlands, Jess made a deal with God. If Connie turned up alive, she'd give hours a week to good works. She'd stop using His name in vain. She'd go to church on Sundays.

The road was interminable, desolate for miles, then dreary, passing through dusty towns of shabby houses and strip-mined hills. Ahead, the brown horizon signalled Los Angeles, and overhead, the sun pounded the car as if it wanted to do Pyramid's job for him.

They stopped at Redlands to telephone. This time, the nurse had news. Connie wasn't missing anymore. She was at the Santa Monica Hospital in a coma. Jess stood with the receiver in her hand, shaking convulsively, her breath coming in short shallow bursts. Michael gently replaced the telephone and led her back to the Jeep. He took the wheel and brought them into Santa Monica while Jess sat beside him in stunned, dry-eyed sorrow.

The intensive-care room was dark, the blinds pulled tight against the glare of the afternoon sun. Connie lay motionless in unfamiliar quiescence, a bandaged mummy pierced by tubes and needles, hooked up to screens that silently traced red and yellow landscapes. They were allowed a single glance from behind glass, then were told to sit in the waiting room and wait. There were others maintaining their own vigils: two families of parents and grandparents and a single young man who sat by himself, unmoving except for a periodic sob that cut shrilly through the silence.

It was almost dinnertime when a newcomer walked in, a tall, very thin man with graying temples and a long, tired, creased face. He stood at the doorway and watched Jess and Michael until they looked up.

"I'm Bruce Legget. Connie's friend."

Michael stood and started to introduce himself and Jess.

"I know who you are." Legget's life hadn't been enriched by the knowledge. "This has something to do with you, doesn't it?"

They nodded silently.

"She was found in the Pacific Palisades. In her car. The wheel had been wiped clean, so the police assume she was driven there by someone else." He paused, making an obvious effort to restrain the desire to strike out. "The Palisades aren't far from Malibu."

They nodded silently again.

"She was going to see you. I was supposed to see her afterwards but she never turned up."

Jess and Michael made no attempt to defend themselves against the insinuation of blame.

"She was beaten to a pulp," Legget continued remorselessly. "She was having trouble with whatever you asked her to do. And, being Connie, she wouldn't give up. I certainly hope," he added bitterly, "that what she was after was worth this."

Jess closed her eyes. Nothing was worth this. Especially not what Connie was looking for, because she and Michael had already found it.

Michael looked as sick as Jess felt. "Will she make it?"

"They don't know. It might take a couple of days to know." Legget turned as if he couldn't bear the sight of them any longer. A moment later, he strode out.

No one else in the room had appeared even to notice the conversation. The heavy silence closed in again, seamless, as if it hadn't been punctured.

Michael could sit still no longer. Jess accompanied him out into the corridor, almost running to keep up with strides made long by frustration and tension and anger.

"We've got to do some thing!"

Jess didn't have a suggestion. He walked another

hospital mile and stopped at a pay telephone.

"We should call Virginia. She'll be worried about us."

"Right." She made herself sound willing and gave the operator the credit-card number. "Mother?"

"Jessica! How are you? How's Michael?"

"We're okay. I'm just calling to say we're fine; you shouldn't worry."

"What happened today?"

"Why do you ask?" Jess answered evasively. The truth wouldn't do her mother any good, and Jess wasn't up to lying.

"Richard's called me three times! He says he *must* see you immediately!"

"Richard wants to find us."

Michael nodded grimly.

Virginia rushed on, "He's tried everywhere — where have you two been?"

"Around."

"He's been thinking about what you said and he's very upset about it. So he talked to Mr. Bowdritch to see — "

"Richard talked to Stephen Bowdritch," Jess muttered. Michael liked the news as much as she did.

"Yes, he wanted to see what's really going on," Virginia continued breathlessly, "and the two of them are looking for you. It must be terribly, terribly important."

"Mother, listen very carefully." She spoke calmly even though the message itself was something less than reassuring. "Do not tell Richard you heard from us. Do not tell him a thing. Not a single thing."

"What?" It was a shriek, followed by dead silence. "Jess, you don't think — "

"Not a thing, Mother. We'll keep in touch." She hung up and looked at Michael. "We don't have any time left at all."

"Let's go." His battered body didn't seem to remember its painful stiffness. "It's time to go as public as we can."

* * *

There were few choices available. Government agencies were out of bounds, political friends were nonexistent, and they knew only one science reporter.

Thomas Burleigh wrote for a weekly, once an underground tabloid for raving radicals and now an above-board tabloid for the settled citizens the radicals had become. It still carried in-depth exposes of scandal, conspiracy, and graft, but far more column inches were dedicated to a lifestyle that required an achiever's income.

It was a gamble, but it was the only game in town. Jess and Michael parked the Jeep in Boy's Town, the gay area of West Hollywood, home to night clubs, good restaurants, interior designers, and precious clothing stores. Burleigh worked regular office hours and cruised regular playtime hours, but early evening fell between the two. There was a good chance he'd be at home.

He answered the door, dressed in jeans and a T-shirt, the uniform established at the tabloid at its inception and still adhered to despite the other effects of the upscale trend. "Jess, Michael. Nice to see you." He was unconvincing; behind him, they could see the reason why. A very young-looking blond boy was sprawled on the floor against the sofa, listening through headphones to something on the stereo that caused him perfect bliss.

"Thomas, we've got to talk to you right now. It's very important." Michael made no apology.

Burleigh frowned and stepped back. "Okay. Let's go into the bedroom." He spared the boy a brief wistful glance and led the way. The apartment was as manicured as he was, painstakingly put together for the sleekest, most up-to-the-minute effect. The man was middle-aged, but in perfect shape, hair tapered, face tanned, smallish body taut with hours of working out. The setting was equally expensive and glossy. Only one wall of the bedroom suggested another dimension: an enormous bookcase of well-thumbed volumes ranging from philosophy to science. Burleigh's libido trapped him in a lifestyle of form; his mind required content as well.

"We're in trouble, Tom." Michael Summed it up quickly. It was an impressive bulk of detail, and Jess found herself surprised at its substance. They'd done a hell of a job. It would be perfect if they could be sure they'd live to boast about it.

Burleigh listened intently, When Michael finished, he nodded without surprise.

"Yeah, I hear you." He rubbed a hand across his hair. "We did a story on the microwave business about a year ago. We talked to some scientists on the East Coast who think the way you do."

"And now there's proof they're right," Jess pointed out. "In Paraguay, and at Dr. Merton's lab."

"Uh-huh. But," he looked around as if to be sure he was correct, "not in here."

"Well, no, not exactly. But once you print the story, we'll be able to get the proof. We'll be safe enough to — "

"Look." Burleigh spoke with genuine regret. "I was as excited about it as you are. Then. Now, I'm not so sure. I've talked to a lot of people, and there are lots of other possible explanations for this so-called Mount Wilson Syndrome. The pill. The air. The — "

"Each single case can be explained away," Jess agreed quickly, "but all together, it's goddam frightening. I'm hardly a hysteric, and I'm scared to hell."

"Jess, be realistic." He looked at her without making a judgment. "You've got no credibility right now. Maybe with me — I've known you a long time. But you're not the kind of source my editor's gonna love."

"Maybe he'd be more impressed with murder." Michael stood up and towered over the reporter. "Thomas, a lot of people are dead right now. One woman's lying in a coma. And we're next on the list if you don't help!"

The speech was a tactical error. Burleigh's world encompassed the wilful violence of the S and M set; it did not extend to accepting the notion of murder. He paled under his tan and stepped back. He was obviously casting around for a way to get rid of them.

The telephone saved him. He looked at it gratefully and leaped for it before the answering machine took away the respite. He said hello, then didn't speak again, his face becoming graver by the moment. Finally, he nodded, as if the caller could see him, and hung up.

Jess was on her feet without realizing it. She and Michael stood very close together. "Was that about us?"

Burleigh frowned at his hands, then assessed them thoughtfully. "Yes. It was a lawyer. Giving me a little lecture on the law of libel."

Jess had to search hard to find her voice. "Was his name Benny Shouldice?"

"That's him."

She bit back the fear, but took Michael's hand.

To do Burleigh justice, he didn't immediately toss them out. He thought about things for a while, then reached a conclusion that made him sigh. "I can't get anything printed without a concrete piece of data. Proof. But if you can get it — bring it to me. I'll print it if I have to put my job on the line to do it."

Jess and Michael were too disappointed to speak.

"I'm sorry. It's the best I can do."

"Tommy." The blond boy wafted into the room. "Are you going to spend the whole night here?"

"No," he smiled, patting the other's arm. "Go back to the living room. I'll be right out."

They all watched the graceful exit. In her thinnest days, Jess's ass hadn't been so perfect. Not that she gave a damn at the moment. The shape of one's ass didn't seem relevant when it was in a sling. "Thomas, we're in terrible danger. Only publicity might help. Once we've gone public, it gives us a chance — maybe they wouldn't keep on coming after us. We'd have done our worst." She hated the plea in her voice.

So did the reporter. He flushed, but he wouldn't meet her eyes.

* * *

They hid out at a tacky bar on La Cienega until dark. The spot was a long, narrow corridor of booths with the bar itself in the back. Jess nursed a Scotch while Michael put away a six-pack of beer, both discouraging the cheerful small talk of the bartender. After-work regulars drifted in and out; cast and crew from the Equity-waived theater next door had pre-performance drinks amidst chipper shop talk. When they reappeared after the show, Jess and Michael figured it was time to move on.

The Jeep came off the freeway and drove slowly up Mission Road, driver and passenger intently scanning the thin traffic for other cars moving at the same un-Californian crawl. When they saw none, they swung into the medical complex and watched the parking lot for a full five minutes.

They finally walked up the stairs into the coroner's building. Jess had never been nervous there before. Never had the security guards seemed so hulking. Never had the corridors looked so dark, the staircase so steep. But then, never before had the chief of investigations arrives with the intention of breaking into the chief medical examiner's private office.

The second floor was deserted. The pathologists worked seven days a week, but only daytime shifts; their patients were not demanding about when they were seen. Even so, Jess fumbled tensely with the key ring, her fingers ten apparently unrelated sausages that took forever to isolate the master key, even longer to insert it into the door. She was almost rigid with tension when the door finally swung open and they were inside.

The room was dark, lit only by dim beams coming from the parking-lot light standards. Their eyes were already accustomed to shadow; they made their way without difficulty to the desk. Michael played a flashlight around the walls, careful to keep it below window level in case a night-guard took it into his head to look up.

"Where would it be?" he asked in a low voice.

Jess looked around. "Maybe the desk?" The drawers were locked, but the key lay in the ashtray. Harper's conscience was clear of sin, or more likely, his mind was not burdened by wit.

Each riffled through one side of the desk. There were notes to himself and clipping files of newspaper coverage that featured movie-star shots of lucky Los Angeles's photogenic coroner. There were personnel records and income-tax receipts. But there wasn't anything about the desert research institute Harper had just been invited to join.

Jess froze suddenly, her hand catching Michael's sleeve. "What was that?" She stared at the door that led to the next office.

"I didn't hear anything."

Reluctantly, she turned her attention back to the room. Michael pointed to the filing cabinet, an oak-veneered two-drawer credenza in the corner. They found it unlocked. Jess sorted through the hanging files, every muscle tight and her skin crawling. Crime was a tough way to make a living. One had to admire those who did it year after year.

"Here!" Michael hissed. He pulled out a folder helpfully marked "Merton"; they skimmed it together.

"Lava Point." Jess glanced up victoriously. "Lorrie was spotted at Lava Point the night before the hit-and-run!" Her grin turned into a gasp. This time, the noise next door was unmistakable, and Michael's *rigor mortis* told her he'd heard it too.

They turned with one motion to look out the window. The van was there, a powder blue that now struck them as more menacing than the red of blood. Michael shoved the folder back into the drawer and took Jess's hand. They dashed toward the door, trying for speed and silence. Jess was clumsy, her stomach protesting the bounces, pulling her down, unbalancing her so that she knocked a chair over. The crash echoed eerily; they were frozen until the connecting door began to open.

They abandoned caution and ran into the corridor, taking the stairs down as fast as Jess's body would permit, careening along slippery-floored corridors, panting as much with terror as with exertion. Michael held onto Jess; "without his support, she'd have fallen a dozen times. The footsteps behind, heavy and confident, grew closer every moment.

The guard at the front door looked puzzled when Jess and Michael skidded into the foyer. She didn't pause, shouting behind her, "Stop the other man!" as they jumped down the entrance steps and pounded to the Jeep.

The guard may have made an effort, but he was no match for the Pyramid. The van was moving out of the parking lot a mere thirty seconds after they slid onto Mission road. Michael took it north, past Lincoln Park, into the unlit hilly streets of Lincoln Heights. The Jeep was top-heavy; at each squealing turn, it threatened to go over. Michael didn't dare touch the brake. The van was unwieldy too, but it was right behind, its engine screaming, as theirs was, with the effort of climbing the slopes.

Jess held on for dear life, her eyes peeled for other traffic. On the narrow pavement, an oncoming car would be suicide, but that was a better chance than they'd have with their pursuer.

"Jess, I don't know these streets," Michael hissed, jerking the wheel as he almost turned up a dead end. "Where do we go?"

She thought fast. "To Broadway. Chinatown. Left here!"

He made the corner on two wheels, straightening out only a few horror-ridden seconds later. They were on a downhill stretch, gaining precious inches, losing them when the van turned too and hurtled down at them. Michael veered again, spinning away as the nose of the van touched their fender. Another corner, tires screaming. A long flat stretch, accelerator to the floor, and the van coming up fast behind them.

"Right!" Jess shouted.

Michael's reaction was instantaneous, and they were on Broadway, scattering cars, braking violently, then shooting ahead. The van took advantage of the space they had cleared, its blunt nose relentlessly bearing down on them. "Where?" Michael asked anxiously.

Jess looked frantically around for a road that wasn't a trap. There wasn't one. The van was closer now; when she turned her head, she could see the Pyramid's face, exultant, nasty. At least someone was having a good time.

The siren didn't filter through her consciousness at first.   She gasped with relief when it did. "Cops!"

Michael's joy matched hers. "Thank God!"

The cruiser was in sight now, a block behind. Michael pulled over fast; the van continued on, braking sharply, but getting away. Jess met the Pyramid's eyes as he passed. She shivered. He as good as told her that they'd escaped this time but it wouldn't happen again.

"Out! Hands up against the car and spread 'em." The cop was a young man, shaking from the car chase, his hands filled with an enormous revolver.

Michael obeyed instantly.

"You too." The officer didn't take a good look at the passenger until Jess had come around. "Oh, shit. You crazy? Driving like that — Oh, God!" His face changed. "You having the baby now?"

Jess shook her head because she couldn't get a word out. She leaned against the car and let the muscles shake their little hearts out.

Michael was frisked and told to stay put. The officer went back to his car to radio in, his eyes never leaving them, and his gun still very much in evidence. Jess and Michael stayed exactly where they were while the police despatcher muttered through the radio static.

"I'm taking you in." He was back, calming down now, but no less wary.

"You're charging me with dangerous driving?" Michael didn't sound alarmed. It was a trivial detail in the life they were now leading.

"You better believe it. Besides, there's an APB out on you, Renfrew." He added, slightly more tentatively, "On you too, uh, ma'am."

Michael looked bewildered.

"All Persons Bulletin," Jess explained swiftly. "All cops are on the lookout for us."

"Oh." His eyes met hers. Neither liked the sound of that.

The paperwork on Michael took an hour and a half. He and Jess were kept in the zoo-like occurrence room while forms were filled out and fingerprints were taken. There was still no explanation for the APB; no one evinced the slightest interest in offering enlightenment, and eventually they gave themselves up to passivity. If nothing else, it was a respite from constant danger.

Jess was actually beginning to enjoy the relaxation when a familiar figure plodded in. She nudged Michael and tilted her head. They should have known.

"Arnheim." Michael looked more irritated than frightened. "Jesus H. Christ, Arnheim, don't you ever sleep?"

The detective grunted and motioned them to follow him. The arresting officer was outranked enough to keep his mouth shut, although he still had another report to type up. Arnheim led the way outside; his car was at the curb.

Jess and Michael looked at each other, then at the detective. "Uh-uh. No way."

Francis pursed his lips at Jess. "You think I'm gonna make you disappear?"

"I've stopped thinking entirely. You'll have to shoot me to get me in that car."

He apparently rejected the notion with reluctance and sighed heavily. "Here's the keys." He handed them to Michael and let the two of them take the front seat while he sat in the back.

The silence wasn't companionable. Michael finally broke it. "Why the APB, Arnheim?"

"You two aren't easy to find."

Which was why they were still alive. Jess glared.

"You got something to say, say it!"

Francis shook his head wearily. "I've been saying it for weeks now, but you don't listen. There are a lot of people looking for you tonight."

"We know that." She stifled the shiver. "Why are you one of them?"

"Because I've had it!" he snapped. "I'm a cop and this is my territory and the bodies are piling up and I don't like that. Ever since you two started to rampage around like bull elephants, the death rate's gone up like a fucking rocket! I want to know what's going on!"

Their refusal to talk made him red-faced with frustration. "You don't trust me and I don't give a shit. I am not going to let the body count mount up! I want to know what's going on. According to Bowdritch, who, by the way, would like to question you himself, you're the only two who can tell me!"

They tensed at Bowdritch's name and avoided looking at each other. Stephen had been a busy boy today, chatting with everyone, from Richard Simon on down.

"I want to know what you know!" Francis leaned forward; the smell of sour sweat filled the car. "To start with, you could let me in on where Consuela Martinez has gotten to. Her parents are hysterical, and I know you know."

"Sure, I'm a bad influence on any unmarried woman," Jess said snidely. "I finally convinced her to spend a night out. Francis, are you holding us under a warrant or something?"

"I'm holding you to save your lives!"

"Uh-huh." Jess and Michael moved at the same moment, each opening the closest car door and stepping out. Francis was trapped in the back seat. It was built for prisoners, and the doors didn't open from the inside.

"Don't be damn fools!" he shouted at them. "Would you feel better if we talked with your crony present? Richard Simon? He and Bowdritch called me a dozen times today! They'll help you."

Jess looked at him. "Francis, I don't know if you're

bought and paid for or just dumb, but we can't risk either." They walked away, speeding up as soon as they rounded the corner.

* * *

They had little cash left, and the Jeep was back at the police station. Jess didn't want to put any other friends in peril, but they couldn't go on without reinforcements and a little rest. She was nauseated and achy, and every few minutes a sharp cramp reminded her that the best medical advice for a woman in her condition was to stay home doing nothing more active than knitting. "Michael, we've got to call Martin."

"I know." He was reluctant too, but he was obviously more concerned for Jess's pale face and labored breathing.

Martin was home, waiting by the phone just in case they called. He'd heard from Richard and Bowdritch too. He'd put them off, but he was almost frantic with worry himself. "What corner are you on? I'll be there in a minute!"

Michael told him, adding somberly, "Martin, be careful."

They waited no more than ten minutes. Silverlake wasn't far away, and Martin's car was made for speed. He leaped out to help Jess inside. She didn't demur. She needed all the assistance she could get. She'd almost forgotten the detective work, now concentrating totally on the baby, holding her stomach as if the comfort would communicate itself to the child inside.

Martin was tact itself until they were inside his house and Jess was tucked into bed. The two men perched at the end of it, glasses of Scotch in hand.

"Okay. Now I want the story." Martin didn't attempt to use a light, amused voice. He was white-lipped and dark-eyed. "What's going on? Where have you been? I've never been so scared in my life!"

"We had a bad moment or two ourselves," Michael pointed out caustically. "But it's nice to know our friends worry."

"Friends!" Martin refused to be placated. "If I'd known what it was going to be like, I'd have stopped this friendship years ago! I can't take all this friendship! I'm too old for all this friendship!"

"Old?" Jess almost laughed. "You're talking to the dame who left Shangri-La this morning a mere slip of a girl, and who's about a hundred and fifty years old now."

Michael leaned over to kiss her. "We'll go to sleep now, babe. Martin, your questions will have to wait till morning. We're out of it."

"Will Consuela have to wait till morning too?"

"What?" Jess sat bolt upright. "Is Consuela here?"

No, she's been calling. It's either urgent or she's got a real thing about me. She must've dialed my number thirty times since four this afternoon. She won't tell me what she wants. She says she'll only talk to you."

"How does she sound?" Jess asked anxiously.

"Tense. Would you call bursting into tears tense?"

"Oh, God." Jess sank backwards.

"Is she supposed to call back tonight?" Michael asked.

"Tonight?" Martin made a production out of looking at his watch. "There is no 'tonight' left. It's now tomorrow. And yes, I assume she will call back, because this phone has been busier than a cathouse number, and everyone calls back."

"We're not here — unless it's Consuela," Michael warned.

"I know that. Jesus, I know how to protect you. I just don't know why, and I think you owe me the whole rundown."

Michael signed and started to nod. The telephone at Jess's elbow shrilled. Martin grabbed it, listened, and then handed it to Jess with a nod.

"Consuela?"

"Oh, God, are you okay? Where have you been? What's happening?" The young woman's voice was ragged.

"Hold on, hold on. We're fine. We'll tell you all

about it. Now, I Want you to — "

Consuela interrupted her. "I did it, Jess. I saw Manuel today — and there are photographs. He told me all about them! It's horrible!"

I know. We know. Consuela, I want you to come here. To Martin's. Do you know where it is?"

"Yes, but . . . " Consuela faltered.

"No buts. Just come here."

"I . . . I think I'm being watched."

Jess swallowed and motioned Michael to come close enough to listen. "Where are you now?"

"At Lou's. The all-night place on Sunset? In West Hollywood."

"I know it. Are you alone?"

"Yes." She spoke softly, the fear louder than the word.

Jess thought for a moment. "Consuela, I used to know some of the pimps who hung out there."

"There's a few here now."

"Okay. There's one called Lincoln."

"Black?"

"Big, black, and beautiful. He's not hard to pick out — he wears all-white suits and violently bright silk shirts."

"There's a guy here in pink sequins and a white suit."

"Pink sequins." Jess was almost amused. "Go ask if he'd like to talk to Jess-baby. If it's Lincoln, he will."

Consuela sounded more cheerful. "Hold on." She returned a moment later. "It's him and he's here."

"Jess-baby, how's tricks?" The drawl was rich and Southern and slow. Lincoln had had some trouble picking it up, seeing as how he'd been educated in his native Chicago, all the way up to Northwestern University. He'd chosen not to make sociology his life, and certainly he lived better than most of his former college colleagues. "Y' all having a party tonight?"

"No, Lincoln, no party. I've got a favor to ask you." She paused fractionally. He was amusing, but he wasn't the sort of person she liked to ask for favors. "I'll owe you."

"Hey, baby, you never owed me nothin' before. This must be some favor."

"That woman who's with you — I'm coming to fetch her, but in the meantime I want you to take care of her."

"On a bad trip?"

"No, no — there are people out to make trouble for her. It could be bad trouble."

"Now, Jess-baby, you know this here's my turf. What kind of asshole's gonna start up on my turf?"

"Maybe no one. But just in case."

"Honey, it must be Christmas. Easiest favor I ever did do. I got a couple of brothers here, and there ain't no dudes that are gonna make trouble around me and my bros without bein' real sorry later."

"Thanks. See you soon."

"Back on the road." Michael was already looking around for Martin's keys. "I bet we've logged a cross-country drive in the past couple of weeks."

Jess nodded as she swung her legs out of bed. She'd have preferred to have logged it the conventional way, actually crossing the country. Most of that would have been in the Midwest and boring. She'd give a lot to be bored.

"What are you doing?" Michael crossed his arms and scowled.

"I'm coming with you."

"No way. You're going to sleep."

Martin nodded his agreement with Michael.

Jess ignored both of them and slipped into her shoes again. "Consuela is scared out of her mind — and Lincoln doesn't know you. I'm coming and that's that. It's not far anyway."

Michael sighed with resignation. "True. West Hollywood's a mere piffle for mobile people like ourselves."

Traffic was light, almost nonexistent, even on the Stripp, which usually hummed after eleven. Los Angelenos ate salads instead of red meat, discoed for exercise rather than pleasure, and got lots of beauty sleep. Life after dark was mainly confined to West Hollywood and Boys' Town, and even there 3:30 AM tended to be subdued. A few curb crawlers were still looking for a little action, patrol cars cruised warily, pretty young men came out of all-night restaurants in pairs. But the night was fading, the tempo dying, and in a few hours the billboards and blinking neon would preside tawdrily over the day crowd, rolling toward offices.

Lou's was a plastic orange-and-brown coffee shop a few blocks down from the rock clubs and a few up from Laurel Canyon. Its parking lot was full, the trade handling the night's receipts over coffee, amateurs trying to disguise their inebriation before taking the freeways home. Michael pulled to the curb on the other side of the street and started to get out.

"There she is." Jess pointed to Consuela and a massive black man already crossing toward them.

Lincoln paused, his attention caught by a beckoning, strutting woman, at least six feet tall without the heels and the six-inch tower of teased blond hair. The only thing small about her was the skirt, an inconsequential strip of yellow velvet that did much more than hint at the contents of the package.

"Hi!" Consuela continued on, pausing to let an oncoming battered hot-rod pass.

"No!!" Jess and Michael screamed together, leaping out to watch with impotently spread arms.

The old car was deliberately picking up speed, aiming directly for Consuela. She saw it too, too late. She was motionless for a fatal instant, then made a run for the other side of the street. The contact was crisp; the metal hit her with a clean loud thud. Her body flew into the middle turn lane and landed with a crack.

Jess was already in the road, breath caught, tears starting to form. She sank to her knees and felt for a pulse. "Call an ambulance! Hurry! Help!"

Michael gently put his hands on her shoulders. "Jess. It's no good. Look at her neck."

Consuela's head was askew, tilted at a crazy angle, as if she had no bones in her neck. Jess was shuddering, one hand on the dead woman's cheek and the other cradling the hair as if she could put Humpty Dumpty together again.

"Jess!" Michael grabbed her and swung her into his arms, running toward the sidewalk with long strides. The killer's car was coming back; it missed them by a fraction of an inch, rolling over the crumpled body again, that Michael turned his face away and buried Jess's in his shoulder.

She felt his body grow rigid again.

"The car's turning around!" He shoved her toward their car. "Get in! Hurry, Jess!"

He tumbled in after her, pulling away before the door was shut, shooting west on Sunset, past the assassin, then hurtling north into the residential hills where the streets were narrow and dark and twisting. Jess barely noticed the speed or the curves or the pain in her stomach. She could only think about Consuela and cry.

Michael finally stopped under a drooping tree at the side of a tiny steep lane. His own cheeks were wet; he was silent.

Jess gradually came back to the present and forced deep quivering breaths of air into her lungs. "Did you see the driver?"

"No."

"Neither did I."

"We can go back and ask Lincoln, if you think it would help."

She shook her head.

"No, I guess not," he agreed wearily. "The driver would just be a hired gun."

"That's not why I don't want to ask Lincoln."

"You think he — ?"

She swallowed and contemplated the high stone wall that enclosed the Hollywood Hills estate on her right. "He was very lucky to get stopped before he walked out onto that street. I don't believe in luck anymore."

Chapter 22

They spent the night at a threadbare motel on Ventura Boulevard, despite Martin's protests. They wouldn't even tell him its name. Being one of their friends had become a fatal pastime, and they couldn't afford any more losses.

It was only a few hours till dawn. They lay stiffly beside each other pretending to sleep, unable to wipe away the nightmares long enough to fall into unconsciousness.

They started out early. It was a scorcher of a day. The air already was gluey with the promise of unbearable heat, and as hot as it was in the Valley, it was going to be a lot hotter in the Mojave Desert. The highway took them north, squeezing between ranges of the San Gabriel Mountains. They saw sallow stone dotted with occasional scrub like dark acne, parched valleys where the only color came from blue sky and green road signs. Gusts of wind did nothing but circulate the heat as they twisted around the peaks and burst through the passes, shaking the car as it climbed.

Defeated by the unrelenting glare, Jess and Michael drove on in depressed silence, through the flats of Antelope Valley, past sour industrial smog in the town of Mojave. Finally, they entered into the grim mining land of the Sierra Nevadas, a desiccated hell of red-striated mountains and endless dust and desolation, although someone had once tried to see it differently. A bleached billboard in the middle of arid nowhere bitterly offered welcome to the "Gateway to Progress." Signposts marked gulches and dry hills: Jawbone Canyon, Last Chance Well, Robber's Roost — sites of long-dead tales, the lies of losers. The sun had always been the winner.

It was almost a relief to return to gaudy Middle America at the Mojave Naval Weapons Center. A strip of neon, polyester, and formica flaunted the twentieth century at the desert. Everything that semi-civilization had to offer was here: BarBQ pits, car dealers, supermarkets, McDonalds, even a hairdressing salon. And behind fences and No Trespassing signs was the ultimate proof that men had vanquished nature: weapons that could blow it away once and for all.

They pulled up at a liquor store for liquid and a break, lingering in icy air-conditioning with cans of Coke. Young military wives moved slowly among the shelves, greeting each other in flat voices, hiding boredom and angry frustration behind dead eyes.

Jess turned away and studied the bulletin board. A wall poster talked about gun control; a petition was attached to it. The petitioners in this town were opposed to it. An old hand-printed notice offered babysitting services, as if there were some-where for mothers to go.

"You ready?" Michael was at her elbow.

"Sure." Jess winced as they stepped back into the furnace, then stared thoughtfully at the base across the street. "Liu Shi figured the research institute would be near a military installation."

"We don't know that Harper's in the right one."

"It is. I feel it in my bones."

He shrugged and unlocked the car doors. It was hot enough inside to boil blood. They sat in torpor as they left the base behind, entering lunar valleys of nubbly brown mountains, a road lined with strangely-shaped rocks that jutted up like tombstones. It was the earth itself that had died, seared and sterile. There were no other cars, no sounds except their engine and the wind battling heavy, smothering air.

"When was Lorrie sighted up here?" Michael asked suddenly.

"Two hours before she died in Mandeville Canyon."

He nodded grimly. "We're in a BMW and we've been going three and a half hours already. She'd have needed a Maserati."

"She had a ten-speed bicycle."

"Oh, super."

The hills rolled closer, became redder. Ahead were the stripped, suede-like Lava Mountains.

"It's a good highway," Michael observed. "Considering the traffic."

"There isn't any."

"I know that, and you know that, but, " he said pointedly, "the engineers didn't seem to know that. They built it to take a lot of cars — or a few pieces of very heavy machinery."

"Cheery, aren't you?" She straightened at the sight of the first intersection in thirty miles. "We leave the highway up there. Make a right."

The road rapidly worsened, degenerating into rubble-filled potholes and cracked asphalt, as welcoming as the landscape, which consisted of denuded hills bristling with abandoned mining rigs. There were gradual hints of a settlement ahead, a few ramshackle hovels and deserted truck shells. And then, Lava Point itself came into view, a motley collection of sagging, forlorn sheds and no-longer-mobile homes. Yards barren of grass or flowers were graced instead by piles of garbage and rotting tires. It was a town that hadn't given up because it had never tried at all.

"I don't think Lorrie was thinking of vacationing here," Michael said sadly. He parked on the shoulder of the road, near a frame slum painted haphazardly in several colors that had in common only their peeling.

"Where is everyone?" Jess asked uneasily. There was only the one street, and it was as lively as the scenery.

Michael pointed to a window covered by a greasy rag that was moving slightly. "They're inside. Someone just looked out at us."

It wouldn't be easy to make friends in Lava Point. Jess felt unseen eyes from all directions. "Got any ideas?"

"Door-to-Door search? There aren't that many doors."

She sighed and opened the car door to be immediately overwhelmed by the gritty, fiery air. "I wish Lorrie had chosen a more desirable locale."

They walked hand in hand to the nearest door. No

one responded to the knock or the call.

They repeated the ineffectual gesture next door, then at the shack beside that.

"Now what?" Jess's mind was blank, drugged by the atmosphere of lassitude.

Michael reached for the door knob. "I can't imagine they've got a finely developed sense of etiquette."

Jess followed him inside. It took a minute for her eyes to get accustomed to the gloom; but even if they hadn't, she wouldn't have missed much. Thus must have lived the peasants of the Dark Ages: a table, three chairs, a cot with ragged blankets, and smells that spoke volumes of unprintable words. There was nowhere to hide and no one in sight.

"Hang out with the Renfrew-Canby clan and travel off the beaten path."

Jess smiled and patted Michael's arm. "They've got electricity, at least. I saw power lines in the hills."

He nodded, unimpressed, and walked back outside. A fat woman in a faded shift was just vanishing into a building at the other end of town, a good two hundred yards away.

"I was beginning to think they'd all been wiped out by the plague." Jess looked at Michael, then back down the again-deserted road. "Shall we? What have we got to lose?"

He tactfully didn't provide the answer.

The building was a frame rectangle, slightly larger than the others in town, but no more spiffy. The front door was a torn screen, just inside of which was a scratched old-fashioned softdrink cooler. Jess perked up immediately. She hadn't realized they'd had Coca Cola in the Dark Ages. She stepped inside first, then stopped so abruptly that Michael barrelled into her.

They both stayed perfectly still in the face of four pairs of sullen eyes and a shotgun.

It would have been a fascinating gathering to an anthropologist. The three men and the woman resembled each other so closely as to be downright eerie, with the same long, square faces, identical flat brown eyes, and pasty skin. The men were differentiated only by generation — young, middle-aged, and old versions of the same model. It wasn't surprising, really. Lava Point wouldn't have enough immigration to widen its gene pool. Jess pushed out her stomach as if it were a talisman warding off evil spirits and let Michael do the talking.

"Hi."

The locals were unimpressed. The eyes hardened and flattened, and the middle-aged clone holding the gun shifted a menacing fraction of an inch.

"My wife and I are thirsty. Could we buy a Coke?"

There was no response. One could only wish that the CIA could keep secrets as well.

"I'd be happy to buy you all a Coke."

"No Coke. The gun-holder's voice was gravelly, as if he didn't use it much.

"How about Seven-Up? Water?"

The man scratched an unshaven cheek, thrown off by the flexibility. Finally, he nodded, and the woman scurried to the back, returning with two bottles of warm grape pop.

"Thanks." They tried to smile, taking their time with the drinks in the hope that, eventually, their presence would become comfortingly familiar.

Michael ordered another two bottles and put a few dollars on the counter. "How about you? Would you like a soft drink? Or beer?"

The men looked at each other. The faces didn't change, and no one spoke, but somehow the woman received a signal. She handed bottles out to all but herself.

"You too," Jess insisted with a smile.

The woman showed her first emotion — surprise. Women's lib hadn't come to Lava Point. She shrugged and accepted the offer.

Michael laid more bills on the counter and stepped forward. The watchers stepped back with the timing of a minuet. Real rapport would take a generation, and Jess wasn't prepared to wait it out. She held up a morgue shot of Lorrie's face. "Have any of you seen this young woman?"

The men shook their heads and looked away; the woman refused even to glance at the picture.

"She was up here about six weeks ago," Michael said easily. "On a fancy bicycle. Someone in town saw her."

And admitted it. Jess was lost in admiration for the interrogator who'd won that admission. It would be easier to break James Bond than this crew. "She was wearing a yellow sweat suit."

Comas were more informative. The store was dark, silent, and hot. Jess suddenly felt dizzy; she leaned against the counter, closed her eyes, and tried to stay calm.

"You okay?" Michael had both arms around her. "Jess?"

The woman interrupted him, bringing out a stool and pushing it under Jess.

"Thanks."

The woman patted Jess's stomach; some connection had been made. She looked intently into Jess's face, then turned and hurried out of the store.

"Michael — can't we — ?" Jess pointed after her new girlfriend.

"Can't talk, her." The leader ran his tongue around his gums.

Before Jess or Michael had come up with a plan of action, the woman returned, dragging along a fat man, a blown-up version of the others. Jess quickly showed him the snapshot. "Have you seen this woman?"

"Dunno."

The mute woman prodded him and nodded.

"Yeah." He scowled. "I seen her."

Jess grinned broadly, pleasing her ally, who did the same. "Wonderful. When was it?"

"Dunno."

More prodding, more scowling. "Mebbe coupl'a months ago."

"Where was she?"

He gestured vaguely. Jess looked out the window through the accumulation of soot, and made out the outline of a slight rise in the road, a few hundred yards north.

"She was with some men?" Michael suggested.

"Two guys, yeah." He scowled without being prodded. "Why're ya askin'?"

"She was my sister." Michael quickly amended the verb tense in case there was a closet grammarian in the group. "She's my sister. She left home a couple of months ago, and I'm trying to find her."

The faces weren't sympathetic. It wasn't personal: they just didn't like strangers. Jess could only hope that Lorrie hadn't begged for help in this town. "Who were the men?"

The eyes blinked.

"You said they were hikers," she insisted pleasantly to the fat man.

"Me?"

"To the sheriff's deputy."

He spat. That was what came from running off at the mouth. You talked to one person, you ended up having to talk constantly. "Not hikers."

"Well, who were they?"

"White clothes. Ya know?"

Jess and Michael looked at each other, trying to decipher it.

"Oh." Michael had a flash of insight. "Uniforms? White uniforms, like doctors?"

Two blinks. Then a faint grudging nod.

"Where did the uniforms come from?"

The men were suddenly edgy, shifting their feet and lowering their heads hike bulls about to charge.

Michael tightened his arm on Jess's shoulder. "Do you know where the uniforms came from?"

"That place."

"The research institute?" The words meant nothing to them. He tried again. "The hospital place with the doctors and the machinery?"

Bingo. All five faces blanked completely.

Jess could feel Michael's pulse racing in time with her own. "Where is it? Maybe my husband's sister is there."

The man with the gun raised it abruptly, pointing directly at Jess's stomach. She bit back a gasp and moved with the tilt of his head. He wanted her outside, and she wanted to make him happy. Michael stayed close to her, their arms touching as they stood motionless on the gravel. The man looked across the road and into the hostile hills.

They followed his gaze; when they turned back, he was on the other side of the screen again, still aiming at them.

"I think we've pretty well exhausted our welcome," Michael suggested. "Let's get the hell out of here."

She could only nod, still dry-mouthed with fear.

She didn't start to relax until they were half a mile down the road. The hills crowded closer, dull taupe rock that looked impenetrable. If there was a road cut through, it would take a keen eye to find it. Jess half-hoped they wouldn't. An institution that inspired the sort of terror felt by all of Lava Point might well be an institution worth missing.

"There it is!" Michael braked sharply. The shadows and littered stones camouflaged the pavement, but it was there, a single lane, winding into the unappetizing wilderness. Michael's excitement faded. "Do we really want to do this?"

"Hell, no."

They turned in without saying anything more. The track was uneven, unkempt for almost a mile. Then it ended at another road coming in from the east, this one solid, heavy, well built, an assurance that they weren't just following the flight of an imagination truly out of control. They wound on through the bleak stone hills that crumbled passively under the beating sun and the dull, listless, hazy sky. It was easy to believe they'd become trapped in a pocket of lifelessness, that they'd never see water or greenery again.

Jess got tenser as time rolled on and the

temperature gauge crept up. She didn't want to think about being marooned, but she was suddenly aware of the infinite varieties of car trouble that she never thought much about before: flat tires, overheated engine, oil leaks, broken axle.

"Jess!" Michael suddenly braked. "Over there! Look."

"Where?"

"Between those two hills."

A flash of white, just a thin line of color squeezed between the hard silhouettes of stone. "You think . . .?"

He was driving again. "What else could it be? Look, have you figured out what we're going to say when we get there?"

" 'I was just passing by and decided to drop in?' "

"It lacks a certain something."

Jess thought about it until they turned a last curve and were facing the building, a long, low white rectangle in what had been a long flat valley. Science-fiction writers couldn't have chosen a more surrealistic setting for malevolent scientists. There were no windows, no signs of people, no cars — just the concrete, man-made box plopped into a dead landscape of geological excrescences.

Jess looked at Michael. "Well. Shall we make a stab at it?"

"Could you put that more optimistically?" He swung his long legs out.

Despite the lack of glass, someone had been alerted to their arrival. By the time they got close enough to knock on the only visible door, it was open, and a woman in a white lab coat was waiting for them. Her face was neutral; the institute wasn't exactly on the beaten path, so she had to assume most visitors had legitimate reasons for being there.

Jess tried to smile casually. "Good afternoon. I'm looking for Dr. Harper." Her hands were clammy and her heart was pounding.

The woman frowned. "He's not here. He left last night."

Jess hoped the relief was hidden behind a sufficiently disgruntled sigh. "Oh, no." She showed her ID. "I'm Jessica Canby, chief of investigations."

The woman looked carefully at the badge and card, then inquiringly at Michael.

"And this is my husband, Michael Renfrew. He drove, so I wouldn't have to do it alone." A rueful wave at the tummy.

"How do you do. I'm Clara Isaacs." She didn't offer her hand or a smile.

"I've been at our regional office in Lancaster. Dr. Harper and I have some urgent business, so he suggested that when I was through, I drive on up here." Lancaster was less than halfway from Los Angeles, but maybe Clara would accept that Harper was a self-centered, inconsiderate, power-hungry employer. That much, after all, was true. "I suppose he assumed he'd be here longer."

Clara assessed the statement and appeared not to find it wanting. "You'd better come in before you drop from the heat. You can call Los Angeles and see what the mix-up is."

"Thanks."

The entrance was unprepossessing, a narrow hallway, pale green walls, and tiled floor of the same shade. At the far end was a heavy glass door that opened only when Clara inserted her identity badge into a scanner. Jess watched her covertly as they strode down long hallway. Clara was in her late forties or early fifties, beginning to spread into matronliness, but fighting it with a girdle and bra. Her face was tanned and creased like a sailor's, alertly intelligent. It wouldn't do to underestimate her.

Michael stayed close to Jess, as if he'd come to the same conclusion. He gazed around with a frank, open countenance. "Quite some place. What exactly do you study here?"

"Radiation." The inference was plain that she meant conventional radiation.

They passed offices and libraries where other

white-coated figures worked, occasionally looking up to greet Clara. The premises were bright, well lit, well tended — obviously well funded. Clara pointed out a few departments. "The computer section is through there. The entire institution is computerized, of course. The newest equipment . . . really a pleasure. That's my specialty — I'm the office manager, which amounts to being chief programmer." She pointed to the left as they turned right. "We keep the zoo down there."

"Zoo?"

Lab animals. Rats, mice, monkeys." She sighed, a human touch. "I try not to think about the monkeys."

Jess nodded without comment. Personally, she was a little more concerned with human beings, including herself and Michael. The journey through the labyrinths was telling them nothing, but it was making her increasingly frightened of running into someone who'd recognize her. With every step, the urge to turn and run out became stronger.

"In here." Clara finally paused and let them precede her into a spacious, brightly decorated staff lounge. "The telephone's over there. Just dial mine."

Michael distracted Clara from noticing that Jess's fingers kept the receiver buttons pressed down. He chatted about vivisection while Jess carried on a mythical, atypically respectful conversation with Harper, the sort he'd always wanted from her. She hung up and shook her head with a martyred air.

"Well?" Clara asked.

"He forgot to let me know. He's sorry, of course."

A flash of amusement came and went in the other woman's eyes. Obviously, she'd taken Harper's measure too.

"As long as we're here," Michael interjected with a bright smile, "would it be possible to have a fast look-around? Jess is used to labs, but I'm not, and I'm fascinated."

He was playing the passive spouse, and Clara was feminist enough to approve. She paused consideringly, then looked at her watch. "I've got a staff meeting in twenty minutes, but I suppose I can give you a whirlwind tour."

"Wonderful." Michael took Jess's hand, and after a moment she forced a pleased smile to her face and stood up. It was Daniel in the lion's den, but Michael was right, of course. They were here, and they had to make the most of it.

Clara whipped them up and down corridors, her patter at staccato pace. Jess hoped Michael was following it; she herself was too busy nervously peering around corners and into rooms, praying she wouldn't see a familiar face. There were laboratories and dissection facilities, offices and word processors, incomprehensible hospital machines, and walls of complex charts. There were technicians and bespectacled researchers and nurses and VDT operators. There was not a single paranoid, hunched-over mad scientist. This was the kosher tour.

Clara finally checked her watch again and said with a convincing display of regret, "Sorry, our time's nearly up."

Jess had never wanted to be shown out of any place so badly, but so far, they'd seen nothing that mightn't be in the Mayo Clinic. She summoned her nerve and took the plunge. "Dr. Harper mentioned you've got microwave hardware, too. I wonder if we could take a look at it? I know Michael would find it very interesting."

Clara shot a sharp glance at her, then at Michael.

He widened his eyes and looked interested.

She bit her lip, thought about it, then shrugged. "No reason why not. But it's pretty standard." She led them to the back of the building; the rear wall looked solid, but after Clara pressed a complicated series of buttons on a nearby console, it slid back to reveal a vast window overlooking a paved field. Three parabolic dishes sat, splayed toward the sky, beside a smaller version of the main white building and a two-story steel structure. She pointed at the latter. "That's the generating equipment. The dishes are receivers and transmitters, of course."

"Do you get nervous around them?" Michael asked, still the dumb blond. "Are the walls lead-lined, like in an X-ray lab?"

"Yes, actually, they are. But," Clara added with a condescending smile, just barely restraining herself from calling him "dear," "X-rays are entirely different from microwaves. Microwaves don't hurt you. We use them to cook food, for example, and send television and telephone signals."

He nodded ingenuously, as if it were news to him. "So what do you study?"

"Oh, we certainly run tests all the time, to be sure that microwaves have no effects. That's simply a precaution, going the extra mile, as it were, because it's so unlikely."

Jess was glad her face was pointed toward the window.

"But mainly," Clara continued, "we study microwaves to find other ways of making use of them."

"What's the other building?" Jess figured it was time to change the subject. Clara wasn't a fool. "Beside the generators."

"Oh, that's another department." She punched buttons again, and the wall sealed itself shut.

"Could we see it too?" Michael asked.

"No, I'm afraid not. It's restricted to red passes," she patted her green one, "and we're strict about it. Government research, you know."

"Oh, yes, of course." Jess affected a throwaway air.

"That must be Dr. Merton's department. Quite some scientist, Dr. Merton."

Clara looked at her with slightly narrowed eyes. "Do you know him?"

There was a tension in the air that Jess didn't like. She smiled through dry lips. "I've heard of him from Dr. Harper. Unfortunately, I've never had the pleasure of meeting him."

Clara didn't answer immediately. Jess and Michael were rooted to their spots. She'd overplayed her hand; if Merton was in the building, they were up the

395

proverbial creek.

Clara must have decided she was overreacting. She relaxed again. "It's a shame he's not here now."

Relief made Michael garrulous. He chatted, slightly flirtatious, all the way back to the front door. Jess was quieter. She wouldn't feel really chipper until they were in another locale entirely.

"Thanks again." Jess held out her hand.

"You were great," Michael beamed. "It was like taking a course."

Michael was a step closer to the exit, reaching for the door, when his eyes fell on a small table in the corner. A pile of parcels appeared to be waiting for the mail, or for a messenger. He nudged Jess back toward Clara, and when she dug in her heels, trying to glare unobtrusively, he beamed blandly and looked back at their hostess. "Oh, Jess, didn't you mean to ask about training staff on word processors?"

She was forced to enter into the charade; it was a wonder that the other woman didn't to hear the thudding of her heart against her rib cage. "Oh, yes. Uh — did you run the training programs yourself or did you bring in experts?" She maneuvered herself so that Clara's back was to Michael. She herself, unfortunately, could watch the whole thing. Clara was impatient, so she kept her answer short, but not short enough to prevent Michael from picking up the top parcel and shoving it inside his shirt.

"Yes. Um. Very helpful, thanks." Jess hadn't heard a single word. She smiled shakily and walked out with Michael to Martin's BMW.

The institute door closed, and Jess's smile froze. "Get this baby moving," she muttered.

Michael needed little encouragement. He gunned the engine, turned the car around, and sped toward freedom.

"You almost gave me heart failure!" she exploded. "You're a cocky, suicidal, reckless sonofabitch!"

"But I'm your sonofabitch, darling," he grinned. "The devil made me do it. I couldn't pass up an envelope addressed to Harper, now could I?" He pulled it out and tossed it onto Jess's lap.

She was still too angry to look at it. She stared instead at the road, as if there were anything in the wilderness worth seeing.

"Quite a little outfit, huh?" Michael mused, cheerfully oblivious to her seething. " 'Radiation studies' covers a lot of territory. Those bastards — pretending they still don't know microwaves are dangerous."

With every passing yard, Jess's terror abated somewhat. She finally sighed and leaned back. "I bet that building of Merton's is where the patients are."

"And where they're doing the real research. Not to see *if* the radiation's dangerous — but what band-aids they'll give us *after* the damage is done." His eyes narrowed. "Jesus, getting in that place would be all we'd need. If we can prove they're searching for ways to protect people — everyone would realize just how dangerous the business is!"

Jess shuddered. "Maybe, but I wouldn't step inside that laboratory without the entire Marine Corps. I've never been so frightened in my life."

"Look behind you."

"Why?" She twisted. "I don't see anything."

He was smiling; his shoulders lost their tension. "Exactly. We're away."

The sweetest words she had ever heard.

Michael came to a halt. "Let's take a look at that parcel."

"Now? I'd like to concentrate on getting someplace else. Anyplace else."

"It'll only take a minute."

Arguing would take longer. She hastily ripped open the envelope, scanned the contents, and whistled. "Well, well, well." She passed it over.

"Well, well, indeed." He met her eyes.

"At current market prices," she hastily calculated, "that's about two hundred grand worth of Berrington Industries stock. I'll say this for Harper, the bastard doesn't come cheap."

Michael snorted.

"You know what this means?" she continued with growing excitement. "It means we just gained our entree! Harper's going to become our very best friend!"

"Blackmail, Jess?   Do I hear you suggesting blackmail?"

"You betcha.   Michael, we did it!" She threw her arms around him. "We did it! We're going to be able to prove it all — the diseases *and* the fact that those bastards have been covering it up! We'll nail them to the wall!"

He laughed at her glee.   "Is this the same person who told me that the powers that be are just plain folks?"

She put away the pang of regret and kissed him. In the middle of it, his body stiffened. Jess froze too, then slowly pulled back. It took a second or two before her resistant mind registered the long black Mercedes coming toward them.

"Oh, God!" Her stomach heaved. "That's Desmond Marchenko! Bowdritch's boy."

They turned and looked behind them. The road twisted, too narrow to let them turn around, too twisting to permit speed in reverse. The Mercedes had slowed down, but it hadn't stopped coming. Michael inched back; the other car got into the spirit of the game and inched forward. Marchenko stared directly into Jess's eyes; her defiant glare was hollow and they both knew it.

The crawl seemed to last for hours. The tension grew until Jess thought she'd snap, the air became heavier and hotter, as if it were resisting their progress too.

Abruptly, Michael braked. He gestured helplessly. Another car was at their rear, another Mercedes. A German steel sandwich, and they were the chopped liverwurst.

Jess and Michael didn't move as two men in white coats approached from the second car. There was nowhere to run, and the men carried guns.   They motioned for Jess and Michael to step out, one on each side, pointing the gun barrels directly into the front seat. There was no point in arguing. Jess and Michael stepped out.

The man on the driver's side shot out an arm, and Michael doubled over with a grunt of pain. Jess gasped and tried to run to him; her guard grabbed her savagely around the neck. Too late, she saw the syringe coming toward her. She struggled, but he was bigger, stronger, and faster. She felt a sharp stab in her upper arm; she had time to feel terror for the baby, and then it all went black.

* * *

It was an expanse of snow, a white field extending as far as the dazzled eye could see; and she was cold, so cold. Nobody came when she yelled; she was the only person alive in the universe.

Very gradually, Jess came back to consciousness, and the white horizon dwindled down to walls and ceiling. The light her hallucination had taken for sunshine glinting on snow was a spotlight focused on her face. She was, however, still cold. She was strapped to some sort of cold metal table in the middle of a brilliantly white square room. With dawning horror, she saw that the table was an operating table, and she was nude on it. Her hands were tied; she couldn't even stroke her stomach to reassure the baby.

Someone was watching, must have seen her eyes open and grow large with fear. One wall opened smoothly to display a recessed object she couldn't place at first. It swiveled slowly on well-greased rollers, making no sound, the movement so deliberate that, at first, she couldn't be sure of it. What seemed like hours later, the object was revealed: a parabolic dish, the concave surface pointed directly at the operating table. At her.

She grasped what that meant and threw every muscle into straining against her bonds. She succeeded only in rubbing skin off her ankles and wrists; to add to everything else, now she felt pain.

"Don't bother."

She looked around to see where the disembodied voice came from. The loudspeaker was invisible, probably hidden behind the sharp white light that hurt her eyes. "Who are you? Let me go!"

The voice came at her again, cold, precise, slightly distorted by the mechanical tone of the broadcasting system. "You were warned; you were given every chance — you still insisted on making trouble for yourself."

It could have been Desmond's voice, or even Bowdritch's, for that matter. She felt a flush of humiliation at being seen like this, spread out naked, the roll of her stomach defenselessly exposed to cold air and colder scrutiny. Then she realized that shame was the least of her problems. "Let me go! Where's Michael? Have you hurt him?"

"We are all very sorry that it required measures like this to talk sense into you."

"Where's Michael?"

"I shall talk and you shall listen." The order was as hard-edged as an axe. "You have noticed the dish on the wall."

Her eyes involuntarily went back to it.

"You are so certain that microwave radiation is harmful — we don't believe it, of course. Perhaps you'd like to put it to the test yourself? Prove yourself right and us wrong?"

She jerked convulsively. "No! Please! You know I'm right — you know it from Paraguay; you prove it every day in the — " She broke off. It didn't matter now, but she just realized where she was. She'd gained entrance to Merton's building, finally. The one she didn't want to come near without the Marines. "Please, don't hurt my baby."

"Well," — the voice was no friendlier, but it was less clipped — "perhaps you're willing to be reasonable now?"

Just don't hurt Michael or the baby!"

"You're a very difficult woman. It was generally

assumed that you were . . . rational. We're all quite surprised at how emotional you've been. Perhaps it's the pregnancy."

The hormone theory again. She didn't object. Whatever made them happy.

"So we're prepared to make one last effort to come to an agreement with you — which is extraordinarily patient of us. We have not always been so patient."

She thought about the people with whom they'd lost their patience. She tried to swallow, but her tongue stuck to the parched roof of her mouth. "We've got friends in Los Angeles. We're not invisible. People will ask questions if something happens to us."

"Of course. Especially after all the fuss you've been raising. No, Ms. Canby — you can't vanish. But if you stayed in sight and had your baby and there was something wrong with the baby, would anyone believe your explanation for it? And if they did, would that make you happy? Would it change the fact that the baby was . . . affected?"

"No." Her voice was dull.

"We will leave you undisturbed if — and only if — you meet our terms."

"Anything."

"You will go back to Los Angeles, you and your husband. You will calm the waters. Completely. You'll tell everyone that you were wrong in your suspicions. That you want nothing more to do with it. That you were overwrought, hysterical, foolish."

"But what if they don't believe me?"

"They'll believe you." He was contemptuous of her naivete. "They didn't want to hear what you were saying in the first place. They'll be delighted to forget it."

She remained silent. God knew, that was true.

"And we will never be far away. We will be watching. For one thing, some of your friends are, shall we say, sympathetic to us. We will know if you try anything fancy. And before you do, Ms. Canby, imagine a lifetime of looking over your shoulder, of wondering what's happened everytime your child isn't where he's supposed to be."

"I'll do whatever you want? We'll do whatever you want! I swear we will!"

The pause stretched into an infinity; Jess's nerves stretched with it. Finally, the dish began to swivel again. She didn't take her eyes off it until it was back behind the wall. Then she closed her eyes and tried to calm her breathing. She opened them again when she felt the presence of another person in the room.

It was a white-clad nurse, holding another syringe.

"No, please — the baby!"

"Now, dear, don't fret." The woman patted Jess's shoulder, her motherly face beaming reassuringly. "It won't hurt the baby. We wouldn't want to do that, now would we?"

Jess turned her face away; the parody of kindliness made her skin crawl. She jerked as the needle went in, and she was almost glad for the fuzziness as it took her over and took away the feeling of the nurse's hand.

Chapter 23

Wooziness ebbed and flowed. There were moments when consciousness was almost within her grasp; then she slipped back into the phantom world. Sometimes she was half aware of movement, of being slung around like a sack of so many potatoes. She had a sense of time passing, as one did in sleep. Perhaps it was from her dreams, so many of them, all disturbed by a vague dread that didn't quite turn them into nightmares.

Then, slowly, her eyes began to open. The universe stopped shimmering, and she came back to the real world. She could tell it was real because of the headache, the grandfather of headaches, a pounding drumbeat that could summon half the tribes of Africa. Her head weighed fifty pounds; the slightest motion threatened to take it off entirely.

She concentrated on other thoughts. The light. Its quality was hard to place, very crystalline, as pure as sparkling white sugar on strawberries. She got it, eventually. Dusk. This was the last golden burst before the sun exhausted itself for the day. But which day? Why was she lying here?

The thought made her sit up, wincing at the protesting crash in her temples, to see where "here" was. Her own living room. Half the drumbeat wasn't inside her head; it was outside, the heavy high surf. She was used to that sound. She was used to this place. She lived here, so why was she surprised to see it?

She forced herself to her feet. The muscles were particularly obdurate; but the task was some sort of test, and she passed it. She went into the kitchen and turned on the tap, waiting until the water was cold, as cold as it could be coming from sun-warmed pipes. Abruptly, she shoved her head under it. The shock stunned the headache and woke up her mind. She remembered it all now, and she wished she didn't.

Her body moved through the house before her mind gave the order to look for Michael. Panic didn't have a chance to set in. She found him in the spare room, apparently drugged with whatever they'd given her, but breathing. Her relief was so great, she was almost grateful to "them", even though she knew how mad that was.

He was starting to stir too, as disoriented as she'd been. Jess went over and over the facts, until Michael seemed to begin to grasp them. She helped him into the bathroom, held him up under the shower. His head cleared enough for him to start to protest at the icy water. She made it warmer, and the two of them stood there for a long time, arms wrapped around each other, eyes shut, as if that would keep them from facing hard facts.

"We're going to drown." Michael finally reached out to turn off the tap.

Jess automatically reached for a towel and handed it to Michael. She watched with growing giggles as he absentmindedly rubbed down his blue jeans and cotton shirt. Eventually, he figured out what was so funny and started to laugh too. It was a release from terror, and the laughter verged on hysteria. Only with difficulty did they stop themselves from going over the edge. Finally they quieted and stood looking at each other, dripping wet, the fear back.

"What now?" Michael asked somberly.

"I want to get out of town. Away from . . . everything." Telephones and televisions and satellite dishes and secret prying eyes.

He was stripping off his clothing and tossing it into a heap in the corner of the shower, as if he'd never need it again. Jess followed suit.

"I don't want to go up against them anymore ," she added after a while. People who could drug you and threaten you and strip you and dress you and take you home again were people who should be allowed to have their own way.

Michael nodded. "They told me they'd zap you and the baby, and I told them I was feeling very cooperative."

"My feeling exactly."

They walked into the bedroom and began to dress again.

Jess was almost afraid to ask. "Did they hurt you?"

He shook his head. "They didn't need to."

"It proves it, though . . . that we're getting the kid-glove treatment."

"Considering everything, I guess we are. Kid glove on an iron fist."

Jess abruptly sat down on the bed. "Just another lifetime organized by Kafka."

Michael leaned down and kissed her. "I can't believe it either — but we have to. We have to pack and get the hell out of here. Call me a quitter if you like, but let's quit."

"I'm with you," she agreed fervently. "It's just that I have to make a few calls."

"They told me about that," he nodded. "I'd do Richard Simon first."

"First and foremost. He can spread the good word." She hated the bile of bitterness that swelled in her throat. Richard. It was almost as painful as when she'd thought her father had let her down.

Michael handed her the telephone. She looked at it as if it were a snake. He eventually picked up the receiver and handed it to her, then dialed the number.

"Hello?"

Jess opened her mouth, and a croak came out. She tried again. "It's me, Richard. Jess."

"I'm so glad you called! I want to talk to you — I even called your mother and left a message."

She vaguely recalled another lifetime in which she'd known that. "We've been . . . away. What day is it?"

"What day — ? Friday. Evening. Jess, what's the matter?"

Friday. They'd gone to the desert on Thursday. Twenty-four hours had evaporated, leaving no trace other than the sour taste in her mouth. "I'm — we're fine."

"Well . . . " He sounded dubious. "Is Michael with you?"

"Yes, he's here."

"Look, I talked to that police officer — Detective Arnheim, you know?"

"Yes, I know."

"I thought it had all settled down when you went back to work — then there was that terrible phone message Virginia got. The threat. And Detective Arnheim said — he came to me, actually — he said that you and Michael were still going around town, asking questions about this . . . conspiracy — "

It was a test, and her voice wouldn't work. Finally, she made the words come; they poured out, tumbling over each other. "No, no — we were doing that, but we're through with it now. I swear. We were crazy; I don't know what got into us — We were wrong; we know that now. We want to be sensible now; we're going to stop. We have stopped. We're going to go away for a while, just relax, stop all this craziness — "

"Arnheim said there was more violence, two more of your friends. He said you probably believe it's connected to the other fatalities — "

"No, no, really, we don't." She was shaking her head as if he could see it.

"Jess, you sound very strange."

"I'm back under control now. I was very strange, but I'm okay now."

"And all the fuss you made — upsetting all of us, upsetting the police — you were wrong about it all?"

"All!"

"I see." He paused. "Well, that's nice to hear."

She bet it was. "I just wanted to let you know. Before we go away."

"And where are you going, my dear?"

Her mind seized up; the only place name she could think of was Paraguay and she certainly wasn't going to let that word pass her lips again. "Uh, we're going to play it by ear." She wanted desperately to be off the telephone. "I'll drop you a line."

She replaced the receiver and took a dozen deep breaths.

"How did he take it?" Michael had packed a flight bag; he was zipping it up.

I don't know. I sounded like a certified moron."

"Better a live moron than a dead genius."

She winced.

"What about the others? Francis, and so on?"

"Richard's in touch with them all. Let's just get out of town — he'll tell them he's heard from me. We can write them — later, from someplace safe."

Michael nodded. "Better get dressed. I'll wait downstairs."

She threw on her maternity jeans, a faded white shirt, and a sweater, and hurried downstairs. It was dark now, and the living-room lamps weren't on. "Michael?" She found the switch; the room was empty. "Michael!"

She stifled a fear that had become as automatic as breathing and went out onto the deck. "Michael!"

"Down here, love." He was sitting, knees up, under the balcony. Saying goodbye to the ocean.

Jess went around the house to the stairs and joined him. The water was glassily smooth. The wind had shifted, and the surf was receding passively. It was a beautiful night, velvet water under soft black sky and sequin stars.

"We'll be back." She didn't know whether to believe her own words.

He put an arm around her. "Where shall we go?"

"I don't care. As long as it's far away and primitive. I don't care if I never see technology again. To hell with the twentieth century."

Michael stood and helped her up. Her jeans rustled, but when she stopped moving, the rustle continued. "Michael." Her voice was as soft as the breeze.

He heard it too.

"There's someone there."

He nodded grimly. "Let's move."

They took a step and froze. A figure stepped out from under the eave of the next house, moving from shadow to the pool of light thrown by the neighbor's beach spotlights. It was a small man, half Michael's size, dark-skinned and balding. He wore jeans and a khaki shirt that looked well-worn, as if it hadn't been bought because it was chic.

"Canby." The voice was musical, accented by Spanish.

Jess nodded very faintly.

The figure made a small gesture, and a second man joined him, as slight as the first, but made very compelling by the gun in his right hand. The newcomer was fair-skinned, glowing white in the spotlight. Neither man was smiling.

"Your husband?" The Spanish lilt was very obvious now.

Jess nodded.

The second man said something in a guttural tone that had nothing to do with Romance tongues. German. Swell. She thought of gentle German types like Attila the Hun and Goering.

The men stepped closer, the German keeping a wary eye on the beach, the other one staring at Jess and Michael. "You ask many questions," the Spanish speaker said softly. "You English say curiosity kills the cat, yes?"

Michael was standing very close to Jess. "Who are you?"

"You are also curious. Very crazy."

There was melodrama here. They were playing roles in a bad movie from the forties, but recognition didn't bring reassurance. Jess had a flash of insight when she remembered that young revolutionaries (or even those not so young) had a great lust for melodrama. "You're Manuel Perreira."

"So." He didn't seem taken aback. He didn't seem anything except in charge. "You make much trouble, looking for me."

"We're sorry about that."

He ignored her inanity. "You feel pleased, now you find me?" It was a sneer.

Jess and Michael looked at each other. Melodrama,

and now irony. A day ago, they'd have felt great, but now he was the last person on earth they wanted to talk to. Both of them quickly scanned the beach, as tense as the German.

"We made a mistake ," Michael finally muttered. "This whole thing is none of our business."

"You talk to my friends of Lorrie Berrington." The name brought a reaction from the gunman. He spat something in German again; Manuel apparently agreed. "She was a stupid, sentimental bourgeois." "Asshole" would have carried no more dislike.

Jess felt as middle-class as Harriet Nelson. Her pulse was stroke high.

"But she was not your friend," he continued coldly. "She had no pig friends."

"I'm not a cop."

"You are with the authorities. I know the authorities, I know all there is to know about the authorities."

"I'm not a threat to you. Or your friends." A quick glance at the second man.

"No." Manuel clearly found the mere thought laughable.

"Why are you here?" Michael asked the question gently, with no urge to offend anyone carrying a gun.

"Not to help you," he snarled. "You ask questions; you are the same as the girl."

"We don't want to ask any more questions." Michael looked intently at Manuel. "We want to go away and stay out of trouble."

"Bourgeois."

They took deep breaths. It would be hard to protest the verdict, standing underneath their Malibu beach house.

"I come here to use you. We have proofs that answer questions you ask."

"We haven't asked any questions," Jess said quickly. "Not lately. We're out of it."

He ignored her and pulled an envelope out of his shirt pocket with a savage fast movement that made both Michael and Jess jump. "It is the proof." He held it out to Michael. Jess might be the authority, but Michael was the man.

Michael's stretch was reluctant. He was afraid to take it and afraid not to.

"There are pictures, reports." Manuel noticed their dubious glance at the very thin package. "Microfilm. We live dirt-poor in Paraguay, but we are not savages."

"No, of course not." She was willing to agree with anything said by someone who could hurt her. "But you shouldn't give it to us. We're — "

He cut her off harshly. "American dogs and the pigs of our government point the machines at defenseless villages. The people sicken and die and no one cares. What they could not do in secret here, they do there and our people cannot fight back. This will prove their crimes — you will make it known." He stepped closer. "You will tell the world what is being done."

"No one would believe us," Michael protested. "We've been saying it all along, and no one — "

"You had no pictures!" His snarl silenced them. In the hush, they could hear their telephone ringing, a sharp summons that heightened the tension and underlined their fear.

Michael tried again. "If this is so — and I'm sure it is," he added fast when Manuel narrowed his eyes, "how can it be hidden? Why hasn't it been made public before now?"

"The girl found out why."

They sighed. They'd almost found out why.

"Lorrie saw the villages herself?" Jess asked quietly.

Manuel shrugged. "Some of them."

"How can you be sure that microwaves are causing the suffering?"

He bared his teeth. "We know. The machines come — and the and the children are sick, the cancer grows, eyes bleed and go dark. The doctors come and study and make notes — it is in there, the machines in the jungles and the doctors and the disease. Ten years

410

of disease, since the machines come."

Ten years. Since the first low voices began to ask what the price of satellite technology would be. Jess felt sick, then remembered the operating room at the institute and felt sicker. "But we're going away. We can't help you."

Michael joined the chorus, talking as if they were all equals.

"Mr. Perreira, you and your friends are skilled at getting publicity. More skilled than we are. You could use the photographs yourself — "

"My friends?" He eyed them assessingly. "What do you know of my friends?"

Michael glanced at the second man and quickly said, "Nothing. Except that he's not South American. I don't know more than that, and I don't want to know more."

The German didn't like the attention. He made his point by gesturing with the gun.

"The pigs of the capitalist press will hear you more clearly than us." Manuel made his voice very threatening. "You will take the — " He broke off, suddenly whirled around. Both men were on the alert, straining into the darkness.

In the silence, the only sounds Jess could hear were the surf and the telephone, shrilling again above their heads. Her eyes tried to pierce the dark shadows of the beach, but she saw nothing, could feel nothing.

"We go now." Manuel breathed the words to blend in with the night. "We find you again if you do not do as I say."

Jess and Michael stepped back from the threat. The men made no move to stop them, not even when they turned and ran for the stairs to the house.

The telephone was still screaming demandingly.

"What should we do?" She gestured at it helplessly. "I don't want them to know we're still here."

"If they're watching, they already know."

She nodded and reluctantly reached for the receiver. She paused. If they're watching. "Michael! If they're watching — they saw — "

He nodded grimly, struck by the same terrifying thought. Two strides brought him to the glass overlooking the beach.

"Answer it; talk normally."

Normal was now tongue-tied. "Hello."

"Ms. Canby? It's Stephen Bowdritch."

She stiffened and waved for Michael's attention. He didn't notice; he was stiff himself, leaning right against the glass to see out. Jess stared at him, then went over, dragging the long cord behind.

"Ms. Canby?" Bowdritch repeated the name several times.

"What? Oh, yes. I'm sorry." The words were meaningless, automatic. All her energy was going into trying to see outside. There were figures down there, more than two. Four . . . five . . .

"Ms. Canby, Richard Simon just called me. He tells me you're going away with your husband."

"Yes, going away." What was happening down there? Two men were running. There were others behind them.

"I wanted to catch you before you left."

Caught. The two men were caught; one, the big one, struggled. She gasped. He was the German, and he was in the grasp of the Pyramid.

"Ms. Canby, are you there? I want to talk to you — I'm very disturbed by what you've been doing."

A noise. A crack like surf crashing down to the ground. But the ocean was demure, and it was the German who fell. The man over him held a gun.

Michael grabbed Jess's arm. "Time to go."

She was immobile, then remembered Bowdritch. "We didn't break our word," she told the receiver frantically. "We didn't know they were coming here tonight — we don't intend to break our promise!"

"Jess!" Michael was insistent. Two of the men were now looking up at the window. He dragged her back and pulled the telephone out of her hands. "They won't listen. They'll shoot first and ask questions later. Come on!"

SIDE EFFECTS

They were in their car and out on the road in moments.

Chapter 24

They took the coastal highway north, with no destination in mind, that knowing only that they wanted to put miles between themselves and Los Angeles. It was busy on the road for the hour and a half it took to get to Santa Barbara; every other car seemed menacing, all other headlights appeared to be pursuing them. They cut away, finally, into the San Marcos Pass, instinctively seeking rugged empty terrain, as if it promised peace and quiet. The pass was the setting of every western ever made: harsh dry hills and gulches, hospitable to no one, unconquerable — the land pitted against the lone cowboy, the taciturn man on horseback who lived simply on celluloid and died in the arms of a gold-hearted whore. For a few minutes, Jess and Michael could pretend their flight was just a film fairytale too.

The narrow road eventually linked up again with Highway 101 and civilization. They turned, instead, toward the dusty inland, instinct taking them away from people. Though it might be a bad instinct, they chose to follow it. There was some relief from constant tension on roads unlit and untraveled.

The hours passed. They spelled each other behind the wheel, stopping only for gas and nervously going on their way again as fast as possible. It was well after midnight when their energy gave out completely. They were too bleary-eyed to see the road and too bleary-minded to figure out if they could risk a motel.

Michael was driving, following small back roads up the side of Los Padres National Forest. He gestured, finally, at a rubble-strewn dirt path that seemed to go nowhere. "Shall we?"

"For a few hours." She leaned back, closed her eyes, and was out like a light.

It felt like no more than an hour later. When the sun woke them both up, Jess's headache was back; Michael's skin was gray, suggesting he felt no better.

"We need a plan."

She raised her eyebrows. "Good thinking. Have

you got one to suggest?"

He opened the map of the state and tried to focus red eyes on it. "I'd say 'go east, young man.' "

"Nevada? Arizona?"

"Whatever." He thought for a while. "We have to buy time. Let things quiet down a bit — then send a message through Martin. Tell them we're out of it; we're really out of it. Explain last night. Promise to stay away as long as they like."

"We've got very little cash."

"We've got plastic."

"They say you shouldn't use credit cards when you don't have a regular income."

He tried to smile. "Into the hinterland? Across the Sierra Madres, then cut east to Nevada? It won't be comfortable, but nobody would expect anyone to choose that. It might buy time."

Or it might buy eternity. East to Nevada was a cheerful way of saying across Death Valley. More people started out to cross it than actually arrived at the other side. She tried not to think of the hours of hell, the heat and the aridity and the immobility that would make her nauseated and crampy. "Sure."

"You think you can make it?"

She met his eyes. "I have to, don't I?"

The hours were interminable, and the drive was more hellish than she'd dreamed possible. The sun rose relentlessly, and appeared to be deliberately aiming at them. Even the car whimpered from the punishment, laboring to climb dry mountain slopes, only momentarily relieved on the downward inclines. They couldn't use airconditioning because they had to husband the gas. Their clothing was entirely damp; even when they removed most of it, there was no relief.

Occasionally other vehicles passed by, long old cars with antique fins, pickups, ancient Dodges, raising clouds of dust that settled on tired scrub and on them. Jess's watch had stopped. Michael wasn't wearing one, but it was some time in the afternoon, and it felt as though they'd been driving for weeks. Her mouth was dry, gritty from dust, sour from lack of sleep and food. Her tear ducts weren't working; she could barely see through caked eyes, but the little she could see told her she wasn't missing much. This wasn't the Southern California of surfing movies and big-eyed starlets. It was the real California, dust and desert and desolation, small grim towns and weather-beaten, god-fearing farmers, hostile to strangers and angry about life. They had every right to be. Life was hard, as hard as it must have been in the thirties; they had no time for frivolities like hot tubs and divorce. Marriage was forever; duty was everything; Coke was just a cola out here.

It was another world, but Jess and Michael had brought their own with them. There was no escaping it; their muscles never forgot the tension. They never relaxed. They pushed ahead, afraid of every shadow, rigid with fear the few times they saw signs of a sheriff.

Once, a helicopter went by overhead, and Michael shoved the accelerator to the ground as if he could get away faster than the whirly bird could follow. It didn't follow; the drone faded within moments, but Jess heard its echo for an hour.

Her body rebelled, finally, in the late afternoon. They were crossing the mountains of the Sierra Nevada; not as far away as they could be if they'd been able to risk major routes; not far, as the crow flies, from Lava Point and the institute's nightmares. Jess tried desperately to hang on at least long enough to pass further north, as if it would be bad luck to stop now. But exhaustion had become aches; aches had become pains and, finally, spasms. Everything was cramping: feet, hands, back, and, worst of all, belly. "Michael."

It was the first sound either of them had made in an hour. He looked over, then skidded to a halt. "Jess, what's wrong?"

"We have to stop. I have to rest."

He gently touched her cheek and nodded, then made the car move on, faster. They passed through gulches and abandoned miners' camps, marked by nothing except notations on the map. It was another half-hour before they saw living habitation. It was primitive. The map called it Goldust Mountain, but if anyone had ever found gold, he'd skedaddled away as fast as he could manage. What was left behind was meager: a few bleached frame houses, a single commercial establishment with a single gas pump and an old sign advertising Hershey's chocolate. Michael stopped and went inside. He returned quickly with an old woman, a big-boned weathered figure who wouldn't look out of place on a covered wagon.

She nodded impassively at Jess, but the voice was kind enough. "You can stop here, Missus."

Michael helped her out of the car; the three of them made a slow, stumbling walk to the back of the structure.

"Bed's in there." The proprietress ran practiced eyes over Jess. "Seven months?"

Michael answered for her. "Yes. But she's had a rough time lately. Lots of pain."

The woman nodded, still emotionless. Life was hard for women out here. No getting away from it. She obviously figured you'd be a fool to try.

The room was small and airless. Dust sat thick on a small cot and a chairless table. Jess thought it was beautiful. She stretched out with Michael's help and sighed at the blessed relief.

"I'll stay with you."

"There's room on the bed," she insisted.

He looked around, faced the fact that there was no other surface on which he could sleep, and lay down with her, half off the bed so as to give her as much room as possible. The heat from their bodies and the cramped quarters made it difficult to nod off, but eventually they managed it.

It was the dead of night when the old woman came back. She leaned over Michael, trying to wake him without disturbing Jess, but it was Jess who opened her eyes first.

"Missus. Phone's for you."

She was bolt upright. Michael jerked awake

instantly and was on his feet. "What?"

"Phone's for you. In the front."

They didn't move.

She misunderstood, took it as a denial. "For you," she insisted. "Described you. Said you was Jess and Michael."

"I'll go."

Jess took his hand. "Not without me."

They walked back around to the general-store part of the establishment, a small room with a wooden counter, an antique cash register, and no more than ten shelves of cans and boxes. The telephone was on the wall, beside a dubious dairy department.

Michael made an obvious effort to regain calm before he picked up the dangling receiver. "Yes."

"Evening, Renfrew."

Jess could hear. She gasped at the voice. "What's Francis doing?"

Michael shrugged and said nothing.

"You're damn fools, running away like that. What the hell are you thinking about, Renfrew? Heading into Death Valley with Jess pregnant. You got rocks for brains?"

She grabbed the receiver. "How did you find us?"

"Took a hell of a lot of doing." He spoke sourly, as if she should apologize for the inconvenience. "You should know better than that. You can't get away from computers anymore.

The credit cards. A trail anyone could follow, if they were powerful enough to gain access to anyone's microchips.

"Look, Jess, you'd better come back. All hell's going to break loose. I can't protect you out in the goddam wilderness."

They shivered at the same moment. "Go to hell, Francis."

She hit the button, holding it down for a long time to break the connection. When she raised it, he was still there, breathing heavily. It was the slightly asthmatic sound of beginning emphysema. Jess marveled at her mind's ability to come up with irrelevancies. "Leave us alone, Francis. We're not going to cause anyone any trouble."

"I want some answers."

"I told you — we're through. We're really through with it. "She tried, but she couldn't keep the panic from showing. "We made our deal, and we're going to stick with it. Please! For old time's sake — let us get away!"

Michael pushed the button this time. They stood there forever while the old woman in the background puffed on a pipe and read a yellowed magazine.

"The credit cards." She finally pulled herself together. "We've got to dump them. They leave a trail a mile wide."

"We don't have enough cash."

"I know." The panic was rising again. "Martin. I don't want to involve him again, but we don't have a choice, Michael."

"He'd want us to — if it meant helping the baby." He spoke reassuringly, as if worry wasn't lurking in his own eyes. Slowly, he released the telephone button and nodded at her. "It's cut now."

The telephone rang at Martin's end only twice. His voice was edgy when he answered it, then rising with the relief of anger. "Jesus H. Christ, Mike! You're a goddam pain in the ass — you know that? You have any idea how scared I've been? Is Jess okay?"

"Shut up," Michael cut in. "Listen carefully. We're in the desert, place called Goldust Mountain, and we're in trouble. We can't use our credit cards. We've got very little cash, and we've got to keep running. I don't have time to tell you about it now. I can't tell you where we're headed, because we don't know. But we need your help. Get some cash together — we'll call again. We'll work something out."

"The bank ," Jess hissed.

Michael nodded. "Yeah. Maybe we'll have you wire funds somewhere."

"Stay put," Martin said tensely. "Stay put — I'll charter a plane and get there fast."

"The people on our tail can get here faster. Besides, there's something we need you to do there. Bowdritch and Arnheim and Simon — they're all in it."

"What?"

"Don't ask questions, lad. Just listen. They think we're welching on a deal we made with them — our lives for our silence. We're not. It's just that, by a terrible coincidence, we got handed proof of what microwaves can do."

"Proof? You're kidding!"

"No, pictures and reports from Paraguay. The point is, Martin, you've got to convince them that we want to keep to the bargain. Tell them Manuel — they'll know who we mean — came to us. We didn't want him. Maybe you can use what he gave us as a bargaining lever. We'll give it up, if they leave us alone." He paused. "Martin, old buddy, be careful. There's a lot of risk involved. We wouldn't ask you, but — "

"Hey, you worry about Jess and the baby, and I'll look out for myself. Hard-nosed bankers do okay. But call, keep in touch," he pleaded.

"We will." Michael hung up. "Jess, let's go. No time to see the local sights."

She ran clumsily back to their brief haven and dumped the contents of her purse onto the cot. She stared sourly at it all: credit cards, driver's license, social security card, coroner's office ID, telephone charge card, birth certificate. Everything linked to the labyrinths of someone's computer. There was no privacy anymore, none. Its passing had somehow escaped her notice, one more nightmare to add to the collection of things she'd worry about some other time.

Michael was filling the car. It was an old gas pump for old cars. Leaded gas. GM's booklet was very stern about that; the catalytic converter, whatever the hell that was, was going to be most distressed. Progress was a pain in the ass.

Jess looked back once; the old woman was standing on the stoop watching them go. The face hadn't changed one iota during the entire visit. Jess waved; the old woman's hand moved, perhaps a farewell, more likely brushing away a fly.

This drive made the earlier one seem a positive joy ride. The sun wouldn't be up for a while, and the roads were mined traps in the darkness, uneven, rubble-strewn, unpredictable. They had to stick to the worst of them, the thinnest strips, the harshest, least-traveled paths, curving in and out of gulches, climbing increasingly formidable mountains and pretending not to know that the blackness on one side of the road concealed empty air.

The sun joined them when they were still in Inyo County; it took away the shadows, but brought its own price, flattening the landscape with angry punishing light. Jess watched the skies while Michael watched the horizon. Every shimmer of the fiery haze made her heart jump, in case it turned out to be a plane.

It was a flight into the surreal, a journey through land that became, with every mile, more and more fantastical, a sorcerer's kingdom: glare looked like cool water, boulders refracted light into dancing colors, mountains slid away from them, then abruptly jutted back, dust settled to reveal ghostly outlines of dead mining shacks and settled again to bury them. It was barren, grotesque, lunar in bleakness. Nothing grew, nothing could live here, and no one still tried.

Jess began to believe they had slipped through a hole in the fabric of the universe, were in a fourth dimension, would voyage forever in limbo. It was no longer simply hot. Air-conditioning was necessary to breathe, and that, with the engine's labor on rough climbs, ate up their fuel with terrifying appetite. They were mute on the subject at first, as if that would make the problem vanish. Jess stole glances at the gauge, her heart sinking as the red pointer did. She had fallen into listlessness, tempted to let fate find them, to stay still in passive fatigue. Only the thought of the baby finally roused her from the trance, gave her the energy to study the map.

Michael was driving like an automaton now; he

didn't seem to hear her at first. She touched his leg, which was burning with dry heat. Sweat evaporated before it reached the surface. It felt as if blood itself was bubbling.

"We've got to go back, Michael. There's nothing on the map — we won't make it through."

"If we go back . . . " His voice was raspy in his parched throat.

She nodded. If they went back, there would be searchers looking for them. By now, the well-oiled money machine would have sent signals throughout the state to God only knew how many sheriffs and gas stations and rest stops.

The red pointer continued to sink.

"We have to risk it." She touched his leg again, then held her stomach, concentrating on the life inside to avoid thinking about death waiting everywhere else.

They had turned not a moment too soon. The car was almost bone-dry empty when they came into a truck stop just east of Highway 395. It was just pumps, restrooms and a shabby refreshment stand, but it was busy. Cars and vans and big rigs pulled in on their way north to Bishop and south to the coast — blue-jawed truckers speedy from the pills that let them drive through day and night; tired, fretful tourist families; brawny tattooed bikers caked with dust, and too road-weary to raise hell.

Jess and Michael waited in line, tense as foxes encircled by the hounds. Every movement made them start, every casual glance raced their pulses. They crept forward, were finally first, were grateful for the bored dead eyes of the attendant. He didn't look at his customers, could hardly be expected to remember what he hadn't seen. Michael ordered an extra can of gasoline to put in the trunk, and a case of ginger ale.

Jess pulled out their money. It wasn't nearly enough to pay the bill. She handed it wordlessly to Michael who nodded and muttered, "Do up your seatbelt."

She knew what he was going to do, but it was still

a shock when he did it. He handed the young man what there was in bills and change, then while it was being counted, before the arm went up in protest, he gunned the engine and shot away. Jess resolutely faced forward, unwilling to watch the pursuit. Michael concentrated grimly on the road, which was at first well-paved; then rocky; he took sharp curves at breakneck speed, twisting the wheel abruptly when the tires skidded on loose gravel, aiming for steep inclines and downgrades that would best hide the car. It wasn't meant for drag-racing; the shock absorbers gave up the struggle early. The seat

belt held Jess in place, but it bit into her stomach and didn't stop her from bouncing painfully. She tried to ignore the fear and cramping, her muscles coiled and rigid. She remained intent on the road as if concentration alone could hold the car safely on the surface.

He finally slowed down and Jess took what seemed like her first breath in thirty minutes. She reached over to wipe Michael's forehead. They were both scratchy with grit that had sifted in from the stirred up dust, their faces lined and gray, and drained of blood. Jess took gulps of thick burning air, trying to hold back the nausea, refusing to give in now. Gradually, her stomach unclenched and her muscles smoothed out.

"How are you?" Michael gently stroked the belly.

She forced a smile. This was not the moment for frankness. "Where did you learn to drive like that?"

"Not bad, huh?"

"I could have lived without discovering your hidden talent, but under the circumstances, not bad." She kissed him; her lips were dry against his grainy skin.

"Try to sleep."

She didn't protest; she couldn't have fought the wooziness of relief had she wanted to.

* * *

The heat was like a drug; Jess passed the day a in

semi-coma. She woke up fully only when it started to get dark. They had stopped on a deeply rutted dirt path that ran through a dry river bed. Michael was massaging his shoulders, his lips pressed together against the pain.

"Let me drive," Jess suggested.

"I'm okay." He lied badly. "I stopped a couple of times to nap. How are you?"

"Numb."

They watched the shadows lengthen as the sky turned purple, then black. It was a dramatic sunset, a desert spectacle that they ought to have enjoyed. They were, after all, lucky to be seeing it. The thought didn't cheer Jess.

Michael apparently felt much the same way. He started the engine again. "We'll drive through the night. We can't stand another full day of sun."

She caught an undertone she didn't like. "There's something else, isn't there?"

He was silent.

"Michael, don't forget your feminist training. Don't hide things from the little woman."

He sighed. "I saw a helicopter a little while back. It may not have seen us, we were sort of moving through rock overhangs. Maybe it wasn't even looking for us, but . . . "

"Yeah." Her adrenal glands had had it. Not even this could spark a flash of energy, but her mind recognized the gravity of the fact. "We'll have to drive without lights."

Michael chose not to comment. What was there to say, short of a burst of terror?

It got cold suddenly, at first a blessed respite from hell's fires. Then it turned bitter, the thin air snapping at goose-bumped skin. When Jess turned to reach into the flight bag for more layers, it hit her.

She turned her head away from Michael and tried to breathe evenly. The cramps were different from any she'd had before, deep-seated, compelling. She denied fiercely to herself that this was labor, but she couldn't deny the sweat pouring down despite the chill, nor then knife twists in her guts. It was too early! This wasn't quite seven months yet. It couldn't be happening, here in the abandoned wilderness, in flight. It couldn't be!

A sound, part hiss, part moan, escaped her. Michael knew immediately. "Jess!"

She tried to say something, but her body was too absorbed in itself to respond.

"Oh, God." He gripped the wheel with white knuckles, gripped his self-control as savagely. "Jess, we're in the middle of nowhere. We'll have to drive . . a while to find help. Can you hang on?"

She wanted desperately to say she could, wanted not to fail them both, but her head shook, more realistic than her will.

He watched her shiver, then convulse again, and reached for the map. They'd been climbing for a while; the ground was rough and bare. Below was dark shadows, desiccated gullies winding through the hills. It was hard to imagine that any other human being had ever been here. The desolation was as complete as if they alone had survived the nuclear holocaust.

Michael put the map aside without saying anything and grimly drove on. Jess didn't know what he was looking for until he took the car down and the gully widened suddenly to an arid plateau. The high beams were on, picking out phantoms that broke the straight line of the horizon; they could be anything — rocks or scrub or illusions.

They were, in fact, the remnants of a camp, shacks of flimsy wood tacked together by crumbling nails and the delusions of defeated men who'd spent years looking for treasure and had probably found only fool's gold.

"Where are we?"

His voice was matter-of-fact. "They called it Deadman's Gulch." She managed a weary smile. The name fit. All the names on the map fit the desolate sites, invariably grim, as if the miners themselves knew what lay in store for them. She pretended not to know what probably lay in store for her and Michael and the

425

baby. "I can't walk."

He lifted her out and carried her gently to a three-sided structure with half a tin roof. There was a ridiculous sense of relief, as if they'd found shelter; the relief fled with another terrible racking pain.

"I'm going to put on the car flashers," Michael murmured, wiping sweat from her cheeks. "And set flares."

"But, then . . " She gasped at another twist of the knife. She had to wait for it to subside before she could talk again. "They'll find us."

"That's our only chance, sweetie." He took her hands in his. "We don't have a chance, here alone."

She writhed again and didn't argue. He was gone only a few minutes; from inside the shed she could see the flicker of light. It was comforting, giving the illusion of warmth, fuel for an atavistic faith that it would dispel the horrors of the night.

Michael came back with the flight bag; he tried to relieve her shivering with layers of clothing laid on her like blankets. They sat together as the hours passed, his warmth given to her while the pains deepened and ripped at her. She tired; it became harder to accept the agony without screaming. Then it became impossible to scream because her voice had gone. She tried to breathe in the deep, regular pants they had learned in the maternity classes, but she'd only attended a couple. She kept on forgetting what the teacher had said. Michael gave her his hands, trying to take some of the torment into himself. He left her side only to nurse the flares.

The night wore on, growing colder every hour. The car battery wore down, and so did Jess. There was a little left to burn; the fires grew smaller, more tentative. They both began to despair, trying to hide it from each other, but knowing their chances were slipping away.

Her water burst before dawn, and then she was bone dry again as the air sucked the moisture away. Michael was lying beside her, full-length, trying to give her strength and warmth. He turned his head away when the car's headlights dimed the final time and went out. There were only two tiny flares now, and they had only minutes left.

"Michael."

"Don't talk. Save your strength."

She wasn't sure she wasn't hallucinating; if so, it was merciful, and she didn't want to stop. "I hear something."

He listened with a burst of hope; it faded, and he shook his head.

"No, I do," she insisted.

Then he did, too. A drone, very faint but distinctly not a night sound of the desert. Michael leaped up and ran outside. Jess gasped through another spasm; the pains were almost continual now. She tried to listen again. It was louder now. Michael was shouting as if he could be heard in the sky.

The minutes passed — or maybe it was hours. Jess had lost all sense of anything except the wrenching and tearing of her gut.

Jess!" Michael was kneeling beside her. "It's a helicopter, two helicopters, in fact! They'll be down in a moment. Hold on, baby, hold on!"

They huddled together and waited, refusing to consider that they might be denied help. They had to have it, whatever the price. They'd get it.

"Jess, Mike!"

They gaped, at first unable to put the evidence of their eyes into their conscious minds.

"It's me, Martin!" He was on his knees with them, shaking with relief. "God, I can't tell you how close we came to giving up!"

Michael shook his head as if to clear it. "What are you doing here? I don't understand."

"The others — Bowdritch and that bent cop — they're looking for you too. I couldn't get to talk to them — I figured I had to find you first."

"I told you to stay in town, and I've never been so goddamn glad in my life to be ignored!" Michael slapped his friend's shoulder. "Have you got a doctor with you?"

"No — but we'll take you two with us. And," — he glanced around nervously — "we've got to move fast. The others could be on our tail."

Michael started to gather up Jess.

"Get the envelope — I hope you still have it," Martin said tensely. "The pictures from Paraguay? We'll need them — they're our only hope, our only bargaining tool."

Michael had forgotten about it. He took a moment to collect his thoughts, then got to his feet. "I think the envelope's in the glove compartment. You take Jess."

"Hurry!" Martin wiped Jess's forehead, held her hand. "How are you doing, honey?"

She shook her head. "The baby — "

"We'll get you to the hospital real fast," he promised. "I spent too much time buying presents for this baby to let you down now."

"The hospital." Her voice was weak; she was straining with him as he picked her up. "Bowdritch . . ."

"It's going to be okay," he crooned, "you'll see. We'll make a deal. It'll be okay."

She arched her back with another terrible spasm. Martin tightened his arms, tried to walk faster. She fixed her eyes on the helicopters, terrified he'd drop her. The door of the second one was open. A stretcher was waiting. As Jess looked back to see where Michael was, she caught a fast glimpse of a face at the window of the smaller bird. It stared at her and then ducked backwards.

She spoke before she thought. "Desmond Marchenko! Why is he here?" She froze at the same moment as Martin did.

No one seemed to notice that the two of them had turned to stone.

"Oh, Jess." He sighed, then laid her on the stretcher.

She looked around, as if to postpone the knowledge. There were other men in Martin's party; a couple of leather-jacketed aces, probably the pilots. Three more were clumped near Desmond's helicopter. It took another beat before she realized that two of them were faces she'd seen before too . . . on the Boyle Heights street corner.

Martin signaled and one of the pilots stepped up to help him raise the stretcher. She was inside the belly of the bird before she knew what was happening. Martin came in after her, his face set and sad.

"Not you, Martin." The words came out with gasps of pain. "Not you!"

He crouched beside her, still gently wiping sweat from her neck and face. "I love you and Michael. And the baby. I did my best to protect you from Marchenko and the others. I warned you; I told you to stop being foolish. I wouldn't let them hurt you — I'd only let them make threats. I hoped you'd see sense. I did my best." It was as if she'd let him down.

"CYMA Corporation. Cyril and Martin. The microwave testing device." She saw it clearly now, despite the torture her body was taking. How could she have been so blind in the bloom of health? "That's how you got Michael his chance — you're very close to Haberman. But, Martin." Her eyes were pained, as much for him as for herself. "how could you go along? You know what happens to people — to babies — "

"We'll find solutions, Jess. It's a question of progress. You can't fight progress. We have to have the satellites; there's no question about it. You were going against the tide of inevitability — we're going to find solutions."

"Afterwards!" she said bitterly. "After you got your satellites up! After you blanketed the cities with microwaves!" She arched again with pain; he held her hands in both of his. "You couldn't see past the billions — money! That's what your progress is!"

"It's not that simple." He shook his head sadly. "America needs the industry. It creates jobs; it's necessary for defense. We're not evil — "

"Oh, yes, you are!" She closed her eyes and lowered her voice, coming to the realization that it was all too late. She and Michael had made one mistake too many, and this was the last conversation she was ever going to have. "You murdered to keep your dirty business safe.

You even killed one of your own."

"Robert." He paused. "That was a horrible choice. He knew, we all knew, there were . . . costs. He tried to shut his daughter. It was his negligence that let her cotton onto our South American venture in the first place. Then," he added heavily, "when we were compelled to step in, he —"

"He finally remembered he was a father." Michael was in the doorway of the copter, looking at Martin with dull-eyed sorrow. Jess hadn't noticed him arrive.

Martin didn't move immediately. He stared back, his right hand still on Jess's cheek. Very slowly, his other hand began to inch its way behind his back. Jess caught a glimpse of the rippling jacket; she didn't understand for a moment. When she did, the hand was already on the gun.

"No! Not Michael!" She lunged her torn, battered body somehow strong with terror. She grabbed at Martin and the gun, grasped it, pinning him against the wall. After a stunned split second of immobility, he fought her, gallantry forgotten, viciously scratching and shoving her away. The cabin was small; there was no room to maneuver, no room for rational fighting. They were in a tangled heap, rolling together and grunting with pain and anger. Michael tried to get inside, but whenever he moved, Jess was in the way. She poured out a final burst of fury, all nails and teeth. The gun went off.

The sound echoed like thunder, and the three of them stopped breathing, statues stinking of sour sweat, overwhelmed by the acrid odor of a firecracker.

Martin moved first this time, putting up a hand to touch Jess's stomach, then sliding down the wall. Jess and Michael were still, they watched a bubble of blood dribble past his lips.

She collapsed. Michael caught her just in time, lowering her to the ground again, frantically asking if she'd been shot too.

She couldn't find her voice, shaking her head over and over again, her eyes glued in horror to Martin's body.

Michael picked up the gun.

"Don't leave me!"

"I won't." He crouched by her side, and they waited for the attack from Martin's men.

There were shouts and shots outside, but no one came. Jess couldn't make sense of the tumult. She didn't bother trying. Every resource was exhausted. Something was torn inside her, causing agony she'd never dreamed possible. Michael said something and quickly dropped out of the helicopter. She barely noticed. The world was coming to an end, and all she wanted was for the finish to be fast so her torture would cease.

Someone was fussing over her. She twisted impatiently. Would they never leave her alone? Why couldn't they let her die in peace?

It was Michael. Eventually, his words got through. "It's okay, Jess. We're okay! Francis and Bowdritch are here; we're going to move you to their helicopter. We're going to take you to the hospital."

She looked around vaguely. There were a lot of people crowding her; she knew she knew some of them, but she couldn't quite get a fix on who they were.

One was talking now, a red-eyed, unshaven, slovenly figure. "Francis." She was proud of herself for putting the name and face together. She began to remember more.

His voice was sour and disgruntled. "Surrounded by goddamn assholes. Nobody wants to talk to anybody till the bodies are knee-deep on the ground. Bloody morons. Bowdritch waits a week to ask why everybody's dead. Simon figures it's cute to see no evil, hear no evil. You two amateur sleuths play Lone Ranger and Tonto in Death Valley. You're goddamn lucky I'm as crazy as the rest of you. Nearly got here too late. Goddamn secretive assholes."

They moved Jess while Francis bitched. She was in the police helicopter on a soft clean stretcher by the time he wound down.

A paramedic was holding a syringe, patting her gently to say she'd be fine now, they'd take care of her, it was going to be all right. Everyone was nodding with worried eyes.

Jess took Francis's hand. "Don't worry about me. I'll be fine, Arnheim." She tried to smile. "But a lot of people are going to be sore at you. I thought you said you had to go along to get along?"

He sniffed. "Shit's gonna hit the fan, all right." The last thing she saw before going under was something akin to a grin on his face.

Chapter 25

"Well, it's about time you deigned to wake up. You've been incredibly slothful." Michael was standing beside the hospital bed, grinning as if he'd won the lottery.

Jess smiled back and tentatively took stock of her body. She wasn't in pain, and it was a wonderful feeling. She widened the smile. "What day is it?"

"Tuesday. You've been out since early Monday morning.

"Michael — " She started to struggle up.

"Shh." He pushed her back. "The baby's fine. A little girl, with the emphasis on little. She's in an incubator."

"Incubator!"

"Not to fret. They've saved preemies a hell of a lot younger than ours."

"And . . . " She didn't quite know how to phrase it. "She's — normal?"

"We're a lot luckier than Betty Drummond," he assured her quietly, nodding.

She closed her eyes and offered up a prayer of thanks.

"And you're going to be fine too," he continued. "Which is just as well, since I really wasn't looking forward to going back to singles' bars. They had to cut, but you're strong as an ox."

"Charmingly sentimental thing to say to the mother of your only child," she grinned.

He kissed her and drew up a chair. "There's been a fair amount of commotion hereabouts."

"I bet."

"Mass hysteria — the public's up in arms, and the authorities are crazed." He passed her the *Times*. "City Coroner Exposes Microwave Conspiracy." She hadn't seen headlines that large since Kennedy died.

"You're a star."

"Only in some circles."

"True," he admitted. "You probably aren't

well-regarded among the captains of industry or in cabinet meetings. The government's beside itself — you should hear them. Simply stunned with surprise: 'We'll get to the bottom of this.' The entire country is being covered with brown stuff."

"What about Haberman and the boys?"

"Lots of criminal charges — conspiracy to commit murder, that sort of thing. You know, Bowdritch really was a pawn. They thought he was — I love their language — soft, so they didn't trust him with the truth. Marchenko was their man in the company after Berrington had to go."

Soft. Jess shook her head. Soft because he might — who knew — ? resent irradiating millions of unsuspecting people. "Martin?"

Michael bit his lip.

"Dead. Martin's dead and I killed him." The thought ricocheted around for a while.

"There's good news, sweetheart."

"I could use it."

"Connie's going to be fine. It'll take months, but she'll be back on her feet, browbeating us."

Jess smiled thankfully. "Thank God for that, at least. What's the bottom line on the rest of it?"

"Well, everyone's blaming everyone else. The White House is shocked at the military, and the military is appalled at business, and business just can't get over the scientists."

"And the scientists?"

"They're still looking for a smaller dog to kick."

"Hello, darlings." Virginia was at the door with Richard Simon. She was cool and collected in the perfect white linen dress. Richard carried an armful of orchids and roses, always Jess's favorite flowers. He was uneasy, looking as if he weren't sure he should be there.

Michael greeted Virginia and kissed her; he ignored the other man.

"Hi, Mother." Jess felt sorry for Richard. She beckoned him in too. "Have you seen the baby?"

"Yes, of course." Virginia kissed her quickly, then sat

down. " She's beautiful."

"Beautiful." Richard shifted uncomfortably. "Uh, I brought these for you."

"Thanks." She looked sternly at Michael who was stony-faced. "Would you see if the nurses have something to put Richard's flowers in?"

Michael left, still without saying a word.

Richard looked at the floor, then at Virginia, and finally at Jess. "Jessica, I don't know quite what to say."

She didn't help, but she didn't throw him out either.

"I wish I'd believed you from the beginning. I found it hard, it sounded so . . . incredible."

"And if you had believed her, what would you have done?" Michael was back; he'd found his tongue.

"You'd have found the 'tactful' way of handling it, the 'smart' way, right? Something negotiated. Don't rock the boat."

Jess thought of all the years of birthday and Christmas presents, trips to the zoo, outings with her father and Richard to party dinners and political meetings. Richard was never too busy to answer her questions, never too tired to read her a bedtime story. "Michael, please don't."

Richard shook his head. "Thank you, my dear, but Michael's question is fair enough. Considering everything." He looked at the other man. "I wish I had an answer. I don't. I don't know what I'd have done."

The room was silent.

Richard moved over to Jess; he looked down with clouded eyes. "I'm sorry." He quickly kissed her cheek, then Virginia's, and left.

Michael stared after him, jaw clenched. "Sorry does a hell of a lot of good."

"Michael," Jess said quietly, "like you said — welcome to the real world. It isn't what I used to think it was, but it isn't what you're making it out to be either. People aren't perfect."

He tried to grin. "Not even politicians? Is this Jess talking?"

"I lost my virginity," she agreed drily. "I can't rely

on Richard's rules anymore, or Dad's, or," she added softly, "yours, sweetie. I'll have to figure out my own."

Virginia wasn't comfortable with the conversation. She fiddled with the flower arrangements. "You must be getting tired, darling."

Jess stifled irritation. "No, I'm fine, Mother."

Her mother nodded stiffly and sat down again. "You've received wonderful press. You're almost as famous as your father was." She was caught by a memory, staring away, smiling very faintly. "He said you would be, when you were born. I was holding you; you weren't more than twelve hours old. My stitches still hurt, and I was tired, but you were so tiny and beautiful . . . I wouldn't let them take you away for hours." She came back to the present, collecting herself, brisk again. "Your father would be very proud of you."

Michael was leaning against the wall, watching Jess watch her mother.

"What about you, Mother?"

"What?" Virginia was taken aback.

"Are you proud of me too?"

"Well, yes, of course I am." She was slightly flustered, distracting herself by picking up a pile of congratulatory telegrams.

Jess's eyes were still on her. The word "mother" had a whole new substance, now that she was one too. This cool, composed woman had sweated and cried and born down in blood and mucus to give Jess life. Flesh of the same flesh.

"Very gratifying," Virginia murmured, replacing the papers and picking up her purse. "Well, my dear, I think I'll let you rest now. I'll call later."

"Mother, you haven't asked what your granddaughter's name is," Jess reminded her.

"Oh, of course." Virginia smiled pleasantly.

"We'll use Rader for the middle name. For Dad."

"Very suitable."

Jess looked at Michael; he smiled gently.

"I want her to be a strong woman," Jess said haltingly. "Strong and dignified. So 'Virginia' seems like the best possible choice."

Her mother didn't move at first. Then she folded Jess in her arms for a long moment, before hurrying out.

Jess grinned at Michael. "Well, it's a start."

He kicked the door shut and joined her on the bed.

"Yup. Maybe we'll grow up by the time our kid does."